Praise for the novels of Rick Mofina

"*Everything She Feared* hooked me from page one and didn't let go. Compulsively readable with twists and turns right up until the stunning conclusion. I loved it." —Amber Garza, author of *A Mother Would Know*

"*Their Last Secret* is Rick Mofina at his edge-of-your-seat, can't-stop-turning-the-pages best as he dives deep into questions of truth, justice, and ultimately redemption. A riveting, moving read." —Lisa Unger, *New York Times* bestselling author of *The Stranger Inside*

"Well-developed characters and an intense pace add to this gripping novel. This latest from a gifted storyteller should not be missing from your reading pile." —*Library Journal* (starred review) on *Missing Daughter*

"Rick Mofina's books are edge-of-your-seat thrilling. Page-turners that don't let up." —Louise Penny, #1 *New York Times* bestselling author

"A pulse-pounding nail-biter." —*Big Thrill* on *Last Seen*

"*Six Seconds* should be Rick Mofina's breakout thriller. It moves like a tornado." —James Patterson, *New York Times* bestselling author

"*Six Seconds* is a great read. Echoing Ludlum and Forsythe, author Mofina has penned a big, solid international thriller that grabs your gut—and your heart—in the opening scenes and never lets go." —Jeffery Deaver, *New York Times* bestselling author

"*The Panic Zone* is a headlong rush toward Armageddon. Its brisk pace and tight focus remind me of early Michael Crichton." —Dean Koontz, #1 *New York Times* bestselling author

"Rick Mofina's tense, taut writing makes every thriller he writes an adrenaline-packed ride." —*New York Times* bestselling author Tess Gerritsen

T0035302

RICK MOFINA

EVERY THING SHE FEARED

mira

Recycling programs for this product may not exist in your area.

ISBN-13: 978-0-7783-3340-1

Everything She Feared

For questions and comments about the quality of this book, please contact us at CustomerService@Harlequin.com.

Mira
22 Adelaide St. West, 41st Floor
Toronto, Ontario M5H 4E3, Canada
BookClubbish.com

Printed in U.S.A.

This book is for
Barbara

Each of us bears his own Hell.
—Virgil, Aeneid

1

SEVENTEEN-YEAR-OLD ANNA SHAW didn't want to die.

Adrenaline surged through every nerve ending, her fingers digging into the tree branch jutting from the cliffside.

This was a nightmare. It couldn't be real.

But it is real.

Anna had been atop the cliff, taking in the breathtaking panoramic view of the river, forests and mountains. Then in a heartbeat she was falling, falling some twenty feet, crashing into the big twisting branch sticking from the cliff face, catching herself, seizing it, struggling to hang on as it bent, now threatening to give way.

Gasping, she looked in horror a hundred feet straight down to the rocks at the banks of the rushing river below.

Wind gusted up, nudging her dangling legs. As she hung on for life, the branch cracked, her body jolted.

"Oh God!"

Anna glanced up at nine-year-old Katie Harmon looking down at her from the clifftop.

"Katie! Get help!"

Transfixed, Katie stared in wide-eyed silence.

Anna strained to move along the weakening branch closer to the cliff face to find a hold on the craggy rocks.

But pulling herself caused the branch to bob and shake, crackling more under her weight. Her hands landed on short branch spikes, like protruding nails piercing her palms with electrifying pain.

Suddenly the branch split and Anna jounced a few feet lower, clawing, clinging on to the fibrous remains.

"Katie!" she shrieked. "Oh God!"

Anna looked up.

Katie was gone.

The branch cracked again.

Run!

Every part of Katie's brain screamed at her to run.

She flew along the trail, twisting, turning through the dense woods, hoping to catch up to the others who had continued moving ahead.

Anna's fall had happened in a terrible instant.

So real and so frightening.

And no one else knows! No one was with us to see!

Katie willed herself to run fast, faster than she'd ever run in her life.

She felt like she was moving in slow motion but she blazed along the trail, coming to the clearing where her group from the Sunny Days Youth Center was setting up.

Katie glimpsed the joyful calm, nearly thirty kids and a sprinkling of adults supervising the day trip from the city, oblivious to the horror now on the cliff they'd all just passed. The boys were moving picnic tables together, others tossed a Frisbee. The girls were opening backpacks, tearing into snacks and drinks while others took pictures.

It all stopped when Katie screeched: "Help!"

Heads turned, smiles melted, the Frisbee crashed.

"What's up, Katie?" said Jackson, one of the supervisors.

"Anna fell!" Katie's chest heaved; she was gasping for air. "Taking a selfie. Fell off the cliff! Hanging on to a tree!"

It took a moment for Jackson and the others to absorb the alarm and snap to attention.

"We'll need ropes," he said, glancing at the other supervisors, Adam and Connie, who'd grabbed a canvas bag, unzipped it and yanked out tent ropes. They turned to Katie, who'd already fled back on the trail, her sobbing echoing in her wake.

"Everyone stay here!" Connie said, starting to run with the two men as she called to another adult with the group: "Dakota, keep everyone here!"

The supervisors struggled to keep up with Katie, all of them racing back on the trail to the area of the cliff. Two backpacks on the ground marked the point where it happened. Katie stood there horrified when she looked down.

Only spear-like remnants of the branch reached from the cliffside.

Katie stepped back while Jackson, Adam and Connie, breathing hard, looked down, their eyes ballooning in disbelief.

"Oh God!" said Connie, her voice breaking.

"No! No! No!" Adam yelled.

Anna's body was splayed on the rocks of the riverbank.

Ribbons of blood were webbing to the water.

2

Near North Bend, Washington

IN THE TIME that followed, events unfolded like a tragic opera.

Connie's 911 call went to the King County Communications Center. Panting with panic, she struggled to report the emergency.

"A girl fell off a cliff! We need—please, we need—"

"Take a breath," said the operator, calm, professional, taking control. "Tell me exactly where you are and what happened."

Connie collected herself, answering questions and following instructions, enabling the operator to dispatch paramedics and deputies from the King County Sheriff's Office North Precinct. The deputies then made a callout for Search and Rescue, setting the response in motion.

"I can't look anymore." Katie covered her face with her hands. Sobbing and trembling, she lowered her hands and asked: "Is Anna dead?"

"We don't know." Connie put her arm around her. "Help is coming."

For their part, Jackson and Adam had found a safe route to hurry down from the cliff. Moving as fast as they could along the rugged riverbank, they came to Anna's motionless body.

Her arms and legs were bent and twisted like a rag doll. She was lying faceup with her eyes open, staring skyward, blood dripping from the back of her neck. Jackson and Adam knelt next to her.

"Anna!" Adam said, knowing the worst but saying her name again.

Her stillness terrified them. They heard nothing but the river's rush while Jackson felt her neck, warm but no pulse.

He began CPR.

Adam saw her palms, bleeding from branch fragments projecting like quills in testament to her fight to hang on. Gently holding her hand, Adam surveyed Anna, almost glowing on the rocks in her bright yellow T-shirt. He didn't know that her mother had had it custom-made for her last birthday with the embroidered motto crowned over her heart: *All We Have Is Today.*

A small tattoo on her inner right wrist said *Fearless,* and on her inner left wrist was a small heart. Her jeans were faded, stylishly torn at the knees. One of her pink sneakers had been ripped away by the impact.

Anna's head nodded in time with Jackson's rhythmic pumping. But both men knew that the effort to save her was in vain.

Still Jackson refused to quit.

Adam's phone rang—it was the emergency operator. She'd gotten his number from Connie.

"Yes... A lot of blood... No pulse... We both have CPR and First Aid... He's doing CPR... Unconscious... Not responding... Tell them to hurry."

Staying on the line to provide directions to the scene, Adam held Anna's still-warm hand while watching Jackson's unrelenting CPR. Blinking back tears. His gaze went from Anna to the rock face, his stomach lifting at the magnitude of the drop, his focus traveling up beyond the broken branch to the cliff, seeing Connie looking down at him.

Adam shook his head slowly.

Connie's hand flew to her mouth. She turned, nearly doubling over before somehow getting enough control to pull Katie closer, comforting her. Slowly they started back to be with the others at their day camp.

Connie's mind swirled as they returned to the clearing; twenty-four kids, aged nine to fourteen, were in the Sunny Days excursion, along with four adult supervisors and three older teen assistants—now, only two.

Moments ago they were all starting a blissful outing, only to see it turn into a day of horrible heartbreak, a day they would remember for the rest of their lives, Connie thought. Everything at their day camp came to a halt when Connie and Katie emerged.

"Is Anna okay?" asked Dakota, one of the supervisors.

Connie searched the group, meeting anxious, expectant faces, feeling Katie's sobs against her. Holding her tight, Connie brushed at her own tears.

"Anna fell," Connie said. "She's hurt bad, really bad."

"Did Anna die?" one of the girls asked.

Connie stared at her.

"I want to see!" said Dylan Frick, a boy who was also in Katie's class at school.

"No!" Connie said loudly, then softened her voice. "We don't know anything yet. We just have to wait."

Some of the kids got on their phones, texting and calling their families, while a few of the girls rushed to Katie and

Connie, encircling them in a group hug, their sobbing soon mingling with the tragic operatic chorus of distant sirens echoing over the treetops.

King County Deputy Rob Hirano's stomach tightened.

It happened to him at every fatality.

Dealing with shocked witnesses and devastated families and friends of the victims, he knew how things could get emotional and chaotic. Often people just lost it, which was understandable. But he had to maintain order, take control, keep his professional distance, concentrate on the job.

As the first responding officer, his work was critical.

Hirano stepped carefully down to the scene with two paramedics behind him carrying equipment bags and a Stokes basket.

With Jackson and Adam watching, the paramedics, their radios squawking as they kept in touch with dispatch, checked Anna for vital signs. All their attempts to resuscitate her failed. Determining Anna had no cardiac activity, they confirmed she was deceased.

"Alright," Hirano said, then alerted the medical examiner to come to the scene just as the sky thudded. The Search and Rescue helicopter began circling the area. Hirano radioed for the crew to stand down for now. They might be needed later, once the ME was finished, to airlift the deceased from the scene.

After Hirano took photos of Anna from every angle, then the area, then the cliff face, he nodded for the paramedics to cover her with a sheet. While the medics notified their dispatcher and waited for the ME, Hirano took Jackson and Adam aside to interview them separately.

Adam Patel, aged twenty-one, held the back of his head in his hands. At times he stared at the sheet covering Anna, his eyes filling with tears, his voice tremoring as he told Hirano all he knew.

Hirano then went to Jackson Jones, aged twenty-three and the group's leader. Continually rubbing his chin, blinking repeatedly, Jackson's voice was steady as he gave Hirano information.

The dead girl was Anna Shaw. She was seventeen, from Seattle and was assisting the Sunny Days Youth Center group with its outing for the day. The SDYC was a nonprofit community organization. They'd left Seattle earlier that morning on a chartered school bus for a day trip here to Sparrow Song Park. The bus dropped them off in the parking lot. From there they hauled gear along the trail to their day camp.

"Anna's one of our three teen chaperones. She was hoping to become a supervisor. Normally we have an adult bring up the rear of the group, but we felt it would be okay for Anna to do it today," Jackson said. "So, she was the last to leave the bus, and she stopped—" he nodded to the cliff "—to take a selfie when she fell."

"How do you know that's what happened?" Hirano asked.

"Katie told us. She ran to us for help."

"Katie?"

"Katie Harmon. She's nine."

"Was Katie the only person with Anna at the time?"

"Yes, I believe so."

"So she was the last person to see her?"

"Yes."

3

"THREE CHEESE WITH HAM, hash browns, sausage and white toast—"

Around the time Anna Shaw fell to her death, Sara Harmon was relaying orders through the pick-up window at the Jet Town Diner.

"And one bacon scramble, hash browns and wheat toast. And then, Mel, I need two BLT combos on white to go. Thank you!"

Amid the clink of cutlery, the hum of conversations, the sounds and aromas of brewing coffee, sizzling bacon, fried potatoes and onions, Sara returned to working her section.

Today, she had gotten up before dawn, remembering Katie was away at a sleepover with Anna before they'd bused off this morning on a wilderness adventure. Sara's heart swelled. Katie was her world. *Just be safe out there,* Sara had thought, telling herself that Katie would be safe because she was with Anna, her babysitter.

That morning, alone at home getting ready, Sara saw the spaghetti sauce that had spilled on her new work shoes at the end of yesterday's shift, which she'd forgotten.

Oh, no. It looks like blood.

She'd washed it off before heading out to start her 6:00 a.m. shift.

Now, her work morning in full swing, when she glimpsed her new shoes, she was glad the stain was gone and for the soothing extra cushioning.

Sara focused on the diner's many customers, who'd been coming in steadily all morning. The Jet Town was in the city's Northgate community, not far from the ramps for the I-5, one the state's busiest highways, and it was a Seattle favorite. The clientele was mostly blue collar, but being close to the freeway, they got commuters, travelers and shift workers, anyone who wanted good food at a good price.

Working at the diner, Sara had met all kinds of people. There were those who scrutinized spotless drinking glasses or polished perfectly clean spoons with napkins, saying: "This place ain't the cleanest. I don't know why I eat here." There were the Goldilocks nitpickers: "Too cold, too hot, take it back."

There were the jokers, the touchers, the grabbers, the asspatters, the jerks who'd read her name tag and say things like: "I can think of other ways you can *serve* me, Sara."

There were families with out-of-control children, people with birthdays, anniversaries, something to celebrate. There were couples on first dates and couples who were breaking up. There were demanding customers who never tipped and silent non-complainers who left huge tips and nice notes: *You're awesome.* There were salt-of-the-earth regulars from the neighborhood, families whose children Sara had watched grow up.

Through it all she'd become something of an expert at dealing with hungry people, keeping her stress in check, learning to prioritize and always going the extra mile.

Now, as she went from booth to booth, topping off coffee and tending to requests, she saw the man alone in the corner at a two-seat table.

Hunched over his plate, he was chewing the last of his lumberjack combo, a big order. His long gray-and-white hair had been wetted, likely in the bathroom, and neatly combed, his effort to look presentable. His denim shirt was faded, dotted with ancient stains. Under it he wore a long-sleeved T-shirt. He had khaki cargo pants and scuffed hiking boots with broken laces he'd knotted together. His gaze went beyond the window to the edge of the parking lot where the sun glinted on a shopping cart overflowing with bags and half-concealed in the shrubs.

Sara watched him look at his check, then reach into his pocket, pull out a couple of coins and set them on the table with one crumpled dollar, the amount far short of what he owed.

Topping up his coffee, she smiled. "Can I get you anything else, Lonnie?"

Toast crumbs and egg bits were trapped in his wild beard. A blend of hand soap, body odor and a trace of alcohol wafted from him.

Lonnie came into the diner a couple times a month. From what she knew, he was in his fifties. Some years ago he'd lost his wife and children, then his job and his house. He didn't like shelters, so now he slept under an overpass or in parks.

"Anything else you'd like?"

He gave his head a slight shake and she put her hand on his shoulder.

"Don't worry. This one's on me. I'll catch ya next time, okay?"

A few minutes later she exchanged heartfelt glances with her coworkers, Polly and Beth, after watching him amble across the parking lot to his shopping cart.

Lonnie was a heartbreaker.

As the morning rolled by, Sara considered her own life as a thirty-one-year-old single mom of a nine-year-old daughter: Katie, the center of her universe.

Sara had lost so much over the years—her husband, then her dad. Now her mom was in a seniors' home, living out her life.

Stop complaining, Sara told herself. *Everyone's hurting. Everyone's carrying something.*

As she worked, she glanced at the gray-and-white flowers blossomed on her inner wrist and lower forearm. *This is what I'm carrying.* For Sara, the tattoo signified who she was—something she thought about every day.

Nothing can change it.

It had been so many years now and the things she feared hadn't happened. Let the darkness stay in the past. She was confident they were going to be okay on that front.

But on the financial front, a clock was ticking down on Sara and she had to do something soon.

She'd started working at Jet Town during high school. It's where she met Nathaniel, the kindest, sweetest, most handsome guy she'd ever known. He had his own motorcycle repair shop in Salem, Oregon, and he had friends in British Columbia. While traveling to see them, he stopped once at the diner. Then he made a point of always stopping, even calling ahead to be sure Sara was working because he wanted to see her. She liked him. After they got married, Sara moved to Salem, where she had Katie. When Nathaniel died suddenly, her world fell apart. Their marriage had been so good because Nathaniel was good. He had such a gentle, solid soul.

After he died, she moved back home and returned to working full-time at Jet Town to make ends meet.

Even Nathaniel never knew the truth about her, and why she'd been reluctant to have children. But he had a good heart, ached to be a dad, and she loved him so much. He gave her hope... And so they had Katie.

But then...why did you have to die on me, Nathaniel?

That was another life, though, and Sara was grateful to work at the diner. It had helped her heal. Now the years had blurred past and Sara was the longest-serving staffer at Jet Town, where she'd seen servers come and go.

"You're a lifer, kiddo," Mel Carver, the owner and chief cook, often teased her.

"You're an institution," Polly always told her.

"You'll never leave," Beth said all the time.

Even Beth and Polly, each going on three years at the diner—way longer than the other servers—were now talking about leaving. Polly was engaged to a pilot and likely moving to Australia. Beth's sister was part-owner of a new motel near Las Vegas and had offered her a position there.

Sara's situation wasn't as rosy. For her, there was more money going out now than coming in, and that scared her, forcing her to take stock of her life. She wanted to act on the encouragement she'd received from two women who were real estate agents. The women were regulars who brought clients to Jet Town to discuss deals. Both had gotten to know Sara and had urged her to get her real estate license.

"You're good with people," one of the women had said. "You can earn a very good living. And think about your fu-

ture. You'll need a college fund for your daughter, a retire-
ment plan for yourself. We can help you with the license."

The women offered to guide Sara on the coursework and
studying for the exam, and help her get her foot in the door
with a good real estate agency. The more Sara thought about
it, the more she liked the idea.

During her break in the staff locker room, which was
cramped with boxes of supplies, she took out her phone. She
scrolled through a site offering information on the steps she
needed to take to earn her license, biting her bottom lip with
excitement at the prospect of a new life. Just then, her phone
vibrated with a text from Connie Atkinson, one of the supervisors with Sunny Days.

It began with There's been a terrible incident...

When Sara finished reading it, she rushed to Mel in the
kitchen.

"I've got to leave!" She was already pulling off her apron.
"Something's happened at Katie's— I gotta go now!"

"Why? What?" Spatula in his hand, he turned. "What?
Go where?"

Sara grabbed her bag from the change room and hurried
out the door. She ran to her car, fishing her keys from her
bag, her heart pounding.

4

Near North Bend, Washington

DEPUTY ROB HIRANO climbed up from the river.

Moving along the trail with other deputies, he reviewed a mental checklist of what he needed to do.

Keep it by the book.

It was far too early to classify this as an accident, suicide or something else. He'd protected the death scene by sealing it at the river and the clifftop, posting deputies and troopers there.

According to Jackson Jones and Adam Patel, no other people had been hurt. To be safe, Hirano had asked the paramedics to look at the two men, then later he'd have them assess Katie Harmon and others in the group as well.

And we may need them when we notify Anna Shaw's family, because her family will come here. No matter what we say, they will come.

Hirano took a long breath, relieved that they had covered the girl's body because by the time he'd finished talking with the adult supervisors on scene and reached the Sunny Days group, the first Seattle TV news helicopter passed overhead. Hirano knew press people monitored police radio transmissions and moved fast.

At the day camp, children were sitting on the grass in small circles. Some were crying and hugging each other. Three boys were off to one side, their expressions grim while tossing a football. Others in the group were at the picnic tables, talking on their phones or texting.

The crackling of police radios signaled the arrival of the deputies. Some of the older kids went to them, their faces taut, intent.

"Is Anna dead?" one boy asked.

"Can we go look?" said another. "Can we ride in a helicopter?"

"What's going on?" one of the girls asked.

Hirano raised his palms.

"I'm Deputy Rob Hirano. What's happened is serious and we need your help," he said. "We'll talk to each of you. Please be patient, this is important. My friends here are going to get started."

As the deputies began gathering statements, Hirano looked at his notebook, then at the group.

"Is Connie Atkinson here?"

She was nearly out of sight, sitting alone with Katie under a tree. Connie heard him, got up and brushed herself off as she walked to Hirano. He took notes as Connie recounted the morning's events.

"Anna and Katie were last getting off the bus. They sort of took their time behind us while we walked the trail here." Connie ignored her vibrating phone. "Then Katie came screaming for help." Raking her fingers through her hair, Connie nodded toward a canvas bag. "We got tent ropes, ran to help but... Oh, God!" Connie covered her face with her hands, sobbing. "It was too late." Connie gasped. "Anna had volunteered to help us for the day. Oh, God!"

Out of earshot, Katie watched them from the tree, never taking her eyes from them.

When Hirano finished talking to Connie, he asked for Anna Shaw's consent form. Her fingers shaking, Connie withdrew a copy from a binder in her backpack.

"I'll need Katie Harmon's, too, before I speak to her."

Connie's phone vibrated again; this time, she pulled it from her back pocket and looked at it.

"Parents are hearing from kids and have been calling nonstop with questions." Connie sniffed. "My God, what do I tell them?"

"Tell them there's been a serious incident, that you don't have all the information," Hirano said. "That help is here and you'll know more later."

Nodding and reading messages, Connie said: "They want to know if they can drive out here and get their kids?"

"Yes, but they must stay in the parking lot until we're done," he said. "We'll bring the kids out when we're done talking to everyone."

Hirano was aware of the challenges, but he knew that under the circumstances, deputies could question the children alone without a parent or lawyer present. He radioed for deputies and troopers to get tape up and post someone at the trailhead.

"Nobody gets in," Hirano said into his walkie-talkie.

Taking a deep breath, Connie got Katie's form for him. And while she sent messages, he went over to the tree and sat alone with Katie.

Her tear-filled eyes took a walk all over him in his patrol uniform. In his black shirt and armor vest, with his body camera, holstered gun and other gear, he realized his appearance might be a concern for a nine-year-old girl amid the horror and chaos.

Still, Hirano couldn't lose sight of the fact he was the first officer to speak to her. This was his one shot at getting her first account. He had to do this right. He checked his body camera to ensure it was recording a video of Katie while he took notes.

"Hi, Katie. I'm Deputy Rob Hirano and I'm here to help, okay?"

She nodded.

"Don't be put off by all my stuff. I have to wear it for my job."

She brushed at her tears. Her face, weighted with anguish. Her hair was half out and half in blond braids that touched her shoulders.

"Are you okay to talk to me?"

She shrugged, crying softly.

"I'm going to ask you some things," Hirano said. "I need you to tell me everything that happened no matter what it was, okay?"

Her blue eyes found his and she asked: "Is Anna dead?"

"She's hurt, very seriously hurt. We have paramedics with her and we still have things to do. But she's seriously hurt."

Her shoulders shook. She clenched her eyes and sobbed.

"I want my mom! I want my mom!" She pressed her fists to her eyes.

"We're going to get your mom here," Hirano said. "I know this is hard, but I need you to be strong, okay?"

Hirano glanced at her consent form for the outing.

"I need you to help me. Your full name is Kaitlyn Jean Harmon?"

"I go by Katie."

"Alright, Katie. And you're nine years old. When's your birthday?"

"June twenty-fifth."

"Your mom is Sara Harmon and you live in Seattle at—" Hirano read her address from the form.

"Yes. Can my mom come and get me, please?"

"We're going to get her here, or we'll take you to her. But only after we're done, and it could take a while, okay?"

She nodded.

"Okay, Katie, I need you to tell me what happened concerning Anna. You can take your time."

Katie swallowed hard. As she began recounting the events, Hirano studied her. He knew children at her age were generally conscientious and truthful. But it was also the age that some became skillful at lying, depending on the circumstances, the stakes and the repercussions. He watched for signs of deception, listening carefully, asking the occasional question.

When Katie came to the part where Anna was taking a selfie at the cliff's edge, she gasped, her words breaking in her throat.

"She fell—I couldn't believe it was real. She screamed and was just gone. I looked down and she was hanging on to a tree, telling me to get help—I was so scared—I ran and ran."

Katie covered her face with her hands and sobbed.

Hirano watched her for a long moment. Her shoulders shook, her head shook. For a brief moment he thought her movements were an overreaction, even exaggerated. It gave rise to his uncertainty as to whether it was due to her shaking, or if she was actually peeking through her fingers, watching him watch her.

He just wasn't sure.

He waited until she calmed down, until her shaking and tears stopped. Then he asked more questions. When they finished, he asked Connie to resume sitting with Katie while the paramedics assessed her.

Hirano walked off for a moment alone.

While surveying the deputies interviewing the others at the day camp, he called his sergeant.

"What do we have there, Rob?"

"I can't be certain," Hirano said. "We need detectives on this."

"You suspect this isn't a clear-cut wilderness accident?"

"Just a gut feeling."

"What's the ME say?"

"They're on their way."

"Alright, Rob. We'll get a detective team rolling. You hold the fort."

Ending his call, Hirano looked down at his open notebook and the words he'd circled after his interview with Katie Harmon.

Possibly deceptive responses.

5

Near North Bend, Washington

DETECTIVE KIM PIERCE didn't see the forests rolling by her window as Detective Carl Benton guided their unmarked Ford Explorer east from Seattle on I-90.

Driving far above the speed limit, the SUV's emergency lights wigwagging, Benton threaded around traffic while glancing at Pierce.

She was concentrating on notes she'd received from the first responding deputy, who was still at the scene. She broke things down: deceased, a seventeen-year-old female; indication she'd taken a fatal fall. Only witness: a nine-year-old female.

Pierce went over other notes while continuing with her own.

Less than an hour earlier, she and Benton were at their desks at the King County Sheriff's Office headquarters at the King County Courthouse in downtown Seattle. Pierce had been completing a supplemental report on an assault when Detective Sergeant Art Acker came to their workspace, undid his collar button and loosened his tie.

"North Precinct just called," he said. "We got a death in Sparrow Song Park, the private place on the east side of North Bend. Kim, this is yours, you lead. I'll put you in touch with the deputy there."

In that moment Pierce caught Benton's reaction, the rise of his eyebrows nearly imperceptible as Acker said to her: "You go with Benton." Acker rolled up his sleeves, looked at the desks nearby. "Grotowski and Tilden, I want you to go, too. Take another vehicle, in case you need to separate out there."

Heading to their car, Pierce had considered Benton's subtle registering of surprise at Acker putting her in charge of the case. It underscored her feeling that Benton and the others were slow to accept her on the team. She was the only woman in an all-white squad of men, having joined three weeks ago after just making detective.

She was the rookie.

Sure, it always took time to settle in, but Pierce sensed their resistance went deeper, thinking back to an uneasy moment.

It happened about three days after she'd joined. She'd stepped away from her desk to get a coffee. When she returned, Grotowski and Tilden were talking with Benton at his desk. Benton, the case-hardened veteran, the team's senior member, was leaning back in his chair, arms folded, holding court. Approaching them, Pierce heard a fragment of Benton's side of the conversation, picking up on two words, *her heritage*, before their murmuring died away. Seeing her, Tilden shifted the subject to the Seahawks.

Her heritage?

The words stuck.

Pierce didn't know what, or who, they were talking about,

or the context. Acting like she hadn't heard, she sat down and resumed working, deciding to let it go.

Days passed, but the incident and those two words gnawed at her.

There'd been a short bio of her in the newsletter when she made detective. Were Benton and the others talking about the fact her mother was Native American and her father had been born in Guatemala?

Do they have an issue with my heritage? Maybe I'm wrong about that. I hope I'm wrong.

No one had said anything about that moment to Pierce. And, on the first day she'd arrived, the team was all smiles and handshakes. Maybe the feeling she'd sensed was in her head. Or maybe it was related to some testosterone-fueled initiation ritual, a way to test her?

If so, then bring it on.

Now, with the Explorer rushing east on the interstate, taking them closer to the death of a teenage girl, Benton whistled through his teeth.

"So Art made you the lead. Do you really think you're ready for this?"

Am I ready for this?

Pierce looked down at her work. Then, for a moment, she turned to the window, the trees blurring by like her life. Her family was always moving, she was always the new kid, and she was often insulted, ostracized. The stench of racism was always near. Her mom and dad telling her: "Push through it, Kim. Use it to make you stronger."

Pierce did.

Her mother and father owned a two-person office cleaning company. Pierce worked with them when she was a teen. When her parents got a contract to clean a police station, a couple officers got her thinking about becoming a cop.

Like her parents, Pierce worked hard, scraped to save, went to college, got a degree in criminal justice, and along the way became a wife, mother and deputy.

She excelled at basic academy training, and while a deputy, she'd completed as many advanced courses as she could, including homicide investigation and questioning witnesses, victims and suspects. And she worked with detectives—learning, always learning.

In her five years as a patrol deputy, Pierce had seen it all: bloated bodies of drowning victims, pugilistic positioning of fire victims, bodies entwined with crushed metal at accidents; beatings, stabbings, shootings, suicides and homicides. So did she think she was ready for this? After several seconds, she turned to answer Benton.

"No, Carl."

"What?" He stared at her, intense, no-nonsense. "You don't think you're ready?"

Her eyes betrayed nothing as she stared back.

"I don't *think* I'm ready. I *am* ready."

He nodded, a smile dawning. "Good," he said. "You should start a running case log, with times."

"Already done."

"Well, look at you, Kim. Good." Eyes on the road ahead, Benton stuck out his bottom lip. "Besides, this is a slam dunk. Sad, but an accidental death, a teen taking a selfie."

Now it was Pierce's turn to raise her eyebrows—she found it interesting that Benton could draw a conclusion without setting foot at the scene, or talking to a witness. She got back to work on her notes, remembering key points concerning a wilderness death.

Always assume criminal intent until proven otherwise.

A wilderness death can be a perfect murder.

6

BENTON WHEELED THEIR Ford into the parking lot at Sparrow Song Park.

News vans, sheriff's units and private vehicles were there. Pierce counted them and made notes along with the time. The medical examiner was there, too.

About two dozen people, including media, were clustered at the yellow tape cordoning off the entrance to the trail where a deputy was posted.

Pierce and Benton were in plain clothes; both wore jeans. They put on jackets with *SHERIFF* on the back and displayed their badges in the front. Gathering what they needed, they left their SUV.

Benton pointed his chin toward an unmarked SUV as it arrived and parked nearby. Detectives Grotowski and Tilden got out and joined them.

"The gang's all here. It's all yours, Kim," Benton said as a news helicopter thudded overhead.

Pierce took a moment to observe the vehicles, the lot, the dome security camera fixed to a light post; she took in the people at the tape, the news cameras, the sense of urgency.

She cautioned herself not to get caught up in the excitement and confusion, to remain calm. Focus on the work, because paramount to everything going on was the fact the investigation into a young person's death was in her hands. Taking a deep breath of forest air, Pierce led the other detectives through the group toward the tape.

"Excuse me," a woman, face taut with worry, said to Pierce. "Excuse me, who are you?"

Before she could answer, a man stepped closer to Pierce, saying loudly: "Are you in charge? Why's the medical examiner here? What the hell happened?"

More people collected around them and another woman, her voice cracking with fear and anger said: "Our children are in there and they won't let us see them!"

Pierce noticed that two TV cameras on the shoulders of newspeople were aimed at her. Other reporters were holding out phones, recording.

"Our son texted me." A woman held up her phone, then pointed to the trail. "He said he thinks someone got killed and police are questioning our kids in there!"

"We demand to know what's happening!" the loud-voiced man said. "It's illegal for you to talk to our kids without us! You can't detain them! We'll get lawyers, we'll sue!"

"Who are you?" a woman asked.

In a moment of silence Pierce jumped in, responding politely.

"I'm Detective Kim Pierce. I understand that you have questions and this is a troubling time. We're investigating a report of an incident. I assure you, we have the authority to talk to your children, to gather information."

"We demand to see our kids," a woman said.

"I know," Pierce said. "We'll reunite you with them right here as soon as we're done. I'm sorry, unfortunately that's all we can say at this time."

Pierce turned to the tape, which the deputy had lifted for her and the other detectives. Passing under it, another question followed her, one from a woman identifying herself as a reporter with a Seattle TV news channel.

"Detective Pierce," she called, "can you confirm the age and sex of the victim?"

The air stilled as Pierce stopped, turned and sought the reporter. Mindful of the parents, the cameras and phones, she said: "I'm sorry but we can't confirm anything at this time."

Pierce and the detectives continued down the trail, tugging on gloves. Deputy Rob Hirano was waiting for them, ensuring they were out of hearing distance from the parking lot. A quick round of introductions, then for several minutes Hirano flipped through his notes, updating them on steps taken so far. He concluded by saying that the Sunny Days group was waiting at the day camp.

"They're upset and want to leave. We've got paramedics and the medical examiner people here, and there are deputies and troopers to help with additional work."

Then Hirano, his hands still gloved, passed a clear evidence bag holding a Washington State driver's license to Pierce. Anna Catherine Shaw, aged seventeen, stared at Pierce from the photo.

"The ME got this," he said.

Pierce signed an evidence tag, studied the license, then tucked it in her pocket and made notes.

"I read your summary on the drive out," Pierce said. "The

only person with her when she fell was Kaitlyn Jean Harmon, and she's nine?"

"Yes. She goes by Katie."

"What made you suspicious that this might not be an accident? You noted *possibly deceptive responses*, concerning Katie Harmon."

"Yeah, she seemed a little evasive," he said. "I could've been misreading her but I thought we should be thorough, bring you guys in."

Pierce nodded and, while she made notes, Benton jumped in.

"Anna Shaw was taking a selfie when she fell, right?" he asked.

"That's our understanding," Hirano said.

"Look," Benton said, "people are dying all over the world taking dangerous selfies. This is a tragic fall."

Pierce shot Benton a look. "How about we let the investigation determine what this is, Carl?"

He held up his hands in surrender.

"Where is Katie Harmon now, Rob?" Pierce asked.

"At the camp, isolated. I've got a deputy with her."

"And she's not hurt?"

"Not physically. Paramedics assessed her. She's pretty shaken up, though."

"Alright, before we get going," Pierce said. "Carl, Lyle—" she nodded to Tilden "—we need to contact the park owner. Arrange to collect any footage from the security camera in the lot. You guys go back, record all vehicle plates, and canvass for dash cams and phone photos in the lot. Then join us at the camp."

"I thought I was partnered with you?" Benton said.

"Just go with Lyle," she said.

"If it's because I said I think this is an accident—"

"Carl—" Pierce stared at him, she didn't have time for this, she had enough to deal with "—just go with Lyle."

"You're the lead." Benton gave her a half-hearted salute.

"Rob," Pierce said. "Walk us through Shaw's steps to the point where she fell."

Pierce used her phone to record a video as the small team moved along the trail. They reached the area, which was cordoned off with yellow tape. The deputy posted there acknowledged them. A few yards beyond the tape were two lone backpacks on the ground.

Beyond them, the cliff.

"Only me and one other deputy have gone in there since the supervisors were here. No one's touched them," Hirano said, pointing to the path they'd taken to the backpacks, lifting the tape for Pierce.

Continuing to record, she went to the backpacks, opening them, conducting a preliminary inventory and finding things like a hoodie, socks, jacket, a phone, earphones and a charger cord in the pocket of one. She also found granola bars, oranges, carrot sticks, apple slices, a water bottle, a small cosmetic pouch, tampons, mints, gum, hand sanitizer, lotion, bug spray, lip balm, a brush and a hair tie.

Pierce noted the contents, then surveyed the area. The section had patches of grass leading to a scattering of stones in the underbrush, then the forest. Near the backpacks she noticed a series of faint partial foot impressions in the soil, took photos and made notes, thinking they'd need casts made as soon as possible.

Then she went to the cliff.

Standing on the edge, Pierce looked out at the view that had cost Anna Shaw her life.

She looked down at the tree branch, some twenty feet below. The remainder of it extended like the twisted, gnarled fingers of a claw. She looked down farther to the riverbank, saw remnants of the branch. Near it on the ground, she saw the sheet over the body and investigators at the death scene.

"Can you get us down there, Rob?"

Hirano led them along the route the Sunny Days supervisors had used.

Several minutes later, Pierce and her group joined Cindy Lehman and Hilary Fung, with the ME's Office. The investigators were suited and gloved, interrupting their work to bring Pierce up to date.

Fung said that they'd checked the body's position, took its temperature and made note of the surroundings, the weather and initial witness statements relayed to them. They'd proceed to photograph the area and take measurements, then they'd take a look at the clifftop as well.

"The most obvious cause appears to be a fall," Fung said. "But we're not making any conclusions until after an autopsy. When we're ready, we'll get Search and Rescue to airlift her out to a secure area where we can transport her."

Fung added: "We'll make a positive ID through dental records, or fingerprints."

"Thank you," Pierce said. "I need to look at her."

They moved closer and crouched down. Fung lifted the sheet and Pierce tensed at Anna Shaw's arms and legs, which were horribly contorted. Blood was puddled at the back of her neck. Then Pierce met her eyes: frozen open, empty of life. It was clear from her driver's license that this was Anna Catherine Shaw.

Pierce took photos of her face, her tattoos, the T-shirt with the embroidered motto, her torn jeans, her feet missing one shoe.

You only lived seventeen years on this earth. Was the picture worth your life, Anna? Is that what happened here?

Pierce wished for Anna's soul to be at peace. Then she nodded to Fung, who lowered the sheet.

Pierce went to the edge of the scene where the two supervisors, Jackson Jones and Adam Patel, were sitting on the riverbank, waiting with Hirano. Interviewing them separately, Pierce obtained their accounts, noting the actions they took and the approximate time they took them.

"Did Anna Shaw say anything to you?" Pierce had asked each of them and in each case the answer was no.

Pierce returned to the death scene where the medical examiner investigators were working. She surveyed it all while taking a video. She saw the broken branch and, yards away, Anna's other sneaker.

But something was missing.

She asked the investigators, then Hirano, then Jones and Patel if anyone had found Anna Shaw's phone.

No one had.

Pierce walked along the riverbank, searching in vain. Then she looked at the rushing water before turning to Detective Larry Grotowski, who'd joined her.

"What do you think, Kim?"

"We need this scene and the cliff where she fell processed— and we need to grid the area, including the water, to find her phone."

"I'll make some calls," Grotowski said.

"Good."

Pierce took a breath. It was time to talk to Katie Harmon.

7

Near North Bend, Washington

KATIE HARMON SHIVERED in the breeze tumbling up from the river.

Someone had given her a University of Washington hoodie that was too big; she was swallowed by it.

With the hood up, Katie had leaned her head on a female deputy's shoulder. They were sitting on the ground under a tree. Katie was watching *Snow White and the Seven Dwarfs* on the tablet the deputy was holding, the faint strains of a song sounding, "Heigh-ho, Heigh-ho…"

Pierce went to the paramedic who was nearby and took her aside.

"How's Katie doing?" Pierce asked.

"Her numbers are still a bit elevated," the paramedic said. "She's cold, pale and anxious. We're keeping her still and hydrated. She's doing okay under the circumstances."

"But she's cognizant, right? I need to talk to her."

"Yeah, it should be okay. I'll stay close."

"Did she say anything about the incident to you?"

"No. She asked me if Anna was dead. I said I didn't know. She's scared, she wants to go home."

"Alright, thanks."

Pierce's mind raced on how best to interview Katie.

She's the last person to see Anna Shaw alive.

Hirano had flagged her as *possibly deceptive*. Pierce needed detailed answers but knew that children who'd been traumatized by sudden tragic events could have distorted or impaired memories. Weighing it all, she went to Katie and sat on the grass with her as Grotowski joined them.

"Hi, Katie, I'm Detective Kim Pierce."

Katie drew her knees to her chest, with Pierce making a mental note of how she'd started swaying slightly.

"This is Detective Larry Grotowski," Pierce said as he sat with them. "He's just recording a video of us. It's part of our job," Pierce said. Grotowski gave her a small friendly wave. "You can call him Larry. He's got two daughters who are pretty much the same age as you. I have a son about your age, too. You can call me Kim. Okay?"

Brushing at tears, Katie said nothing.

Pierce reached into her pocket and passed Katie fresh tissues, which she accepted. As Katie wiped her face under the hood, Pierce saw Katie's ice-blue eyes, the pretty side braids of her blond hair.

"I want my mom to take me home now."

"She's on her way."

"Everyone says Anna's dead— When I saw her at the bottom of the cliff—I thought—" She took shaky breaths. "Is she really dead?"

"Anna's hurt bad, very bad, and there are a lot of things

people have to do to take care of her. And we need you to help us. Do you think you can help us?"

Katie gave a weak shrug, tightened her arms around her knees, and this time she began rocking gently.

"I need you to be brave and strong so you can tell me everything that happened, okay?"

"But I told the other policeman everything."

"I know, honey, but I need you to help me understand exactly what happened so we can take care of everything and get you home with your mom."

Katie sobbed a little.

"I know, I know, Katie, this is so hard, but it's important because nobody else was there but you."

Katie continued rocking.

"Let's start like this," Pierce said. "What did you do when you got up at home this morning?"

"I had a sleepover at Anna's last night."

"You woke up at Anna's house?"

"Anna's my babysitter."

"How long has she babysat you?"

"A long time, I guess."

"A couple months, a year, longer?"

"A year, I guess. She wanted to help today and we got up early."

Pierce nodded, encouraging her to keep talking.

"We got a ride to Sunny Days and got on the bus with everybody."

"Where did you sit?"

"In the back."

"Did you and Anna talk?"

"Yes, about music and stuff."

"What kind of stuff?"

"She just broke up with Tanner, her boyfriend."

"Tanner? What's Tanner's last name?"

"Bishop, I think."

"Was she sad about that?"

"Yes, I guess, but she was happy to be on the trip."

"Okay, were there any incidents, anything that happened on the bus?"

Thinking about the question, Katie stared down at the ground and shook her head.

"Are you sure?" Pierce asked.

"Nothing happened."

"Okay, okay, you're doing good, Katie. What happened when the bus got here?"

Katie gave a little shrug. "We were the last to get our backpacks and get off and follow everybody down the trail. The others were pretty far ahead."

"Was anyone else walking with you?"

Katie shook her head. "They were far ahead."

"It was just you and Anna alone?"

"Yes, well, there were butterflies, birds, and we saw a rabbit."

"What did you talk about?"

"How pretty it was. Anna was taking pictures."

"So you're walking from the bus. Do you meet or see anyone else?"

"No."

"So, it's just you and Anna. Then what?"

Blinking, Katie said, "We came to the cliff part."

"Then what?"

Katie looked down at her hands, fidgeting with her fingers.

"Anna says, oh, it's so beautiful here, Katie, I want to take a selfie."

"A selfie? That's what she said?"

"Yes."

"Alright."

"We took off our backpacks to stay there for a bit. She got her phone." Katie nodded at no one. "And I said—" her voice softened to a whisper "—I said, okay, be careful, Anna."

"You said that?"

"Yes, because of the cliff."

"Those were your exact words?"

"Yes."

"Then what happened?"

"She turned around and started walking backward to get a better picture from the cliff." Katie wrung her hands and licked her lips. "I said be careful but she kept saying it was so beautiful and stepped back and then—"

Catching her breath, Katie forced the words out.

"She just fell, she screamed, she wasn't there anymore!"

Katie stared straight ahead, focusing on nothing. "But I heard her voice. I looked over the cliff and she was hanging on to this tree that was sticking out. She was begging me to get help! I was so scared I didn't know what to do! So I ran!"

Katie sobbed, her voice weakening to a whisper.

"I got here and I screamed for help. Jackson, Adam and Connie came, but when we got to the cliff—" Katie's face creased in anguish. She clenched her eyes shut. "I saw Anna at the bottom on the rocks. It was awful!"

A long moment passed before Katie resumed speaking.

"I want my mom! I want my mom to take me home now!"

"We're almost done," Pierce said.

"Please!"

"Only a few more things to help us, sweetie," Pierce said. "Now, when you ran for help, was Anna still holding on to the branch?"

"Yes."

"Was Anna holding her phone at the time she fell?"

"I don't think so."

"Did you see where it went?"

Katie shook her head.

"Did you take any pictures with your phone?"

"No, mine was in my backpack. Anna took better pictures."

"Did you see or hear anyone else near you when Anna fell, or at any point after you got help?"

"No."

"Did you see if she slipped on anything?"

"No."

"Was it windy?"

"I don't know."

"Did you have any arguments or disagreements with Anna before this happened?"

"No."

"Not even a little one?"

"No, she's my friend."

"Did Anna say anything before she fell?"

"Just that she wanted a picture—" Katie struggled with her words "—and, and, and I kept telling her—" Katie's voice broke. "I kept telling her to be careful."

Pierce let a long moment pass, then patted Katie's arm.

"Katie, you did good helping us. We're done for now. We'll let the paramedics take a look at you, and then we'll get you home."

Pierce left Katie with the paramedic and the deputy, stepping away to review her notes, taking a deep breath and surveying the other kids.

They were huddled in groups, some talking with deputies and troopers. Some consoled each other in a portrait of despair.

An innocent outing ended in tragedy. *At least, that's what it looks like*, Pierce thought as her phone rang.

It was Benton. She answered.

"Pierce."

"Anna Shaw's parents have arrived in the parking lot," he said. "Word's getting out. They need to know."

"Did you tell them anything, Carl?"

"No, you're the lead."

She pressed the phone harder to her ear and steeled herself for what she had to do next.

"I'm on my way."

8

Near North Bend, Washington

WORRY WAS ETCHED in Lynora Shaw's face.

She clutched her phone over her heart; her other hand dug into her husband's arm.

The backs of Chuck Shaw's tanned hands were scarred, splotched with dried concrete after rushing from a jobsite. His eyes like bullet tips drilling into Pierce.

Whenever she faced the families of victims in the moment their lives would be changed forever, details would burn into her memory—like a nick on someone's chin from shaving that morning, or the way fists banged down on kitchen tables, or how people recoiled, staggering from her with aching groans, refusing to let the horror in.

These moments would haunt Pierce on sleepless nights, in quiet pauses of her day.

For her, this was the hardest part of her job, but one of the most important, and today she was determined to do the best she could under the circumstances. Rumors were flying among parents in the parking lot who were reading texts from their kids still in the day camp. Speculation was swirling in news and social media posts.

Pierce had requested Anna Shaw's parents be taken to a far corner of the lot between emergency trucks and an ambulance, and that the section be cordoned off with tape, shielding them from media and others. She wanted to afford them some privacy.

Benton and Tilden had escorted the Shaws and their in-laws to the area. The two paramedics with the ambulance had been alerted and stood ready nearby. Minutes later Pierce arrived with Grotowski and Hirano, and as she neared Anna Shaw's mother and father, she began absorbing their demeanor, locking in details and readying herself.

"I'm Anna Shaw's mother," Lynora said to Pierce. "Where is she?"

"Are you in charge?" Chuck said. "What the hell's going on?"

"Is Anna hurt? People here are saying things!" Lynora's eyes searched Pierce's. "Tell us what's happened!"

Reading their faces, Pierce knew that they knew.

The families always knew just before they were told. They knew from the police activity, the scope, its intensity, the overpowering alarm in the air. They knew. But they didn't want to know. They begged to Heaven that they were wrong, because like every parent, deep in their hearts, they prayed that it couldn't be true—that the worst thing in the world wasn't happening.

But they knew it was.

And it was Pierce's job to tell them.

"I'm Detective Kim Pierce—" she started.

But Chuck Shaw pressed on. "Listen," he said, fear and

anger carved deep into his face. "Lynora gets a call from a parent that something's happened to Anna. I leave my work site, get her at the bank—the whole time we're driving here no one's telling us a damn thing!" Shaw cast around at the distant helicopter. "Are you going to tell us?"

Pierce blinked several times, her eyes softening as she reached into her pocket and showed them Anna's driver's license.

Lynora's hands flew to her mouth.

"Mr. and Mrs. Shaw, is this your daughter, Anna Catherine Shaw?"

Lynora clamped her eyes shut, squeezing out thick streams of tears.

"Yes," Chuck said, his voice shattering.

"I'm so sorry, but I have bad news."

"Oh, God, no!" The words scraped up Lynora's throat.

The man and woman behind the Shaws, Lynora's sister and her husband, stepped closer, putting their hands on their shoulders.

"I'm sorry to have to tell you," Pierce said calmly, her voice firm but warm. "Anna was on a cliff when she fell a great distance. She was so badly hurt she didn't survive. I'm so sorry."

Lynora crumpled. Chuck, his brother-in-law and Lynora's sister caught her. Then a soft moaning escaped from Lynora's very marrow, growing into a banshee wail that exploded from the enclave, blowing out over the parking lot, knifing through the trees and shooting into the sky. Chuck held her, a deep low groan quaking through him.

Paramedics had already opened the rear doors of their ambulance and, with the help of Lynora's sister and her husband, they got the Shaws seated on the rear entrance.

Pierce and the others stood with them, helpless. Paramedics shrouded the couple with a blanket. Lynora's sister lowered herself, rubbing Lynora's and Chuck's legs, minutes passing, their grief consuming them.

Lynora's face was buried in Chuck's chest. He held her head, his eyes blank, until his jaw began working, trying to push out words.

"How—how— Why did she fall?"

Pierce looked into his anguished face.

"A witness told us she was taking a selfie."

"A selfie?" he repeated in a weakened voice. "A selfie? Our daughter died because of a freaking selfie?" He shook his head. "Who was the witness who saw her?"

Pierce hesitated, but decided to tell them. They'd find out soon enough.

"Katie Harmon."

Chuck shut his eyes, nodding. "Anna babysits Katie. She slept at our house last night for this trip. They were up early with me. I drove them to the Sunny Days bus." He dragged a hand over his face. "The last thing Anna said to me was 'love you, Dad.'"

He began sobbing.

Lynora lifted her head, speaking as if her words were too heavy.

"I have to see Anna. Where is she—take me to her."

"I'm so sorry," Pierce said. "But it's not possible at this time."

"Why not?" Chuck asked. "She's our daughter. We want to see her."

"The medical examiner's team is with her. And at this time, with these cases, it's procedure for the medical examiner's team to transport her to their office at Harborview. Their staff will talk to you there, at their office on Jefferson, about next steps and arrangements."

Pierce allowed a few seconds, then made eye contact with the Shaws' brother-in-law.

"Would you be able to take them to Harborview?"

"Yes, we can take them," he said.

"Mr. and Mrs. Shaw," Pierce said, "we'll investigate further to answer all the questions about what's happened to Anna. We're sorry for your loss. Our condolences."

The Shaws may have nodded in thanks, or not.

It didn't matter.

They held each other tighter under the blanket, pulling even closer, fused in their pain.

Pierce touched each of them on the shoulder before stepping away.

She found a private space where she took a deep breath and kept herself together before resuming her work.

This was the part of the job she hated the most, because each time she told a mother, father, husband, wife, sister, brother or friend that a loved one was dead, a piece of her died, too.

9

Near North Bend, Washington

SARA HARMON SLOWED her Trailblazer at the entrance booth for Sparrow Song Park.

No one was inside.

She accelerated past it down the paved ribbon of road, her pulse racing, glancing at her phone for updates, finding none. A helicopter thudded by low to the treetops, hammering her with dread.

I've got to find Katie and bring her home.

Earlier, that was all Sara could think about while she drove along the interstate, weaving her SUV around cars and trucks. Using the hands-free option and voice commands on her phone, she'd sent a barrage of messages to learn more about what had happened.

Back at the diner, in that first text, Connie Atkinson, one of the supervisors, had said there'd been a terrible incident at the camp and that Sara should come right away. After that,

Connie's messages were sporadic. The next said: There's been a tragedy. Katie's shaken but okay.

Tragedy? Katie's shaken? What kind of tragedy?

Sara's request to speak with Katie went unanswered.

Sara's calls to Katie's phone went unanswered.

Sara's calls to Connie's phone went unanswered.

Sara's calls to Anna's phone went unanswered.

Tragedy? What tragedy?

Then, in Connie's most recent message, she'd instructed Sara to wait for Katie at the police line in the parking lot at the trailhead.

Police line? Dear God!

Now Sara was losing her mind as she came to the lot. The havoc of emergency vehicles, their lights flashing, with news trucks, cameras and people gathered at one end.

No spots were available. She parked on the shoulder, grabbed her keys, her phone, her bag and, still in her dark shirt and dark jeans for work, she ran.

Sara rushed to the end of the parking lot and the trailhead, where she'd glimpsed yellow police tape. Distraught parents were leaving with their kids, comforting them while walking to their cars. She pinballed from group to group, searching for Katie and for Anna, asking about them. No one knew anything.

Why hasn't Anna contacted me? She's so responsible.

Seeing TV reporters interviewing people, urgency mounting, Sara went to the nearest camera. Its lens and bright light were aimed at a woman holding a boy close to her. She was among a small group, talking to a woman who had coiffed hair, lots of makeup, and was gripping a microphone.

"From what we're hearing," the woman was telling the reporter, "a girl fell from a cliff and died…"

"Who fell?" Sara asked others nearby. "Does anyone know

who fell?" Most shrugged. Sara said a bit louder, "Please, I need to know!"

The reporter, watching from the corner of her eye, stepped toward her, thrusting the microphone toward her face. The camera and light were now on Sara.

"Excuse me," the reporter said. "Would you talk to us?"

Anger and fear rising in her throat, Sara shook her head and moved off, bumping and shouldering her way toward the police line and the deputies there.

"Can you please help me?" Sara said to a deputy with a clipboard. "I was told to come here to get my daughter."

"Yes, ma'am. Her name?"

"Katie Harmon. Kaitlyn Jean Harmon, she's nine, with the Sunny Days group."

He focused on the name sheet, then said, "Your name, ma'am?"

"Sara Harmon. I'm her mother."

"Could you show me some identification?"

Sara withdrew her driver's license from her wallet. The deputy then flipped to a page and turned the clipboard and his pen to her.

"Sign here." He tapped a spot.

After she signed, he stepped away, turning, reaching for his shoulder microphone and saying something into it. Then to Sara, "Please stand aside, ma'am. They'll bring her out shortly."

"Can you tell me what's happened?"

"I'm not authorized, ma'am."

Sara nearly choked on her words.

"My daughter's in there! Tell me! Is she alright? Tell me!"

"I'm sorry, ma'am, but I don't have any information. Please stand to one side."

Stunned, Sara moved trance-like, watching other parents

getting their kids. Some parents she knew, like Daria Ahmadi, who'd worked at the diner years ago.

Daria was helping her daughter, Leila, who was about eleven, pass under the tape.

"Daria." Sara touched her arm. "What's happened?"

"Oh, Sara. It's awful, just awful. It's going around that one of the children was killed."

"Oh, my God, no! Who? Do you know who?"

"No, Mom," Leila said through tears. "It was a supervisor."

"A supervisor? Who?" Sara asked.

The deputy stepped closer, saying, "Ladies, I'm sorry, but you need to keep moving. Please."

"We have to go, Sara," Daria said.

Her mind racing, Sara stepped back, clasping her hands together, entwining her fingers and touching her knuckles to her lips as if in prayer. Then a man and woman wearing jackets with *SHERIFF* on the back arrived. They spoke quietly with the deputy at the tape, then followed his gaze to Sara before approaching her.

"Are you Sara Harmon, Katie Harmon's mother?" the woman said.

"Yes, I'm here for Katie. She's on this trip with her sitter, Anna Shaw."

The man and woman traded a serious look.

Sara felt her scalp tingle.

"I'm Detective Kim Pierce, this is Detective Larry Grotowski."

"Is it Katie? What's happened?" Sara asked.

"I'm very sorry," Pierce said. "It appears Anna Shaw fell to her death and your daughter was with her at the time."

Sara covered her mouth with her hands. Eyes filling with horror, she thumped back against a Washington State Patrol SUV. She was frozen for a moment before hugging herself, fighting tears, struggling to cling to a measure of composure as Pierce rubbed her arm.

Then, her voice barely above a whisper, Sara asked: "Did Katie see it happen?"

"We believe so," Pierce said. "We've spoken with her."

"How is she?"

"Pretty shaken—paramedics have looked at her and say she's holding up, given the situation."

"What about Lynora and Chuck, Anna's mom and dad?"

"They're here and they know."

Sara shook her head. "Oh, my God, this is so—so horrible!"

"Will you be okay?" Pierce asked.

Sara got tissues from her bag.

"I don't know, I just—oh, God—I just want to get Katie home."

"Is there someone we can call for you?"

"No, I'll be okay once I get Katie."

Pierce continued staring at her, assessing her until Sara's attention shifted to the trailhead, the tape and Katie under the arm of a female deputy. Katie looked so small in the large hoodie, her face nearly concealed.

Spotting her mother, Katie broke away from the deputy.

Sara lowered herself and Katie flew into her arms. Holding her tight, Sara felt Katie's convulsed sobs, muffled against her, for several moments before her crying subsided. Sobbing herself, Sara wiped her daughter's tears and let Katie catch her breath.

"Everyone's saying Anna's dead," Katie said.

"I know, sweetheart. It's so awful, so terrible. Are you alright?"

Sara stroked Katie's hair as the detectives watched and listened.

"I saw Anna fall. She was taking a selfie, and I told her

to be careful. Then she fell." Katie gasped. "She fell but she was hanging on to a branch, just hanging on. I ran for help. I ran as fast as I could and got Jackson and Adam and Connie. But when we got back, Anna was at the bottom and oh—oh, no—she looked broken!"

A TV reporter and camera operator had quietly inched closer to record Katie and Sara. Grotowski noticed them first. "Back off!" he said.

"We're not intruding," said the reporter, the same woman who'd tried to interview Sara before.

"Back off," Grotowski repeated.

Deciding not to push the issue, the reporter and camera operator retreated and turned to hunt for people to interview in the parking lot.

"Thank you," Sara said to Grotowski.

Pierce took a business card from her badge wallet, jotting numbers and information on it. She then touched Sara's arm.

"I know this is a painful time but we'll need to talk to Katie again sometime later," Pierce said. "We're hanging on to her backpack and phone for now. I didn't see any medications, but if there's something in there she needs, let me know."

Sara nodded.

"Can we go home, Mom?" Katie said.

Sara stroked her hair.

"Yes. Our car's this way."

"You're sure you're okay to drive back to Seattle?" Pierce asked.

"I think so." Sara touched her tissue to her eyes. "Yes, I think so."

"One more thing," Pierce said. "While you're free to do what you like, we'd suggest you not talk to media or post things about this while we're investigating."

Arms around each other, Sara and Katie walked across the

parking lot. Driven by the need to see Anna's parents, Sara searched for Lynora's Malibu, or Chuck's truck. Cars were coming and going in the lot. The yellow school bus that had delivered the group to the park that morning had just returned for those who needed a ride back.

Unable to find the Shaws' vehicles, Sara and Katie continued to their car. They were steps away when a horn sounded behind them.

"Sara!"

They turned to the SUV that had stopped next to them. Chuck and Lynora got out of the back and they all embraced in a long tearful hug.

"Oh, God!" Sara said. "Oh, God, I'm so sorry!"

Chuck no longer resembled himself, his face a mask of pain. Lynora's face was crumpled, her eyes swollen, drowning in agony. Suddenly Lynora seized Katie's hand in desperate anguish.

"You were with Anna! You were the last to see her!" Lynora's voice rasped.

Katie's eyes widened, tinged with fear at the depth of Lynora's grief.

"What happened, Katie? Tell me what happened?"

Pulling Katie tighter to her, Sara said, "Honey, you don't have to talk about it now if—"

"It's okay. I want to," Katie said, swallowing hard. Her voice breaking over her words, she relayed what had happened on the cliff, how Anna wanted to take a selfie.

"She started walking backward and I said be careful, Anna, then she just fell and screamed."

Still clasping Katie's hand hard, Lynora's body trembled.

"What..." she began. "Katie, please, what was the last thing Anna said?"

Katie bit her bottom lip.

"It's so beautiful here."

A few seconds passed before Lynora groaned and threw her arms around Katie, the last person who'd been with Anna, in the last moment of her life. Lynora welded herself to Katie with such force, releasing a wild animal wail that rose over the parking lot.

Fused to Katie, Lynora wouldn't let go. It was as if she felt by some metaphysical force she could reach through Katie to hold Anna. Gently, Chuck, aided by his sister-in-law, pried Lynora from Katie and got her back into their car, then they drove away, bound for the morgue in Seattle.

Standing alone with Katie on the roadside, Sara noticed people nearby, staring at them. News cameras and phones had captured the scene. Moving quickly, Sara got Katie into their car and drove out of the park.

Before they reached the interstate, she pulled over to the shoulder of the on-ramp, stopped and undid her seat belt, then Katie's. She took Katie into her arms and they cried together. Several minutes passed before Sara released Katie, got tissues for both of them and refastened their belts.

As Sara resumed driving down the ramp and onto the highway, she reached out, taking Katie's hand. But Katie only watched the forests rolling by. The drone of the highway was soothing. When Sara gave her hand a tender squeeze and glanced at her, she could feel that Katie was still trembling while staring into the trees.

"It's okay if you want to talk to me about it, sweetie."

Katie swallowed, then shifted in her seat, slipping one hand into her front pocket. While driving, Sara saw a metallic flash in Katie's hand, then the fine chain of a gold necklace.

Katie caressed its tiny gold heart with her thumb.

That's not Katie's necklace.

Eyes shifting from the road back to Katie, Sara tried to recall where she'd seen that necklace before.

"That's so pretty, honey," Sara said. "Where did you get it?"

"Anna gave it to me."

"Anna?"

"Yes."

"You never showed it to me. When did Anna give it to
you?"

"Before she fell."

10

Seattle, Washington

FOR MUCH OF the drive Katie held the necklace, often touching the tiny gold heart to her cheek.

As Sara watched, anguish and anxiety pounded at her in waves, stirring old fears. With every mile, she forced herself to focus on getting them home.

But her troubling thoughts raged.

Anna's death was horrific.

That Katie had been the last to see Anna and now had her necklace only deepened it. Watching the traffic and the suburbs flowing by, Sara wanted to ask Katie more about the necklace, but she held back.

Don't start anything now. You're not thinking clearly.

During their drive Sara's phone pinged with messages and vibrated with calls, but she didn't respond. *I'll deal with them later.* Closer to the city, Katie turned to Sara.

"How long will they keep my phone?"

"I don't know."

"I need my phone, Mom."

Even though Katie was only a kid, Sara had wanted her to have a phone. She got her one for her ninth birthday and had put all the parental controls on it. Being a single, widowed mom, Sara never wanted to be out of touch with her daughter, and knowing she had a phone gave Sara peace of mind.

"Mom, why do they need my phone? It's my private phone and I want it back."

"Maybe we can get you a temporary one later, but we won't worry about that now."

It wasn't long before they'd reached their North Seattle neighborhood tucked between Lake City Way and the interstate. A community of hardworking families and well-kept homes shaded by tall trees, it felt like a small town.

Sara had grown up here.

She found a measure of relief when they came to their two-story seashell-gray house. It had belonged to her parents, just like the SUV. Sara got them both after her dad died and after her mom went to a seniors' home. Her parents' life insurance and savings went to support her mom's care, with just enough left so that, with Sara's job, she and Katie could survive. But lately the cost of her mom's care was rising to the point where they would soon be unable to afford it.

I can't think about that now.

She parked the Trailblazer in the driveway.

They entered the house in silence. Sara grappled with a numbing sense of unreality, striving to find order in something mundane.

"Have you eaten anything?" Sara asked.

Katie shook her head.

"How about a banana smoothie?" Sara said.

Katie shrugged.

Sara started making it, preferring the activity to the raw quiet and her jumbled thoughts and emotions. She made enough for both of them, then checked her phone.

News of the tragedy had moved with viral speed. Friends offered concern, condolences and support.

I just saw the tragic news about Katie's group, Val Rossi, her friend and neighbor, had texted. Let me know what I can do, dear.

Sara took a second, then texted back: I will. Thank you, Val.

Another message was from a paramedic, relayed by Detective Pierce. It reiterated that Katie was experiencing mild shock, advising Sara to keep her calm and rested. Then she got an email from the Sunny Days Youth Center.

Dear Parents and Guardians:

It is with deep sadness that we inform you about a recent loss to our Sunny Days community during a day trip to Sparrow Song Park. The death of one of our volunteers will raise many emotions, concerns and questions for everyone.

We're arranging for a Crisis Intervention Team made up of professionals specially trained to help at difficult times such as this. The team of counselors will be available at no cost for any child, parent, relative, friend, staff member or volunteer who may want help or any type of assistance surrounding this loss.

We've enclosed details of the times and dates the team will be available.

We are profoundly saddened by the loss and are making every effort to help everyone involved.

Sincerely,
Violet Juarez
Director

Sara's phone rang. It was Mel from the diner, so she answered.

"Hey, Sara, we've been trying to reach you. It's online and all over the news that a girl was killed at Katie's camp."

Sara stifled a sob and left the kitchen to talk.

"Are you alright, kid?" He'd called her *kid* since the day he hired her.

"Not really. Katie was there. She saw the girl fall."

"What? Damn! Oh, geez!"

A second passed and Sara turned to ensure Katie couldn't hear.

"Do you need help? What can we do?" Mel said.

"No," Sara said, fighting for control of her emotions. "No, thank you. I think I'm going to need a couple days, you know?"

"Absolutely, take whatever you need. We'll cover your shifts."

"Thank you."

"Okay, just let me know if you need us, or anything."

"I will. Thank you, Mel."

Collecting herself, Sara returned to the kitchen and Katie, who was swirling her reusable straw and looking into her smoothie.

"That was my work, honey."

Katie didn't say anything.

Sara's phone vibrated with two new messages, both from reporters. One from TV, *Channel 7 News*; the other from the *Seattle Times*. They were requesting interviews.

Sara left them unanswered.

How did they get my number?

Katie suddenly got up and hugged Sara so hard she nearly lost her balance. She hugged her back, unable to dismiss thinking that at times Katie had seemed somewhat distant. Perhaps it was all stemming from the shock, she thought, before Katie raised her head and looked at her.

"My tablet's in my backpack. Mom, can I use yours to talk to my friends?"

"I don't think it's a good idea, honey. Everything's a little chaotic right now. We need to keep things calm."

Sara could feel Katie trembling against her.

"Are you cold, sweetie?"

"A little."

Stroking Katie's hair, Sara considered the paramedic's advice to keep her rested. Sara needed to fill the silence with something for Katie. "Let's go upstairs to my room and watch your favorite movie."

They got onto Sara's bed, propped up pillows and got under the big quilt Sara had bought last fall at a fundraiser, and she started *The Wizard of Oz* on her tablet. Seeing Dorothy's house spinning in the tornado, Sara tried to make sense of Anna's death.

She'd been in our home so many times to watch over Katie. She was like a big sister to her.

The tornado kept churning and the house kept spinning, like Sara's thoughts. She held on to Katie but nothing was real anymore.

Please let it all be a dream.

While they watched the movie, the doorbell rang. Looking from her bedroom window, Sara saw a news truck out front but didn't go down to the door.

"Who is it, Mom?"

"Reporters. We're not going to talk to them." Sara stepped back from the window. "After they leave, I'll fix us something to eat."

Later she made grilled cheese and tomato soup. Good comfort food, as Mel always said. But they had little appetite. Afterward, the hours seemed to evaporate in a sorrow-filled fog with the evening coming fast.

Sara persuaded Katie to take a hot bath. She knelt next to her at the tub, washing her back, soothing her. Katie sat as if she were in a trance.

"Mom," Katie said, her voice low and despairing. "What's wrong with me?"

Her question caught Sara off guard before she recovered.

"What do you mean?"

"I feel like I'm a bad person."

"Why do you say that?"

"Because Anna died."

"Oh, honey, no. What you're feeling is normal. Honey, it's like the paramedics said, you're shaken. You saw a horrible thing, an awful thing that was beyond your control."

Katie didn't answer. With the gentle trickling of the water, Sara decided now was her chance to press a little.

"Maybe we could talk a bit," Sara said.

Katie didn't respond.

"What happened has taken a toll on your nerves." Sara swallowed. "You saw Anna step backward off—" she cleared her throat "—off the cliff. She just backed up, right?"

Katie nodded, as if in a hypnotic state, watching the tragedy replay on the tiled wall in front of her.

"She was taking a selfie?" Sara said.

Katie nodded.

"That's what really—I mean, that's all that happened?" Sara asked.

Suddenly, the water splashed as Katie thrust her hands to her face.

"Help me, Mom! Make it all go away!"

Sara hugged her, shushing her.

"It's okay, it's okay."

Katie froze, then asked: "Do you think it hurt when Anna fell?"

Tears filled Sara's eyes. Katie was struggling to comprehend what was incomprehensible.

"No," Sara said. "I think it was fast, that she didn't suffer and went straight to Heaven."

"Really?"

"Yes, sweetie, I really believe it."

Katie stared at the tiles.

Sara continued, gently pressing, "It was so nice that she gave you her pretty necklace."

"I love it so much," Katie said.

"You said she gave it to you before she fell. When was that exactly?"

A long silence passed, punctuated by the drip from the faucet.

"It was on the bus."

"On the bus?"

"Well, first she showed it to me on the sleepover last night. She said she just broke up with Tanner and he wouldn't let her give it back, but she was so mad at him she didn't want it. Then on the bus this morning she showed it to me again. She was saying she would throw it off a cliff or something but I said no, don't, and that's when she decided to give it to me."

"So she gave it to you then, right there on the bus?"

Katie nodded. "I said it was pretty and I liked it so she gave it to me on the bus before we got off and I put it in my pocket because we had to get off."

"Did people see Anna give the necklace to you?"

"I don't know but I put it my pocket because I didn't want to lose it and everyone was excited to get their backpacks on and get off the bus, and we were at the back."

Sara thought for a moment.

"Do the police know you have Anna's necklace?"

"It's my necklace, Mom. She gave it to me."

"Yes, but later, did you tell, or show, the police how Anna gave it to you?"

"No, they never asked me. I kept it my pocket. I didn't want to lose it." Katie slapped the water with both hands. "Mom, please, it's not important anymore."

"I know, honey, I know." Sara had another idea. "Maybe I should hold on to it and we should think about giving it back to Anna's parents?"

"Why?"

"I'm sure Anna's mom would like to have it."

"But it's mine."

Sara didn't know what to say. She looked at Katie for a few worried seconds before finally reaching for a towel.

Katie slept in Sara's bed that night.

In the darkness, Sara was listening to her breathing when suddenly a noise rose from the street.

Plastic scraping against pavement.

Sara went to her window, looked down at her black and blue trash containers on the curb. Tomorrow was collection day. It sounded as if someone had moved them. *Weird, no one's there.* In the past, she'd occasionally seen a homeless person sifting through the neighborhood garbage. *But no one's there.*

She returned to bed.

Settling back under her sheets, listening to Katie's breathing, the tragedy, and the dread compounding it, tormented Sara.

While Katie slept, Sara inserted earphones and connected them to her tablet so she could listen to news reports on what had happened. A photo of Anna from one of her social media accounts blossomed on the screen as a report began:

"A Seattle teen died today after falling from a cliff while

reportedly taking a selfie on a trail during a group outing in Sparrow Song Park east of the city…"

Dramatic shaky aerial footage showed the tarp near the river, then cut to reaction shots of parents in the parking lot. Sara and Katie were in a few of them, including when they had consoled Anna's parents. But the reports only named Anna and in most reports Katie's face was blurred—a few showed Sara's face, but her head was turned.

"Sources have identified the victim as Anna Catherine Shaw, seventeen, of Seattle. At this stage, her death appears to be a tragic hiking accident. King County detectives are investigating. We'll update you as more information becomes available…"

Other reports Sara watched and read were similar.

Then she checked other social media, to see some of the things people were saying.

How horrible. My heart goes out to her family.

What a waste. She was so young.

WTF, dying for a dumb picture.

Shutting off her tablet, her stomach in knots, Sara looked at Katie.

This can't be happening.

The gray-and-white flowers of Sara's tattoo stirred troubling memories.

All these years, without anyone knowing about us.

She closed her eyes because her worst fears were looming.

Now, with today's tragedy—please don't let it be true! It can't be true!

11

LATER THAT NIGHT, while Sara Harmon's neighborhood slept, a vehicle moved slowly down her empty street.

No dog walkers, late-night joggers or delivery people to see it, only crickets chirping in the stillness.

A solitary cat padded down the sidewalk.

The vehicle came to a silent stop near but not directly in front of Sara's house, as if to avoid any home security cameras.

It sat there, idling quietly.

The driver's side window lowered, giving whoever was in the vehicle a clearer view of the house and the Trailblazer parked in the driveway.

They watched without fear, without a need to hurry away.

They watched with the patience of a hunter.

They watched for nearly twenty minutes before the vehicle pulled away as slowly as it had emerged, vanishing into what was left of the night.

12

ACROSS THE CITY in the hour before sunrise, Detective Pierce was home, poring over case files, statements, videos and notes.

She'd gotten in late last night.

Her son and husband had already gone to bed. She'd tried to sleep, too, but had risen after three hours, working under the glow of her desk lamp and leaving the rest of the house in darkness.

As she sipped coffee, her thoughts went back a few hours to when she and the team had returned to headquarters. She was there with Grotowski, Tilden and Benton. She'd started debriefing Detective Sergeant Acker when Benton jumped into the conversation.

"I'm telling you, Art, this is a wilderness accident. Tragic, but she fell."

Grotowski and Tilden watched in silence, but Acker saw Pierce's jaw muscles bunching.

"Carl," Acker said. "Kim's the lead. Go on, Kim."

"There's an indication she'd just broken up with her boyfriend but—"

"Are you saying she jumped?" Benton said.

"No. But we can hardly draw a conclusion at this stage," Pierce said.

"Our only witness is a nine-year-old girl," Benton said. "I can't see criminal intent here, so…"

"Carl." Acker glared at him before nodding at Pierce to continue.

"The boyfriend is only one element," Pierce said, flipping through her notebook. "We still have to get warrants. The forensic work isn't complete. The scene needs to be processed. The area needs to be gridded for her phone, the medical examiner's not finished and we still haven't canvassed every person who was in the park at the time of Anna Shaw's death."

"Alright," Acker said. "We're just getting started. We've got a long way to go before we nail this down. We all know that it's part of the job to challenge each other, and some of you are still a bit jacked—it's been a long day. Go get some sleep. Get back to it in the morning."

Pierce had arrived home to find a note from Webb, her husband, on the kitchen table.

There's pizza in the fridge. We held the onions for you.

She'd smiled—she liked cold pizza and ate a slice before heading to bed.

Now at her desk, in the tranquil predawn light, Pierce estimated that she still had an hour before Webb and Ethan would be up.

She drank more coffee and got back to work.

Once more chronologically with key points: Anna Shaw is Katie Harmon's babysitter. How did they get along? There was the sleepover. Katie says Anna broke up with her boyfriend.

Pierce went to her notes for his name: Tanner Bishop.

We need to talk to him. What happened between them? What was Anna's state of mind at the time she fell? So then Anna and Katie take the bus with the group to Sparrow Song Park. But no one's at the park's entrance booth. We finally got to Dave Kneller, the park owner.

Pierce found Kneller's statement.

We staff the booth. But our person went home sick real early. I told him to leave the gate up. We knew the Sunny Days folks were coming, so it was no problem. The gate was up so it would've been free admission until I could get someone to work the gate. It was fine with me. We don't have plate readers or anything like that. So, yeah, we likely had a few early birds come and go, hikers, joggers, etc. We're a laid-back operation. We do have a camera in the parking lot for liability. But it's an old one. This is just a terrible thing. We'll do all we can to help.

Pierce bit her bottom lip and went online. Notice and details of the excursion to Sparrow Song had been made public, posted on the Sunny Days site. Anyone could've seen it.

And we don't know who was in the park before or after the Sunny Days group arrived. We have a list of plates the team collected after the fact at the scene to run down and canvass, but the key question is, did anyone get by us, anyone from earlier?

Pierce moved to the videos and photos that followed Anna Shaw and Katie Harmon's path to the scene, studying the terrain and area around the clifftop. She saw the cluster of stones several yards from the point where Anna fell. Partially concealed by underbrush and loosely spread around.

Maybe used in a campfire years ago. I can't put my finger on it but there's something about these stones.

Pierce moved on to the video and photos of the broken branch, the cliff face and the bottom of it. Her heart broke again as she looked at the area, the riverbank, then Anna's lifeless body.

Pierce paused for a moment.

Was this all for a selfie, Anna? Is Benton's assumption correct? Or is there more to it?

Pierce had no key facts, no evidence to support anything yet. One important item was Anna's phone, which still hadn't been located. They'd called the number without success, and tracking apps had failed. The phone may have been damaged or swept away down the river. Other work was ongoing. Much of the forensic analysis was still to be completed. They had the backpacks and they had warrants in the works for them and one to look at Katie Harmon's phone.

Pierce went online to check Anna Shaw's social media, which had a lot of posts related to music, fashion, celebs and food. Not a whole lot of selfies. If Anna was trying to become a Sunny Days supervisor, why would she stop to take a selfie? Seems a little irresponsible, even odd, or out of character, Pierce thought.

What we have is a dead seventeen-year-old girl and the account of one child witness.

As she reread other statements and reports, a pinging sounded at the back of Pierce's mind.

I've forgotten something, overlooked something.

She couldn't pinpoint it.

Kneading the tension in her neck and shoulders, she weighed what she had to do today when the floor creaked near her.

"Hey." Webb kept his voice low, whiskers brushing Pierce's cheek as he kissed her. "I didn't hear you come in. You get any sleep?"

"A little."

"Guess being the lead on a case means no sleep for you."

She stared at the screen of her tablet.

"I can't make mistakes. I have to get this right, Webb."

"You can do this, hon. You're a detective, you've got this."

"We'll see." Pierce paused, closing the file of a photo of Anna's corpse. "A girl is dead and it's on me to prove without a doubt exactly what happened, and there are things going on."

"What kind of things? Is Acker giving you a hard time?"

"No, Art's fine."

"Is it the others? What about that Benton guy you mentioned?"

"Oh—" she waved it off "—Benton's being Benton. I've dealt with people like that all my life. No, I just need to do this right and I can't shake the feeling that I've missed something."

"You're smart, Kim. You'll do a good job. I have faith in you."

"You'd better. That's what you signed up for, buddy."

"Listen, I've got your back. I'm just coming off twenty-fours and don't have to be at the firehouse for a few days. So there's no problem with Ethan. After that we'll get my mom."

Pierce nodded as he rubbed her shoulders and neck.

"You're tense. Have a shower. I'll get breakfast and fresh coffee going."

Hot needles of water felt good on Pierce's skin.

Images of Anna Shaw rose in the wisps of steam as the full weight of the investigation pressed down on her.

After dressing to the aroma of fresh coffee and the sizzle of bacon frying, she went to her son's bedroom.

A Seahawks poster was on one wall, a framed mosaic he'd made with dazzling colors on another. She sat on the edge of his bed and kissed his cheek.

"Time to get up, Ethan."

He clenched his eyes tighter and she kissed him again.

"Come on, get up."

Groggy, he rolled over, rubbing his eyes and smiling at her.

"Guess what?" he said.

"What?"

"I'm making a drum for the next time we go to Arizona."

"That's cool. Sounds like fun. Your uncle will love that." Pierce stood. "Dad's got breakfast going, let's go."

She glanced around and began picking up Ethan's clothes to get ready for the next load. While she was in the laundry room, emptying his pockets, it struck her.

I forgot to get Katie Harmon to show me what was in her pockets.

Maybe Hirano did that, she thought, returning to her desk, scrutinizing reports and finding nothing.

She took a breath, cursing to herself.

I can't go back in time.

Pierce cued up Grotowski's recording of her interview with Katie. She replayed it, scrutinizing Katie's demeanor and body language under that big hoodie.

Are we getting the whole story from her? Hirano thought she was being deceptive. Certainly she was traumatized, but I got a sense that she was holding back, not telling me everything.

And as for a juvenile committing a crime?

Well, for the most part, Pierce knew that state law considered young children legally incapable of committing a crime, except when it came to murder. That meant a child Katie's age could face a murder charge if there was proof and evidence that she understood her actions were wrong.

Don't be making any assumptions.

"Breakfast," Webb called from the kitchen.

Switching off her tablet, Pierce joined her husband and son at the table. She was happy to be with her men, absorbing the moment, hearing what they had going on today.

"Math test," Ethan said.

"Are you ready?" Pierce asked.

He gave her a thumbs-up. "I studied."

She turned to Webb, wanting to know what he was doing today.

"Going to help Raylon restore his old Dodge pickup."

Finishing her toast, Pierce said she was getting back to the case, leaving out today's first order of business: attending the autopsy of Anna Catherine Shaw.

Big Skyline Library Network Data Services–Montana News Archives 1994

Family of Missing Massachusetts Couple Fear Worst

TOM GANNON
World Press Alliance 25 August 1994

Officials in Boston have asked police across the western US to help locate Lydia Worrell, 67, and Frank Worrell, 68, a retired couple making a cross-country dream trip to the West Coast in their motorhome.

The Worrells have been reported missing by their son, Phil Worrell of Springfield, Mass., who hasn't heard from his parents in over two weeks.

"We feel something's wrong, that something happened, somewhere," Worrell, 42, told the *Boston Globe*.

He said his dad, Frank Worrell, a retired bus mechanic with Massachusetts Bay Transportation Authority, and his mom, Lydia Worrell, a retired bank teller, left their South Boston home in late July.

"They talked about taking this trip for years."

Worrell said his parents were looking forward to seeing landmarks across the country on their way to visiting their daughter and her family in Spokane, Washington, then driving along the west coast to see their son and his family in California.

"Once a day, every day, my mom, or my dad, would call one of us to let us know where they were, where they were headed and that all was well."

Worrell said the last time the family heard from the couple was August 4. They called from Great Falls, Montana, and were ready to start driving through the mountains, across Idaho and into Spokane.

"Since the call from Great Falls, none of us has heard a word," Worrell said. "We're a big loving family. My parents have six kids and eleven grandchildren. Every day they'd call from campgrounds or gas stations because they didn't have a mobile phone. But they go from calling one of us each day to absolute silence? We're sick with worry."

Worrell and his brothers and sisters have called police, hospitals, motels and campgrounds, and even contacted trucking companies to ask drivers traveling along the route their parents would have taken to check for any accidents, incidents or sightings. He said his family is preparing to fly to Montana to start searching for their parents.

"We know with hundreds of miles to cover it's like a needle in a haystack, but we're not giving up until we find them."

The couple's last known credit card transaction was for gas and food at a gas station near Missoula, Montana, on August 4. But investigators found no record of the missing couple making phone calls or using their bank or credit cards beyond that date.

"We tracked their credit and bank card use across the country, but it stops cold at Missoula," said Sgt. Whit Newsom of the Boston police. "We've issued missing person alerts, along with details and photos of the Worrells to every police agency in the western US and the FBI."

The couple is driving a 1992 Chevrolet Class C 21-foot motorhome with Massachusetts license plate AAA02AX

Police are urging anyone with information about the couple's whereabouts to contact their local law enforcement agency.

13

Seattle, Washington

SOFT CLASSICAL MUSIC floated in the somber air of the North Seattle community hall.

Sunlight streamed through the windows, gleaming on the polished wood floors. The building was often rented for corporate meetings, community gatherings, banquets and wedding receptions.

Today it was crisis counseling.

Watching people entering and leaving the hall, Sara accepted the risk in bringing Katie here. But given what Katie had experienced, Sara wanted her to talk to someone who knew about these things. She also secretly hoped that in some way coming here would allay her own deepening fears that went beyond the tragedy, to something so dark it was unimaginable.

"Welcome," Violet Juarez, director of the Sunny Days

Youth Center, greeted Sara and Katie. "Please sign in and we'll set you up."

At a table nearby, an SDYC volunteer gave Sara a consent form to fill in. Upon completing it, Sara and Katie waited in the reception area where Connie, Dakota and a few others from the group were talking. Seeing Katie, they swept around her in a flutter of tearful hugs.

"Oh, Katie," Dakota said.

"I'm so glad you're here." Connie embraced her, then clasped Sara's hand briefly.

"I felt we needed to come," Sara said, putting her arm around Katie, pulling her close. "Are Lynora and Chuck here?"

"No," Connie said. "But word is the service might be next week."

A woman emerged from a room nearby and said: "Sara and Katie Harmon?"

The woman was in her forties, wearing black-framed glasses and holding a tablet. A laminated ID card hung from a chain on her neck.

"Sally Mehta," she said. "I'm with the crisis team. Sorry if I'm interrupting."

"It's okay," Connie said, excusing herself with the others.

Sally Mehta turned to Sara and Katie. "Please come with me."

As they walked with her, they saw some people leaving, including Dylan Frick and his mom. Dylan appeared to give Katie a cold look, which she returned as they passed each other, leaving Sara unsure what to think of it. In the main room, the hall dividers had been employed, configuring the area into several small rooms that afforded privacy. Each had folding chairs around a folding table with a box of tissues, a pitcher of water and plastic glasses.

"Not the warmest, most ideal setting," Dr. Mehta said. "But it's the best way for us to help the most people the soonest."

Everyone sat and Dr. Mehta poured them water while smiling.

"I'm a psychiatrist. I teach a class at the University of Washington. I have a practice and I volunteer with the crisis network. There are a number of us here today. You can call me Sally, if you like. Do you have any questions before we start?"

"This is confidential, right?" Sara said. "Whatever we discuss stays with us?"

"Absolutely," Dr. Mehta said. "For us, this is doctor-patient privilege."

Sara nodded. "We're here for help," she said. "I brought Katie here because after what happened, and after we got the note about crisis counseling, I felt it would help if she talked to someone."

"Of course." Dr. Mehta smiled. "Katie, do you have any questions? I might not have all the answers but it's good to ask."

Katie lowered her head, looking into her hands.

"Just that I'm really, really sorry for what happened."

Dr. Mehta observed her, then said: "I can understand how hard this is."

"Sally, are you familiar with what happened?" Sara asked.

"We've been given a summary, but not specific names or details to protect privacy."

"So you're probably not aware," Sara said, "but Anna was our babysitter, our friend, and Katie was with her on the cliff. She saw it happen."

Katie lowered her head. Sara hugged her.

"I was not aware." Dr. Mehta took a moment, processing Katie's connection to the tragedy. "I see."

"Last night," Sara said, "Katie had a nightmare about it."

"Would you like to tell me about it, Katie?" Dr. Mehta asked.

Looking into her hands, Katie began.

"I just keep seeing Anna hanging on to the branch and she keeps begging me to get help, then in the dream I'm having all these bad thoughts and Anna's screaming why, why, why, and I don't know why, and I feel like it's my fault Anna's dead..."

Katie buried her face into Sara as she consoled her.

Dr. Mehta leaned closer to them.

"Katie—" Dr. Mehta's voice was soft "—this is a normal reaction. It's okay to have these thoughts and feelings after such a terrible event."

Dr. Mehta waited for a few seconds.

"Part of this, the way your mind mends itself and helps you heal, is to relive the tragedy, to blame yourself for what happened, to feel guilty for things that you were never really in control of."

Dr. Mehta paused.

"You may feel this way for a while because the pain, the hurt, is part of the way our hearts heal. But over time, you'll stop feeling it so much."

Katie, still burrowed into Sara, blinked through tears at Dr. Mehta, who continued for several minutes about what to expect and the things Katie and Sara should and should not do.

"Like don't watch or read the news reports on what happened," she said. "And remember, you'll never forget your friend, you'll always remember her, and when you're healed, your happy memories will erase the difficult ones you're holding now."

Sara cleared her throat.

"Sally, the service for Anna is happening soon. Should I take Katie to it?"

"If Katie wants to go, that's okay. It's good to say goodbye and honor the memory of your friend," Dr. Mehta said. "If Katie prefers not to go, that's okay, too."

"Thank you, Sally," Sara said. "This has been helpful."

Dr. Mehta reached into her pocket for her card.

"I'm happy to have follow-up sessions with Katie, if you like. No charge."

"Thank you."

"Katie, do you have any other questions, anything you'd like to know?"

"So I shouldn't feel like what happened to Anna was my fault?"

"It was a tragic accident that happened close to you."

"Just like with that boy," Katie said.

"No," Sara said, placing her hand on Katie's lap. "No, nothing like that."

Puzzled, Dr. Mehta blinked.

"What boy?" she asked, reaching for her tablet and swiping the screen. "I'm sorry, I don't understand." Dr. Mehta searched her summary. "There was a boy?"

"No." Sara was shaking her head. "She's confused things. It's a complicated, unrelated matter. Nothing to do with this. No, honey."

Dr. Mehta pulled her focus from her tablet, to look at Sara and Katie. An awkward silence passed between them before it was broken by Sara.

"We'll go now." Sara stood, taking Katie's hand. "Thank you again, Sally."

"I'll go that way with you."

They walked without talking and before Dr. Mehta took up the form for the next session, she stood at the hall door, watching Sara and Katie go down the sidewalk.

14

GIFTS WRAPPED WITH festive paper and bows formed small mountains around her at their Christmas tree, her mom beaming, taking pictures while her dad's booming laughter filled the house.

Sara was three, no, maybe four, at the time, and it was one of her earliest happiest memories.

Savoring it now while driving in the rain, she glanced at her tattoo, which catapulted her back through her life even further, to a hazy memory that she fought to keep out of her head...*driving at night in the rain...wipers swiping like a beating heart...the scream...something seizing her...*

Sara pushed away the painful thoughts until she was rescued by reflections of her parents: George and Marjorie Cole.

Her mom was an office administrator; her dad was an electrician. They were honest, hardworking, loving people, who lived their faith. Always volunteering to do whatever they could. Sara remembered the aromas of their kitchen, remembered standing on a chair after washing her hands, after Mom cut the onions and celery. "You scoop them into the pot, honey." Helping Mom make sandwiches, soup and chili, then driving with Dad to deliver the food to a church basement or mission. "You have to help people, that's what we do."

But there were moments, in those early years, when they looked at her, that she saw dread behind their eyes, a fear of something coming.

A darkness.

Sara turned to her daughter in the car beside her.

It's the same way I look at Katie.

Sara had been startled when Katie told the grief counselor about the boy. *I should've expected it as part of the risk.* Thankfully the session was confidential. Sara didn't want to think about the boy, because the matter had been resolved long ago, and it didn't fit with anything.

But maybe it does now.

Maybe it fits because of Anna's death. No. Stop. Don't think about it.

Sara took in the trees of the countryside.

"Isn't this pretty, hon?"

Katie nodded.

"Grandma always loved driving this way," Sara said. "When I was little, we'd come here to buy apples and Grandma made pies."

After several more miles, Sara came to the Silverbrook Hills Senior Living Home and parked. They registered at the desk, then went through the lobby. Along the way they saw Bella Spencer, a woman in her fifties who volunteered at Silverbrook. She had large glasses and was pushing a wheeled cart filled with books.

"Well, if it isn't Sara and Katie."

"Hi, Bella," Sara said.

EVERYTHING SHE FEARED 87

"Let me know if your mom would like a book today. Got some new John Grisham and Stephen King."

"Alright. Thanks, Bella."

Bella glanced around, then whispered a warning. "Hetta's here today."

Sara nodded. They passed by residents in cushioned chairs or wheelchairs playing cards at a table. A few steps down the hall they met Hetta Boden, Silverbrook's manager.

"Hello, Sara," said Hetta, her hair pulled into a tight bun, her smooth face holding little warmth.

"Hello."

"You've received our notice about the adjustment in our rates?"

"I have, thank you," Sara said, continuing with Katie to the elevator.

"A deadline is approaching," Hetta called after her.

"I know. Thank you," Sara said as they stepped inside the elevator.

They ascended to the fourth floor. The air in the hall held a mix of perfume and hospital. Suite 404 had a sign with large letters: Mrs. Marjorie Cole. The door was open.

"Grandma!"

Marjorie, sitting in her wheelchair at the window, was wearing a print dress. Katie rushed into her open arms.

"I saw you driving up." Marjorie held her tight. "Oh, that feels good!"

"Hi, Mom." Sara kissed her mother's cheek, then sat on the bed with its quilted spread.

"It's so lovely to see my two girls!"

"We brought you a present," Katie said. "Can I give it to her, Mom?"

Sara shifted her bag on the bed. Katie retrieved a box of chocolates and gave it to her grandmother.

"The kind you like, Grandma, milk chocolate."

"Oh, that's so nice." Marjorie kissed Katie. "Thank you. Why don't you have one right now? Go right ahead and open the box."

Katie's fingers found the seam of the cellophane wrapping and tore it away from the box.

"You look nice, Mom," Sara said. "How are you?"

"I had my hair done yesterday."

"I like how they feathered it."

Still working on the box, Katie said: "Mom, should we tell Grandma what happened to Anna? How I saw her body bleeding on the rocks. Sally said it was okay to talk about it."

"Oh, no," Marjorie said.

Sara's focus flicked to her mother and in that second, she saw the sparkle in her mother's face dim. Sara never doubted for a moment that her mother had learned of the tragedy. The residents of Silverbrook were news-watchers in the common room. Marjorie had a TV in her room, and she used the laptop Sara had given her two years ago almost every day.

In an attempt to shift the subject, she reached for the chocolates. "Let me finish opening the box, honey." She shook the tight lid loose and lifted it. "Take one."

"You go first, Grandma."

"Oh, I'll have one a little later, dear. Go ahead."

Katie picked a chocolate and bit into it.

"Now—" Sara got her tablet and a pair of small earphones from her bag "—Katie, why don't you go over to Grandma's table and finish watching the movie we started yesterday while I visit with her?"

"But I want to finish watching Snow White, first, and can I have one more chocolate?"

"Okay, Snow White and only one more."

After selecting another, Katie settled in on a chair at the

table on the far side of the room and inserted her earphones. When the movie came to life on the tablet, Sara sat closer to her mother and lowered her voice.

"Mom, do you know what happened at Katie's day camp?"

"Yes, when I saw it on the news, I sent you that email."

"Oh, I haven't read it yet. I'm so sorry—things have been so hectic."

"It's okay. This is all just so horrible."

Sara nodded, her chin crumpling.

"You don't know all of it. Anna Shaw was Katie's sitter, and when she fell, Katie was there."

Marjorie Cole drew a breath. "Katie was there when she died?"

Sara nodded, tears rolling down her face.

"In what way was she there, Sara?"

"She was the only person with her, the last person to see her alive."

Marjorie blinked, wincing slightly.

"Mom, I can't even say the words. I just don't know how to deal with it."

Marjorie lifted her wrinkled hands, taking Sara's hands into hers, while looking at Sara's tattoo.

"Mom, it can't be true, can it?"

They both turned to watch Katie across the room, sitting at the table with her legs crossed, finishing her chocolate. Her tablet was angled; they could see the movie. It was playing the part where the wicked witch queen was offering Snow White a poisoned apple.

"Tell me it's not true, Mom." Sara's whispered voice cracked.

Marjorie's face filled with trepidation, then tender compassion.

"I know you're afraid. I know what you fear. But you have to stay strong and trust your heart. Katie's a good girl."

15

HERE'S ANNA SHAW, a toddler blowing out candles on a cake.

Now here's Anna, front teeth missing, a pink helmet, gripping the handles of her bike. "Watch me, Daddy, watch!" And here's Anna, hugging Jon, her little brother, laughing with her mom and dad at the Grand Canyon.

The video played on the screens in the chapel of the funeral home, along with one of Anna's favorite songs, Sarah McLachlan's "Angel." One wall was lined with photos of Anna, always smiling, eyes bright like stars.

Fragrant flowers everywhere.

Anna's urn and candles were centered at the front on a table.

It was all Sara could do to hold herself together. Katie had wanted to come, so they'd joined the mourners filling the chapel. Most were teens wearing black or dark clothes and holding hands or gripping tissues, amid soft sniffles, whispers and shuffling of fabric.

The service was livestreamed and began with Reverend Arturo Santos from Anna's family's church at the podium, welcoming everyone, including those online, reviewing the program agenda.

He paused a moment before continuing.

"In gathering here today to celebrate Anna Catherine Shaw, we may ask why—why was her young life cut short? Parents are not supposed to grieve their children. This is not supposed to happen.

"But it did happen and we don't have the answers, and it hurts so much for all of us who loved Anna."

The reverend paused, holding the edges of the podium.

"But, in many ways Anna's death lights a path for us, a path to find meaning in our lives. Our pain reinforces the truth in our hearts of how strongly we are connected to each other. And now, our bond to Anna takes on a new spiritual form, a glorious transcendent understanding that she will always be a part of us..."

Reverend Santos continued for several minutes before concluding.

Then, one by one, others came to the podium to give eulogies.

Paige Kendall and Charlotte Cook, two of Anna's school friends, stood together, offering their memories.

"Anna was always there to fix you when your day sucked," Paige said.

"Yeah, *we need ice cream* was her solution to everything," Charlotte said, causing a ripple of laughter.

"Anna was the best of us," Paige said.

"She really was," Charlotte said as they consoled each other.

One of Anna's teacher's spoke next. Then the principal

of her school, then Anna's aunt Dolores, from Reno, who'd taught her how to play poker.

"It wasn't long before she was cleaning up. She was so good, so good."

The eulogies concluded with Chuck, Lynora and Jon, her little brother. At the podium together, supporting each other, they worked through tears to say what they needed to say.

"I was honored to be your dad," Chuck said.

"You were a perfect daughter," Lynora said. "I was blessed to be your mom."

Then Jon, now fourteen, moved to the microphone.

"She was so good at being a big sister that the angels asked God if they could have her to be their sister."

The program neared the end when Anna's friend, Will Naya, from her music class, played the piano and sang another of Anna's favorite songs, "Someone Saved My Life Tonight."

As he played, Sara brushed her tears and turned to Katie, putting her arm around her, giving her a sad smile, then shutting her eyes and praying.

Sara prayed with all her heart.

I cannot think what I'm thinking because it isn't true. I have to stay strong, like Mom said.

Sara clasped Katie's hand.

Because Katie's a good girl.

People congregated in the building's expansive entrance hall.

At times Sara sensed a few mourners were looking at her and Katie, but she could never catch them staring. *It's like they know.* Or maybe Sara was only imagining it, with her nerves in overdrive.

Navigating through the gathering, Sara and Katie passed

near a group of teenage girls, their whispers spilling over their circle.

"I can't believe Tanner came!"

"After breaking her heart? No way!"

"Maybe he still loves her?"

Funeral home staff gently guided everyone into a long line that flowed to Anna's family, close to the reception room where a buffet had been prepared. Sara and Katie soon found themselves in the line, sandwiched ahead of some teenage girls and behind two tall teenage boys in suits.

"Hi, Tanner," one of the girls whispered.

One of the boys, his tie a little crooked, turned and saw the girl. "Hi, Aubrey," he said. Turning back, Tanner glanced at Sara, then Katie, nodded politely, then did a double take, registering what Katie was wearing.

The necklace Tanner had given Anna.

He turned to face forward again, but unease rattled up Sara's spine.

I shouldn't have let her wear it here.

But Katie had insisted. As they dressed, she'd said: "Anna gave it to me, Mom. It's so pretty. Please, please let me wear it, to show how I miss her so much, to help my heart."

Sara had surrendered, but now, seeing Tanner's reaction underscored her discomfort as they advanced in the line. Drawing closer to the family, they could hear people offering condolences. Then Tanner stood before Anna's mother and father.

"I'm so sorry," he said, his voice tapering, "for everything."

Lynora looked at him.

Seconds passed before she accepted his words with a slight nod.

Chuck shook Tanner's hand. "Thank you."

Then Tanner nodded and moved on.

Upon seeing Sara and Katie, Lynora embraced them. "Thank you for being here today," she said.

"It was a beautiful service," Sara said.

"You look so nice, sweetheart," Lynora said to Katie.

Light glinted off the gold heart of Katie's necklace.

Lynora stared at it.

"That's a pretty heart," Lynora said. "Anna had one like it."

"This was Anna's." Katie held out the tiny heart. "She gave it to me."

A question was rising on Lynora's face.

"When did she give it to you?"

"On the bus at the park. Anna said she didn't want it anymore and that I could have it."

In the seconds that passed with Lynora looking at the necklace, Sara's nerves tingled. Then the corners of Lynora's mouth lifted into a weak smile.

"That sounds like Anna. Cherish it. I know she loved you, Katie."

"I loved her, too."

"That's why—" Lynora reached for Katie's hand "—it comforts us to know that you were the last—that you were with her when—that you were there, Katie."

Lynora gasped into her husband's chest; he held her as Jon rubbed his mom's shoulders.

"Thank you," Lynora exhaled.

Sara touched them. Then, with her arm around Katie, they began making their way out.

Moving toward their SUV, Sara spotted the news cameras and TV trucks across the street and walked a little faster.

16

Online

THE STRAINS OF the opening score for a 1940s noir movie play over a montage of desolate big-city streets at night.

Then the title *Tell-Tale Hearts with Sonya and Shane* blossoms on screens around the world.

It dissolves to an image of a woman with oversize red-framed glasses and a bearded man in a ball cap. Both are wearing headphones and are sitting at a table, poised for a broadcast.

Their room of book-filled shelves, framed photos, plants and posters of the covers for *In Cold Blood* and *Crime and Punishment* make for a warm, homey backdrop as they smile, wave and begin.

"A big hello to everyone. I'm Sonya and this is my brother, Shane."

Shane taps the brim of his hat in salute.

"And we are live," Sonya says. "Welcome to our ninety-ninth—can you believe it, bro?—our ninety-ninth episode of *Tell-Tale Hearts*."

"It's wild. And look at everyone joining us today, from Birmingham, England; Miami; Ottawa, Canada; Denver; Santiago, Chile; and Perth, Australia. Boy, some of you are up at all hours, talk about the real dark night of the soul, I love it."

"So," Sonya says, "a little background for those of you joining us for the first time. Shane and I are amateur sleuths who became obsessed true-crime aficionados. We started out reading classics like *In Cold Blood* and *Helter Skelter* and *The Onion Field*, then studying cases like the Boston Strangler, Ted Bundy, the Yorkshire Ripper and tons of others."

Photos from those cases flash on the screen.

"Since then, we couldn't get enough and started this channel to discuss cases new and cold with like-minded folk."

"Right," Shane says. "And a warning—we are unfiltered, our shows get very dark, very gross and very disturbing, because whenever and wherever possible we will show and discuss everything about a case. And we mean *everything*. If you are hardcore, we recommend a legendary primer, *Practical Homicide Investigation* by Vernon Geberth."

"This week we're joined by a special guest to discuss our featured case," Sonya says. "But before we start, we have some news. Thanks to you, we've surpassed five million views a month!"

"That is freaking amazing. We really want to thank you, our followers."

They cut to a blip of stock footage of mass crowds, oceans of people cheering and applauding.

"Today we're going to look back several decades to the case of one of the world's most prolific serial killers," Sonya says. "A soulless monster, active for over a decade before he was captured."

A photo of a bald man with a wide-eyed maniacal grin appears.

"This man," Shane says, "is Andrei Chikatilo of Russia."

"This case gave me chills."

"After he was arrested for killing, mutilating and, in some cases, eating parts of fifty-two boys, girls and young women, in the time between 1978 and 1990," Shane says, "Chikatilo called himself a freak of nature."

Photos of the young faces of victims appear.

"Chikatilo used to carry a frying pan and other cooking implements with him in his bag when he hunted his victims," Shane says. "Russian investigators noted that in one case the victim was so horribly destroyed, they initially ruled out homicide because they were convinced the victim had fallen into a harvesting combine."

Graphic crime scene photos appear.

When the photos vanish, the screen is split with the hosts on one side, a white-haired man with glasses and a headset, sitting at his office desk, on the other.

"Today we are honored to have with us Professor Anton Belyayev," Sonya says. "I hope I pronounced it correctly, Professor."

"You did."

"Thank you and welcome. You're joining us from Los Angeles where you're a visiting professor of history at UCLA."

"I am, and thank you for inviting me to your program."

"Professor," Shane says, "you have a personal connection to this case."

"I do. My uncle was one of the detectives who had a part in the investigation that resulted in Chikatilo's arrest."

A photo of Belyayev's uncle appears.

"Let's begin at the beginning," Sonya says, "starting with Chikatilo's life, then take us through the case history."

For the next hour Belyayev gives an account of how Chikatilo came to be, his career as a teacher, then clerk, along with his evolution into a serial killer of more than fifty known victims. The professor discusses how Chikatilo thrived as a murderer under the old Soviet system for more than a decade. Finally a five-year investigation led to his capture, trial and death sentence. He was executed with a bullet to the back of his head at a military prison in western Russia in 1994 and buried in an unmarked grave.

The professor discusses the case with Shane and Sonya while taking questions texted to the show from its worldwide audience. The episode winds down with the hosts thanking Belyayev, who logs off.

"That was fantastic," Sonya says.

"Incredible case. We were so fortunate to have Professor Belyayev as our guest. He was excellent."

"Now, a few notes about future episodes before we sign off," Sonya says. "In one of our upcoming segments, we'll take a deep dive into the case of Herman and Magda Vryker. They were a husband-and-wife team responsible for several murders in 1994 and 1995 across Montana, Idaho and Washington."

"In this case, the bodies of their victims were never found," Shane says. "I'll let Sonya give you some details."

"In prison, Magda changed her story about knowing the locations of the victims. She served her time and, after her release with no further conditions, remained silent before disappearing off the grid. Our guest will be Beatrice Clearfield with the social media group *The Hunters—Finding Magda*. In the time since Magda's release the group has dedicated itself to seeking justice by tracking her and posting information on where she may be and what she's doing. This horrible case has left the anguished families desperate to find the remains of their loved ones while fearing Magda gamed the system and is now smarter and out there possibly killing again under a new identity."

"You won't want to miss it," Shane says.

"Finally, friends, if there are cases you want us to consider for the show, or there's information you think needs to be shared, you know how to reach us. That's our show for this week."

The same opening music plays against the empty city streets at night as the screen fades to black.

17

BACON SPUTTERED IN the pan the morning after Anna's funeral.

Sara hadn't slept well.

Her thoughts continued pinballing from Anna's death, to Katie, to the necklace, and the worry knotted her stomach.

None of it's real. None of it's true.

Standing at the stove in her robe, she took a breath, tried to relax and sort things out. Katie hadn't come down for breakfast yet. Turning to the fridge for eggs, Sara spotted the note on her calendar for the mission.

Helping at the mission.

The mission.

Seeking refuge from the fears tormenting her, Sara reached for her tablet. She played an older video of Katie, with her, at the mission.

Katie was smiling at the mission's guests. "Welcome," she

said while assisting families. She carried trays of food for smaller children to their family's table. "Would you like me to get you anything else?" Katie asked them, then brought them napkins, utensils and drinks. The children liked Katie and she was totally dedicated to being there.

Seeing Katie embody her family's spirit of giving warmed Sara, especially the moment when Katie went to a little girl who was sitting with her dad. The girl appeared sad and wasn't eating.

"What's wrong?" Katie asked her.

The little girl whispered in Katie's ear. Katie patted her hand and went to Mr. Yang, the mission's manager. He went into the storage room filled with donated items and came back with a doll. He gave it to Katie, who gave it to the little girl.

"She's your dolly now," Katie told the little girl, comforting her. "She loves you."

Katie and the girl smiled at the camera.

The video ended, leaving Sara to think, *Was this really Katie?* Her smile in the video now seemed a little too sweet.

A chair scraped on the floor behind Sara.

Katie had come down to the kitchen in her pajamas and was seated at the table. Sara stroked Katie's hair.

"How're you doing, honey?"

Katie shrugged.

Sara kissed the top of her head, noticing that Katie was wearing Anna's necklace as she served up their breakfast. Neither of them had much of an appetite. They ate a few forks of scrambled eggs, a few bites of toast and nibbled at bacon. Katie spent most of the time staring at the small gold heart of the necklace.

"It was so awful on the cliff, Mom. So awful."

"I know, honey."

"I miss Anna and it hurts so much."

"I know." Sara lowered herself next to her chair, took Katie in her arms and held her. "I know."

Minutes passed, then Katie went upstairs to get dressed. After cleaning up, Sara went upstairs to get ready, too.

Opening her closet, she glimpsed the flannel of one of Nathaniel's beloved L.L.Bean shirts. Taking a moment, she studied it, took it from the hanger and pressed her face into its softness, breathing in its scent. On those agonizing nights when she'd first lost him, Sara had sprinkled his cologne on his side of the bed.

Tricking myself into thinking he was still here.

More memories pulled her back until suddenly, standing at her closet, she heard Nathaniel.

"Come on, Sara, we have to." They were driving through the city, a car had pulled over, the hood raised. Nathaniel stopped to help. It didn't matter, day or night, rain or shine, the interstate, the city, if someone needed help, Nathaniel, the Good Samaritan, would render aid. "You got to show a little kindness." That's how he was raised and that's how he lived.

Sara needed to believe, as her mother did, that Nathaniel's virtues were woven into Katie's DNA.

After she showered and dressed, she paused for a moment outside of Katie's bedroom door.

Katie was sitting at her desk, bent over her spiral-bound sketchbook. She was drawing carefully, pencil in hand, the chain of the necklace folding on the paper, lost in her work.

Let her be, Sara thought.

As she headed downstairs, she thought she heard Katie humming.

18

LYNORA AND CHUCK Shaw were on their knees, working in the garden of their front yard.

It had been several days since their daughter's funeral and Pierce's heart broke again for them.

Benton slowed the unmarked SUV at the Shaws' house. The garage door was up and Pierce recognized Anna's bike inside, having seen it in her social media posts. She imagined Anna growing up here, dreaming all of her dreams in the short time she lived in this world.

Pierce shut her eyes briefly, her thoughts pulling her back several days, before the funeral, back to Anna Shaw's body on the cold polished steel table; Mia Ryu, the medical examiner, working to the sound of her tools; the formaldehyde smell dominating the room. "It appears death was caused by blunt force trauma to the head and massive internal injuries," Ryu said later in her office, giving Pierce and Benton her prelimi-

nary assessment. "Consistent with a fall from the height indicated to rocks below." Ryu then discussed other aspects of
her findings. Pierce noted it all before the detectives returned
to headquarters, where Detective Sergeant Art Acker nodded
as he listened to Pierce's update.

"Looking at what the ME says, where are we?" Acker asked.

"I think we're done," Benton said. "No foul play, an accidental fall."

"No," Pierce said. "Ryu didn't rule out other possibilities.
We still have loose ends, locating everyone who was at the
park at the time of her death. We haven't recovered her phone
and we haven't fully processed the parking lot security video.
There's a glitch with the park's system."

"Alright, keep working and keep me posted," Acker said.

Then, earlier today, he'd notified Pierce and Benton that
forensics had finished processing Anna Shaw's backpack and
its contents.

"We have all we need, should it be deemed evidence later,"
Acker said. "We don't need to hold it."

So now here they were driving up to the Shaws' North
Seattle home to return Anna's property and ask her parents a
few more questions.

Benton eased the Ford to a stop and they got out. The
Shaws watched, their focus going to Pierce, who was carry-
ing the large brown paper bag into which forensics had placed
Anna's backpack.

Chuck stood to greet them while Lynora remained on her
knees, holding a gardening trowel.

"Your garden's beautiful," Pierce said.

"Some friends sent live plants for the funeral," Lynora said.

"What do you have there?" Chuck asked.

"We're returning Anna's property. May we talk?"

They went inside to the living room. Jon had gone to a

movie with friends, Chuck told them. The house was empty. Sitting in the quiet with the Shaws, Pierce felt their pain in the grief creasing their faces, the helplessness in their eyes, drained of joy by the toll of their agony. The silence was broken with the rustling of the paper bag as Pierce gave Anna's backpack to her mother.

Lynora released a soft groan. She touched the canvas tenderly, slowly unzipping it, reaching inside to run her fingers over some of Anna's belongings, a cosmetic pouch, a brush and a hair tie.

Touching the last things her daughter touched.

"Thank you," Lynora whispered, hugging Anna's backpack as Chuck moved his hand soothingly up and down her back.

"Does this mean—" Chuck cleared his throat "—that you're done?"

"Not yet," Pierce said. "We've got things to follow up on."

Chuck nodded.

"Forgive me for this imposition," Pierce said, "but would you allow us to take a look in Anna's room?"

Chuck looked at Lynora, who found her voice.

"What for?"

"To give us a better understanding," Pierce said. "It may help."

"Help with what?" Lynora said. "Will it bring her back?"

"Honey," Chuck said. "They have a job to do."

"It's alright," Pierce said. "I'm so sorry."

"I'll take you up," Chuck said. "Give us a moment."

Allowing the Shaws privacy, the detectives waited in the kitchen.

Benton was shaking his head as he scrolled through his phone. Pierce turned from him, uncertain if he was shaking his head at messages or the fact they were here.

Pierce looked at the calendar on the backsplash, appointment notes—one for Anna at the dentist next month. An array of family photos fixed with souvenir magnets to the fridge door. Happier times over the years with the Shaws at Niagara Falls, Disneyland and New York City.

In each of them, Anna's smile was like the sun.

Chuck entered the kitchen.

"We're both very tired. She's resting on the sofa."

He led them upstairs to a small hallway and a door he opened to a pleasant hint of lilac.

"It's been untouched since Anna—" Chuck stood at the entrance, looking into it. "Lynora slept on the bed the first nights."

The detectives nodded.

"We'll be downstairs when you're done," Chuck said.

It was a pretty room, Pierce thought, done in very light lavender. The floating shelves were the same color as the walls and held books, trinkets and a Polaroid camera. Anna's space had a grown-up feel while still being a bit girlie, judging by those curlicues in the chair at her desk.

Pierce had taken out her phone to record a video for her files.

She looked at Anna's dresser, with a small jewelry box holding a few rings, bracelets, earrings and a couple pretty necklaces, one with a pearl, another with a star. Looking at Anna's laptop on her desk, Pierce considered getting a warrant for it, too. But getting another one might be a challenge because Pierce had no strong indication, no reasonable cause to suspect a crime had been committed. Then, looking at the bed, neatly made, she went to the upholstered storage bench at the foot of it. She opened it to find a sleeping bag, comforter and foam mattress.

Likely used by Katie for their sleepover, she thought.

Benton, hands on his hips, stood before one wall, studying

a display of photos. Pegs had been attached to the ends of the wall, with lines of string tied to them like rows of clothes-lines. Dozens of Polaroid photos of Anna and her friends were clipped to the lines, making for a selfie wall.

Benton turned to Pierce, then pointed his chin to the wall. "See?" he said. "She loved taking selfies."

Pierce studied the wall, noticing gaps with empty clips on the lines, suggesting photos were missing. Thinking, she went to the desk and the wastebasket. In the trash she saw pieces of torn Polaroids of Anna and a boy, glimpsing an ink caption on one fragment: *Tanner & Me.*

Pierce recorded all she could before they left the room.

Chuck and Lynora were at their kitchen table when the detectives returned.

"Would you like some coffee?" Lynora's voice was raw.

"No, thank you," Benton said. "We should be on our way."

"Thank you," Pierce said. "Before we go, can I get your thoughts on something?"

"Okay. Are you sure you don't want some coffee? It's fresh," Chuck said, seeming to want the detectives to stay.

"No, thank you," Pierce said.

"What do you want to ask?" Lynora said.

"We went over some of this, but we understand that Anna broke up with her boyfriend, Tanner Bishop, in the time before?"

"Yes," Chuck said.

"Do you think Anna was despondent over the breakup?"

"Despondent?" Chuck threw a glance to Lynora, who was shaking her head.

"She was upset," Lynora said, "but it's not like you're think-ing. She was not suicidal."

"Do you know why they broke up?"

"Tanner was cheating on her with another girl," Lynora said. "She was upset and ended it with him."

"Did Tanner see Anna in the time leading up to the outing at Sparrow Song? Did he go to the park?" Pierce asked.

"No," Chuck said. "At least not that we know."

"A week or so before," Lynora said, "Tanner gave Anna a necklace with a small gold heart to try to get her back."

Pierce took a quick mental inventory, unable to recall a necklace with a small gold heart in Anna's room, or with Anna's belongings inventoried from the scene.

"Anna refused to accept it," Lynora said. "But he wouldn't take it back."

"Where is the necklace?" Pierce asked. "I didn't see it in her room."

"Katie has it."

"Katie Harmon? The girl she babysat—the girl who was here for the sleepover, the night before?"

"Katie, yes. Anna loved Katie," Lynora said. "Katie liked the necklace so she gave it to her."

"Did you see Anna give her the necklace? Was it at the sleepover?"

"No, she didn't give it to her here."

"Where did she give it to her?"

"On the bus, on the way to the park," Lynora said.

"That's what Katie told us," Chuck said.

"And Katie wore it to the funeral."

"She wore it to the funeral?" Pierce said.

"To let us know how much—" Lynora began to cry "—how much she loved her, too."

As Chuck comforted Lynora, several thoughts shot through Pierce. The first was realizing the consequences of her mistake of not getting Katie to empty her pockets at the park.

Katie could've had the necklace in her pocket when she first interviewed her.

Katie never mentioned receiving the necklace from Anna on the bus. Why? I asked what she and Anna talked about on the bus, yet Katie said nothing about the necklace. Why? There were no witnesses, no cameras, just Anna and Katie at the cliff, and now Katie has Anna's necklace.

Benton was behind the wheel. They drove several blocks from the Shaws' house without speaking, but Pierce couldn't hold it in any longer.

"Why're you hampering me on this, Carl?"

Eyes forward, he didn't answer.

Pierce stared at him, noticing the veins in his neck had risen.

"From the get-go you've been determined to clear this as an accident," she said. "You seem intent on not letting me do a proper investigation."

She continued staring, waiting for an answer.

"Because…it's just not there, Kim," he said. "We're intruding on the family's grief, wasting everyone's time, when there's no point. The girl died taking a selfie. The ME said her injuries were consistent with a fall. So, it was a tragic accident."

"Are you dismissing what else the ME told us?" Pierce said. "She said Anna Shaw could've jumped, or could've been pushed off the cliff?"

"Follow the evidence and the facts, Kim. They point to a fall."

"But we're not done looking for evidence."

"You're making a rookie mistake, trying to build a case that isn't there."

"We still have a lot of unanswered questions."

Pierce turned away from him, letting out a slow silent breath.

ARCHIVED

Department of Justice-Federal Bureau of Investigation

MISSING PERSONS

Carrie Arleen Gardner and Willow Eve Walker
May 10, 1995
Tempe, Arizona

DETAILS
The FBI's Phoenix Field Office in Arizona is seeking the public's assistance in locating Carrie Arleen Gardner and Willow Eve Walker, who have been missing after departing from Tempe, April 12, 1995, bound for Alaska.

Gardner and Walker were last seen in Idaho Falls, Idaho, April 14, 1995, leaving the Burger King in Walker's blue 1992 Ford Aerostar Minivan with Arizona license plate Q959VMN3. Neither have been seen nor heard from since. Gardner and Walker are students at Arizona State University and are driving to Fairbanks, Alaska, to start jobs.

Descriptions:
Carrie Arleen Gardner
Date of Birth: February 21, 1973
Place of Birth: Hartford, Connecticut
Hair: Light brown
Eyes: Blue
Height: 5'3"

Weight: 115 lbs.
Sex: Female
Race: White

Willow Eve Walker
Date of Birth: April 6, 1973
Place of Birth: Baltimore, Maryland
Hair: Black
Eyes: Brown
Height: 5'5"
Weight: 115 lbs.
Sex: Female
Race: Black

REMARKS

Walker occasionally wears glasses and has a scar on her right
ankle.

Gardner is asthmatic and uses an inhaler and has a birth-
mark on the back of her left thigh.

If you have any information regarding the whereabouts of
Carrie Arleen Gardner and Willow Eve Walker, please contact your local FBI office or the nearest American Embassy
or Consulate.

Field Office: Phoenix

19

THE SCREAM IN the night woke Sara.

She rushed through the darkness to Katie's room, finding her asleep, blankets kicked off and askew. She was curled tight, almost fetal, her hands balled into fists.

Sara tried to conceive the visions tormenting Katie after all she'd seen that day on the cliff with Anna.

And what could've really— No, oh, no, don't think about it.

Sara looked upon her daughter, her flawless skin, her upturned nose, her angelic face.

What could've really— Stop. Stop thinking what you're thinking.

Katie just had another bad dream, something to be expected, *something normal*, even now, almost three weeks after the tragedy, according to Dr. Sally Mehta, who'd been having regular sessions with Katie alone in her office.

Sara smiled down at Katie. "I love you so much," she whispered, then untangled Katie's sheets, covered her, kissed her cheek and went back to her own bed.

But Sara couldn't sleep.

Plagued with her own thoughts, she needed to believe that Katie would be *alright*—that she *was alright*—and searched for assurance in memories of Nathaniel, Katie's father.

He was a soft-spoken man whose parents died not long after he'd turned twenty. His dad dropped dead from a brain aneurysm and four months later a heart attack claimed his mother. Nathaniel had no other family. He was a quiet, good-hearted man, and it was so easy for Sara to fall in love with him.

Before they married and she moved to Salem, Oregon, Sara had made it clear to Nathaniel that she didn't want children. He accepted her feelings, respected them. But after they were married, she saw how he looked longingly at other couples with their babies. One day when they were sitting in a park, she brought up the subject.

"You really want kids, don't you?" Sara said.

"Sure, but I know how you feel."

"I don't think I could do it. I don't think I'd be a good mother."

"That's where we disagree." He smiled. "I know you'd be a good mom because you're a good person. And it's no surprise. Look at George and Marjorie. You were raised by two people who are the salt of the earth."

But Sara could never tell Nathaniel the truth—*the whole truth*—about why she didn't want a child. She couldn't bear for anyone to know, not even Nathaniel. Still, Sara saw the yearning, the aching for a child, in his eyes and it broke her heart to deny him a baby. She knew he'd be the best father.

Nathaniel's goodness had given her hope that maybe, just maybe, she *could* be a good mother. And with Nathaniel, she felt she might conquer her fears and gain the strength to one day tell him the truth. So she agreed to start a family and they had Katie, with Sara praying, begging God to make everything okay—*in every way.*

And it was okay. It was better than okay. Nathaniel was overjoyed. He was there for Katie's birth. Nathaniel said his feet never touched the ground that day.

"Holding her is like holding a bundle of Heaven," he said.

Sara's parents were thrilled.

Then came that rainy day around the time Katie was two years old. Sara was working as a cashier at the Grocery Corner-Mart when Nick Papas, her manager, called her to his office, where two police officers were waiting. Something was wrong. *Very wrong.* They pulled out a chair for Sara to sit. Her heart skipped as they told her that Nathaniel had been on his motorcycle when a big rig blew a tire, lost control and struck him.

"We're so sorry," the officer said, "but Nathaniel was killed."

The earth shifted under Sara; hands steadied her as she stared into Nick's big calendar with its stunning picture of the Greek Isles and the glowing shrine on the swooping hills overlooking the Azure Sea. The whole time, her screams rattled off the walls.

Nick got Donna, the head cashier, to help him get Sara home. She never remembered being back in their house. Numbed and overwhelmed with grief, sights blurred, sounds deadened as if she were at the bottom of the Azure Sea looking up at the surface and the sun.

Everything was a haze and after Nathaniel's funeral Sara only went through the motions of living, clinging to the one thing she could hang on to: Katie.

In time, Sara, a widowed young mother, left Oregon and moved back to Seattle to live with her parents. Mel Carver hired her back at the Jet Town to work full-time. The routine and sanctuary of living with her mom and dad helped. And every few months or so Sara would take Katie to see Nathaniel's friends in British Columbia.

They were always warm, loving times.

Until two years ago, during one of their visits to Greater Vancouver when Katie was seven, the incident with the little boy happened. It was so, so awful. What struck Sara was how Katie wasn't fully empathetic. *How she seemed almost "satisfied."* Sara told Katie that they should never talk about what had happened to the boy. But that didn't make it go away, for it became something that dwelled in a corner of Sara's heart.

Sara recalled how shortly after the incident in British Columbia, she'd sat alone one night in dim light at the kitchen table of her parents' home—*this home*—her thoughts swirling. Her mother, still living at home then, had heard her, sat with her and eventually got Sara to tell her what was on her conscience.

"I'm so afraid," Sara said.

"What are you afraid of?"

"This won't make sense, but I fear that losing Nathaniel is the price I'm paying for having Katie. For going against my plan never to have a child because of our secret, because of who I am."

Her mother listened.

"It's like our curse, the keeping of secrets," Sara said. "How I'm forever looking over my shoulder for the forces out there—and those even closer to us here, now, after what happened with the boy." Sara's voice broke. "I'm scared."

Her mother took her hands. Sara could feel them trembling, betraying the internal turmoil her mother battled.

"Now, you listen to me. I am your mother. I love you with

all my heart. I will always be your mother and Dad, God rest his soul, will always be your dad."

Sara nodded.

"You have goodness in you," her mother said. "You are Katie's mom. Nathaniel was her dad. And all the virtues you both have are in that little girl. You must believe that because it's true."

Sara nodded.

"You love Katie, don't you?"

"With all my heart. She's my world."

"Then that's all that matters."

"But, Mom, Nathaniel was taken from me, Dad was taken from you and there's what happened in Canada—"

"No," her mother said. "What happened to Nathaniel and Dad, that's part of life, not some curse. And what happened in Vancouver, happened. It has nothing to do with you, Katie or anyone else. There's no need to ever bring up what happened with that boy. You remember that and you make sure Katie does, too."

That night with her mother was two years ago.

Now, alone in her bed, Sara turned to the clock on her night table. It was so late. She had to work in the morning and needed sleep. But she couldn't stop thinking about that boy—*and Anna.*

Now, like wolves emerging from the edge of darkness, the horrific secrets of her past and her fear of what was coming gnawed at her.

Please don't let it be true.

20

Seattle, Washington

"ARE YOU STILL having nightmares about Anna?"

Katie nodded.

She had been walking slowly around Dr. Sally Mehta's office, touching her plants, her books, before stopping at the small figures on her shelves: a hand-carved giraffe and elephant.

"How often do you have the bad dreams?"

"Almost every night." Katie touched the carvings. "Sally, where did you get these?"

"When I was at a conference in Africa."

"They're nice."

"I like them." Dr. Mehta looked at her. "We didn't talk about your nightmares much on your last visit. Do you feel like telling me about them now?"

As Katie lifted the elephant to inspect it, she shrugged, which Dr. Mehta took as an invitation to continue.

"What happens in your bad dreams?"

Katie set the elephant down.

"I'm at the park with Anna and she stops by the cliff to take a selfie and she starts backing up and she's getting so close to the edge. I say, be careful, Anna..."

Katie stopped talking.

She was rooted before the shelf, staring at the elephant and giraffe. Dr. Mehta knew Katie was ordering her thoughts and waited for her to continue.

"But," Katie said, "Anna's holding her phone up, looking at it, saying it's so beautiful and she keeps backing up. I tell Anna to stop, be careful, but she keeps backing up and I want to—I want—"

Katie stopped.

"What is it you want to do, Katie?"

"I want to run to Anna and—and—"

Katie stopped.

Dr. Mehta went to her, gently helping her onto the sofa chair. Ice cubes clinked as she poured water for Katie. Drinking some, then gasping, Katie's brow furrowed.

"She didn't listen to me. Why didn't she listen to me?"

Dr. Mehta waited for her to continue.

"I see her hanging on to the branch," Katie said, "screaming for help and I run so fast for help but it's too late—and—and I feel like it's my fault."

"No, Katie, no, it's normal for you to think that," Dr. Mehta said. "Katie, it was a terrible accident that happened to your friend right in front of you. You had no control over the events. What happened is not your fault."

"But I feel like it is. It's really in my head that it is my fault, and this feeling won't go away."

Katie looked at the tiny gold heart of the necklace she was

wearing, taking it gently between her fingertips as Dr. Mehta watched.

"That's the one Anna gave you that day?" Mehta said. "It's pretty."

Katie nodded.

"You wore it the first time we talked. What does it mean to you?"

Katie blinked, thinking.

"It means I'll remember Anna all my life and that I'm sorry for what happened."

"In time, when you think of Anna, your memories will become happy ones, and soon you'll understand that what happened was not your fault."

"Will the nightmares go away?"

"Yes, they will.

"I'm curious about something you told me," Dr. Mehta said. "I was hoping you could help me understand it. Remember when we first met and you said that what happened to Anna was just like what happened to *that boy*? What does that mean?"

Katie's face whitened.

"Mom said it's better if I don't ever talk about it."

Dr. Mehta removed her glasses, tapped the arms to her chin.

"Tell me about your family again, as far back as you can remember."

"Well, my dad died when I was little, so I don't remember him so much. Sometimes Mom shows me videos of him holding me when I was a baby and stuff. Then later my grandpa got sick and died, then my grandma is in a place for old people where we visit her."

"What about relatives on your dad's side of the family, your dad's mom and dad, your other grandparents?"

"We don't have other relatives. We have friends."

"And do you see them?"

"Not all of them. I mean, we used to visit, but not so much anymore, especially after—"

Katie stopped herself as if she'd opened a door to a forbidden room.

"Especially after what?"

Katie shook her head.

"Katie, whatever you tell me is private. I'm not allowed to tell anyone. I want to help you, but you have to help me. Okay?"

Katie looked at her.

"It's okay, Katie."

Katie swallowed. "Well, I think, it's because of what happened to that boy I was with."

"What happened to him?"

Katie blinked several times.

"I don't want to talk about it."

21

IN THE SCATTERED light of the dawn, the stranger in the vehicle parked far down the street watched Sara Harmon's North Seattle home through binoculars.

A shadow fell along Sara's front sidewalk.

The view through the binoculars blurred, shifting and locking onto a woman and a dog, a leashed retriever, approaching the front door. The woman rang the doorbell, the sound carrying softly.

A few seconds later the door opened.

Sara appeared and hugged the woman.

A thread of their indecipherable voices echoed in the still morning air, floating down the street to the vehicle enveloped in the dark shade of maples.

The woman and her dog entered the house.

The windows of other rooms illuminated.

The binoculars raked over the house, the yard, the street and back to the house.

Ten minutes later the front door opened. Sara, bag in hand, appeared and was walking toward her SUV in the driveway when she stopped dead in her tracks.

Did she forget something?

Sara took a few steps toward the front sidewalk. She looked along the street. Her head tilted as she looked in the direction of the vehicle parked in the darkness down the street, nearly a block away.

Why? Why was Sara looking?

Was there a glint reflecting a streetlight in the lenses?

The curiosity on Sara's face was evident through the binoculars. She took another step toward the sidewalk and stopped as if debating further investigation.

The person in the vehicle didn't move.

Sara raised one hand slightly, triggering a distinct chirping as the lights of her SUV flashed. She got in, started it, then drove away.

The stranger watched her taillights until she disappeared.

Then the binoculars raked the house—searching every window.

Watching.

22

SARA SET DOWN an order before the man at table nine.

"Fish and chips," she said. "Can I get you anything else?"

He was alone in the booth working on his laptop and glanced to the plate, then to Sara.

"Well, no, but I ordered a club."

"No, it was fish and— Wait—" Pulling her order pad from her pocket, she saw what she'd written for table nine: *club / w / wheat / fry / slaw.* Her face sank, reddening as she picked up the plate. "I'm so sorry. I'll take care of that."

"It's okay, no problem."

Sara headed across the dining room. Her worries about Katie, about everything, were deepening to the point of paranoia about being followed. It was distracting her.

I need to concentrate on my job.

Pushing through the swing door, she stepped into the

kitchen. It was steamy and bustling with lunch orders. She put the fish and chips on the counter.

"I messed up. I need a club on whole wheat, fries and slaw for nine."

Without stopping their work, Mel and Brenda, the new cook, glanced at her from the sizzling grill, the churning deep fryer and the stove. Mel looked at the plate, then at Sara, his face telegraphing both his concern and thinning patience at cutting Sara slack in the wake of the tragedy.

Then he nodded to her. "Whole wheat club coming up, kiddo."

Brenda put up two plates at the pick-up window. "Small veg soup and half chicken sandwich on rye for number seven."

"That's me," Sara said, leaving the kitchen to go around for her plates when her phone vibrated with a notification about fees from the Silverbrook Hills Senior Living Home. Sara glanced at the message. Not an emergency but still alarming. Skimming through the legalese and payment plan now showing detailed options, she went to the number telling her exactly how much more it would cost *monthly* to keep her mother at Silverbrook Hills.

Way more than we can afford.

The increase would start in six months.

Putting her phone away, Sara picked up her order. The soup and sandwich went to an older woman sitting by herself at a small table. When Sara had first taken the woman's order, she'd thought she looked familiar but couldn't place her. The woman was staring over her glasses at her clear plastic wallet of photos. Sara thought she embodied loneliness.

"Creamy vegetable soup and a half chicken sandwich on rye. Here you go." She set the order down. "Nice pictures. Your family, I'm guessing?"

"Yes, thank you."

"Family's everything," Sara said.

"Goodness, that's so true. Do you have children?"

"A daughter."

"Ahh." The woman smiled. "A daughter is a daughter all of her life."

"So the saying goes." Sara smiled. "Anything else?"

"No, thank you."

Relieved she'd gotten the woman's order right, Sara moved on. Then it struck her and she glanced back. Had she seen the woman at Anna's funeral? Had she been one of the people looking at her and Katie? Sara wasn't sure. She didn't know her. The woman had to be a friend of the Shaws, she thought while clearing plates from table six. Table two wanted apple pie and more coffee.

While working, she grappled with the ever-increasing financial strain she faced, and how she needed to find a new *affordable* sitter for Katie. Friends, like her neighbor, Val Rossi, a retired flight attendant, were helping. Val was up before dawn each morning to walk Bingo, her retriever. After hearing of the tragedy, Val had come to Sara's house with lasagna and insisted on watching Katie and getting her to school during Sara's morning shifts.

As Sara worked, a tiny ringing in the back of her mind got louder, forcing her to confront the one thing she feared most: Anna's death.

What had happened on that cliff? How had Katie ended up with Anna's necklace? Why was Sara even questioning it? Maybe she was being too paranoid. Her thoughts spun. Were Katie's sessions with Dr. Mehta helping? Or would they open a door to something more terrifying than Sara could ever imagine?

Will the truth be exhumed?

Some press reports had included photos of Sara and Katie—but none identified them. Still, newspeople had come to her home and called her phone the day it happened. Sara figured they'd gotten her number and address from other parents in the Sunny Days group.

But no news outlet and nothing online had publicly identified Katie or Sara and their link to Anna's death.

None had dug deeper.

They can't know who I am.

Not yet, at least.

And since then, news media coverage of the tragedy had waned. Social media chatter about it had also subsided. Still, Sara couldn't shake the feeling she was being watched, followed.

"Sara?"

She turned to see Beth and Polly huddled in the alcove near the kitchen door. She stopped to join them.

"What's going on? Are you okay?" Polly asked.

"You look a little uneasy," Beth said. "Everything okay?"

"I'm fine."

Beth and Polly traded disbelieving glances.

"You've been through so much," Beth said.

"If you want to get together later at your place and talk..." Polly said.

For a second Sara considered finally confiding the truth, *the whole truth*, unburdening herself of the immense weight she had carried all these years. But no, she could never let that happen—*never*.

She killed the thought as quickly as it rose.

"Thank you, guys, but I'm fine. Really."

"Our offer stands if you change your mind," Polly said.

"Thanks."

"Hey, Sara." Beth was looking elsewhere. "You're being watched."

Sara followed Beth's gaze across the dining room to table nine, where the man had shifted his focus back to his laptop.

"Oh, yeah, that guy," Polly said. "Kinda hunky."

"Mmm," Beth said. "Gives off an Ethan Hawke vibe."

"You think so? More like a Jake Gyllenhaal to me."

"Either way," Polly said, "he's got his eye on you, Sara."

Sara rolled her eyes, smiling at her friends.

"Order up!" Mel said. "Club on whole wheat."

Sara took the correct order to table nine, where the man was still working on his laptop.

"Here we go." Sara set the plate before him. "Again, I'm sorry about the mix-up."

He smiled at her. She noticed his long eyelashes as his focus flicked to her name tag.

"No problem, Sara. It gave me more time to do some work."

"Oh, what are you working on?"

"I'm researching some local history." He shrugged. "Maybe for a book."

"How interesting. Seattle history?"

"A bit, yeah. It's complicated. I have to sort it out." He nodded to her wrist. "I like your tattoo."

They both looked to the gray-and-white flowers on her inner wrist and lower forearm.

"Thanks," she said.

"What's the story behind it?"

"Oh, it's complicated."

"I'd love to hear it sometime, Sara."

She looked at him, not knowing what to say, just as her phone buzzed in her pocket.

"Oh, I've prattled. I better let you eat. Enjoy." She smiled and left for the pick-up window to get her next order. Before reaching it, she glanced at her message.

It was Detective Kim Pierce.

We'd like to talk to Katie again. Can we set up a time?

23

Seattle, Washington

SARA FELT UNEASY.

Detective Kim Pierce was sitting at her kitchen table, explaining why she and her partner, Carl Benton, had come.

Pierce was striking in a subdued way, but Sara perceived something dangerous behind her smile.

"First," Pierce said, "we wanted to return your daughter's backpack with her tablet and phone. They may need charging."

"Thank you. She'll be happy to get her things," Sara said, setting Katie's aqua canvas backpack on the counter.

"And, as I indicated, we wanted to follow up with her."

Sara took note of their tablets, the detectives' binders, how they'd arrived as if prepared for an exam, *or court.*

"But we also need to outline the terms of the situation," Pierce said.

"The terms?" Sara said.

"It's a formality that we're legally required to do," Benton added.

"A legal formality? I don't understand."

"It's because Katie is a minor," Pierce said, "a child witness, and, things are a bit different now because we're removed from the event, or scene, and you're present. All to say, we'd like your permission to interview Katie here, but alone."

"Oh, my God, is— Are you going to read her her rights or something? Does she need a lawyer?"

"No," Pierce said. "No, this isn't a custodial interview. Katie isn't under arrest, nothing like that, no. She's a witness and we're required to outline your options in order to talk to her further here."

"But she's told you everything and she's still grappling with the trauma of it. She's still getting counseling."

"We understand," Pierce said. "But children who've experienced sudden tragedies like this often forget details."

"What're my options here?"

"You can refuse to allow us to talk to Katie. That's your right. You can be present during the interview. Or, you can have a lawyer be present. Or you could agree to allow us to talk to her alone, which would be the most helpful as we'd like to wrap things up. Again," Pierce said, "she's already talked to the deputy and to me at the scene without you being present but with other adults watching over her, so it's your choice."

An icy prickling scraped at the walls of Sara's stomach.

If she said no, it would look suspicious. If she got a lawyer, which she couldn't afford, Katie would look guilty. *If you have nothing to hide, why get a lawyer?* If she sat in on the interview, she'd look controlling, as if she had something to hide.

I want what's best. But, oh, God, I thought they were done. Why're they so careful, so insistent? What do they know—or think they know? If I asked them that, I'd look suspicious. What happened to Anna was an accident, an awful accident. It has to be.

She bit her bottom lip.

"I guess it would be alright, since you've already talked to her."

"It's routine, just a follow-up," Pierce said.

"We want to help any way we can."

"We have your permission to talk to her alone?"

"Yes. She's upstairs in her room. Let me go tell her."

Moments later Pierce and Benton entered Katie's room while Sara held the door.

"Hi," Katie said.

She was sitting on her bed, cross-legged with a laptop. Her bed had a quilted white bedspread and an emerald bed frame. The pink-peach walls had a floral pattern and the room smelled of fresh linen and soap.

Very neat and ordered, Pierce thought.

"Hi, Katie," she said. "You remember me, Kim, from the park? This is my partner, Carl Benton. He was there, too. You can call him Carl."

Benton gave Katie a friendly little wave as he looked around the room.

"Okay if I sit here?" Benton indicated the chair at Katie's desk.

She nodded and Benton turned it and sat, dwarfing her workspace.

"I'll leave you guys to talk." Sara forced a smile, then left, closing the door behind her.

"May I sit with you on your bed?" Pierce asked.

Katie scooched over.

"Thank you. You pretty much told us everything about

Anna. But we're here in case you forgot, or we forgot, anything, and to ask you some new things. Will that be okay?"

"Okay."

"And because we want to get things right, Carl's going to record us, make a video on his phone for our notes, like before. Okay?"

Katie nodded.

"And we'll keep this confidential, private, which means we can't tell people what you tell us and you shouldn't tell anybody what we ask you, okay?"

"Okay."

Pierce then casually relayed a summary of the events, confirming details with Katie from the previous interviews she'd given to her and Deputy Hirano. Katie listened, answering Pierce's occasional questions, clarifying aspects leading up to and after Anna's fatal fall. As Katie spoke, she gently twisted the tiny gold heart on the fine chain around her neck.

"I like your necklace," Pierce said. "Where did you get it?"

"Anna gave it to me, that day."

"It's pretty. Can you hold it so I can take a picture on my phone?"

Katie raised it and it sparkled in the light as Pierce took a photo.

"Thanks," Pierce said. "We didn't know that Anna gave it to you. When did she do that?"

"On the bus, just before we got off. She told me the night before, on the sleepover, that Tanner gave it to her and that she didn't want it. He wouldn't take it back, so she was, like, going to throw it away."

"She wanted to throw it away, why?"

"Because she was mad at Tanner."

"Why?"

"I think he had another girlfriend."

Pierce weighed the information.

"Katie, do you remember at the park, I asked you what you and Anna talked about on the bus and at the park, but you never mentioned her giving you the necklace. Why's that?"

Katie thought, shrugged, then lowered her head.

"I guess I forgot. So much stuff was going on. I'm sorry."

"Where did you put it after Anna gave it to you?"

"In my pocket."

"And this was on the bus?"

"Yes."

"Was Anna wearing it at the time?"

"No, she had it in her backpack."

"Did anyone on the bus see Anna giving the necklace to you?"

Katie shrugged. "It was pretty busy, we just got to the park and everyone was, like, hurrying to get off and stuff."

Pierce sorted her thoughts before continuing.

"I need your help going over a few more things again. So, you and Anna were the last to leave the bus?"

"Yes."

"When you started on the trail, you were far behind the others, but she wanted to stop to take a selfie?"

Katie nodded.

"And no one else was around you. It was just you and Anna?"

"Yes."

"And she fell walking backward while framing her selfie?"

Katie's shoulders dropped.

"Yes, I keep telling you." She shot out a breath of frustration. "And I kept telling Anna to stop, to be careful. She was so close to the edge. I told her to stop but she didn't listen to me!"

Pierce leaned a little closer to Katie. "And when she fell, did she fall all the way down to the ground?"

Katie shook her head. "She was hanging on to the branch."

"Then what happened?"

"She was screaming and I ran for help."

"So Anna was alive, hanging on to the branch when you left to get help?"

"Yes!"

"Is that what really happened, Katie?"

Katie recoiled a little, her face whitening as if stung. Then she lifted the tiny gold heart and gazed at it.

"Yes."

Pierce let her answer sit in the air, allowing her time to adjust it if she needed to. Katie outwaited her in the silence, then Pierce continued.

"We understand you're seeing a counselor."

"Yes, Doctor Sally, near the university."

"Does talking with Doctor Sally help you feel better?"

"Yes, she's nice."

"Is there anything that you tell her about that day, that you maybe haven't told us, and maybe we should know, to help us, too?"

Katie pondered Pierce's question, then shook her head.

"Is there anything that your mom, or anyone, told you not to tell us?"

Katie's nostrils flared slightly as her breathing quickened.

"No."

"You're sure?"

"Yes."

"I know this is hard. Just one last thing—is there anything you think we should know, or that you want us to know?"

Katie found Pierce's eyes and looked into them. Almost imperceptibly Katie's eyes narrowed.

"It's not my fault!"

"What do you mean? What's not your fault?"

"What happened to Anna and to— It's not my fault!"
Katie turned, thrust her face into her pillow.

Pierce traded a glance with Benton, then put her hand on
Katie's shoulder.

"Okay, Katie, it's okay, we're done for now."

Idaho FOIA request (Sec 74-113, Idaho Code)

BONNER COUNTY SHERIFF'S OFFICE, WITNESS STATEMENT FORM

Case# 5276

Date: 21 June 1995

Time: 1:30 p.m.

Statement of: ██████████████

Phone#: 604-████████

Address: ████████████████ Creston, BC, Canada

Date of Birth: 3 April 1965

I certify and declare under penalty of perjury and under the laws of the State of Idaho that the following statement was given by me under my own free will.

I am a Canadian citizen and resident of Creston, British Columbia. On June 19, 1995, I left my apartment to visit ██████████ *my friend, who is six months pregnant and resides in Coeur d'Alene, ID. I left Creston, BC, driving alone in my 1989 Honda Civic, after my last evening shift as a shipping yard clerk at* ██████████ ██████. *I was starting four days off. I entered the US at the Porthill, ID, border crossing about 10:00 p.m. No traffic at all. It was raining heavily and windy as I drove south. The roads seemed deserted. I'd only traveled a few miles when I came to the flashing lights of an emergency road crew. The storm had knocked down trees for several miles along the highway. A crew boss said I could detour onto a secondary road that was clear, then get back on US 95. The detour ran for several miles south to Naples, ID, through dense national forest* and the state park, parallel to the Kootenai River. The crew boss said it was unpaved but otherwise clear. I thought about turning back and returning home, but my friend had argued with her husband who'd left her to go hunting and needed me to come as she was in a bad way and really needed me there.

I kept going. The road was extremely dark with hardly any traffic. I didn't know this back road. I couldn't see any towns, gas stations or houses. I kept going, watching the miles on my odometer. The rain had not let up. I had gone about six miles when my lights caught the reflection of a vehicle stopped far ahead on the shoulder. Getting closer, I saw that the hood was raised, like it had broken down. Then I saw that it was a van and had a Montana license plate. No one was around so I didn't feel comfortable stopping. But as I slowed to pass it a woman got out of the driver's side, waving like she needed help. She was holding a child on her hip. She must've had the child on her lap, as if waiting to show they were alone and needed help. The child looked to be about two. Both of them were in the rain lit up by my headlights. Because she had a child, I pulled over, stopped and rolled down my passenger window.

She leaned into my car, thanked me for stopping and asked me to help. I said I didn't have a cellular phone (they were too expensive for me), and she didn't have one either, to call the AAA or someone. I offered to call for a tow truck when I saw a gas station. But she said that the van was her brother's and it had a loose battery cable or something and she needed help and if I got behind the wheel, she could hold the cable, like her brother showed her and could get her van running again. She had a long drive to go with her child. I decided to help her. I got in the van behind the wheel, leaving the van's driver's door open. She put her child in the van passenger seat like a sign to tell me I was safe. I couldn't tell if it was a boy or girl; it had a woolen cap on. The woman had a flashlight and worked under the hood, tapping. Then she told me to wait a moment before turning the key. At that point I felt a shift of weight from the back, a noise, then a sudden dark blur *from behind like a large animal coming at me and in a heartbeat a rope was around my neck with a powerful force pulling from behind, crushing my windpipe. I couldn't breathe. Somehow out of fear and a burst of adrenaline I slid down in my seat, my arms flailing clawing at anything, fighting the rope, hefting my legs out the open door, twisting my body with the rope burning, scraping my neck, my chin, grinding at my jaw, tearing at my nose and scalp. A hand seized my hair and shoulder but I broke free.*

With my feet on the ground, the next seconds were hazy. I was screaming and running for my life straight into the woods, into the darkness. I couldn't see, I slipped, stumbling into trees. Branches pulled and yanked, tearing at my clothes, my hair, my face. I could hear the screech of the toddler or baby crying, then voices behind me, then two flashlights played into the woods. I heard one of the voices, deeper, a man's voice, saying that the woman screwed up letting me leave the driver's door open. I could hear panting as they came into the woods, searching for me, sweeping their light beams. I pushed deeper into the darkness, then fell on the rain-slicked ground, rolling, thrashing. I rolled and rolled, knocking against trees and rocks until I came to a stop. Fighting shock, gasping, fighting terror, my stomach spasmed but I never moved. I listened and listened but heard nothing. I don't know how much time passed before I slowly covered myself with branches and leaves. I stayed that way until the sun came up. In the morning the rain stopped and my body ached. I hurt all over but I climbed back carefully, watching through the branches until I got to the road. No one was there. The van was gone. My car was gone. I found a child's shoe. I began walking down the side of the road. That's when a forestry truck stopped for me and called police and took me to the hospital where they took photos of my injuries, the rope burns, ligature marks, bloodied face. I looked frightful. I recovered, then was taken to here, to Sandpoint, to write my statement. I gave the deputy the shoe and told him what happened. I will never forget when I saw the rear license plate and a little voice told me to remember it. I managed to burn it into my memory and told police the last digits of the license of the people who tried to kill me was ███████.

I have read the above statement and have had an opportunity to make any changes or deletions I have felt necessary. I certify and declare under penalty of perjury and under the laws of the State of Idaho the foregoing is true and correct.

Signature: ████████████
Date: 21 June 1995
Witness: BCSO Deputy Bob Elam
Place: BCSO Sandpoint, ID

Idaho FOIA request (Sec 74-113, Idaho Code)

24

Seattle, Washington
True Ocean Auto Dealers in Lake City

PIERCE AND BENTON were walking through the expansive lots with rows of new and used cars, and vehicles in for servicing.

After leaving Sara Harmon's home, Pierce wanted to talk to Tanner Bishop, Anna's ex-boyfriend.

While Benton drove, Pierce consulted Tanner's statement and contact information, then made calls. Tanner was here, at his part-time job.

Pierce's concerns, after seeing the torn Polaroids of Tanner in Anna's room, and her parents' revelations about the necklace, had mounted after they'd interviewed Katie Harmon for her account of how she'd come to possess it.

In the statement he gave to Larry Grotowski, Tanner had acknowledged the breakup with Anna. But there was nothing about a necklace. It also left Pierce doubting herself for not interviewing Tanner directly.

"I still think you're reaching with all of this, Kim," Benton had said when they wheeled into the dealership.

"I want to be thorough."

At the counter, the service manager had eyed their badges, listening to their request to talk to Tanner.

"Is this about that girl he knew who fell in the park by North Bend?"

"Yes, we'd like to talk to him alone for a moment," Pierce said.

"Well, he's alone in the far west lot, washing cars or moving them in and out of the service bays. He's got on a neon lime shirt. You can't miss him."

Now, threading their way around cars, they glimpsed a flash of a bright T-shirt. Pierce was glad Tanner had turned eighteen a few months ago. It would make questioning him less complicated.

A hose hissed and a rainbow appeared in the spray as Tanner rinsed perfumed soapsuds from a Jeep Wrangler, pausing when the detectives approached him with badges and introductions. They requested Tanner show them his driver's license to confirm his identification. After Pierce photographed it, Tanner leaned against a dry car and listened.

"Just a few questions on your relationship with Anna Shaw," Pierce said.

"What about it?"

"In your statement you acknowledged she broke things off a few weeks before her death."

He dragged his forearm across his forehead.

"Yes."

"Why did she break up with you?"

Tanner looked at Pierce, then Benton, then back at Pierce.

"It was a misunderstanding."

"A misunderstanding?"

"Shelby, my ex-girlfriend, wanted to talk to me. She was hurting about her parents' divorce. I met her at a park. She was crying. I hugged her. She kissed me. It got back to Anna and that was that. But I wasn't cheating."

"After Anna broke it off with you, did you do anything to win her back?"

"I gave her a necklace." Tanner blinked and looked to the sky. "The breakup destroyed me. I loved her and wanted her back. I would've done anything to get her back, to make her see I wasn't cheating."

"Why is none of this in the signed statement you gave to Detective Grotowski?" Pierce said.

"Tanner," Benton said. "It's a crime to give a false statement."

Tanner's face whitened.

"It was all so personal, so embarrassing," he said. "Anna had just died. I was messed up."

The detectives gave him a few seconds.

"How would you characterize Anna's mood or demeanor after she broke up with you, believing that you'd cheated on her with Shelby?" Pierce asked.

Tanner shook his head at the memory.

"Pissed at me. Angry with me. Heartbroken, I guess."

Pierce cued up a photo on her phone and showed him.

"Is this the necklace you gave Anna?"

Tanner looked at the photo of Katie's necklace with the tiny gold heart.

"Yeah, that looks like it."

"Did she like it?" Pierce asked.

"No, she was too pissed off. She didn't want it. She wanted

me to take it back, but I told her she had to keep it because I was so sorry."

"What happened?"

"I don't know. She must've given it to Katie, the girl she babysat. I'm pretty sure I saw her wearing it at the funeral."

"Alright, we're almost done," Pierce said. "Where were you on the morning Anna was killed?"

Tanner licked his lips.

"Home, sleeping in. I only had late-afternoon classes." He shook his head, fighting tears. "This whole thing's so messed up. I just wanted Anna to know the truth—I just—" He turned away, rubbing his eyes.

Pierce and Benton waited until he'd regained some composure.

"Thank you," Pierce said.

As they walked away, they heard a key fob's chirp and turned to see Tanner resume work, moving a car toward the service bay doors.

When they returned to their SUV, walking to either side, Benton stopped to talk to Pierce over the hood.

"I really don't know where you're going with this, Kim. This was a tragic accident. We're done. We've got cases backing up."

Pierce met Benton's gaze and self-doubt flared in a corner of her mind.

Is he right? Am I pushing it too far because this is my first case? Am I trying to prove something? No. That's not it. Every instinct tells me something about this case just doesn't sit right. I've got to do this by the book.

"I don't think we have the full picture of what really happened, Carl. I think Tanner was holding back on us. Maybe Katie, too. I've got an unsettling feeling about all of this."

Benton cursed under his breath, then said, "Evidence, Kim?

There was nothing on Katie's phone. Nothing anywhere else. No solid evidence."

"That's true. *So far.* Earlier this morning I was looking at the forensic stuff from the scene, the video inventory they took."

"And?"

"We need to go back to the park."

25

Online

THE MUSIC AND montage for *Tell-Tale Hearts* plays on phones, laptops and monitors around the world.

It's followed by Shane with a Blue Jays ball cap and Sonya in her red-framed glasses, both wearing headphones and seated at their microphones.

"A massive hello to everyone," Sonya says.

"Welcome to another episode of our true-crime show."

They acknowledge their global audience, run through the show's background and give their advisory about graphic content, then get started.

"Today we have a special guest for our featured case," Sonya says.

"I'm fascinated with this one. We did a little reading up on it and even though it goes back years, it really still hasn't ended," Shane says.

"That's right. On today's *Tell-Tale Hearts* we're looking at

Herman and Magda Vryker, a husband-and-wife team linked to at least seven murders in 1994 and 1995 in the US, across Montana, Idaho and Washington," Sonya says. "But their victims were never found. To beat the death penalty, or life in prison, for an easier sentence, Magda made a plea deal with prosecutors to locate the bodies," Sonya says.

"But she outsmarted them," Shane says. "Once she had the signed deal, Magda failed to locate their victims, claiming a faulty memory. She served her time and, after her release with no further conditions, remained silent before disappearing off the grid. To take us deeper into the story of the Vrykers, Beatrice Clearfield joins us from Tampa, Florida. Beatrice is with the social media group *The Hunters—Finding Magda*. Welcome, Beatrice."

The screen divides to show a woman in her late forties, early fifties. Missing person posters of victims in the case serve as her backdrop. "Thank you for having me."

"Tell us," Shane says, "how you got involved in this particular case."

"Well, before moving to Florida, I was living in Montana when it emerged. It just haunted me that part of it took place not far from where I grew up. I followed the case and, seeing that justice was never really served, I wanted to do something about it. So that's how *The Hunters* got started."

"Now, in the time since Magda's release, your group has dedicated itself to seeking justice by tracking her and posting information on where you think she may be and what you think she may be doing?" Sonya says.

"Yes, we have five-thousand members from across the US and around the world. Most are concerned everyday people. We also have retired cops, reporters, professional researchers, legal and forensic experts, you name it, using their skills to actively search for Magda over the years."

"What are the challenges in finding her?" Sonya asks.

"Well, many records concerning Magda, especially those that relate to her daughter, are sealed by court orders."

"So, you haven't located Magda or her daughter?" Shane asks.

"Not officially."

"Not officially?" Shane repeats.

"No, but we believe we're close."

"Now, before we get into why your group is doing this and its objective, can you outline the case for us and how it broke?"

"In 1994 and 1995, several reports surfaced of people missing in Montana, Idaho and Washington," Beatrice says.

"Sadly, countless numbers of people are reported missing each year in the US," Sonya says.

"That's unfortunately true. But a connection to these cases came to light in late June 1995. A Canadian woman who'd crossed the border from British Columbia into Idaho gave a Bonner County sheriff's deputy a chilling account. The woman had narrowly escaped with her life after she'd spotted a van on the shoulder and stopped to aid a woman and her child on a back road during a storm."

"The Canadian woman broke the case?" Shane asks.

"Yes, the sole survivor. Remarkably, and this is so rare, she remembered a good part of the van's plate. It led investigators to a mobile home on the outskirts of Billings, Montana, the residence of Herman and Magda Vryker and their toddler daughter, Hayley."

"Amazing," Shane says.

"Police showed the Canadian woman photos of Magda. She said it resembled the woman she tried to help that night. It was enough for police to get a search warrant."

"So things got moving," Sonya says.

"Police also had other pieces of evidence tied to the case, including items belonging to the missing victims."

"This is frightening," Sonya says.

"Among the items found were rings belonging to Sharon Lance and Jeremy Dunster—British tourists reported missing in '94 after they disappeared in their rented car north of Spokane. And they found a ring belonging to Brent Porter, a long-distance cyclist from Denver, Colorado, last located in Butte, Montana, before he was reported missing.

"But the Vrykers only faced charges in the attack on the Canadian woman," Beatrice says. "Police believed they were involved in crimes against the missing people, but they had no crime scenes, no witnesses and no bodies. They knew Herman was a long-range trucker and an ex–doomsday cult member. Magda worked at a slaughterhouse near Billings."

"That alone presents some chilling scenarios," Shane says.

"They used cadaver dogs, searched and dug up their property in vain. Everything was circumstantial," Beatrice says. "Then while they had them in custody, a couple of sharp investigators questioning Herman and Magda separately, employed a strategy whereby they strongly suggested one was poised to betray the other and both would be executed for their crimes."

"Clever," Sonya says.

"That's when Magda made a shocking move," Beatrice says. "Through her lawyer she said she was a victim of Herman's abuse, stemming from his twisted cult beliefs. Magda said she was forced to participate in Herman's crimes as a matter of self-preservation and to protect their daughter. Then Magda and her lawyer offered a deal—a full confession to seven murders in which she would give up her husband. In exchange she would avoid the death penalty. She'd serve a maximum of twenty years at a minimum-security prison, would have absolutely no restrictions or conditions upon her release, and she would be given a new identity that wouldn't be made public. And, she'd sign a confession and help locate the bodies."

"Wow," Shane says.

"The prosecution saw it as the only way to put the Vrykers behind bars and accepted the deal.

"Herman attempted to portray Magda as the driving force behind the crimes. It failed. He was convicted of seven first-degree murders and sentenced to death. But, unable to accept Magda's betrayal, he took his own life in his cell. Some called him Magda's last victim."

"That's wild," Shane says.

"Wait," Sonya says. "From our reading Magda used her child to lure victims. It's so cold and calculating. Who's not going to help a mother and her toddler when their van breaks down?"

"That's right," Beatrice says.

"So what happened to the daughter, Hayley?" Sonya asks.

"Social services took custody, she was adopted and nothing more is known about her, although some speculate about where and who she is."

"Imagine being the kid of a serial killer?" Shane says.

"That's a subject for another show," Sonya says.

"And what about the deal Magda made to locate the bodies?"

"She was escorted out of prison several times to sites that she claimed were the graves of their victims. But each expedition yielded nothing. It became obvious to investigators that she would never lead them to the actual graves, which enraged and deepened the pain of the families of their victims."

"Oh, my God," Sonya says.

"Magda was sentenced to twenty years in '96 when she was twenty-four. During her prison time she also earned a couple of university degrees and became extremely well-read and learned to speak Spanish and French. After twenty years of soft time, she was released at age forty-four, started a new life under a new identity and vanished. She's been invisible for about seven years now."

"This brings us to your group, Beatrice," Sonya says. "You believe that even though Magda served twenty years, she cheated the system."

"We know there are many arguments—that the prosecution accepted the deal, she did her time and we have to give offenders a chance at rehabilitation."

"But?" Shane says.

"Well, let's start with her sentence. She negotiated the terms and served less than three years for each life she and her husband took. So many people do harder time for less. Then let's look at her deal. She failed to hold up her end. When officials took her to sites, she claimed she couldn't remember, got confused, disoriented, never revealed a shred of evidence. Yet her lawyer convinced the court she was keeping up her end of the deal. Privately, investigators believed Magda knew exactly where they were. So yes, some see her as a monster who cunningly gamed the system, absolutely. This is a person who faced the death penalty, or at least should've been locked away for life, and has been living a new and free life."

"So the goal of your group is...?" Shane asks.

"Our goal has a couple of aspects. We want to find her, confront her and get her to reveal what happened to her victims and where they are."

"That's one," Sonya says.

"More important, we believe that Magda has not, nor ever will be rehabilitated. We believe she is a threat, a danger to society and could kill again. Look, there's so much we don't know about her early life—it's shrouded in mystery. Some members say it's as if Magda dropped from the sky to earth, or clawed her way up from a netherworld beneath the surface. One last point, and I put this to the millions of people in your audience, what if Magda was living next to you and your family?"

Several seconds of silence fill the air.

"I think that was a collective gulp," Sonya says.

"Thank you so much for an amazing episode, Beatrice. Anything you want to say as we wrap up?"

"I invite people to join our group, become searchers, help us find Magda, find justice, peace and healing for the families. Thank you so much for having me on *Tell-Tale Hearts*."

"Thank you, Beatrice Clearfield of *The Hunters—Finding Magda*. All the information is on our site. That's our time."

Sonya and Shane wave.

The same opening music plays against the empty city streets at night as the screen fades to black.

26

Near North Bend, Washington

BENTON SWITCHED OFF their SUV's motor in the parking lot of Sparrow Song Park.

"What're we doing here, Kim?"

He turned to Pierce. She was still focused on a forensic video of the scene playing silently on her tablet. From the moment they'd left Lake City and their interview with Tanner Bishop, her nose had been in her file notes.

"Really, Kim, why did we come here?"

Pierce closed the folders on her tablet, gathered her bag and things, and turned to Benton as she reached for the door handle.

"We're here to investigate, Carl."

They headed to the trailhead, neither of them speaking until they got to the clearing.

"I'm going to check the time to run the distance from here to where the group was setting up," Pierce said.

"It was done by Tilden and Grotowski."

"Time me."

Pierce ran as fast as she could, gripping her phone and timing herself, imagining Katie Harmon, terrified and running at top speed. Arriving at the day site area, Pierce allowed ten seconds before running back. Getting the time from Benton and checking it on her phone, Pierce put the time gap between when Anna was left clinging for her life to the branch and when she was found on the rocks at a total of five to seven minutes.

"This is a pointless waste," Benton said.

Bent over, catching her breath, Pierce glared up at him. At every step of the investigation, she felt him suppressing anger, and with every step, her patience with him was thinning. Pierce moved to the open area and the cliff where Anna Shaw fell and stood there, surveying the area.

Benton came up behind her. "This whole place was processed a couple weeks ago," he said. "It makes no sense to come here."

Pierce took another deep breath, released it, closed her eyes, then opened them.

"Something doesn't feel right."

"Doesn't feel right? How long you gonna play that record?"

"I've been studying everything and I think the answer's here."

"Answer to what? She fell, end of story." Benton swore under his breath and turned away.

Pierce looked to the section with grassy patches and underbrush that bordered the forest, several yards away. The scattering of stones there was barely visible, but you could see it if you looked.

That's why she'd wanted to return.

Something about the stones nagged at her.

She went to them and lowered herself. She counted seven coconut-sized stones, each rounded, smooth and spread in a loose circle, remains of a campfire. But not recent, no, years ago. The stones were weathered, with each one blackened on one side.

In studying the photos and the forensic videos of the scene taken the day of Anna Shaw's death, something about these same seven stones gnawed at her.

And here it is.

Just as it was in the photos and video, among the seven stones: a bowl-like impression in the earth.

A stone is missing.

But the impression was not weathered; it looked recent.

She lifted some of the other stones. Each left a similar cupped impression. Benton joined her, watching in silence, absorbing her work, seeing what she was seeing.

Pierce took photos with her phone, then walked to the cliff and the spot where Anna Shaw fell. Pierce drank in the glorious view of the mountains, the forest and the river. Wind gusted up the cliffside, beckoning her to look down twenty feet to the twisted, speared remnants of the tree branch where—according to Katie—Anna clung in the last moments of her life.

Benton stepped beside Pierce at the cliff.

She turned to him and said, "I think we're missing something."

Benton was ignoring her because he was looking at his phone.

She'd had enough.

"Have you got a problem with me, Carl, with my gender, or maybe my *heritage*?"

He stiffened, clenched his jaw and put his phone away without answering her.

Pierce looked to the mountains, then said: "When I was a kid in school, about eight or so, my teacher, a nun, took me into the bathroom and started running my hands under the water."

Benton looked at her, a little puzzled.

"'You missed all this dirt on your knuckles,' she told me. And I said, 'No, sister, I didn't.' She made the water hot and scrubbed at my knuckles until it hurt. I said: 'Sister, it's not dirt, it's my skin.' And she said, 'No, you're dirty. You're a dirty little—' She stopped but we both knew how the sister was going to end her sentence. I pulled my hands away and I told her, 'It's not dirt, it's my skin. It's me. It's who I am.'"

Pierce turned to Benton.

"I'm telling you this, Carl, because this is who I am. And I'm proud of who I am. The nun was not going to scrub me away and neither are you."

Benton nodded slowly. "Yeah, well, I don't care."

"Excuse me?"

"No, it's not—" he scrambled. "I know what you're doing," he said. "And I think what that nun did to you was unforgivable."

"Really? Is that what you think? Is that why you clammed up that day when I heard you talking about my heritage?"

"This is messed up." Benton shook his head.

"It's messed up?"

"We were talking about that John Wayne Western with Natalie Wood, when she was just a kid."

Pierce thought a moment, then said: *"The Searchers?"*

"Yeah."

"What about it?"

"We were talking about Natalie Wood's heritage, being Ukrainian and Russian, and some other stuff about race in the film, when you walked in. It was awkward." He grimaced with self-disappointment. "I know I made you feel uncomfortable. I was wrong. I should've handled it better. I'm sorry," he said. "Look, Kim, I'm a cop, you're a cop. I don't care about your gender or heritage. I don't— It's just—"

She looked at him, deciding if she should believe him.

"What is it?" she said. "Let's have it out now, because you're starting to piss me off and we need to focus on this case."

Benton looked at her like he was seeing her for the first time. A shadow crept over his face. He swallowed hard and looked down at the river rushing below.

"I've been a prick to you. I've behaved like an ass since you caught this case. Even now, I'm not handling this right, look—"

"You're stating the obvious."

Pierce looked at him gazing down at the river. She watched his face crease, watched him rub it hard as if coaxing another truth to the surface.

"My wife, Elizabeth," he started. "It's almost certain she's terminal. She's had a lot of tests, we're waiting for results, so every message I get, I just—you know?"

Pierce exhaled, then nodded, letting him go on.

"I've been raging at the world," he said. "Not giving a damn or seeing the point in anything."

"I get that, Carl, but it's no excuse to act the way you did."

"No, no it's not and I just didn't care, you know?"

"Does Art know about Elizabeth? Any of the other guys know?"

Benton's chin crumpled as he gave his head a quick shake.

"No one. Just our family. And now you. I want to keep it that way."

Pierce took a moment to accept that, alone with her here, he was being sincere. But the sting of his behavior had not fully subsided.

"You've got to tell Art. There're programs, benefits, counselors... You could take time off. Carl, you shouldn't be working—you should be with her—"

"No." Benton shook his head. "No. She absolutely doesn't want that. We've been very private, practically said all our goodbyes. She wants me to keep working." He shook his head. "Instead, I've become a bitter bastard."

"You say her condition is *almost certain*, which tells me you still have hope, Carl. Hang on to that hope."

He nodded and looked away.

Pierce touched Benton's shoulder and found his eyes.

The look on his face told her that he recognized the depth of the racist wound, even if unintended, that he'd inflicted and that he was sorry.

The look on her face told him that, while forgiveness would come, he was her partner now.

Benton nodded, cleared his throat.

"I think I know where you're going on this." He indicated the stones. "Let's get down there."

They found the safe route down to the river, the one used by everyone at the outset, from the camp supervisors to the investigators. The rush of the water was loud as they walked carefully along the craggy riverbank, coming to the spot where Anna Shaw was found. Minutes ticked by as they searched the uneven rocky ground, looking for something, something that would be easy to overlook. From time to time, they'd take stock of the rising cliffside, the broken branch protruding from it. Noting their bearings, they'd double-check their position on the rough riverbank.

Then Pierce found it.

"Carl!"

Nearly invisible, wedged a foot down between two large rock sheets.

A single coconut-sized round stone, just like the others on the clifftop.

Pierce got down on her knees to inspect it without touching it. Benton arrived and turned on his flashlight.

The stone showed signs of being charred on one side, just like the others.

"So," Pierce said, "how does this stone go from being up there, to down here?"

27

THIS IS THE TIME.

Sara gripped her shopping cart handle, pushing it down the aisles at the Safeway. Helplessness rippled through her in the wake of the detectives interviewing Katie.

Alone in our home. I should've said no. I should've sat in or called a lawyer. Why did they come?

After the police left, Sara wanted to know what the detectives said to Katie and what she told them, but she didn't want to put pressure on her by reinterrogating her at home. They needed groceries. Taking Katie on an errand would give them some distance and divert attention, or so Sara hoped.

In the car Katie was distracted, checking out her phone. Sara held off asking her about the detectives, even with sun finding the tiny heart of the necklace—flashing on it like an accusation. Sara, afraid, bought time, letting the drive serve as decompression while waiting for the right moment.

This is it.

Sara reached for a box of pasta, placing it in her cart. She glanced at Katie, who seemed happy to have her phone back. It had partially charged in the car, and she was quietly swiping and tapping away.

"Mom, when can I go back to school?"

"You want to go back?"

"Yes, I miss my friends."

"I'll call Mrs. Hadley and tell her you're ready."

They continued to another aisle.

Keep it calm and casual, Sara told herself.

"How did it go with talking to the police?"

"Alright, I guess."

Sara glanced around. No one was within earshot.

"What did they ask you?"

Ignoring her, Katie asked, "Mom, do police always know when people lie?"

The question took Sara by surprise and she adjusted her grip on the handle.

"They're good at finding out things, sweetie. Why do you ask?"

Katie remained focused on her phone as Sara checked a sale on canned vegetables.

"Why do you ask about that, honey?"

"Just wondering."

"You seemed a little upset after they left," Sara said.

Katie remained silent.

"Honey, I'm your mom. I should know what they asked you." Sara placed two cans of corn in the cart.

"They asked me about how Anna gave me the necklace."

"Oh." Sara reached for peas. "What about it?"

"Like, why I didn't tell them about it at first, then stuff

about Anna breaking up with Tanner. And when and where did Anna give me the necklace, stuff like that."

"I think we need some ketchup," Sara said. "What else did they ask?"

They stopped in front of the shelves for ketchup. No one was near, except for an older woman far off, browsing.

"They asked me for the millionth time what happened." Sara paused. Ketchup was on sale.

"I see. Were they double-checking details, that sort of thing?"

"I guess."

"What did you say?"

Katie lowered her phone, her chin wrinkling as she looked to the ceiling.

"Geez, Mom, do I have to keep talking about it?"

Sara looked down the aisle. The older woman remained distant from them. Sara lowered herself before Katie and stroked her hair.

"Sweetie, I know this is hard." Sara blinked quickly. "It's hard for me, too, but I'm doing this to help you, and it helps me, too. That's why I need to know everything."

"Everything?"

Sara drew back slightly.

"Yes." Sara looked at Katie for a moment, then repeated, "Yes."

"They wanted to know what I talked to Dr. Sally about and if there were things that I told her that they should know."

"They asked you that?"

"Yes, and they asked if there were things you told me not to tell them."

Sara swallowed.

"What did you tell them?"

"I said no, there was nothing. That's what I'm supposed to say, right?"

Sara's thoughts whirled.

"Excuse me."

The older woman appeared beside them, wanting to pass. Smiling, Sara stood to make room. The woman rolled her cart by them, disappearing around the end of the aisle. The interruption ended Sara's questioning of Katie and they resumed shopping. But for the entire time, Sara struggled to process her concerns over what Katie had told her.

At the checkout, while placing her items on the conveyor belt, Sara's heart flew back to Salem, Oregon, to when she was a cashier and the day she lost Nathaniel. Then her mind shifted to what had happened only two years ago when she'd taken Katie to visit friends in British Columbia—another tragedy.

And now this one with Anna.

"That'll be forty-one forty."

Sara got her card from her wallet and, after paying, noticed that the older woman she'd seen in her aisle was now watching her and Katie from the next checkout line. When Sara stared back, the woman looked away.

Their groceries bagged and in their cart, Sara and Katie moved through the parking lot. Once everything was loaded into their Trailblazer and the cart was returned to the corral, they got in. Before starting the motor, before they buckled up, Sara turned to Katie.

"Honey, I have to know what really happened to Anna."

Katie lowered her head, took the heart of the necklace between her fingers, twisting it tenderly.

"I had bad thoughts, Mom."

"Like you did with the boy?"

Katie shook her head slowly. "Worse thoughts than that."
"Did you have these thoughts after Anna fell, or before?"
Katie whispered.
"Before."

Pursuant to Resolution 10242

Pursuant to Montana Code Annotated § 44-5-103
Records Bureau Archive Retrieved: Copied from original
Great Falls Police Department report number ███████████

Great Falls Police Department
Incident Report Abandoned Child
INTERNAL USE ██████████████████████████
PERSON MAKING REPORT:
NAME: ████████ ████████
ADDRESS: ████████████████████
PHONE: ████████████████
DOB: ████████████ 1956
AGE: 20
SEX: F
EMPLOYER/SCHOOL: ████████████
PHONE: ████████████████
ADDRESS: ████████████████
DATE: 17 June 1976
TIME: 8:45 a.m.
INCIDENT LOCATION: Bus depot
ADDRESS: 1st Avenue S & 4th Street S

DESCRIPTION OF INCIDENT
At approximately 8:45 a.m., I responded to a dispatched code
████ call to the bus depot. Upon arrival met with ████████
depot manager and ████████ in the depot's main office. A
white female child, name N/A, estimated 3–5 yrs was with

them. ███████ stated she had arrived very early before her bus to Salt Lake City and reported seeing the child enter main doors at approximately 7:30 a.m. along with several people. ███████ assumed the child was with one of the adults who'd entered. Members of the group eventually left as various buses departed. The child remained, seated alone. Being concerned, █████ asked child about parents or family and the child cried. ███████ alerted the depot staff, who checked bathrooms, and made an announcement in the depot to negative results. ███████ radioed drivers of the three buses that departed within the period in question to alert passengers to the child at the depot in an attempt to contact parent/guardian, who may have left child. Results negative.

I attempted to interview the child for her name/parent/relative name/address/telephone. She managed to tell me she was four years old but could not or would not provide any other information. A search of the child yielded no information that would serve to identify her. Child was tearful but did not appear to have a physical injury or be in physical distress. Child accepted a sandwich and milk from depot staff. Other units called through dispatch conducted a canvass of all businesses and residences nearby with negative results. I alerted Child & Family Services Division (CFSD) who dispatched ███████ # ███████████ a child protection specialist (CP specialist) to take temporary custody of the child as this appeared to be an abandoned child case. Further investigation to be conducted.

OFFICER: ███████
OFFICER SIGNATURE: ███████
DATE: 17 June 1976
SERIAL NUMBER: ███████
INCIDENT NUMBER: ███████
SUPV INITS: █████

28

Seattle, Washington

IT RAINED THAT NIGHT.

Sara made Katie's favorite supper, baked mac and cheese.

Later while cleaning up, Sara's phone vibrated. Another notification from the Silverbrook Hills Senior Living Home on the increase, advising her that she hadn't yet selected a payment plan and time was running out.

I can't select a plan because I can't afford a plan.

Sara thought about alternatives for financing her mother's care. Maybe selling the SUV—*but Dad loved the Trailblazer. It was his baby. "Always check the oil. It's still golden when I change it and it runs like new."* She could take out a home equity loan or sell the house—*but Mom loves this house.*

Sara put her phone away.

I can't deal with this now.

Her anguish over Anna's death and Katie eclipsed everything.

She joined Katie on the sofa, trying to maintain control while they started watching *Frozen*. But Sara brooded so deeply she didn't see the TV. She couldn't escape her increasing fear over the detectives' questioning of Katie today.

And that woman in the store staring at us. Why was she staring?

Sara picked up the remote and stopped the movie.

"Mom?"

"Sorry, honey, but I need to be sure about some things, okay? Did the detectives ask you about the boy in Canada?"

Katie kept her eyes on the TV. "No, I keep telling you, they didn't."

"What about Dr. Sally? You've had several sessions with her now. Did you tell her about the boy?"

Katie was silent.

"Did she ask you about the boy?"

Katie nodded.

"What did you tell her?"

"I told her I didn't want to talk about it."

"Did you tell her what happened? Did you say where it happened?"

Katie shook her head.

"I didn't tell her anything, Mom, I didn't. You told me not to talk about it ever, so I didn't."

Sara struggled, probing Katie on how much she actually recalled.

"Do you remember what you said to that boy?"

Katie nodded without looking from the screen. "He was so mean."

"Do you remember everything that happened after?"

Katie nodded.

"And that what happened after had nothing to do with what you said?"

Katie nodded and kept staring at the TV.

"But today, in the car at the grocery store, you talked again about having had bad thoughts. You said that they were worse than what you had with the boy."

Katie said nothing.

"You said you had them before Anna fell."

Katie said nothing.

"Did you have them at the time she fell?"

Katie said nothing.

"Honey?"

Katie's breathing quickened, making her nostrils flare. She pursed her lips, snatched the remote from her mother, resumed the movie and turned on the sound.

Sara closed her eyes, then opened them.

"I'm trying to help you, honey."

"My thoughts scare me, Mom. They really scare me."

Sara swallowed hard.

"Did you tell Dr. Sally about them?"

Katie shook her head and raised her voice. "No. I already told you, no! Geez, Mom!"

"Did you tell any of your friends about them?"

Katie shook her head.

"Do you want to tell me about them first? It might help?"

"No."

"Do you want to try?"

"No, no, I can't! Please don't make me tell!"

"Okay, it's okay." *For the time being.*

Nothing more was said on the subject for the rest of the evening, and they continued with the movie. After it ended Katie went to bed.

Downstairs Sara dimmed the lights and sat near the window, watching the rain web down the glass as she wrestled with confusion and dread.

No one will understand, after Anna, after Katie and the boy. How could they? I don't understand it myself.

It was late when Sara padded upstairs and into Katie's room, looking down at her daughter and the necklace on her nightstand.

What really happened on that cliff, Katie?

Turning to the rain-streaked window in the room, Sara clenched her eyes as her own dark thoughts reached from the night to drag her back...

...driving in the rain...screams in the darkness...

29

Seattle, Washington

THAT SAME NIGHT across the city from where Sara Harmon grappled with her life, work continued.

Rain glistened on the streets near an apartment building on a hill. An upper window was lit in bluish white from a laptop screen and a lamp. In the room, on the desk, stacked next to the computer, was a mountain range of files, dog-eared pages of records, articles and documents.

A ceramic mug of fresh black coffee sat next to a yellow pad with handwritten notes. Soft steady tapping on the keyboard resumed. A few clicks, and a PDF blossomed:

**Child and Family Services Division (CFSD)—
Child Protective Services (CPS)
Update RE: Assessment and Investigation Report
Case Number:** ▮▮▮▮

CP Specialist: ▮▮▮▮▮▮▮
DATE: 25 September 1976
Pursuant Mont. Code Ann. § 41-3-4

Further to neglect/abandonment case #▮▮▮*., female child taken into temporary custody of CFSD via foster home / while assessment and investigation conducted.*

Subsequent to female child's abandonment at the Great Falls bus depot 17/06/76, medical examination determined no signs of physical or sexual abuse, or inadequate nutrition. Child's demeanor: anxious/nervous. Attempted interviews with child yielded few results. Child gave age as four, but was unable (or unwilling) to provide information regarding parents, guardian, address, tel., etc. Examination of child's clothing/labels show acquired from US retailers but no indicators of child's identity.

Investigators had temporarily named child "June," for the month she was found. Psychological assessment indicated that June's cognitive development of episodic memory may have been "stalled" due to possible traumatic occurrence, resulting in "blocking" or a degree of amnesia.

Investigation by CPS and law enforcement encompassed an area canvass of businesses and residences and search for possible items related to the case, checks with hospitals, accident reports, suicides, shelters and support groups. Investigation also included questioning and background checks of all passengers by respective law enforcement at arrival destinations of buses departing from Great Falls bus depot on day June was abandoned. No information linking any individual(s) was obtained.

Law enforcement alerted all local, regional, state and federal agencies, including the FBI and Royal Canadian Mounted Police, to the case. Extensive searches of missing children's cases, databases, and various agencies and organizations were consulted. Search of all prison records was conducted for any po-

tential links to an incarcerated, sentenced, or paroled parent in the system. The outcome was negative. Local media reported on the case, consequently several individuals stepped forward requesting to adopt June but no information concerning family or relatives emerged.

CPS has made diligent effort to identify and locate June's birth parents, or possible relatives. Efforts included: consultation of all registries; alerting of all CFSD offices state-wide and social services agencies in other states and Canada; conducting a Family Finding Search through the search center.

CPS has submitted the attached affidavit with all required supporting documentation.

MONTANA JUDICIAL DISTRICT COURT, COUNTY

IN THE MATTER OF: (JOHN DOE AND JANE DOE),

AFFIDAVIT FOR YOUTH IN NEED OF CARE.

STATE OF MONTANA COUNTY OF (Name), being first duly sworn on oath, states:

1. That (Name) is a Child Protection Specialist for the Department of Public Health and Human Services.

2. That natural birth parents of child in case # ▇▇▇▇▇ cannot be identified or found for service of process in this matter.

3. After due diligence, unknown parents cannot

be identified, or located, despite all efforts with all resources available to CPS and law enforcement.

4. That the State of Montana has a valid cause of action, which in the interest of the above-child must be fully pursued before this Court.

DATED this day of ▉▉▉▉▉
(Child Protection Specialist: ▉▉▉▉▉▉)
State of Montana
County _____
On this _____ day of _____, __ personally appeared before me a notary public for the State of Montana; personally known to me to be the person whose name is subscribed to this instrument, and acknowledged that s/he executed the same.
NOTARY PUBLIC FOR THE STATE OF MONTANA
Printed name of Notary Public
Notary Public for the State of Montana
Residing at _____
My commission expires _____

Case # ▉▉▉▉ *referred to district court. Update to follow.*

Case # ▉▉▉▉ *status notes*

17 April 1977—No information on June's family / relatives / circumstances leading to abandonment of 17 June 1976 has emerged.

26 June 1977

Upon review district court judge found that the Department has made reasonable efforts to identify and locate the birth parents of child, known as "June," efforts that have proven fruitless. Further efforts by the Department would likely be unproductive, and reunification of the child with the parent or guardian would be contrary to the best interests of the child. The court judge ordered CFSD/DPHHS to implement a plan for June's permanent placement through adoption or guardianship.

Update Case # # ▮▮▮▮

Child and Family Services Adoption Case # # ▮▮▮▮

Adoption / Pre-Placement Process: A prospective adoptive family xxxxx residing in ▮▮▮▮ *in* ▮▮▮▮ *County has been selected through the process found in section 603-2.*

▮▮▮▮*, family resource specialist, is working with the prospective adoptive family to coordinate a pre-placement process.*

NOTE: Documentation being a major part of this process, all records of information of all parties are to remain confidential, subject to unsealing by court order. ▮▮▮▮ *CPS arranged for pre-placement visits with child and her prospective adoptive parents, to become acquainted and to ease the adjustment of all parties as the child moves into a new home. A written visitation agreement was drawn up and included place, frequency and number of visits; purpose and goals of visits, along with roles and responsibilities. (SEE ATTACHED VISIT AGREEMENT #* ▮▮▮▮*.)*

Update Child and Family Services Adoption Case # xxxxx

CAPS Entry
Pre-placement process successfully concluded with decision to place the child in the adoptive home with the prospective adop-

tive parents with ███████████, *a placement worker supervis-*
ing the adoptive placement and completion of all documentation,
including all brief known medical and psychological history of
the child. Noted exceptions in Case # ██████ *no information*
concerning the social history, psychological evaluation, medical
information and background of the child's birth parents could
be provided.

Adoption Process Procedure / Removal of Child from State
██████████████████████

Post-Placement Evaluation
████████████, *assigned caseworker, conducted first visit two*
weeks after placement, then conducted monthly visits with the
child and the pre-adoptive family in the family's home during
the post-placement period. All visits documented. The wait-
ing period has been complied with. Maiden name of the pre-
adoptive mother and the correct spelling of the name of the child
and adoptive parent(s) that will appear on the amended birth
certificate to be verified by the pre-adoptive parent(s); adoption
to be finalized with attorney.

Adoption is finalized. Order of Adoption Decree April 1978.

The ceramic mug was raised, coffee was sipped.

Obtaining these decades-old confidential records was difficult. Of course, all the identifying information in the case
of the abandoned-adopted girl had been redacted, in keeping
with privacy laws.

But if you knew where to look, how to look and who to
ask for help, you could get closer to the truth.

Tapping on the keyboard resumed, a few more clicks and
another file blossomed.

★ ★ ★

May 1978

Yellowstone River Community Newsletter

UPCOMING EVENTS

3rd Live Music at the Sky Riders Museum: Big Country Cowboys 7:00–9:00 p.m. in the Honor Hall $20 per ticket
4th Farmer's Market 8:00 a.m.–12:00 p.m. in Split Rock Park
8–9th Flat Ranch Rodeo Finals: Friday 6:00 p.m.
9th High Plains Classics Car Show & Shine: 11:00 a.m.–3:00 p.m. at Split Park
23rd Clear Plains Wildlife Banquet: 5:00 p.m. at BillTown
Tickets: Terry Lisher or Jed Ford

ANNOUNCEMENTS & HONORS

BIRTHS

William Jackson, 9 pounds, 7 ounces, a male born April 17, 1978, to Clarisa Dacks and Venner Kerdhal at the Health-Care Complex.
Rhonda Allen, 7 pounds, 5 ounces, a female born on April 15, 1978, to Valeria Martin and Shawn Mcartey at the HealthCare Complex

NEW FAMILY MEMBER

Nelson and Scarlett Kurtz of Lone Tree Ranch in Big Sweet Water welcome Magdalena Ursula, age 6.

JUNE WEDDING

Franklin and Louise Learner of Scottsdale, Arizona, are pleased to announce the engagement of their daughter

Maria Rose to Chet Granger of Miles City, Montana, son of Leo and Ruby Collins also of Miles City.

HONOR ROLL

Abraham Lincoln Middle School has posted its honor roll. An asterisk denotes a 4.0 grade average.

ON THE DEAN'S LIST

Tilly Rickert of Circle has been named on the Dean's List at the University of Kansas in Lawrence, Kansas.
Jordan Falkner of Miles City was named on the fall Dean's List at the University in Syracuse, New York.

HAPPY BIRTHDAYS THIS MONTH

Larry Carr
Penny Miner
Nancy St. Dennis
Wanda Simms
Leonard Krieger

Let us know about your events and activities!

The mug was set down.

The cursor highlighted the announcement of the six-year-old girl named Magdalena becoming a new member of the Kurtz family.

30

ONE BY ONE, the Magdalena Kurtz files were closed on the laptop.

Now, Carrie Gardner smiled from the screen in pictures taken at the photo booth at the Westfarms mall near Hartford, Connecticut. She's sixteen and hugging Ryan, her five-year-old brother, who's sitting on her lap. They're sticking out their tongues or laughing with big-eyed expressions in the series taken on a shopping trip with their mom.

Carrie is radiant, the life in her overwhelming.

Ryan can feel her holding him, hear her laughter and smell her Love's Baby Soft perfume.

It was a perfect day.

Rubbing his eyes now, Ryan scanned the folders towered next to his laptop. His files were growing ever thicker with new information and the records he was continually gathering and studying over and over.

How many years have I been doing this?

Then, as it often did in these lonely hours, the memory came to him:

...with Mom and Dad, seeing Carrie off with a flurry of hugs and kisses at the Hartford airport. She's returning to Arizona after coming home from college for a brief visit. Mom's anxious for Carrie's upcoming trip, driving from Arizona to Alaska. "Call us every day," Mom says. "Promise." Carrie with her bright smile says: "I promise, Mom."

At the last minute, Dad surprises Carrie with a roll of cash. "Fill the tank every chance you get." Carrie saying, "I'll be home for Christmas or Thanksgiving." Telling Ryan, "Watch over Mom and Dad for me and be good. You're the best little brother in the world." She crushes him in her arms. After pulling away she turns back, searches his face, hugs him again, harder, whispering, "I love you."

Like she knew.

Like she knew it was the last time they would see each other.

He was eleven years old.

Carrie had flown back to ASU, then left Tempe for Alaska with her friend Willow Walker in Willow's van. Their long journey would be a vacation, an adventure, before they started summer jobs in Fairbanks.

On the first day of their trip, Carrie called home from Orderville, Utah. On the second day she called from Idaho Falls, Idaho. But she didn't call on the third day, the fourth or the fifth. Ryan remembered how the air began tightening at home, his mom and dad sensing something was wrong. How in those first days, concern rolled through them in small waves until his mom called Willow's family. The Walkers hadn't heard from Willow either and, yes, they were worried.

With each day the fear grew, leading to calls to police in Idaho, police in Arizona, Montana and Canada.

Ryan's dad and Willow's dad, who was a Baltimore cop, flew to Arizona to search for their daughters, renting a car, following their route into Idaho, then continuing into Montana. ASU student friends put up posters, held candlelight vigils, and a collection was started for a reward for information about the girls. Every day Ryan's mother prayed for them.

All of it was futile.

Three months after Carrie and Willow left Tempe, a sedan pulled into the driveway of the Gardners' home. A man and woman came to the front door. Grim-faced, they presented ID, confirming they were FBI agents.

"We have an update on your daughter's case," the woman said.

Ryan's parents sent him upstairs to his room, but he sat at the banister where he listened and watched through the spindles.

The agents were invited into the kitchen. Ryan had a direct view from the banister and he watched as the female agent unzipped a leather portfolio bearing an FBI seal, then withdrew large photos, placing them on the table. The pictures showed, in large dramatic, crisp detail, a yellow actuator, a canister and a capped mouthpiece of an asthma inhaler. Ryan's dad groaned and Ryan's mother stifled a squeal. The agents said the prescription label on the canister held Carrie's full name, her date of birth and other medical information, then showed it to his parents. Without speaking, their eyes carried their terrifying question to the agents.

"We're certain this is Carrie's inhaler," the agent said. "It was found near Billings, Montana, in the residence of Herman and Magda Vryker."

"Where's Carrie?" Ryan's mom's voice sounded strange.

"We haven't located her at this time," the agent said.

"Who're these people in Montana?" Ryan's dad bristled.

The question went unanswered for what seemed like a long time.

"There's little we can say because we have an ongoing investigation," the agent said. "We can tell you that the Vrykers are facing charges in the recent assault of a woman in northern Idaho. Her case led us to the Vrykers and evidence linking them to the disappearances of several other people, including Carrie and Willow Walker."

"Oh, my God!" Ryan's mom said.

"What're you saying?" Ryan's dad asked. "Is Carrie dead?"

"We never give up hope," the agent said, "but you must brace for the worst."

And the worst came, weeks later when the agents returned.

Again they sat at the kitchen table where they told Ryan's mom and dad that Magda Vryker had made a plea deal and confessed to investigators. She and her husband had murdered Carrie, Willow and five other people.

To this day Ryan maintained that the windows in the house rattled at the fury of his mother's screams. Watching it all from upstairs, Ryan gripped the banister spindles so fiercely he was certain they'd snap.

Murdered? Carrie's dead? I'll never see my sister again?

Ryan went numb, raced down the stairs and flew to his mother, welding himself to her as she convulsed with sobs, his dad trying to comfort them. One of her hands reached to the empty space at the table where Carrie sat, Carrie's spot. The space where Mom had set down birthday cakes before Carrie, glowing with candles that made her eyes shine like stars; the space where she had helped Carrie with homework; the space where she had taught Carrie needlepoint; the space where Carrie had opened her letter of acceptance into Arizona State University.

Oh, God, it hurt. It hurt so much.

It was as if the earth beneath their feet had collapsed.

It may have been a month, or longer, of his parents pushing through their agony, of continually asking when they could bring Carrie home for her funeral. That's when the FBI relayed events: How they still hadn't found any of the victims. How Herman Vryker, facing the death penalty after his wife's betrayal, had died by suicide in prison. And how Magda, who as part of her twenty-year-sentence plea deal had made an agreement to locate their victims, was now claiming that she couldn't remember.

Despite trying other options, investigators couldn't locate the remains of the Vrykers' victims. And Magda Vryker's sentence meant she would serve less than three years for each person she murdered. Taken together, the situation increased the pain for Ryan's family.

The days passed into weeks, the weeks into months, with Thanksgiving and Christmas passing like wakes. Ryan's mom insisted on setting a plate at Carrie's empty chair. Then, when Carrie's birthday came, she spent much of it alone in Carrie's room while Ryan's dad sat in the dark, ice clinking in his glass.

Carrie was gone and they would never bring her home.

The horror had ripped a hole in the fabric of their lives. Ryan's family would never be the same. As the years went by it seemed that all he could do was look at the pictures from the photo booth and cherish his memories of the airport. His grief became anger. By the time he entered Manchester Community College, he'd resolved to acquire the skills that would lead him to Carrie.

He excelled at research. When he graduated, he got a job as a reporter at the *Hartford Courant*, where he refined his skills, learning how to be more effective at mining public databases and archives, and how to use the Freedom of Information Act to access records at every level of government.

While Magda Vryker was in prison, refusing to reveal the locations of the people she and her husband had murdered, Ryan began digging into the case and her life, with the patience and precision of a hunter. Sources pointed him to possible leads. Some of his requests to government agencies for information took months, even years. Some were denied, which led to appeals or had him consider lawsuits.

Some records were leaked to him, arriving in unmarked envelopes.

After several years he left the *Courant* for a reporting job at the *Chicago Tribune*, where he continued pursuing Magda Vryker as Carrie's death continued exacting a toll on his family.

His parents had separated. His dad had moved to Bridgeport and found contract plumbing work but was lost to his drinking. His mom, a lab technician, lived alone like a spirit in their empty house. Devastated, Ryan hung on to one thing: his belief that if he could find Carrie and bring her home, he could somehow reassemble the pieces of his family, that in some dimension they would be together again—fractured, but together.

He intensified his work but paid a price for it. For years he'd lived with Olivia Sanders, a fellow *Tribune* reporter. They'd planned to get married, but Ryan's deepening obsession to find his sister's remains drove a wedge into their relationship—"I thought I could handle it," Olivia told him one night driving home from a party, Chicago's skyline glittering. "But I'm sorry, I can't. I'm so sorry."

A few years after Olivia left him, Ryan took a buyout and left the paper, using the time and his savings in a full-bore pursuit of Magda. He consistently wrote to her in prison, requesting she agree to an interview. Prison officials informed him that his requests had been denied. He continued writing until eventually his letters went unanswered.

Ryan traveled to Montana, visiting key locations he'd discovered in Magda's life. He talked to people who had any association or memory of her. Some shared photos, letters and journals; most wanted to help, always pointing him to other possibilities.

And like his dad and Willow's father did years before, Ryan traveled the route the girls took. Only he went all the way to Fairbanks, Alaska, and back in an effort to make a spiritual connection with Carrie. Then he drove the routes of the other victims in Montana, Idaho and Washington.

His files and expertise on the case growing, Ryan wrote an article for *Vanity Fair* about his quest, which the magazine featured and pegged to Magda's then-upcoming release from prison.

Not only did his *Vanity Fair* piece pay well, it yielded other dividends.

Literary agents contacted him with potential publishing deals. They said his story could be made into a network true-crime series.

"But it's not over yet. It doesn't have an ending," Ryan told them, deciding to hold off.

Inspired by Ryan's article, amateur sleuths took up his cause, giving rise to a number of online groups outraged at how Magda had beat the system. Fearing Magda had not been rehabilitated and could kill again, they were devoted to locating her wherever she tried to resume her life and warning her community that a murderer lived free among them.

Many people in the online groups passed theories, speculation and leads to Ryan. Much of it led nowhere, but he looked at everything because upon her release, facing no terms or conditions in her legally binding deal with prosecutors, Magda had vanished. And despite all of Ryan's sources and efforts, he couldn't find her. He'd learned that while in prison she'd earned a number of degrees and planned how she would disappear. Rumor among the online groups held that Magda had changed her appearance and her name, learned other languages and may have fled to another country to live out her life in peaceful anonymity.

Some thought that Magda may have reconnected with her daughter, who'd been taken from her as a toddler at the time of Magda's imprisonment. Given the magnitude of Magda's crimes, prosecutors were steadfast in ensuring Magda lost custody.

In the years since her release from prison, Ryan's search for Magda had been futile. He'd traveled to Panama, Canada, Germany and the UK, in searches that had dead-ended. Following leads in the US, he'd searched for her in Denver, Dallas, Minneapolis, Pittsburgh and Brooklyn.

He survived by taking whatever jobs he could: Uber driver, warehouse worker, reporter. He'd house-sit, couch surf, work out long-stay rates at cheap motels, all while scouring a location for Magda and researching every aspect of her life.

Now he clicked on a news picture of Magda taken at her arrest: she's handcuffed and staring into the camera, her eyes telegraphing bone-chilling malevolence—*something dead behind them.*

Ryan stared at Magda for the longest time.

I will go to the ends of the earth to find you.

Ryan turned from his laptop to the window and the rain and sipped the last of his tepid coffee.

Now he was in Seattle following a lead arising from his research and his sources indicating that Magda's daughter was living and working in the metropolitan area, and that it was possible Magda was also here.

Have to admit, that's a first, a tip putting them both in the same area.
He'd gone to the diner in North Seattle.

I'm just not sure about the woman working there. So many times he'd been convinced he was on the right track with other women in other cities. He was wrong every time. No, he couldn't be sure until it was a certainty.

Ryan paused to consider a tip he'd gotten long ago from a police source in Montana. In her life-and-death struggle, the Canadian woman who'd survived had flailed wildly in the Vrykers' van, gouging the wrist of Magda's daughter so severely it left a permanent scar.

Ryan looked through his files. He had information for other women in other locations in the area that he was working on.

But his thoughts went back to the diner. The woman appeared to be the right age and her tattoo—if meant to hide a scar—was in the right spot.

I just don't know. I've still got a lot of work to do until I am certain.

Among the skills he'd learned from his sources, who were detectives and private investigators, was how to surreptitiously collect and sift through people's trash for useful items and information. He'd also learned how to acquire cast-off, or shed, DNA from such things as discarded napkins, gum and hair, which could be analyzed.

All of the tactics were legal and could prove to be critical. But they took time.

He yawned and rubbed his eyes. Before shutting everything down, he went to his photos from the photo booth of Carrie holding him in her lap and smiled at them. Then he turned to the window and watched the rain.

In his heart he felt something, a sensation, telling him to keep going.

I feel I'm closer now, closer than I've ever been.

31

Seattle, Washington

AT RAINIER PINE ELEMENTARY, Katie's desk was covered with cards and drawings made by her classmates.

Colorful pictures of broken hearts, butterflies with tears and people hugging. They had handwritten messages that said things like: *I'm so sorry for you* and *I said a prayer for you and your friend.*

Before Katie had returned to school, her teacher, Mrs. Hadley, called Katie's mom to offer her condolences and determine how Katie wanted to be welcomed back to class. After a discussion, they decided that Katie didn't want to draw too much attention to herself but wanted Anna's death to be acknowledged in some way.

"Hi, Katie. Welcome back." Mrs. Hadley lowered herself at Katie's desk while other students settled at their desks.

"Hi."

"I'm very sorry that Anna died. I'm a good listener and I'm here if you ever want to talk."

"Thank you."

"The class wants to do something for you, then we'll carry on, okay?"

"Alright."

Mrs. Hadley gave Katie a little hug, then went to the front of the room.

"We're happy to have Katie back, class. All of us are sad that her friend Anna has died. We talked about this, so now, if you want to give Katie a hug, you may. Is that okay with you, Katie?"

Katie nodded.

One by one, row by row, every student in the class but one came to Katie. They hugged her and told her they were sad for her, too, but happy she was back. When they finished and everyone was back in their seats, Mrs. Hadley started with a math lesson.

Later, outside at recess, Katie was talking with two other girls when Dylan Frick interrupted them by standing close and staring at Katie.

Dylan was in Katie's class and the only person who hadn't hugged her. He was also in the Sunny Days group and had been at the park the day Anna died.

"You're being creepy and rude, Dylan," one of the girls said.

His eyes burned into Katie's.

"You know," Dylan said, "some people are saying your friend didn't fall taking a stupid selfie."

Katie's eyes narrowed and she began breathing hard.

"They think you're a liar!" Dylan said.

"Don't say that!"

"What're you going to do to me? Liar!"

The muscles in Katie's jaw bunched and she pushed Dylan's chest with both hands.

"Whoa." Dylan grinned. "Looks like you push people when you get mad."

Katie held one finger of warning to Dylan's face.

"You better stop telling lies."

Katie eyed him coldly before she walked away.

32

PIERCE LOOKED TO the investigators on the teleconference screen and those settling in at the table in the King County Sheriff's Office headquarters.

Detective Sergeant Art Acker spoke first. "We've got developments to discuss. Let's get to it." He nodded for Pierce to begin.

"Alright, you should all have our updated summary." Pierce started the case-status meeting. "Our forensics people have collected and analyzed evidence we discovered recently at Sparrow Song Park."

The partially blackened coconut-sized rock appeared in photos on the screen at the end of the room and on teleconference screens. Pierce outlined the details of where and how the rock was found: it was nearly seven inches in diameter, seventeen inches in circumference and weighed six pounds.

"Now—" Pierce used her laptop's cursor to circle areas

"—forensics found hair and blood traces on the rock here and here." Pierce's cursor went to the circled spots. "Analysis shows they're consistent with Anna Shaw's hair and blood. The medical examiner said blunt force trauma to the head was a factor in Shaw's death. In further consultation, the ME said the rock could be considered a weapon."

"Are we calling this a homicide?" Deputy Rob Hirano was on the screen.

"We're calling it suspicious," Pierce said.

"Did we get latents from the rock?" Hirano asked.

"Not yet," Pierce said. "As we know, it's difficult to get prints from rough, porous surfaces. Forensics advises that they're trying some new techniques, but it'll take time and they'll get back to us."

"I see a problem," Oscar Neale, a commander from the North Precinct, said. "You found this *weapon* long after the fact, after the scene was processed, then opened to the public. It might not be admissible or hold up in court."

"We always find guns after the fact and away from a scene," Benton said. "Then prints and ballistics tie it to a crime."

"Oscar's point is a valid one," Acker said. "But we've got date-stamped photos and video of the scene that show the impression of a missing rock at the top of the cliff. And even though we missed it at the time, you can see the rock wedged deep between cracks at the bottom at the riverbank."

"Your summary suggests other factors, potential players like the ex-boyfriend," Hirano said.

"We can't place him in the park at the time," Pierce said.

"The park has a security camera in the parking lot," Neale said. "That should be able to determine who else was there at the time. Where're you with that?"

"It's an aging, faulty system," Benton said. "It was record-ing at the time but any images we can recover might be unusable, if we can recover images at all. Our techs are working with the camera company. It's going to take time."

"What about Anna Shaw's phone?" Neale asked.

"We still haven't located it," Benton said.

"Did you go through Katie Harmon's phone?" Neale asked.

"We did, and there was nothing there of any significance," Pierce said.

"Your thoughts, Heidi?" Acker said.

"Thanks, Art." Heidi Wong, with the Juvenile Division of the King County Prosecuting Attorney's Office, was on the screen flipping through notes on a legal pad at her desk.

"It appears you're thinking Katie Harmon, who is nine, may have struck and pushed Anna Shaw off the cliff, possibly for the necklace?"

"It's a theory with some supporting evidence," Acker said.

"It's compelling, I grant you, but you're not there yet," Wong said. "Our unit has a high volume of cases right now. This one presents a challenge, starting with Katie's age. We have to prove she was capable of committing the crime and knew what she was doing. Cases of children who have killed other children are rare. And prosecuting a case like this as a Murder One or Murder Two is extremely difficult. We need solid evidence of the crime and clear evidence the child understood that what they did was wrong."

Acker, Benton and Pierce nodded.

"Now," Wong said, "your evidence, as it stands, is weak and your case is circumstantial. You have no witnesses. You can't polygraph Katie because polygraphs aren't effective on children her age." Wong tapped her pen on her pad. "Reading your case notes, Katie Harmon's statements thus far have been consistent, that Anna Shaw fell taking a selfie. We see Anna Shaw's parents were not alarmed that Katie had Anna's necklace. We don't see a conflict between Katie and Anna, who was Katie's beloved babysitter. We see that Katie's statement of Anna clinging to the branch is supported by the traces of material embedded in Anna's hands. And you estimate the gap in time when Kate ran for help at four to six, or even five to seven, minutes. While it may be a short time frame, it could be enough to weaken certainty. We don't see that Katie has a known history of violent acts, and other aspects of the investigation appear not to be nailed down yet, leaving room for a lot of reasonable doubt, which you need to remove."

"But we have the rock as a murder weapon," Benton said.

"At this stage, that's all you have," Wong said. "Have you even established that Katie Harmon can lift a rock of that weight and carry it that distance, what, about six or seven yards? And can she raise it high enough to use as a weapon on a teen?"

"Not yet," Pierce said.

"Bottom line this for us, Heidi," Acker said.

"This case is suspicious and it remains open," she said. "You've done good work. But you need to eliminate all areas that raise doubt. Keep going on Katie Harmon. Keep nailing down the open elements wherever possible—the prints on the rock, finding Anna's phone, the security camera. Strengthen your case."

The meeting ended, and Pierce and Benton returned to their desks.

"I'm going to the kitchen for coffee. Want me to get you one, Carl?" Pierce placed her files, notebook and tablet on her desk. They slid, sending her framed photo of Webb and Ethan to the floor with a crack. "Oh, shoot." She picked it up, studied the fractured glass. "I'll have to replace that." She set the broken frame in her drawer. "So, coffee?"

Benton was looking at his phone.

"Thanks, I'll go with you." He put his phone away.

"Everything okay?" she asked.

"Still no word."

"Hang in there."

"Kim, you've been on the right track on this, right from the get-go."

She shrugged as her phone rang. She looked at the number.

"Heidi Wong is right. We've got a lot of work yet and we can't get tunnel vision. Hello," she said into her phone.

"Detective Pierce?"

"Yes."

"Andy Newell, forensics. I was hoping to get this update on the parking lot security camera to you before your meeting. But we just got this. We've finally been able to clean up the footage recorded at the time of the fatality."

"How clean?"

"Still working on it, but we should get plates."

33

Seattle, Washington

SARA TOOK KATIE to Kerry Park. From a slope in Queen Anne Hill, it offered an unbroken view of downtown Seattle and the Space Needle.

Taking it in from the bench where they sat, Katie seemed lost in a thought and was humming softly to herself. Sara had brought her here to get out of the house, hoping to talk. She was searching for a way to start when Katie beat her to it.

"Mom, does it hurt to die?"

The question cut into Sara, but before she could answer Katie continued.

"Because I was wondering like how much pain Anna felt when she fell."

"I don't think she—"

"I was wondering like what her very last thought was before she hit the ground. Like, if she knew she was going to die and how awful it would be."

"Oh, honey." At a loss, Sara turned away, then said: "Have you talked to Dr. Mehta about it?"

Katie nodded.

"What does she say?"

"She said what you said, that Anna didn't feel anything. And she said nobody will know what Anna's last thoughts were."

Sara nodded.

"And she said it's normal for me to have lots of questions because I was with her."

"That's true, and it sounds right, don't you think?"

"Yes, Mom, but I can't stop thinking it was my fault." Katie was staring at the skyline.

"It wasn't your fault."

"But I *feel* like it is."

"Why?"

"It just does, Mom. It just does."

Sara put her arm around Katie. "Didn't Dr. Mehta tell you that you would have all kinds of feelings about it but it wasn't your fault?"

Katie nodded. *Now,* Sara thought. *Now's the time to press a little.*

"Has Dr. Mehta asked you to tell her more about the boy?"

"She said that it would be okay if I wanted to talk about it with her."

"What did you say?"

"I said I didn't want to because—even though—even though—"

Katie couldn't finish. Sara coaxed her gently. "Even though what, honey?"

"Sometimes I feel like what happened to the boy was *my fault,* just like I feel like what happened to Anna was *my fault.* Like something's wrong with me, Mom, and I don't know what it is."

"Are you still having bad dreams?"

"Yes."

"And bad thoughts?"

She needed Katie to reveal more, accepting that she might not be able to handle what it was—*what I fear she's locked away. But I need to know.*

"Have you told anyone what your bad thoughts are?" Sara asked.

Katie shook her head.

"Maybe if you told me, I could understand them, then together we can work to make them go away?"

"But they're scary, Mom."

"I know, but I can't help you if you don't help me understand."

Katie pulled away; Sara looked at her. Katie's expression shifted.

"Did you ever have scary thoughts when you were a girl, Mom?"

Taken aback at how Katie had turned things around to her, Sara swallowed. "Yes, I suppose a lot of people have troubling thoughts at one point or another. That's just human nature."

"Tell me about your bad thoughts when you were a girl."

Searching her daughter's eyes, the truth hit Sara full force. *I can't tell Katie—just like she can't tell me.*

"I'm not sure about when I was a girl, but I had some very sad thoughts when your dad died, then when Grandpa died. I guess you'd call them dark thoughts."

Analyzing Sara's answer, Katie was quiet. If she'd concluded that sad memories were not the same as bad thoughts, that Sara was not being entirely honest, she didn't say. She withdrew and remained silent.

Sara left things there.

Both of them were in pain. For a while, they gazed down

to the water, watching the ferries crossing Elliott Bay. Then Sara said, "We should get home. Tamika and her mom will be coming soon."

"Thanks for this."

Standing in her driveway, Sara embraced her friend Adina Nichol, who'd worked with her at the Jet Town Diner years ago. Adina waved off Sara's thanks as they watched Adina's daughter, Tamika, and Katie buckling up in the back seat of Adina's Tesla.

"It'll be good for Katie to hang out at our place for the afternoon, and good for you," Adina said. "How're you doing?"

"One day at a time."

Adina's eyes filled with empathy.

"You will get through this."

"Thanks, I hope so."

"So, how're Mel and the gang?"

"Good. Same old, same old."

Adina smiled, casting back. "We had some times, didn't we, Sara?"

"We sure did."

Then Adina said: "Stay strong, for Katie and for you."

Sara smiled.

"Alright," Adina said. "We'll get going. I'll have her back on time. And if you need anything or just want to talk, call me."

"Thanks, you're an angel."

Watching them drive off, Sara waved, marveling at how Adina had put herself through college while working at the diner to become a nurse, enduring the pandemic and a divorce from an unfaithful husband. Sara was fortunate to have Adina as a friend, she thought.

Turning to her house, she caught a wink of bright light,

like a small reflection, flashing from a vehicle parked down the street. *Is that the same one as before? Is someone watching me?* Squinting, she looked toward it. She knew most of the neighbors' cars on her block. Unable to pinpoint the source, she let it go. Likely the sun on a windshield, she reasoned.

But inside her house she couldn't shake off the feeling of being watched.

Was it the detectives? The media?

She tried shoving it out of her mind, but it gnawed at her. For most of her life Sara had feared that people were looking for her, following her—*because of who I am.*

Yet nothing had happened.

Maybe I let my imagination take over.

But Anna's death had deepened her fears, making them more real.

Sara went online, checking the latest news reports on Anna's death. In some of the early stories, she found news pictures of her with Katie, but none had named them. In a couple of cases, they were identified as *a mother comforts her daughter at Sparrow Song Park.* The press may not have published Sara's and Katie's names, but they knew enough to call Sara and come to her house in attempts to get interviews.

But it seemed like that had happened a long time ago.

Now the news stories had faded away, along with the social media chatter on the case. Sara found herself going back to one of the earliest comments on Anna's death.

Taking a breath, she reread it.

Two people on a cliff. One dies. No witnesses.

The post, signed by *Anon E. Muss,* underscored Sara's anguish about Katie; and how Katie now had Sara's necklace, how Katie had revealed having *bad thoughts,* forcing Sara to admit to herself that she had lied about her own bad thoughts—*I'm trying to protect her.* But now, like a claw, the truth seized her, pulling her back across time to...

...the night...the rain...the dark forest...stopping, waiting and waiting...then the heart-wrenching screams...the pain...oh, God the pain...the horror of being caught up in a whirlwind of evil...

Tensing her body, Sara pulled out of the memory, massaging her wrist, looking at the flowers of her tattoo, then at her laptop's screen. Steeling herself, she began clicking her mouse and typing.

Still rattled by the memory, she had to check again, but not about Anna. Sara had to go online to the places she hated. She went to the sites and social media pages of the people hunting for her and the link to her dark past: the justice hunters, the finders or whatever they were now called.

They were the self-appointed, self-righteous searchers obsessed in their pursuit of every aspect of a life, a lie and a nightmare that had nothing, and yet had everything, to do with Sara.

She opened a page:

Can't believe she's been free so many years, she should be in prison.
—Louise from Omaha

A friend with a women's support agency is hearing that she now lives in Wichita.
—Rolinda B.

That could be outdated because my cousin in law enforcement has her in Cleveland, maybe Shaker Heights.
—Lynn R. from Dayton

Check out this security still we got from a friend last month.
We think this might be her walking into this Houston 7-Eleven.
—Jock from San Antonio

No. Look at the height strip at the door. It doesn't fit with
her height.
—Chris from Norfolk

Didn't she find her daughter and move to Birmingham, England? That's what we heard from a friend at the US Embassy.
—Polly from Arlington, VA

We heard she died in a house fire in Medicine Hat, Alberta,
Canada, like 4–5 years ago.
—May from Toronto

How fitting for her to burn. Good riddance.
—Zelda from Utah

Sara breathed a small sigh of relief because there was nothing recent about Seattle, or even Washington. As always, the
sites were awash with rumor and theories.

As always, they were wrong.

*But what if I'm wrong this time? What if somehow, in some way
someone drew a connection from Anna Shaw to my past? What if
those online searchers have gone from being ridiculous to being right,
and right down the street? Watching? Waiting to do—what?*

*I can't be found and I can't be found out. If the world discovers
the truth— Stop this!*

Sara got offline, got away from her computer.

Deciding to clean her house, she dusted, vacuumed, then
changed the sheets on her bed, then Katie's. The mundane
tasks gave her a sense of accomplishment, a sense of control, re-
storing a measure of order to her life. She found it therapeutic.

Maybe I'm overthinking this.

Anna's death was horrible, but maybe the detectives coming back was nothing more than a routine follow-up? And, like Dr. Mehta had suggested, maybe Katie's reactions were normal responses to witnessing a traumatic tragic event.

I just need to get a handle on everything.

Since she was changing the sheets, Sara decided to do laundry and began collecting clothes in the hamper. In Katie's room, clothes were scattered helter-skelter. Sara was forever picking up after her.

Getting down on her knees, she checked under the bed for any fugitive socks or underwear. Nothing, but she did a double take.

Some pages were hanging down, wedged into the bed frame.

Katie's spiral-bound drawing book.

Sara pulled it out and began flipping through her sketches of birds, trees, butterflies, hand tracing.

I've seen these drawings. Katie's shown them to me. But why hide this book under her bed?

Sara continued turning pages, coming to the last one on which Katie had sketched, gooseflesh rising on Sara's arms from what she was seeing.

In Katie's scrawl, she'd titled the drawing: *The Park.*

It showed two stick people, one labeled *Anna*, her mouth agape, tilting, falling from a cliff. The second one, labeled *Me*, arms outstretched toward Anna, her face wide-eyed, her mouth open.

The balloon of dialogue from Anna said: *Help!*

The balloon of dialogue from Katie: *Why, why, why!*

34

Tacoma, Washington

THE WOMAN BEHIND the counter at the drugstore handed a prescription to a man with a cane. She rang up the transaction, the man left and Ryan Gardner approached her.

"Could you help me?"

She was wearing a white smock. Her name tag said *Sherry Evers.* "What would you like?"

Ryan indicated a shelf nearby. "Could you recommend something for a backache?"

She came around the counter, led him to the display. A source had tipped Ryan that he'd find his subject working at Giger's RX Pharmacy, an independent store in Tacoma, and that her name was Sherry Ursula Evers.

As Ryan had done so many times with so many other leads over the years, he'd checked out the pharmacy until he found her on duty. Now, with Evers so close to him, he absorbed every detail. She was the right age, the right height.

"I was thinking about this." He pointed to a box on a higher shelf.

Eyeing her, he studied the wrist extending from her sleeve as she reached for the box. She had flawless skin. Not a mark. And all he could think was that he'd struck out, again.

Then something happened.

She raked a free hand through her hair and a single strand caught the light as it fell, floated and coiled, landing on the bottom display shelf. Evers hadn't noticed. Ryan pretended to listen as her glossed fingernail tapped the medicinal ingredients on the box while she told him about the remedy.

He thanked her and she returned to answer the phone behind the counter.

Pretending to ponder a purchase, Ryan lowered himself at the shelf and collected her rogue strand of hair without anyone noticing. What luck, he thought, like when he'd collected a toothbrush recently discarded in the trash of another target.

Of course, he was uncertain Evers was Magda's daughter.

Maybe she'd had surgery to remove the scar, he thought, consoling himself while driving back to Seattle. And maybe her middle name didn't reflect Magda's but was, in fact, coincidence.

Still, he couldn't rule her out.

Not just yet.

Besides, he had her DNA to test, and he still had another possibility to pursue in Redmond. And there was that woman at the diner in North Seattle. He hadn't given up on her. *There's something about her—a vibe, something.*

I can't give up on any of the women in the Seattle area yet. I need to be thorough. I need to be certain.

Deciding to return to the apartment, Ryan regrouped, taking stock of all the research he'd collected over time, reminding himself that he'd come a long way. He always had setbacks and successes.

At his desk, to reassure himself, he reread files, opening a PDF.

Montana Child and Family Services Division (CFSD)—Child Protective Services (CPS)
Update RE: Post-Adoption Follow-up Assessment / Evaluation
Case Number: ▆▆▆▆ // CP Specialist: ▆▆▆▆▆▆
// DATE: 30 May 1979
Pursuant Montana. Code Ann. § 41-3-4

Attached is a supplemental note to the post-adoption assessment. At this writing, more than a year after the finalization of the adoption, it appears placement and adjustment has been largely successful, with one known exception. This note concerns an incident.

It has been determined that ▆▆▆▆▆▆▆, the adopted child, aged seven, was invited to a birthday party attended by six children of similar age at the residence of the host child at a neighboring ranch. The mother hosting the party had discovered that her daughter's favorite doll was missing after the party guests had departed. The host mother contacted the guests' families, asking them to check with their children, politely suggesting the doll had been accidentally "misplaced," the implication being that it was taken from the host child.

▆▆▆▆▆▆▆, the adopted child, was asked by her adoptive mother about the doll. ▆▆▆▆▆▆ denied any knowledge. However, after the adoptive mother searched ▆▆▆▆▆ room, she discovered the doll and ▆▆▆▆▆▆ confessed to taking it but demanded to keep the doll, stating that the doll "likes me

more, so I should keep it." It was only after the adoptive mother's insistence that ▇▇▇▇▇▇ agreed to return the doll.

The adoptive mother took ▇▇▇▇▇▇ to the ranch to apologize and return the doll, which ▇▇▇▇▇▇ had packed into a shoebox. In the presence of both mothers, ▇▇▇▇▇▇ handed the box to the child. Upon opening it, the child screamed for ▇▇▇▇▇▇ had placed the doll in the box decapitated and handless.

Supplemental Note: The biological parents of ▇▇▇▇▇▇, the adopted child, and their history, are unknown factors. CP Specialist ▇▇▇▇▇▇ consulted with departmental psychologist about the incident. Without interviewing ▇▇▇▇▇▇, the adopted child, psychologist could only hypothesize about a possible genetic predisposition to violence in ▇▇▇▇▇, the adopted child. Psychologist noted that research showed that in some few cases the offspring of violent adults were at risk of acts of violence when their wishes were thwarted. Subsequent communication with the adoptive parents of ▇▇▇▇▇▇, the adopted child, resulted in the adoptive parents declining to have ▇▇▇▇▇▇ seen by a psychologist. The adoptive parents were provided information on adoption support groups and services that are available through agencies or organizations.

Ryan sat back in his chair.

How many times had he read these files—the documented beginnings?

He needed fresh coffee. Then he would move on to the video recordings.

There was more to come about the early years.

35

Seattle, Washington

THE SUNNY DAYS school bus arrives at Sparrow Song Park and the group gets off. Anna Shaw and Katie Harmon are last to leave. The bus pulls away. Not long after, a man, appearing older, moving slower with a slight shuffle, emerges from one of the trails. He walks across the parking lot to a blue Toyota Camry, gets in, then drives out of the frame.

"That's the first. I'll call him Camry Man." Detective Andy Newell typed commands on his keyboard, freezing a frame on the Toyota's Washington State license plate.

Newell had called Pierce and Benton to view the video recovered from the park's security camera. The detectives were encouraged, determined to follow up on and clear any outstanding investigative threads. Newell's office was jammed with monitors, computer towers and cables; one wall bore a poster of Newell's hero, Charles Babbage.

It had taken so long to extract anything from the park's

faulty security system that the detectives had given up hope the camera would yield anything useful. Applying his never-say-die attitude, Newell had worked tirelessly with the manufacturer and IT experts to get usable footage.

"We plowed through a lot of problems," Newell said. "Resolution and compression issues. The lens was dirty with moisture and particles. It was tedious, but with some new technology we got these three potentials."

Newell tapped on his keyboard. His monitor resumed playing the video.

A woman appears, leaving a trail and walking across the lot, getting into a Ford Focus. She begins driving away before the footage freezes.

Newell typed more commands, enlarging the Washington State license plate on the Ford.

"She's the second. I'll call her Focus Woman."

Newell entered more commands. This time his monitor rewound footage to the start, then resumed playing.

"Watch." Newell pointed to the bottom of the frame. "This is interesting."

The Sunny Days school bus arrives; all the passengers begin disembarking. At the edge of the footage, a Chevrolet pickup crawls partially into the frame and stops as if watching. The driver is not visible. Moments later, Anna Shaw and Katie Harmon get off and disappear down the trail. At the edge of the frame, the pickup wheels around to exit before the footage freezes on its Washington State license plate.

Newell's chair creaked as he leaned back.

"That's the third. I call it Sketchy Pickup," he said. "The truck wheels in as if watching the bus, then pulls away."

After considering the image, Benton said: "Maybe the driver wanted to avoid the security camera."

"That's what I was thinking," Newell said.

"When the pickup left, it could've parked outside the lot,"

EVERYTHING SHE FEARED   209

Pierce said. "The driver could've entered the trail outside of camera range."

"All good theories," Newell said, typing on his keyboard. "I'm sending you the three plates and copying the footage."

The detectives' phones pinged.

"What you now have," Newell said, "are three vehicles that were in the parking lot within the time frame of Anna Shaw's death. But all three left before we got there and sealed the park."

"This is good," Benton said.

Back at their desks, Pierce and Benton got to work.

"So none of these three have been checked, interviewed or cleared," Benton said. "You take Camry Man and Focus Woman. I'll take the pickup."

Pierce consulted her open notebook. "Remember, Dave Kneller, the park's owner, said no one was at the entrance gate. It was left open because his staff member went home sick."

Keyboards clicked as the detectives entered the plates, submitting them to several law enforcement databases, including ACCESS, a central computerized system.

"Okay, Focus Woman is Marilyn Leanne Hamilton, aged sixty, resides in Seattle. And Camry Man is Gilbert Conroy Croft, aged seventy-nine, resides in Issaquah," Pierce said.

She continued running their names through other databases that were part of the ACCESS network, including local and state systems with warrant data and NCIC, which was managed by the FBI.

Hamilton and Croft had no criminal history, no records, no offences and no warrants.

Taking a moment to study their driver's license photos, Pierce tapped her pen on her notebook. She thought how several trails webbed in the park to the one used by the Sunny

Days group. What were Hamilton and Croft doing in the park at that time? Did they see Anna and Katie?

Maybe they witnessed something concerning the girls?

"My guys came back clean," Pierce said. "What about yours?"

Concentrating on what was on his monitor, Benton didn't answer.

"Carl?"

"This could change everything," he said.

"What do you have?"

"My guy is John James Smith, forty-one, a registered sex offender. He resides in Seattle, ten blocks from the Sunny Days Youth Center."

"What the—?" Pierce said.

"My words exactly."

36

"CAN WE GET PIZZA, MOM?"

Tired from cleaning the house and masking her alarm from what she'd discovered earlier under Katie's bed, Sara forced a smile.

"Sure, honey. We'll get the usual, okay?"

"With dipping sauce, please."

Katie had gotten home around 5:30 p.m. Tamika was going to her father's place for the night, so there was no chance for a sleepover. When their pizza came, Sara asked Katie about her visit while they ate.

"Tamika's got this mosaic kit and that's what we did."

"You made mosaics?"

"Uh-huh, a panda, a butterfly and a tiger. They're pretty. It was fun."

"Cool, what did you guys talk about?"

"You know, songs we like, our friends, movies and stuff."

Chewing her last bite of pizza, Sara looked at Katie.

"Wasn't Tamika curious about what happened at the park with Anna?"

Studying the crust of her piece, Katie shrugged. "Not really."

"Seriously, she didn't ask about it?"

"I didn't want to talk about it. Can we have some ice cream?"

After they finished eating, Sara began clearing things, putting plates and cutlery in the sink. She sent Katie upstairs to wash her face and hands. Then with the pizza box in the recycling, dishes done, Sara went to a drawer. She sat on the sofa in the living room, struggling to remain calm.

Katie bounced down the stairs to the living room, her eyes going to the spiral-bound drawing book Sara had on her lap. "What are you doing with that?"

Following her gaze to the book, Sara said: "I found it when I was picking up your clothes in your room."

Katie reached to take it, but Sara placed her hand on top.

"Give it to me."

"No, I think I better hang on to it."

Katie looked at Sara. "It's mine."

"I'm keeping it for a little while, honey."

"Why?"

Sara patted the sofa beside her.

"Sit with me. I want to talk about the pictures you drew."

Hesitant, Katie sat as Sara turned the book's pages.

"Why're you snooping on me?"

"I wasn't snooping, honey. I found this when I was picking up your clothes under your bed for the laundry." Sara turned more pages to the birds, trees, butterflies and hand tracings Katie had made. "I remember these—they're nice."

Sara continued to the next pages.

"Why did you put the book under the bed like you were hiding it?"

"It's private."

"But you've shown me the birds and things you've drawn before," Sara said, turning the page to the stick people. "But not this one, you've never shown me this new one."

Sara blinked as she and Katie looked at Katie's depiction of the tragedy at the park with two stick people.

The house fell silent.

"Honey, why did you draw this? What does it mean?"

"It's private. You spied on me."

Again Katie tried seizing the book from Sara.

"Give it back, it's mine!"

"Stop." Sara pulled the book back. "I wasn't spying on you. But you have to tell me why you drew this."

"I already told you. I have bad thoughts."

Sara couldn't stop now. Jabbing her finger at the sketch, she said: "Katie, I need you to tell me the truth about what happened."

Katie shook her head, clamping her mouth. Watching her, Sara feared the answer. Maybe because she now believed *she knew* the answer. And all this time, since the day she rushed to Sparrow Song Park, she could never bring herself to say the words. Until now, glimpsing at the sketch, feeling the words rising in her throat, like an eruption she couldn't control. Sara stabbed at the sketch as if it were the horrible truth.

"Are these your bad dreams, your bad thoughts? Did you— Katie, did you push Anna?"

Katie screamed. "Stop it! Stop, stop, stop!"

Katie blasted from the sofa and thudded up the stairs, slamming her bedroom door, leaving Sara alone on the sofa.

Her skin numbed, the tiny hairs on the back of her neck stood up. Through her tears she stared at her daughter's notebook—feeling its weight pressing down, its heat burning her.

37

SIPPING COFFEE AT his desk, Ryan Gardner scrolled through folders on his computer, stopping at the video of his interview with Cody Barlow, retired sheriff of Tall Tree County, Montana.

Ryan had located Barlow in a mobile home park near Tucson, Arizona, and called. Barlow agreed to talk to him but only in person, so Ryan made his way to Tucson. A few years after he'd recorded the video, Barlow died from colorectal cancer.

But he came to life now on Ryan's laptop.

Here was white-haired Barlow on a recliner in his double-wide trailer, black-and-blue-plaid Western shirt, black-framed glasses and with a small smile under his gray walrus mustache. Ryan found his gentle, almost high-pitched voice calming.

"You have good sources tracking me down on this, son. Word on the law enforcement grapevine is that you're a good guy. That, and your personal connection to the whole damn thing, made it an easy decision for me to help you."

"Thank you. I appreciate it."

"Aside from Bill Hooten, who was sheriff at the time, and Cal Nixon, who was deputy, no one knows the *whole* story I'm going to tell you. Are you all set there, Ryan?"

"We're all set. Go ahead."

"Well, like I said on the phone, it was late summer that year and still warm when the four children, all of them about seven or eight, had decided to explore and play at a secluded corner of a neighboring acreage."

"Can you confirm who they were?"

"Sure, it's been so long and there are no statutes, and given what we now know, what the hell. I got my old notebooks to help me. Here—Judy Ayers, Bobby Rickard, Nancy Vaughan and Magdalena Kurtz. I'll copy the spellings down for you."

"Great, thanks."

"So the kids go out to this section, some people called it the Old Settlement, because it was first settled by immigrants. But there's nothing out there except for a few rickety outbuildings, overgrown by tall grass.

"The kids get out there. They said they were looking for treasure in the old buildings and playing around the property when it happened—Nancy just vanished from the surface."

Barlow stopped to blink at the memory and stroke his mustache.

"She'd fallen down a well. It took forever for the kids to get help. Bobby ran to Red Wheelock's place and Red called us. We soon got a team out there, paramedics, fire department, well-service experts. We could see her, and we had her mother call down to her, but she wasn't responding, wasn't making a sound. The rescue crew lowered listening devices but couldn't pick up a sign of life.

"Working as fast as we could, we rigged things up, fashioned a harness chair and lowered Billy Dix, this skinny firefighter, down on a rope with water, medicine. Billy musta went down a hundred feet. We could hear him gasping, shouting—it's bad, it's bad!—saw his camera flash. We needed pictures for the case and for possible rescue, but—"

Barlow paused again.

"It was a recovery, not a rescue. She was deceased. Her parents were there—their screams... They wanted to go down the hole to get her. We had to hold them back. Lord, it was just so damned awful. Eventually we got her out. Later I looked at Billy's pictures, at how she was all twisted, her feet up by her ears. Doctor said her spine was snapped."

Barlow removed his glasses, drew his sleeve to his eyes.

"Something like that you never forget," he said. "Later, as part of our investigation, talking to Nancy's folks and the kids, we learned there was a bit of history between Nancy and Magdalena, or Magda, as she was called."

"Is this about the doll?"

"You know about it?"

"I'd heard something about it. I'm trying to get a copy of a confidential report."

"I've seen it and may be able to help you with that," Barlow said. "I'll tell you what we learned about the whole thing."

He related an incident that happened several months prior to Nancy's death. It concerned Nancy's birthday party and a missing doll that Magda had stolen. When forced to return it, Magda had removed the doll's head and hands.

"So there was some bad blood between the girls. That explained why Nancy was at first reluctant to go to the Old Settlement that day. It turned out Magda wanted her to come. Magda had convinced Bobby and Judy that she'd been to the old buildings earlier with her dad and there was likely jewels and money hidden in the building."

"She made it sound exciting," Ryan said.

"She did, convincing Bobby and Judy, who were Nancy's best friends, to come, and they convinced Nancy to come. When they got there, they looked around inside, then Magda told Bobby and Judy to stay inside while she and Nancy looked outside."

Barlow adjusted his glasses.

"Not long after, Bobby and Judy heard Magda shouting 'I found some treasure!' They left to join her, seeing Magda standing still and waving for Nancy to come closer to her. The place was overrun with wheat grass up to their waist so when Nancy approached she didn't see how it canopied over a few rotting wood planks, gaps between them, covering the well. She stepped on them and went right through."

"Bobby and Judy witnessed it?"

"Yes. The thing was, they said Magda just stood there looking down, not reacting, while they were crying, screaming down to Nancy, hysterical."

Ryan thought for a moment.

"What was the treasure Magda found?"

"A couple of quarters."

"Quarters?"

"Yeah, but they were newer ones, not old timeworn coins."

"Really? What was going on in your mind as you investigated?"

"You first look at the facts, or the facts as we know them."

"Which were?"

"It's a fact the well was dug by settlers, then abandoned. Landowners are supposed to locate unused wells, seal and cap them. But along the line, other than a few planks, that wasn't done with the Old Settlement well. So we had a dangerous

well. Magda and her father told us they had no prior knowledge of the well."

"So it was a tragic accident?"

Barlow adjusted his glasses and stroked his mustache. "I
think Magda lured Nancy to her death."

"Why would she do that?"

"Payback for the doll."

"But she's, what, seven years old or so, just a child?"

"We couldn't ever prove a damn thing. Nothing came of
it, so yes, on the books, it's an accidental death."

Barlow's jaw tightened, he gritted his teeth and he looked
off, leaving Ryan to think he was recalling those disturbing
photos of Nancy.

"It's hard for me to explain," Barlow said.

"That's okay."

"When I questioned Magda, my gut told me this girl wasn't
like any other child. Something about her was not right. And
now, when I think to what Magda and that husband of hers
went on to do to innocent people, like your sister and her
friend, I realize as I stood at that well, watching them lift
Nancy Vaughan's body from the ground, I was witnessing the
birth of something monstrous."

38

A FOURTEEN-YEAR-OLD GIRL walked Buddy, her beagle, every day on the trail through the park near her home in Olympia. On one walk she failed to secure his leash and Buddy chased a squirrel.

She couldn't find him.

John James Smith was in the park that day and saw that the girl was upset over her dog. Smith was a stranger, but the girl had seen him in the park occasionally when she walked Buddy. Smith offered to help look for Buddy, suggesting they go in different directions. In a short time Smith said he'd found the dog and called the girl to a dense thicket.

Not seeing Buddy, or hearing panting or the jingling of his leash, the girl hesitated. But Smith urged her into the thicket, saying Buddy looked hurt. Concerned, she proceeded. When she got to it, she didn't see Buddy. Smith pulled her to the ground.

Two female joggers, marines who'd served in Afghanistan, heard the girl's screams. Rescuing her, they subdued Smith, fracturing several bones in the process. The women called police and paramedics. In the chaos Buddy returned to the girl and was a source of comfort as paramedics and police tended to her.

Smith was charged with assault. Olympia detectives investigating Smith linked him to other attacks where he had stalked girls, learning their routines, waiting for the chance to strike, then assaulting them in wooded areas or empty buildings and lots.

Smith was convicted and served time in prison.

Reading the report, Pierce studied Smith's physical description again: white, six feet tall, one-hundred-eighty pounds, with a scar running over his left eye to his cheek from a victim who'd scratched him.

Looking at his photo in the offender registry, Pierce thought, *Why was Smith at Sparrow Song Park at the time of Anna Shaw's death?*

Benton slowed their SUV, then said: "Here we go."

The license plate captured by the park's security camera matched the plate of the pickup parked on the street in Ballard.

A white 2012 Chevrolet Silverado 1500, two-door with a regular cab, belonging to John James Smith, a released inmate and registered sex offender. Pierce and Benton checked the truck's interior.

Neat. Spotless.

Trading glances, they continued walking.

With the forensic analysis of the rock indicating Anna Shaw's death was intentional, they still hadn't ruled out Katie Harmon. She was the last known person to see Anna alive. But there was that gap in time when Katie ran for help. Someone else could've been involved. And placing Smith at the park, at the time of Anna's death, had turned their investigation around.

The detectives found Smith's truck after Pierce reached Rawley Grimes, Smith's community corrections officer, a gravel-voiced man who sounded like he was scraping his way through the phone line.

"Why're you asking? Has he deviated from his conditions? As his CCO, I need to know."

"We just have a few questions."

"What questions? 'Cause I got him adhering to the program."

"We'll let you know how things go when we're done."

Smith's Silverado sat a few doors from a 1950s house that was enveloped with scaffolding and ladders. The front yard was covered with stacked sheets of lumber, shingles, bricks and other building material. A symphony of staple guns, power saws and hammering filled the air with clouds of sawdust and the smell of fresh-cut wood.

A van and pickup with the logo *Diamond Ocean Remodel* sat in the driveway as workers in jeans, T-shirts, hard hats and tool belts moved about.

Pierce stopped a worker inspecting a sheet of plywood.

"Excuse me. We're looking for John James Smith."

"J.J.?" The worker pointed his chin to a table saw.

The saw whined as Smith pushed a four-by-four-inch beam to the blade. Finishing the cut, he looked up to see Pierce's and Benton's badges. He switched the motor off.

"Got a minute?" Benton said.

Smith eyed them without speaking.

"Your CCO told us you were here," Pierce said. "We got a couple of questions. Could you show us your identification?"

After showing them his license, Smith stood there waiting. Pierce pulled out her notebook, paged through it.

"Where were you on the morning of the tenth of this month?"

Smith's focus shifted as he thought and blinked once. "Here at work."

"You want to rethink your answer?" Benton said.

"What's this about?"

They turned to a bearded man about six two, his eyes going to their badges, his expression going cold.

"Who are you?" Benton said.

"Venner Robson. I'm the contractor. J.J.'s boss."

"Could you show us some identification?" Benton said.

Robson pulled out his worn wallet. While Benton checked his driver's license, Robson said: "What's going on here?"

"We want to establish John's whereabouts on the morning of the tenth."

Robson thought for a moment. "Yeah, he was here. We've been on this site for several weeks."

"Can you prove that?"

"I'll swear to it in a statement."

Benton's eyebrows rose. "You'll swear to it?"

"And so will the other guys on this site." Robson turned to the house. "And the coffee truck guy who comes here every day, and our suppliers. So what's this about?"

"You're a bit protective," Benton said.

"Cut the crap, okay? I know J.J.'s done time. I did time, so did most of my crew. That's in the past. We're straight and we're clean. Yet whenever you guys get any kinda beef, you jam us up."

"So you'll swear J.J. was here working on the morning of the tenth?" Pierce said.

"Absolutely. I picked him up that morning for work."

Pierce threw a silent question to Benton to indicate something was off with these guys. She got her phone, cued up a clip of the video showing Smith's pickup truck in the lot at the park.

"Explain why the camera at Sparrow Song Park, with this time and date stamp, recorded his pickup behind the Sunny Days school bus moments before a teenage girl in the group was killed?" Pierce said.

Smith and Robson leaned closer to the phone as Pierce replayed the video, pausing on Smith's plate.

"You've got a history with teenage girls in wooded areas, don't you, John?" Benton said.

The blood drained from Smith's face; he shot a look at Robson, then the detectives.

"What the hell is this?" Smith said. "Some kinda setup? Some kinda joke? I wasn't there. I was here."

"Clearly you were at the park," Benton said.

Smith shook his head, then raked his hands over his face.

"I did all the programs, took all the treatment. I stick to the conditions. I'm working, doing everything I'm supposed to do. Why're you doing this with some kinda doctored video? I'm telling you I was never at that park."

"That's right," Robson said. "I picked him up that morning because he didn't have his truck."

"Your truck is in this footage, John," Pierce said. "You going to tell us it was someplace else?"

"It was in the shop, getting the transmission fixed."

Pierce and Benton stared at him, their faces filling with doubt.

"I can prove it," Smith said.

Robson, Benton and Pierce walked down the street with Smith.

Coming to Smith's truck, the detectives took no risks. Because Smith was a convicted felon, they took his keys from

him, then patted him down. Benton then unlocked the pas-
senger door and Smith directed him to look in the glove box.
Tugging on gloves and rummaging through the compartment,
Benton withdrew a folded yellow sheet of invoice paper.

Pierce took a photo of it.

It was all there: transmission repair, parts, labor, drop-off
and pick-up dates. Benton and Pierce looked at the name of
the auto shop at the top of the invoice.

True Ocean Auto Dealers in Lake City.

The same shop where Tanner Bishop worked moving vehicles in and out of the service bays.

39

SARA WAS LOSING her grip.

She'd nearly spilled a plate of lasagna and a bowl of tomato soup on two screeching boys, each about six years old, who were racing around tables, bumping into her.

The boys' parents sat in a booth, faces in their phones, indifferent. Then one of the two older women in the corner booth, who'd seemed nice, tapped her spoon to her cup, her way of requesting more coffee. Meantime, a man glared at Sara from his seat because the detailed special order he'd made off the menu was taking too long—"No salt must be added in the preparation. Is that clear? No salt."

But Sara was detached, her mind spinning with thoughts of Katie's drawing, of Anna falling to her death, the horrifying truth growing into an internal cry.

Someone brought her back by saying her name.

Beth and Polly called her into the alcove near the kitchen door.

"Yes?" Sara answered.

"What's wrong?" Beth said.

"Nothing."

"Bull," Polly said. "You look like the world's fallen on you. What is it?"

"Is it Katie? Is it your mom?" Beth said. "Talk to us."

"Lean on us, Sara," Polly said.

Feeling Polly take her hand amid the din of the dining room, the clatter in the kitchen, Sara welcomed the heart-felt concern in the faces of her friends. Breathing evenly, Sara wanted to embrace them, collapse into their arms before she broke into a thousand pieces from her secret crushing fear. Maybe, just maybe, talking about it with them would help. At the brink of revealing it, her jaw opened slightly to form the words but—

No. No, I can't risk telling them. I can't bring myself to say out loud that I think Katie may have killed Anna and that even worse, I— No, I can't...

"Order up," Mel said, setting two plates with fish and chips at the pick-up window.

Sara touched Polly's and Beth's arms before they got back to work. "You guys are the best," she said. "Thank you, but I can handle it."

But Sara couldn't handle it.

When her shift ended, she called her neighbor, Val Rossi. If there was one person Sara could lean on, it was Val. She'd moved into the neighborhood a few years ago, after her husband's death. Sara and Katie met Val while she was walking her dog, Bingo. Ever since then they'd been friends. Val struck Sara as a little lonely. She didn't have kids and took to Katie right away, often telling them: "You girls are like family to me."

When Sara reached Val on the phone, she asked if she could watch Katie for a few hours as soon as Sara got home from the diner and Katie got home from school.

"Absolutely."

"I'm sorry to impose, I just need some alone time."

"No imposition. Happy to help. You've had a lot happen in the last little while."

"Yes, a lot."

"I'll come to your house to get her. I'm dropping Bingo off at the groomers for some spa treatment. Katie can come with me."

"She'll love that."

"I'll take her out for a cheeseburger after, then some shopping before we pick up Bingo."

"Sounds good."

"How's your mom doing?"

"She's doing okay."

"I've been meaning to get out to Bothell and visit her. Please give her my love, Sara."

"I will."

"Is there anything else I can do?"

"No, but thank you so much, Val."

Rain webbed down the windows of Sara's house.

Home alone, she clasped her hands around her ceramic cup of hot tea in a futile effort to subdue the icy dread inside her. She glanced at the cup with *World's Best Mom* printed in colorful letters. Katie had made it for her at a Sunny Days craft class.

Sara then glanced at Katie's drawing book on the kitchen table, opened to the sketch of Anna and Katie on the cliff.

Sara stifled a sob.

Why did Katie make this drawing? Is she trying to confess?

Sara thought back to the detectives, Pierce and Benton,

sitting at this table not so long ago. They'd come to talk to Katie, a follow-up, they'd said. But they'd come with their binders, presenting Sara with options, and were so formal, so *careful*, as if laying legal groundwork.

What do they know?

She'd heard nothing from them since.

Sara pulled her laptop closer, went online and for several minutes searched news sites, social media posts. Then she went to the pages of the people mining rumors and conspiracies tied to her dark past.

It appeared that nothing new had emerged.

She looked at Katie's drawing again.

Could it be some sort of evidence? Should I burn it? Should I get a lawyer? I can't afford a lawyer. Who can I talk to? What should I do?

Sara buried her face in her hands.

I have to face the truth.

The truth.

Sara's eyes flicked to the ceiling.

The truth is up there.

She left the kitchen and a moment later was on the second floor, looking down the hall to a closed door. Behind that door were the steps that led to the attic.

Sara hated going to the attic—*knowing what was there.*

Rooted before the closed door, glancing at her tattooed wrist, rubbing it, thinking of Katie having bad thoughts stirred her own...

...*the rain...the pain...the screaming...*

Sara turned from the attic door and hurried downstairs.

40

"I'LL NEVER FORGET that day." Stephanie Leal's voice rose from the recording playing on Ryan Gardner's laptop as she recalled her former high school classmate Magda Kurtz.

That's the file I want. That's the one.

Ryan paused it and went to the kitchen. He made a ham and cheese sandwich, got a glass of milk, then came back to the recording. While eating, he surveyed the files listed in the folder where he'd stored it among additional material he'd obtained years ago that had belonged to Julie Carter, a Montana journalist.

Ryan had learned of Julie through a colleague at the *L.A. Times*, who knew of his pursuit of Magda.

"She was a freelancer based in Billings, and my wife's distant cousin," Dan Morden, an *L.A. Times* reporter, had told Ryan at the time over the phone from California. "She'd written for us, for everybody. She'd started working on a feature when Magda and her husband were arrested. Julie located nearly everyone in the region who knew them and was hoping to sell her article to the *New York Times Magazine* and turn it into a book."

"I got an email from her once, but we never talked," Ryan said. "You said she *was* working on a feature, past tense?"

"Several months after she got going, Julie was hiking in Glacier National Park when she was killed by a grizzly."

"Oh, man, that's awful," Ryan said.

"Yeah, so she never wrote the piece. But she'd done massive research, it's just boxed up. I thought of you and that maybe I can help you get access to it."

Dan contacted Julie's dad and set things up for Ryan to talk to him. After hearing Ryan recounting how Carrie, and her friend Willow, died, Julie's father agreed to give him Julie's research.

A few weeks later, Ryan pulled his rental up to a modest home in Billings. Julie's dad, Butch Carter, a semi-retired welder who looked like a beat-up prizefighter, took him into his garage. He raised the door and in the center sat two plastic storage bins containing court records, statements, transcripts, notebooks, documents, USB keys, newspapers and more, all on the case.

Carter helped Ryan place the bins into his rented Jeep. Then he shook Ryan's hand while clamping the other on his shoulder. His face was creased with grief, but he attempted a smile.

"Julie would've wanted someone like you to carry on her work. You see this through, son. By God, you see it through."

For years, Ryan drew upon Julie Carter's files, and added his own, in his search for Magda and her daughter, for any links to where they may be.

Now, taking the last bite of his sandwich, he went over everything in his head.

Okay, I'm not sure yet about Sherry Evers at the pharmacy in Tacoma. It's not uncommon to have scars removed. And I'm not sure yet about Sara, the server at the Jet Town Diner. Maybe it's because I've struck out so many times before. And I still need to follow up on the woman in Redmond. I'm not done here yet.

Finishing his milk, Ryan wiped his mouth with the back of his hand. Then, being a former reporter, he did a quick scan of the local news, to see what was going on. He saw that officials were considering a plan to build a Seattle-to-Vancouver high-speed train. Scrolling further, he saw that the Seahawks were seeking a new quarterback. There'd been an engine fire on a ferry. Thankfully no injuries. Then: that case he'd been following of the Seattle teen who died taking a selfie in the park east of the city. A photo of the victim, Anna Shaw, seventeen, accompanied the story, along with file photos of emergency units, police and families in shock at the park. *Does that woman look like the server from the Jet Town Diner?* It was hard to tell. He couldn't be certain. He stared a second before dismissing it. He read the short update, which said that Shaw's death was believed to be accidental but the investigation was ongoing.

Interesting, he thought before he returned to Julie Carter's files and her interview with Stephanie Leal, who'd gone to high school with Magda.

"I'll never forget that day," Leal said. "We were in our first gym class, sitting on the floor, twenty-five girls. Miss McCoy, our gym teacher, says, 'Everybody listen up carefully. When I blow my whistle, everybody jump up and touch all four walls the fastest way you can, then sit back down.'

"She blows her whistle, and the class tears around the gym, slapping the walls, everyone except Magda."

"What's she doing?" Julie asked.

"She's running diagonally, touching two walls in one corner, then running diagonally to the opposite corner and touching two walls. Then she sits back down alone, waiting and watching the rest of us trample around slapping walls."

"What did the teacher say?"

"After we finished, we're sitting on the floor, panting, gasping. Miss McCoy smiles right at Magda and says, 'There's one in every group.' I'll never forget Magda sneering at us with an air of superiority."

"What did the teacher mean by *one in every group*?"

"Someone asked her later, and Miss McCoy said it meant Magda had genius-level intelligence or something. But when I think back on it, and how I used to sit next to her in class and how she went on to kill those people, I mean, God, it turns my blood cold."

A moment later the recording ended, and Ryan clicked on another video Julie had made with another former student, Sandra Hinson.

"It was a high school dance in our senior year," Sandra said. "I was dating this cute boy, Jake. It was a starry night, so pretty, and we left the dance for the slope."

"The slope?" Julie asked.

"Our football field was in a valley. We called the grassy hill next to it the slope. We watched the games, from the slope. But this was at night, totally dark, no one there, if you know what I mean?"

"Got it," Julie said.

"After we got there, we saw someone alone, lying on their back, not making a sound. We thought maybe they were hurt, or passed out? We walked over quietly. That's when we saw it was Magda Kurtz. She was lying on the ground, staring at the stars. She knew we were there but didn't move or speak. Jake nudged me and I said, 'Magda, are you okay?'"

The recording hissed for a moment.

"Magda didn't answer," Sandra continued. "Then after about a minute, she looks up at us, and says: 'You have no idea what I can do. One day you'll all be in awe of me.'"

"Wow."

"Then Magda got up, walked away, vanished in the dark. To this day, it still freaks me out."

Ryan pulled a file folder of Julie's typed interviews with people who knew Magda. After she graduated from high school, she fought with her parents, left home, moved to Billings and into an apartment with two older women. Julie had tracked down one of the women and wrote this note:

PENNY WOMACK
Roommate in Billings

We lived together for a time. Magda answered our ad for a roommate. My friend Kit Lee and I thought she was young, but we took her in to save on rent. Magda was smart and had a thing about numbers. Her room was full of calendars. She read weird books about mystics and the cosmos. She was quiet, a loner. She had a job at a poultry processing plant. Kit and I were office girls. One night we were all watching TV when Magda started talking about her job.

Lord, she went into such detail, how the birds, as she called them, are shackled upside down on a moving conveyor line, then electrically stunned before moving on to where their jugular veins were automatically severed. Magda said it was her job to ensure this stage ran smoothly, that the process was quick, effective and humane. But she was grinning, and her eyes were gleaming when she told us: "I just love watching them bleed."

Ryan pulled out another of Julie's notes:

JANINA RIMKUS
Poultry plant coworker

Magda was good at her job. She enjoyed it. She kept to herself until she met Herman Vryker, a trucker from Idaho, who moved shipments in and out of the plant and drove all over the country.

Herman was good-looking with intense eyes. But he was an outcast, or so the story went. He was a prepper who followed wild conspiracies and got kicked out of a doomsday cult. But Magda seemed to fall for him. She would suit him up and sneak him into the plant to watch the process. Magda told me that Herman thought it was "poetic," that was his word, *poetic*, the way the blood flowed. Those two were made for each other. No one was surprised when they got married and moved into a double-wide at the edge of town.

Paper-clipped to the Rimkus note was another.

CAMILA DIAS
Poultry plant coworker

Magda and Herman didn't get many visitors. I don't think it bothered them. They didn't care much for people. When word got around that Magda had a baby, a couple of us visited to fawn over her little daughter. They named her Hayley, a play on the name of Halley's Comet, Magda told us. She was a beautiful baby. While we cooed over her, Magda said odd things, like "Hayley's birthdate was an important sign for us to make use of her." None of us knew what the heck she was talking about. "Make use of her?" We thought, who says things like that about their child? At one point Janina nodded to all the calendars, charts and numbers on the wall. It was strange. We'd heard the rumors about Magda's borderline obsession with some sort of cosmic relationship with dates and events and numbers, I'm not sure, maybe like some sort of occult, numerology thing? But being there, hearing her and seeing her home, well, we left there a little shaken. I'm still uneasy talking about it because, well, of what they were planning.

Leaning back in his chair, Ryan exhaled, rubbed his eyes, then reached for the folder of information that had drawn him to Seattle, flipping through it for the millionth time.

Am I really getting closer to finding Magda?

He typed a few notes into his phone.

He had more work to do.

41

TANNER BISHOP LOOKED at the handcuffs around his wrists.

"You're still under the Miranda warning," Pierce said.

Nodding, Tanner turned to his father's stern, sober face, then to that of Whitney Bowen, the $400-an-hour attorney he'd hired.

A few hours earlier, Pierce and Benton had located Tanner near his home, eating at a McDonald's, where they arrested him. They brought him downtown to the King County Sheriff's Office headquarters.

Tanner was photographed, fingerprinted and permitted to make calls. He'd summoned his dad, who'd hurried to headquarters with Bowen. The detectives allowed them to consult privately with Tanner in a holding cell for nearly forty minutes.

Now all five were gathered at the table in a large meeting

room. Pierce tapped commands on her tablet, then turned it so Tanner, his father and his lawyer could view the screen.

Clear video recorded by the security cameras at True Ocean Auto Dealers in Lake City played. It showed Tanner getting into the white Chevrolet Silverado pickup belonging to John James Smith and driving away.

The video was time- and date-stamped.

Pierce then played footage from the camera at Sparrow Song Park. It showed the Sunny Days school bus arriving. Then a Chevrolet pickup came partially into the frame, stopping as if watching the passengers disembark, the last being Anna Shaw and Katie Harmon walking far behind the others as they disappeared down the trail.

At the edge of the frame, the pickup wheeled around to leave before the footage froze on its Washington State license plate, confirming it was the vehicle Tanner drove from True Ocean Auto. The footage was also time- and date-stamped, falling within the distance and driving time from Lake City in Seattle to the park near North Bend.

Pierce let Tanner consider the evidence.

"Let me lay it all down for you, Tanner," she said. "We investigated with the people at True Ocean. They hired you as a favor to your dad, who knows the service manager, didn't they?"

Tanner didn't answer. His dad cleared his throat. Pierce continued.

"The people at True Ocean were very cooperative. We know you know all the keypad codes to the locks on all lot gates, and you have access to all the keys to all vehicles in for servicing. You can even see the invoices that show when someone will pick up their serviced vehicle."

Pierce glanced at her notebook.

"You would've known the Silverado was serviced ahead

of schedule and that the owner wasn't picking it up until the end of the day. You also knew about the security cameras on True Ocean's lots. In fact, you switched one off that morning. But you missed the safety feature it had to protect against outages, so it was actually never off."

Pierce paused.

"You're facing charges for theft of a motor vehicle, a felony with a maximum sentence of ten years and a twenty-thousand-dollar fine."

Pierce let that sink in.

"Here's where it gets worse, Tanner," she said. "You weren't even supposed to work that day. Yet you went to the dealer early that morning and took the Silverado and drove it to the park. We know the Sunny Days trip to the park was posted in advance online. It wasn't a secret. Your actions suggest planning, premeditation."

Pierce looked at Tanner, then her notes. "You told us that Anna had broken up with you because she thought you'd cheated on her with Shelby. You said she was 'pissed at me. Angry with me. Heartbroken.' Correct?"

Tanner licked his lips and swallowed, said nothing.

"As far as Anna was concerned, you two were done. It was over," Pierce said. "But you were desperate to reconcile, to get her back. Is that why you stole a vehicle and followed her to the park that morning, to get her alone?"

Tanner's face whitened.

"Did something go wrong in your attempt to talk to her at the park? Maybe things got heated, she shoved you, then you grabbed something to strike her and shoved her back. You didn't mean it—it was an accident."

Tanner shut his eyes for a moment and Pierce kept going.

"How can you explain that you, you of all people, Tanner, you with this emotional tornado in your heart, committed a felony, pursued Anna and got to the park at the same time Anna was killed?"

Tears rolled down Tanner's cheeks; he wiped them with his sleeves.

Pierce twisted her pen in her hand while Benton eyed the teenager, his poker face betraying nothing.

"If Anna's death was an accident—" Benton said, halting when Tanner started shaking his head. "Tanner, if you didn't mean for it to happen, now's the time to tell us the truth."

Tanner's chair creaked, and he turned to his father, meeting the face of a man battling anger and fear. Through gritted teeth, Tanner's dad said: "Tell them."

Tanner looked to the lawyer, Whitney Bowen, who nodded.

"Go ahead," she said. "Tell them what happened."

Tanner searched his empty hands for the words.

"I kinda lost my mind," he began. "I couldn't handle losing Anna."

Benton leaned closer, and Pierce studied Tanner, noticing him squeezing his eyes shut and wincing as he spoke.

"I'd put a dent in my dad's SUV, so he banned me from using it. I knew Anna was going out to the park with Sunny Days, and I knew the time. I woke up hurting so bad, aching to talk to her, to make her understand. So it was like an impulsive thing, something I just had to do that morning.

"I needed a car, so I went to True Ocean, checked the invoices, then just drove off in that pickup, figuring I'd have it back before anyone knew.

"I followed the school bus from Seattle to the park. The whole drive out I'm thinking about what I want to say to her. I need her to believe me, that I never cheated. And to make her see that we belong together.

"But when I got there and watched all those people getting

off the bus, it's like my brain's sizzling. There's so many people in the group, I'll never get her alone and she'll freak out. It feels like I'm stalking her when I should just talk to her later."

Tanner stopped, his eyes going around the room as if the walls were closing in on him.

"It's like I snapped out of a spell or something, like the whole thing's a stupid idea. I mean, I even stole a truck. So, I pull out and drive back to the city to put the truck back and ride my bike home. And that's when—"

Tanner raked his hands through his hair.

"Rumors start flying, texts and stuff, on social media from Sunny Days kids that something bad happened to Anna, then they say she's dead. And I'm like what the hell? I don't believe it. I mean, I just saw her get off the bus. Then I see the news reports, the police and helicopter, and I get texts from friends who know, and it's true. They say Anna's dead, she's freaking dead!"

Tanner's eyes widened. His breathing heavy, his composure slipping.

"I got to the bathroom and puked—my whole body went numb." Choking with emotion, gasping, Tanner struggled to continue. "The whole time I'm thinking that maybe if I had gone to her, I somehow could've saved her, and that, that, that Anna died hating me."

A full minute passed with the detectives watching Tanner until he gained a measure of composure.

"Alright," Pierce said. "To start, we'll proceed with charges for stealing the truck. You'll be processed, held, then go before a judge to see if you can bail out and if your attorney can help you."

Opening her file folder, Benton passed formal documents to Tanner's lawyer.

"These are warrants allowing us to seize all of Tanner's

phones and devices, to search the Bishop residence and other areas."

"You're going to take my phone and laptop?" Tanner turned to his lawyer. "Can they do that?"

"Yes, they can," she said.

"That's right," Benton said. "And don't worry, Tanner, if you deleted anything. Our people can find anything that has ever been there."

42

Redmond, Washington

THE ESPRESSO MACHINES GRINDED, banged, hummed and gurgled; the milk steamer reached a high pitch; and the coffee machines sizzled, cracked and dripped.

The aromas of dark chocolate and cinnamon floated over the bustle behind the counter at the Chiming Bells Café.

Waiting in line to place his order, Ryan scanned the employees. Each was wearing a name tag. A tip from one of his sources held that the woman he was looking for was named Avis Brook, and she worked here as a barista.

As he'd done with the diner in Seattle, and the drugstore in Tacoma, Ryan studied the café, off and on, subtly stalking it, asking a harmless question or two of customers or staff, as he zeroed in on his subject.

He needed a close look at Avis Brook.

The fact employees wore name tags helped, but what really helped was that names and schedules were posted on the in/out staff board, near the back but visible to customers.

Standing in line, Ryan read it to be sure he had the correct day. His eyes ran down the list: Sandy, Aaron, Hayworth, Ashley, Rosa, Lucas, and there it is: Avis, marked as *in*.

While waiting, he looked at the female staff members, trying to read their name tags as they moved about—ringing up orders, filling them, calling them out. When he got nearer to the counter, he spotted Avis and his pulse kicked up. This was the closest he'd gotten to her.

Examining everything about her, his thoughts swirled.

Is this the daughter of the woman who murdered Carrie?

Avis Brook appeared to be in her early thirties, so her age was right, but Ryan couldn't see her wrists clearly.

When his turn came, the barista named Ashley smiled at him.

"How can I help you?"

Ryan ordered a vanilla latte, then paid. When Ashley stepped away to make it, Avis came to the counter holding a take-out cup.

"Order for Eric," Avis said.

Ryan was about three feet from her and now had a clearer view. Avis had a double nose ring, studs in her pierced ears. She wore a beige bib apron over a black T-shirt. He could see her arms, and her tattoos: latte art and stars but nothing on the spot of her wrist.

No scar, no tattoo, nothing. His staring was interrupted.

"Have you been served?" Avis looked at Ryan.

"Yes, thanks."

Ashley brought him his order and he went to a table nearby, sitting so he could watch the staff behind the counter while contending with what he sensed was another miss.

The scar should be noticeable on her left wrist.

But there was also another key fact to consider about Avis. According to Ryan's source, she had a six-year-old daughter, named Hailey.

Names again. Coincidence? Maybe.

He didn't know.

Frustrated, Ryan left the shop.

He calmed down outside, sipping his coffee. A car passed with a John Denver song spilling from the radio, one of Carrie's favorites. He couldn't give up. He got into his SUV and parked a distance away, but kept his eye on the shop for the next two hours until Avis's shift ended.

He saw her leave, sipping a drink from a bright yellow can as she walked to the bus stop. He watched her toss the can in the trash before the bus arrived, creaking to a stop.

Ryan walked to the bin and collected the yellow can.

Another DNA sample to ship overnight.

Another possibility.

43

HEIDI WONG SURVEYED her laptop's screen, then her notes on her yellow legal pad at the King County Prosecuting Attorney's Office.

Several days had passed since Tanner Bishop had been charged with stealing a pickup truck, which had put him in the park at the time Anna Shaw died.

At the conference table, rereading updates on the case, Wong shook her head slowly before she raised it to the investigators.

She'd called Acker, Pierce and Benton, along with Grotowski and Tilden, to her building. She'd requested to speak to the main team on the case because of a development.

"So why this meeting?" Acker asked. "You said there's been a turn of events?"

"Earlier today I was on a call with Bishop's attorney, Whitney Bowen. Also on the call, we had John James Smith's lawyer and the lawyer for True Ocean Auto Dealers."

"Why weren't we informed?" Acker asked.

"Sorry, Art, it came about quickly," Wong said. "Smith, due to his own status as an offender, insists that he not be linked in any conceivable way to Shaw's case."

"Meaning?" Pierce said.

"Meaning he wants all theft charges concerning his pickup dropped. He has his truck in good running order. And that's the end of the story, as far as Smith's concerned. For their part, the auto dealer will refund the repair cost and provide Smith free maintenance service, or something. It's up to them how they want to handle it."

"What?" Benton said.

"Bishop has been terminated and will make restitution to the auto dealer on terms acceptable to all parties."

"Can we knock the charge down to taking a vehicle without permission?" Acker said.

"Smith won't support it," Wong said. "I'm sorry. And after looking at everything, you definitely don't have enough for a murder case against Bishop."

"Hold on," Benton said, sitting straighter, jabbing the table with his forefinger. "None of this takes away from Bishop's admission to pursuing Anna Shaw to the park to confront her in the moments before her death. We have the video."

"And we have the rock with Shaw's blood and hair," Pierce said.

"Again, circumstantial," Wong said.

"Bishop admitted to being an emotional powder keg," Benton said.

"But it doesn't erase the cracks in the case," Wong said. "We have no conclusive trace evidence putting Bishop on the cliff."

"The video puts him in the park," Pierce said.

"But not on the cliff. His defense will flip the video to their advantage, saying it proves that Bishop turned away, left the park, as he's stated. And that his denial is supported by the fact none of the statements we have from the group, including from Katie Harmon, put Bishop at the cliff. You have nothing to even raise the possibility he stepped out of the truck. You've got nothing from his phone or other devices that builds a case. And there's the gap."

"The gap?" Acker repeated.

"Katie left Anna to run deeper into the park for help, returning with the supervisors to see Anna Shaw had fallen. You estimate the total time to be four to six minutes or seven, thus creating a gap in time when no one was with Anna."

"Right," Benton said. "Just a few minutes."

"The defense will stress that a lot can happen in that time. They'll point to the faulty cameras in the parking lot, state that someone else could've arrived or been in the park within that time."

Wong clicked on her laptop, reviewing files.

"For example, you haven't ruled out other possibilities, such as Marilyn Hamilton and Gilbert Croft, who were identified on security camera footage as being in the park."

"Focus Woman and Camry Man," Benton said.

"Who?" Wong said.

"Their vehicles," Pierce said. "Hamilton and Croft are on our list, but Smith and Tanner became priorities."

"And," Wong said, "you haven't ruled out Katie Harmon."

"Not yet," Pierce said. "As you suggested, we're endeavoring to eliminate all other possibilities before we concentrate on her."

Wong looked at the detectives.

"Keep doing that. You're doing good work, guys," she said. "You just need to keep nailing down every loose end."

★ ★ ★

They stepped into Acker's office for a post-meeting huddle.

"These things are never smooth." Acker cursed to himself, undid his collar button and loosened his tie, then turned to Grotowski and Tilden.

"Lyle, get in touch with North Precinct. We need to make another search for Anna Shaw's phone at the scene."

"Again?" Tilden said.

"Again," Acker said. "And, guys, before we go back to looking hard at the Harmon girl, let's chase down the two others on the footage, Hamilton and Croft. We haven't spoken with them yet."

"Sure," Pierce said.

"You okay with that, Carl?"

Benton looked up from scrolling on his phone.

"I'm okay with it."

"Good. Stay the course, hang in there," Acker said.

At their desk, Pierce searched her computer for contact information and called Gilbert Croft. She gave him a brief explanation on the investigation into the death at Sparrow Song Park and set up a time to visit him at his home in Issaquah. Then she called Marilyn Hamilton and arranged to meet her later.

Upon ending the call, she noticed Benton sitting across from her, leaning forward, elbows on his knees, talking softly into his phone.

Allowing him privacy, Pierce got her bag and the new frame she'd purchased at Walmart. She opened her drawer to the glass-framed photo of Webb and Ethan she'd broken earlier in the week. The new frame was a plastic rounded poster frame. It held a paper stock photo of a little girl in a bright yellow raincoat holding a rainbow-colored umbrella and splashing in puddles with her blue rubber boots.

Pierce smiled at it, then removed the stock photo and tossed. it in her drawer, intending to put it in recycling later. When she inserted the photo of Webb and Ethan, a pang of guilt shuddered through Pierce. She'd been working longer hours than usual, and she missed them. Softly she touched the restored picture, then placed it on her desk.

Benton ended his call, stared at his feet and rubbed the bridge of his nose. Ensuring no one was near, Pierce said: "Bad news?"

"No news. Still waiting on the latest test results."

"Carl, did you tell Art about Elizabeth?"

"No, no one outside our family knows, except you."

"It might help if you let Art know."

"I'll think about it."

Pierce nodded with a warm smile. Before she could say anything more, Benton said: "Right, let's get busy."

44

FINISHING HIS TAKE-OUT fish and chips on a bench at Alki Beach Park, Ryan took in the view as gulls glided in the salt air.

Puget Sound, the Olympic Mountains, freighters, ferries, Seattle's skyline and the Space Needle.

Nothing had panned out yet. Not the coffee shop in Redmond, the drugstore in Tacoma or the diner. For now it had come down to a waiting game.

He sought a measure of optimism in the fact he'd sent off another DNA sample. He hadn't received the results of the others. These things took time. His heart sank a little. Could he realistically expect different results after so many years of strikeouts? After all these years, and all the cities he'd searched, would he find the answers here?

Or am I chasing ghosts in the wind?

★ ★ ★

Back at his apartment, Ryan made coffee and settled in to work, doing what he always did to recover from a setback.

He reviewed his research material.

Deciding this time to study Magda and her husband's downfall, he opened a folder on his laptop labeled *MAGDA ARRESTED.*

It had the videos that had been recorded in the FBI's office in Billings, Montana. He'd obtained them with the help of court clerks.

The first started with Magda in a barren room with cinderblock walls. She was wearing orange jail clothes, sitting in handcuffs at a table across from a man and woman in business attire, FBI Special Agents Joe Avelar and Erin West.

They informed Magda everything was being recorded.

"You don't have to answer our questions," West said. "Anything you say can be used against you. And you're entitled to have a lawyer at any time. But first, we'd like to talk. Is that okay? Do you agree to talk to us first?"

Magda remained silent.

Her focus flicked up at the camera, like a snake's tongue.

Ryan's stomach tightened as he stared at her. How many times had he watched these videos? Here was Magda at twenty-three, practically the same age as Carrie and Willow. Magda wore no makeup; her tousled blond hair framed her face. And with her high cheekbones, she was attractive. But her eyes. Those stone-cold, dead eyes.

Were they the last thing Carrie saw?

"Magda," Avelar said. "If you're going to help yourself, you need to help us."

"Where's Hayley?" Magda asked.

"Before we answer that," West said, "are you agreeing to talk to us?"

"Yes, I agree. Tell me what you did with my baby."

"She's safe," West said. "She's with the people at Family Services until you and Herman help us sort things out."

"What things?" Magda's voice broke. "I have no idea why I'm here."

"Magda, it was all in the warrants," West said. "You read them. You and Herman were present when they were executed at your home."

Avelar opened a file folder and set down before Magda, one by one, color photographs of an engraved watch belonging to Frank Worrell of Boston, then Carrie's inhaler. Then the rings belonging to the British couple, Sharon Lance and Jeremy Dunster of Manchester. Then a ring belonging to Brent Porter from Denver.

"These items are the property of people reported missing by their families, people last seen in Montana, Idaho and Washington," West said. "Why did you have them?"

"I don't know." Magda shook her head. "I don't know anything."

"You don't know?" West said.

For the next few hours, the agents detailed each of the missing person cases and the astronomical odds of their items being discovered with Magda and Herman Vryker. Over and over, with tears brimming, Magda said, "I don't know anything. I want my daughter and I want to go home."

Finally Avelar said: "We've talked to Herman, you know."

Magda's eyes registered a glint of surprise.

"What did he tell you?" Magda asked.

"Oh, he had a lot to say," West said.

Thinking for a long moment, Magda's tears evaporated.

"Did Herman tell you he got the items at flea markets?" Magda said.

The agents let her statement sit in the air.

"You know that's not true," West said.

"It is. He told me not to say anything because they could've been stolen. That's why you searched our place."

"Enough," Avelar said. "You're lying. You and Herman killed Lydia Worrell and Frank Worrell, Carrie Gardner and Willow Walker, Sharon Lance and Jeremy Dunster, and Brent Porter. And you kept their property as trophies."

Magda shook her head.

"We know," West said, "because there's a living witness, a survivor, from your failed attack on her in Idaho, a few miles south of the Canadian border."

"That's not true," Magda said.

Avelar turned to West, who put another photo on the table. It showed a single toddler's shoe, white with pink stripes.

"This shoe was found at your residence," West said. "But not its mate. Now, you may have thought it was misplaced and would turn up."

West set down another photo of the missing shoe, white with pink stripes.

"It did turn up," West said. "In Idaho, where you faked car trouble and flagged down a woman while holding your daughter so you and Herman could kill her. But she fought back, she survived, and here you are, facing multiple first-degree murder charges."

"You'll likely never see Hayley again. And in this state," Avelar said, "the death penalty's a certainty for you."

Magda's eye twitched.

"Magda," West said. "This case will proceed, with or without your help. It's pretty much guaranteed—you'll never be free again."

Realizing she was trapped, all the blood drained from Magda's face.

"Now's the time for you to take control, here," West said.

"Tell us everything, tell us the truth. And we'll make sure the county attorney knows that you cooperated. No guarantees, but it could help."

The agents stood.

"We'll give you a moment to think it over," West said.

"Remember," Avelar said, "Herman could beat you to it. He could work a deal and walk free with your daughter. The clock is ticking."

Magda began rocking back and forth. The handcuffs jingled as she covered her face with her hands. A few seconds later she looked up to the camera, then to the agents, stopping them cold at the door.

"Herman killed the couple from Boston. He killed the Arizona college girls. He killed the British tourists and the guy from Denver. He killed them all. I couldn't stop him. He beat me and would've killed me and Hayley if I didn't obey and do what he said. I had no choice. It was not my fault."

"Are you prepared to tell us everything, Magda?" West said.

"First, I want a lawyer. I want a deal and I want my daughter back."

45

RYAN EXHALED.

The next recording he cued up was labeled *HERMAN ARRESTED.*

Herman Vryker, aged twenty-six, parents divorced, raised by his uncle in Hayden Lake, Idaho. Herman was a long-haul trucker with a long record of moving violations that included: speeding, an improper lane change and twice he'd bumped cars on the highway.

Herman sat in the drab interview room, wearing an orange prisoner jumpsuit. Unshaven, eyes bloodshot, his unwashed hair matted, he was handcuffed along with a leg iron attached to the metal table. Beside him, his lawyer, Heinrich Butler, read documents while they waited without speaking, both unaware what had transpired with Magda in the previous days.

Watching them, Ryan reflected on how at that time the investigators had considered their case a bit shaky. Outside of the failed attack in Idaho, they had no bodies and no murder scenes. The fact Magda and Herman possessed items belonging to missing people was not enough. They needed admissions from Magda and Herman to tie together the evidence and facts they had.

In most jurisdictions the law allowed detectives to be deceptive with a suspect in pursuit of the truth. So they'd gone to Magda first, having not yet questioned Herman. Telling her they'd spoken to Herman, they wanted her believing her husband had turned against her. They also planted the seed that Magda was facing execution and would likely never see her daughter again, which was true.

It worked.

With her attorney beside her, Magda was questioned for hours, during which she detailed the killings and her role in them. In exchange she would plead guilty but wanted to be reunited with her daughter. Magda wanted a light sentence, five to seven years, in a minimum-security prison with access to college courses of her choosing. After which she'd be released with no conditions. Once she started serving her time, she would help locate the bodies, so the families of their victims would have some peace.

Days passed as approval was sought from the county attorney, right up through to Montana's Attorney General's Office. Lawyers for the office consulted with their counterparts in Idaho and Washington. Given the scale and horrific nature of the case, the state revised the deal to a take-it-or-leave-it final status.

The state said Magda would serve twenty years. She'd be released with no conditions, no parole, no reporting and—given how Magda had used her baby daughter in commission of first-degree murders—there would be no mother and child reunion. The state would become Hayley's guardian and she would be put up for adoption to start a new life with a new name. Magda would not be given any details. There would be no contact. Her daughter would be taken away from her.

Magda was outraged.

But if she rejected the deal, she'd face execution.

"You have no choice," West told Magda, echoing her claim in the killings.

Magda's lawyer advised her to accept the terms. The deal was signed by all parties and approved by the court.

When Magda left the small interview room for the last time, she shot a glance up at the camera in what Ryan thought was a smirk.

Now, in the video Ryan watched, the door opened to the room where Herman and his lawyer were seated. FBI Special Agents Joe Avelar and Erin West entered.

After a perfunctory round of introductions, Heinrich Butler started complaining. "Why keep my client in custody all this time? So you can prolong the process? You're infringing on his rights."

"No, we're not, Mr. Butler," Avelar said. "My colleague will update you."

"Herman, we've spoken at length with Magda," West said. "She told us everything."

Herman glanced to Butler, then at the agents.

"What do you mean?" Herman asked.

West placed photographs of the victims on the table, then photos of the items found at Herman and Magda's residence.

"She told us everything you did," West said.

Herman swallowed.

"We got those things at flea markets," Herman said. "One in Billings, one in Miles City. Are they stolen? That's what I was afraid of. You need to check those places, investigate the vendors, because—"

"Herman," West said. "You need to listen to something."

West took out a microcassette recorder, set it on the table and played a long excerpt of Magda speaking to them.

"...he's a trucker, he grew up in the northwest. Herman knows every back road, logging, mining road, pioneer trail in the region. He'd take us out to remote, isolated areas he selected and then dig graves to use later..."

Herman's face whitened as it played.

"...he had these scary beliefs, that he had *dominion over lower life forms* and *every creeping thing that creepeth upon the earth.* Sometimes at night he'd lie on the ground and stare up at the stars. I think it exaggerated his sense of self-importance, because he started embracing these strange ideas about how he was superior to all others, that he should rule over who lives and who dies, because he feels nothing wrong about a necessary death. I think that's why, when we met, he insisted I sneak him into the slaughterhouse where I worked...so he could watch death..."

Butler scribbled notes quickly on a legal pad.

"...Herman started talking about how a day of deliverance was nearing, and how people who stood in the way of foretold events had to be removed. He'd take action according to dates, numbers, weird formulas and things he'd calculated, then we'd go out to find potential victims..."

Herman clenched his jaw as he listened.

"...it was his idea to use Hayley to lure people to stop—no one would feel threatened by a woman with a toddler needing help on a lonely stretch of road—and he'd lie in wait and kill whoever stopped..."

"What would happen after that?" West asked Magda.

"Herman would load the bodies into their vehicle, drive it to a selected, prepared site, miles and miles away, with me following with Hayley. I'd help him bury the bodies in a pre-dug grave. Later he'd hide their vehicles, alter the VINs, then sell them to his friends in trucker world. He told me they'd transport them to resell in Central and South America."

"Why didn't you stop or report him?"

"I was terrified. Herman beat me all the time."

"Did you make a criminal complaint?"

"No, I was frightened. With my lawyer's help, I'll be making one now."

"Alright, continue," West said.

"Herman hit me all the time and said if I didn't do what he said, he'd put me and Hayley in one of those graves. Yes, I participated in the murders, but I had no choice."

West switched off the recorder.

Avelar set down a photo of a child's shoe.

"This was found at your home," he said, setting down a second photo of an identical shoe. "This one was found at the site of your attempt to kill a woman in Idaho. She's our surviving witness who got your plate. And we have Magda's admission."

"It's over for you," West said.

Tears rolled down Herman's face.

"She's a liar," Herman said.

Butler touched his handcuffed wrists. "Don't say anything."

"They have to know the truth."

"Go ahead," West said.

"As your attorney," Butler said, "I advise you to remain silent, Herman."

"Magda," Herman said, ignoring his lawyer's advice, "lied to you. She's smart, very smart. She always thought she was above other people. She's the one who reads strange books. She's the one who believes in the stars and power in numbers."

His handcuffs jingled as he pressed his palms to the table, bit his bottom lip to push down on his anger.

"She's the one who planned it all—it was her idea to use

Hayley to lure people. And she loved it. From the time I met her at the slaughterhouse, she told me how she loved the killing, the power over living things. Yes, I did what she wanted. But she stared into the eyes of people as we killed them. She loved watching them die. She told me there was no greater feeling than watching life drain from a living thing."

"Now, please," Butler said. "None of what Magdalena has told you is admissible under Title Twenty-Six. It's spousal privilege—neither spouse can testify against the other without consent of the other. Your case collapses."

"Mr. Butler," West said, "you heard on the recording that she's in the process of swearing out a criminal complaint against your client, so the privilege will not apply."

"Herman," Avelar said. "You'll be charged with multiple counts of first-degree murder. The prosecution will seek the death penalty."

"I can't believe it." An intense visible change rolled over Herman; he appeared to deflate and break before their eyes. But it was not about facing execution. "I can't believe she betrayed me."

Much later, Herman's case went before the court. Butler's attempts to secure a deal—a commutation to life in exchange for his cooperation to find the bodies—had failed. The state wanted Herman executed. It wasn't interested in another deal. They already had Magda's.

Herman's death sentence was passed. Within days of it being issued, death row inmates near Herman heard bedsheets being torn and alerted guards.

But it was too late.

Herman Vryker had hung himself in his cell.

It was during this time that Magda, handcuffed and shackled under heavy escort, led officials in Montana, Idaho and Washington to isolated areas to find the graves of their victims. Huge contingents involving helicopters, search teams and dogs failed each time to find any remains.

Locating them was difficult, Magda explained, because often she'd only seen the sites at night. She had been so terrified that now she couldn't remember *the exact* locations. After nearly a dozen attempts, it became evident that she either could not, or would not, locate the remains of their victims. Frustrated, investigators went to Herman Vryker's relatives, friends, and trucking and business associates, thinking he may have confided in someone. It was another futile effort to locate the remains.

The state appealed to the court to declare its deal with Magda invalid and subject her to a harsher sentence. Magda's attorney, Katherine Marie Powell, argued that even though no remains had been located, Magda had made every effort to fulfill her end of the agreement. Powell cited precedents. Magda ultimately won. The deal could not be changed. Magda would be released in twenty years, with no reporting conditions or terms.

A free woman at age forty-four.

Ryan was seething at his desk.

He went back to the part in Magda's video where she was smirking at the camera, as if to say she'd won.

No, I can't let you win!

He stared at Magda.

"You know!" His fist came down on the table. "You know where they are because you put them in the ground!"

46

MARJORIE COLE LOOKED through the window of her room at the Silverbrook Hills Senior Living Home.

"Hi, Mrs. Cole." Bella Spencer stood at her open door. Marjorie kept it open most times. The hall traffic and occasional visitor eased the lonely days. Bella had her laundered towels. "I'll set these on the counter for you."

"Thank you, Bella," Marjorie said. "Is Hetta here today?"

"I think she's out at a meeting. Enjoy her absence while you can."

"I don't know why that woman is so, so, I don't know what."

"God wires us all differently." Bella smiled. "I'll check back with you later, dear."

Marjorie gave a little wave and turned back to the window.

Her thoughts carried her from her wheelchair beyond the surrounding woodland, back years, back to a time when the highway rushed under her. She was sitting next to George, her husband, in their truck, her heart nearly bursting as they departed Montana.

She was sad to leave their friends and the life she and George had had in Great Falls. But a new life awaited them in Seattle where George had accepted a fantastic job offer. It was exciting, but Marjorie was anxious.

Tenderly she stroked their daughter Sara's hair. Sara was seated between them. Watching her, Marjorie was convincing herself that the move would be good for all of them.

It would be a new beginning.

Sara flipped through the pages of a Dr. Seuss book, *Horton Hears a Who!* She'd been in their lives for more than a year at that point. She had come to them with a terrible history; and being her new parents came with challenges, but it didn't matter. Marjorie and George were prepared to meet them.

Sara was their answered prayer and they loved her unconditionally.

Their love had arisen out of the painful realization that they could never have children biologically. The wait on adoption lists for a child was unbearable, and surrogacy was too expensive for them. Devastated, they had abandoned their hope for a child of any age when the stars aligned.

Marjorie had a close friend at their church. That friend's uncle was a detective. He'd mentioned a gut-wrenching complex situation involving a little girl who needed new parents.

Calls were made to the little girl's caseworker at Child and Family Services to establish Marjorie and George as a prospective adoptive family. Procedure was followed, forms were completed, and assessments and evaluations were conducted.

Marjorie and George received a summary of the girl's tragic story from the detective, and it gave them pause. Then, at home in the evenings, George and Marjorie digested news reports they'd photocopied at the library. Reading them, Marjorie gasped at times. And early in the process the caseworker, having advised them of confidentiality laws, relayed details of the girl's life that were unknown to the public. She stressed difficulties they could face as her parents.

Marjorie wept for the little girl.

"With this knowledge," the caseworker had said, "would you like to withdraw your application? Or do you still wish to be considered?"

That afternoon, weighing their lives, George took Marjorie's hand. "I see the answer in your eyes," he said. "Heaven moves in ways we can't understand. That little girl needs us."

"And we need her," Marjorie said.

In time Marjorie and George were informed they'd been selected to become the girl's adoptive parents. They were overjoyed as the next steps in the process were set in motion, and they met with experts who advised them on what lay ahead.

"The child has fragmented memories of her early years," one psychologist said. "And she'll question you about her birth parents."

The psychologist removed her glasses and continued.

"Her history and the truth about her birth parents belongs to her and she will need to know. That truth should come from you, her adoptive parents, to establish trust."

The psychologist warned about the harm of lying or not telling her, guiding them on what, when and how to tell her.

"It'll take time, you'll need to lay the groundwork and plant seeds of truth at the appropriate ages of her life."

Marjorie and George listened carefully as the psychologist, and later other officials, warned them about a crucial fact.

"As you know, the girl's father is deceased and her mother incarcerated," one official said. "The criminal court has ruled that there must never be contact of any kind between the girl and her biological mother, deeming it a risk to the girl's safety. Therefore, all identities, all private information about the girl and her adoptive family, have been sealed and kept confidential, to protect the girl and her adoptive parents."

The placement process went well, and Marjorie and George's attorney helped with finalizing the adoption and ensuring the little girl was given a new legal name: Sara Dawn Cole. Marjorie had always loved the name Sara, and Dawn was chosen as a middle name to signify a new start. The psychologists had suggested they start calling the girl by the name Sara casually, as a nickname. That way it would naturally eclipse, and ultimately replace, the name her birth mother had given her in another severing with her past.

But, as predicted, as soon as Sara started living with Marjorie and George, she asked questions.

"Why aren't I living with my mom and my dad? What happened to my mom and my dad?"

Guided by the experts, Marjorie and George began filling in the blanks in Sara's life.

"Your mom and dad had big, grown-up problems," Marjorie said.

"What kind of problems?"

"Well, it's hard to understand, but their problems were so serious they started hurting other people."

When they first told her that, Sara looked at the scar on her wrist, as if remembering, and it took everything Marjorie had to hold herself together to help her child.

"Sara, their problems had nothing to do with you," Marjorie said. "It had to do with their problems."

"But how come you're my mom now?"

"Well, a judge—that's the person who can make things official, like a law or rule—decided it was best for everyone to put your mom and dad in a place where they couldn't hurt anybody anymore. And, to make sure you were safe, a judge decided it would be best if you lived with us because we wanted to have you in our family more than anything, and because we love you very much."

"And you don't hurt people?"

"No, we don't hurt people," George said. "We like to help people."

"But will I ever see my mom and my dad again?"

"Honey, the judge said with their problems, they can't take care of you. That the best way to keep you safe is for you to not see them."

Sara thought for a while, withdrawing, just as she was during their drive from Montana to Seattle, looking from her book, up at the highway, the forests rising around them.

Until the episode.

A few miles after stopping for gas and topping off the oil, a rattling sounded from the truck's motor. "I bet the oil cap's loose," George said, pulling over and getting out. The moment he raised the hood, Sara's head snapped up, her eyes widened. Twisting in her seat she looked behind her repeatedly. When a car stopped and a man offered to help, Sara's breathing quickened, her face flushed with alarm.

"It's happening! It's happening again!"

George thanked the driver, declining his offer. The man waved and drove off, but Sara exploded in sobs as Marjorie took her into her arms, shushing and calming her. Having tightened the cap and dropped the hood, George got into the truck. Taking in the situation, his eyes met Marjorie's. As she rocked Sara, they silently acknowledged that their daughter's trauma was bubbling under the surface.

They continued driving.

Life went well for them in Seattle.

The electrical contracting company that hired George

helped him upgrade his certification and license to earn more. They found their dream home in a pretty neighborhood in North Seattle. Marjorie got a job as an office administrator for an accounting firm. Marjorie and George volunteered at shelters and missions. Sara helped, learning and applying their morals and beliefs to always think of others.

But given Sara's history, they continually told her to never talk to, or go anywhere alone with, strangers "no matter how nice they seem, no matter what they say." It was a caution they underscored. From time to time, Sara would ask more questions about her past. Often they had no answer, or didn't think she was ready for one.

"It's complicated," Marjorie would say. "I'll explain when you're older."

Early on they frequently told Sara that it was *very important* she always remember: "Not everybody's family is like our family. There are things we must always, always, keep private in our family. Remember that."

One Sunday afternoon they'd taken Sara to a Seahawks football game, seating her between them. During a lull in the play, she asked questions.

"You said a judge put my mom and dad in a place so they won't hurt people. Is that place jail?"

George traded a look with Marjorie, then leaned closer to Sara's ear and said, "Yes, prison."

"How long will the judge make them stay there?"

More looks were exchanged, then Marjorie said, "Honey, we can talk about it later in the truck."

Driving home after the game Marjorie said, "Your mom will stay in prison a long, long time."

"What about my dad?"

"Well, you see, his problems were too much for him to handle and he died in prison not long after he was put there."

"Oh."

Absorbing the information, Sara stared ahead. The traffic and buildings flowed by, as did the years.

In keeping with the advice of experts who'd studied the research, Marjorie and George gradually finished telling Sara all about her birth parents by the time Sara was ten years old. Psychologists had told them that Sara's history should be established before adolescence, because by then she'd be going through enough, trying to figure out who she was.

During those years, they reinforced the fact their family was unlike others.

"There are things we don't ever discuss outside our home," Marjorie said. "No one knows who your birth parents are, but people who are angry at what they did will want to know. They might be angry at you, or us, even though what your parents did has nothing to do with you at all. And if we keep things private, no one will ever know about the past."

Marjorie and George prayed that Sara understood as she continued asking questions.

"When my mom comes out of prison, will she hurt people?"

"Nobody knows that."

"When I grow up, will I hurt people like they did?"

Marjorie looked at her; it was the first time Sara had ever asked that question.

"Do you ever think about hurting anyone?"

"No," Sara said, "never, because it's wrong."

Marjorie took Sara into her arms, holding her.

"No," she said. "You will never hurt anyone."

Marjorie believed it with every fiber of her soul.

Still, while Sara was growing up, Marjorie had been plagued with dread about her. Because of the disturbing history of Sara's biological parents, deep down Marjorie always worried that Sara would inherit their traits.

But she didn't.

When George was dying, he told Marjorie that Sara was a blessing in their lives, and it was true.

But now, after all these years, Marjorie's faith was shaken.

For in a dark corner of her heart, she still held secrets.

Yes, Sara was a good person. And Nathaniel, God rest his soul, was a good person.

But Katie.

At first, after what happened to the little boy, Marjorie believed Katie had nothing to do with it. But now? Now with the girl on the cliff.

I fear the worst. I fear it because I lied to Sara. I haven't told her everything about her birth mother.

Marjorie drew her hands to her face. She sat that way until a shadow fell over her. Then she felt someone touch her shoulder.

"Mrs. Cole, are you okay?"

Hetta Boden had lowered herself beside the chair, concern in her face as she studied Marjorie.

"May I get someone, or get you some water?"

"No, thank you." Marjorie politely waved off the offer and found her composure. "I was just lost in my memories."

47

Seattle, Washington

THE STEPS CREAKED as Sara climbed them to the attic, guided by the weak light spilling up the narrow stairway from below.

Anxiety had tormented her for days before she overcame it and found the will to come up here—uncertain of what she would awaken.

At the top, she opened the attic door and tried the light switch. It didn't work. She used the flashlight on her phone and glanced around. Dust mites swirled above boxes of old clothes, Christmas decorations and cartons of items jettisoned from their lives.

Sitting on a wooden chest filled with old blankets, Sara slid a carton closer and pulled out a photo album. Her mom had one or two albums at Silverbrook Hills, but most of them were here.

The laminated pages crackled as Sara looked through the

images of her family taken over the years, coming to happy times with Nathaniel. Sara had her favorites of Nathaniel downstairs in her room, and on her phone. But there were more family pictures here.

She traced her fingers over Nathaniel's face, smiling at her from his motorcycle, so handsome. Here he was at his shop. There he was helping at the shelter. Here he was holding Katie when she was born. Here he was with Katie on his shoulders, looking up at her; she was laughing down at him.

Sara smiled back at the photos of her mom and dad, Christmases, birthdays.

Closing the album, she glanced at a cardboard box, one she rarely opened.

Because I know what's there, waiting for me. The truth.

It contained old things: a lamp, bookends and candlestick holders. But under them, hidden, was a box.

She opened it to faded clippings, photocopies and printouts of old newspaper reports. Sara scanned the headlines:

Survivor's account unearths link to troubling case
FBI to lead probe of several disappearances across several states
Husband and wife tied to multiple slayings
Hearts of Darkness: Murder Suspect's Wife Seeks Deal

Sara couldn't go any further.

Why didn't I get rid of all this stuff long ago?

She put the box away, unable to silence the shrieks from the recesses of her mind, pulling her back...*the rain...the pain... the screaming, kicking...clawing...bleeding...the thudding...the digging...the blood...*

She shook her head to drive the images from her.

I know who I am! I'm not them! I'm not them!

Sara fought a great sob.

But Katie?

The drawing, Anna, and there was the boy, and how Katie had said at the time: "It's sad what happened to him." But it was *the way* Katie had said it. Like she didn't mean it.

Oh, God! What do I do? Please tell me what to do!

48

Issaquah, Washington

THEY FOUND GILBERT Croft's house in a terraced section of the neighborhood known as Montreux, on the slope of Cougar Mountain.

A blue Toyota Camry stood in the driveway. Its plate matched the plate of the Camry recorded at Sparrow Song Park, a thirty-minute drive away.

Pierce and Benton went to the door and rang the bell.

No one answered.

Pierce rang it again.

Nothing.

She checked the time.

Benton nodded to the pathway leading around the house. Following it to the backyard, they saw an older man working at a flower bed, next to a wheelbarrow with precast gray-white bricks. Grunting, he hefted one and, with the slowness of age, placed it on the grass.

"Mr. Croft?" Pierce said.

He turned. "Yes."

"Detectives Kim Pierce and Carl Benton, King County Sheriff's Office."

"Oh, yes." He brushed his brow. "Let's go inside."

Croft's living room had a cultured stone fireplace, floor-to-ceiling bookshelves and comfortable chairs.

"Can I get you anything? Coffee?"

"No, thank you," Benton said.

"I lost track of time. My wife wanted me to finish the garden edging." Croft sighed as he sat in a sofa rocker. "So, you want to talk about that girl who fell in the park?"

"Yes. A few things we'd like to go over with you." Pierce reached into her bag for her laptop. After relating another summary, she cued up the video showing Croft at the park. He slid on his glasses and then she passed her laptop to him. Holding it, he watched the video carefully.

"Yes, that's me, alright. These days we seem to see cameras everywhere."

He passed the computer back; she closed it. Then, sitting back down, Pierce said: "Did you know Anna Shaw?"

"Anna who?"

"Anna Shaw, the girl who was killed."

"No, I'm afraid not."

"Do you know her parents, Lynora and Chuck Shaw?"

"No, I don't know them."

"The video shows you were at Sparrow Song Park the day of Anna's death, walking to your Camry at the time of Anna's death."

"Yes, such a terrible thing, her falling."

"What time did you arrive at the park?"

"Oh, gosh, let me think. I usually get up at six a.m. or so. Not sure exactly, sometime after that."

"Why were you at the park that day, Mr. Croft?" Pierce asked.

"My wife likes to walk through it. We go every week or so. It's beautiful. And I was there that day out of routine, I guess."

"Routine?" Benton asked.

"Yes, my wife is away, visiting her sister in Maine."

Benton's attention focused on the spines of the books filling Croft's shelves. A set of binoculars stood on one shelf. Nearly all of the books were related to true-crime cases, serial killings, infamous murders, texts on police procedure and forensic investigations.

"That's quite a collection of books," Benton said.

"Most of them belong to Dolores, my wife. She's a fan of all those murder shows, *Dateline, 48 Hours*."

"And you? Do you read the books and watch the shows with her?" Benton asked.

"No, no, I like puzzles. In fact, I'm working on one of Lake Louise, Alberta, a thousand pieces. We went there for vacation once."

"Who do we have here?" Benton nodded to another shelf with an array of framed photos.

"My wife, our children and grandchildren. Our son lives in Atlanta, our daughter's in Cleveland." Croft picked up one of a girl about the same age as Anna Shaw. "Miranda, our granddaughter. She's a teenager now and you know how teen girls can be—boy crazy, rebellious." He replaced the picture. "She's quite a handful now. You have to be stern with teens."

Pierce surveyed the photos. "You have a nice family."

"And you and Dolores have been retired a few years?" Benton asked. "From where?"

"Yes, I worked at Boeing. She was in accounting at Costco."

"Getting back to the park," Pierce said, then got her laptop again. She took it over to Croft, cued up a map of Sparrow Song and handed her device to him. "Can you show me where you walked that day?" Leaning closer this time, she caught a trace of Old Spice as Croft held the laptop and studied the map's trails.

A finger with gnarled knuckles traced a line that was not the trail used by the Sunny Days group, but webbed to it, near the trailhead.

"Did you see or hear anything that day to cause you concern?"

"No."

"Did you hear a cry for help? A scream?"

"No. I walked on the trail Dolores and I usually take, then got to my car and came home."

"You say you walk in the park every week or so with Dolores, but that day you went alone. Why's that?" Pierce slid her laptop back into her bag.

"Like I said, routine. I guess I want to maintain a routine while she's away."

"But, Mr. Croft," Pierce said, "why drive down the interstate to a park when you have so many parks right here in Issaquah with views of the mountains, the lake?"

"Dolores likes the park and it's good for us to get out there."

"When did you become aware there was a tragedy at the park that day?" Pierce asked.

"The first inkling was when I got on ninety-five to come home. I saw police cars with their sirens going and lights flashing, heading in the direction of the park. Then I saw the news and that's how I knew. It's just terrible. They said she was trying to take a picture of herself and fell."

The detectives looked at Croft for a moment.

"Mr. Croft—" Benton indicated the small table next to Croft "—why do you have two phones?"

"Oh, one belongs to Dolores."

"May I?" Pierce picked up the phones, then made note of the two, their brand and color.

"But Dolores is visiting her sister in Maine?" Pierce said. "Wouldn't she take it with her?"

"Right, right." Croft tapped his palm to his cheek, staring at the two phones Pierce had set back down beside him. "She forgot it. We're not as young as we used to be."

Pierce and Benton asked Croft questions for several more minutes before wrapping up the interview and thanking him.

Walking to their SUV parked on the street, they saw a woman in her fifties, passing by on the sidewalk with a leashed white cairn terrier.

"Oh, hi," she said. "Is everything okay with Gil?"

"Excuse me, who are you?" Pierce asked.

"I'm Mave Garland. I live two doors that way. Are you with the senior outreach group?"

"No. Why're you concerned?"

"We, I mean, the neighbors, sort of watch out for Gil. His children live across the country. He's getting more forgetful. He's likely going to lose his driver's license. He hasn't been the same since Dolores, well, you know."

"What about Dolores?"

"She passed away almost a year ago now. Who did you say you're with?"

49

TWISTING HER PURSE STRAPS, Sara waited with Katie in Dr. Mehta's reception room, listening to the tranquil bubbling of the aquarium.

Katie stood before the tank watching the brilliantly colored fish darting and gliding in the glowing water.

Sara was thinking of Nathaniel, his gentle kindness, his good heart. And her parents, so selfless, so giving and loving.

She looked to Katie.

She must have their goodness in her, like Mom said.

Sara tensed at her own horrible memories of driving in the rain, the thrashing, the screams, churning with the unbearable truth in the attic of her home.

Katie must have her family's virtues. Sara repeated the thought, as if it were a plea, her *real* family's virtues. Or had she inherited the worst of her family's history? And after the incident with the boy in Vancouver, after Anna's death, and being plagued with bad thoughts—*is Katie trying to tell me with her drawing what really happened on the cliff?*

Is she confessing?

Sara didn't know where to turn or what to do. That's why she'd requested to see Dr. Mehta privately in advance of today's session with Katie.

"Sara?" Nadia, the receptionist, gestured to the open door down the hall. "Sally will see you now."

"Thank you."

Nadia then went to Katie at the tank. "Want to help me feed them? We can give them names, how about Nemo for that one and..."

Dr. Mehta met Sara at the door, holding her folded glasses in one hand.

Her office was softly lit and filled with bookcases, art pieces, ferns and plush chairs.

"Have a seat, please."

After they sat, Dr. Mehta smiled.

"You wanted to talk?"

"Yes. I think you're helping Katie."

"These things can take time. We've had some bumps along the way but overall, she's coming along."

"Yes," Sara said. "Well, the reason I wanted to talk is I need your help to understand something."

"What is it?"

"This stays confidential like you said before, right?"

"Of course."

Sara twisted the straps on her purse.

"This is hard for me."

"Take your time."

Sara withdrew Katie's drawing book, flipped through it

beyond the birds, the trees, butterflies and hand tracings. She stopped at the sketch titled *The Park.*

"This is Katie's sketchbook. She usually leaves it on her desk, but I found it hidden under her bed after she drew this one."

Knitting her brow, Dr. Mehta took the book to her lap, put on her glasses and examined it.

"Katie drew this after Anna's death?" Dr. Mehta asked.

"Yes. What does it mean?"

"Did you ask Katie about it?"

"I did. But she refuses to discuss it and was upset that I'd found it."

Dr. Mehta weighed her thoughts. "May I take a photograph of the sketch?"

Sara hesitated.

"For my own reference," Dr. Mehta said.

"Okay."

Dr. Mehta used her phone to photograph the sketch, then leaned back in her chair, studying Katie's drawing.

"What do you think it means?" Sara asked.

"It's difficult to say off the top."

"Does it look like, like Sara's pushing Anna?"

"Not necessarily," Dr. Mehta said. "She could be reaching to help. It could be any number of things."

"Katie told me she's been struggling with bad thoughts about Anna's death."

"Yes, she told me that as well."

"Maybe the drawing's related, some kind of confession, or cry for help?"

"Sara, don't read too much into it. This sketch could be Katie's crude depiction of what happened. Or it could be a manifestation of her trauma, an image reflecting a dream or a combination of things. It's difficult to say without talking to her about it. Is she aware that you've brought this to me?"

"Yes."

"Do you want me to raise it with her?"

"Yes. Maybe you can find out more. I'm concerned. I'm worried."

"I understand."

"Because there's more." Sara paused. "I don't know how to put this—it's so difficult."

"Sometimes it helps to just say it."

Sara nodded and took a deep breath.

"If there was a history of violence in our family, part of our family, could that be passed down? Could it be inherited?"

"Violence?" Dr. Mehta looked at her for a long moment. "Has there been abuse in Katie's family?"

"What?"

"Do you suspect Katie's been abused?"

"No, I—"

"Sara, before you go any further, I need to inform you that I have a legal obligation to report any suspected abuse to police."

"No." Sara's face whitened; she began shaking her head. "No, please, you misunderstood."

"I'm sorry."

"No, no, nothing like that. No, Dr. Mehta, this must remain confidential. Please."

"Alright, just so you're aware of my mandated duty. Please, continue."

Sara took a moment to collect her thoughts.

"I'm sorry this is so complicated. It's hard for me."

"I understand. Take your time."

"What I'm trying to say, to ask you, is if, if someone in Katie's family history was a violent person, could Katie inherit that, that violent trait? Could it be passed down through her genes, or something like that?"

Dr. Mehta nodded, processing the question, removing her glasses and tapping them to her chin as she thought.

"Let me ask you something that may or may not be related," Dr. Mehta said. "Within the context of Anna's tragedy, Katie had referenced *a boy*, but declines to elaborate. Is it related?"

Sara shook her head. "A few years ago, Katie was present when a boy died, and it troubled her."

"She was present when a boy died? Could you tell me more about the circumstances?"

Sara was silent.

"Sara." Dr. Mehta leaned forward. "It might help me understand the entire context of Katie's trauma."

"It was tragic. But that case is not related in any way."

"So why not tell me? Katie brought it up, so it might be related. It might help if I know a little more about it."

"No! No, it wouldn't. Please, it was complicated. Please, Dr. Mehta, we must keep this confidential. I don't want to discuss that. My worry in coming to you was about inheriting violent family traits."

"Okay." Dr. Mehta held up a palm. "We'll set aside the boy for now."

Dr. Mehta let a moment pass, slid on her glasses and continued.

"There's been research on the question of genetic predisposition, or children inheriting violent characteristics," she said. "Some studies examined the childhoods of adults arrested for serious crimes and found that in many cases their biological parents were violent. Researchers observed that it's quite possible that children can inherit violent, antisocial behavior, or impulsive aggressive behavior, from their biological parents."

"What about children raised apart from their biological parents?" Sara asked.

"The research shows that even children raised apart from their violent biological parents exhibited similar violent traits."

Sara's eyes glistened.

"However, other research has shown that being the child of a parent, or parents, who've committed violent acts, like assaults and murders, is no guarantee of inheriting the violent characteristics of their parents. What it comes down to is there's no certainty about inheriting violent traits."

Tears rolled down Sara's face.

Dr. Mehta passed her tissues from the box nearby.

"Thank you," Sara said.

"You're welcome."

Dr. Mehta glanced at the time.

"Is there anything more you want to tell me or discuss, Sara?"

"No. Thank you."

Nodding, with a little smile, Dr. Mehta subtly regarded Sara with a degree of puzzlement, as if she had not made up her mind about their conversation and Sara's revelations.

50

DRIVING EAST OUT of downtown, his nerves gnawing at him, Ryan glanced at the skyline in his rearview mirror.

Was Seattle going to be another washout?

Stopped at a red light, he checked the touchscreen of his SUV. No messages. Nothing yet on his requests for help with DNA analysis. Sometimes his sources were quick to get back with results.

Sometimes it took longer.

Ryan accepted the odds of him finding Magda's daughter were astronomical. But he had three possibilities and despite the setbacks, deep in his gut, he still believed he was close.

Isn't that what I told myself in Panama, in Canada, in Germany, the UK? Isn't that what I said after searching in Denver, Dallas, Minneapolis, Pittsburgh and Brooklyn?

So what?

I can't give up. I'll never give up.

The reality was his financial situation was not good. He'd need to find work again soon. But he'd set that issue aside until he was done, really done, in Seattle.

And he wasn't done.

The light turned green. He adjusted his hold on the wheel. He was following a weak tip that Magda lived in this region of Seattle. It was weak because his source, a retired federal agent, kept revising the name Magda was using, then the Seattle address where Magda supposedly lived.

The most recent put her in Madison Park.

He was heading east on Madison. He'd passed a branch of the Banner Bank, then a chop suey restaurant near 14th Avenue, when he got a call displayed on his touchscreen from Sonya Rule.

The name's familiar.

He used the voice activation feature to answer and said: "Hello."

A woman's face appeared.

"Hi, is this Ryan, Ryan Gardner?"

"Yes." He kept his eyes on the road.

"Hi, Ryan, I'm Sonya Rule. My brother, Shane, and I host an online true-crime show called *Tell-Tale Hearts*. I'm not sure if you've heard of it?"

"I've heard of it. Hang on, I need to pull over."

After pulling into the parking lot of a fast-food place, he said: "Okay, we're good."

"Okay, good. Ryan, we'd like to have you on as a special guest."

Surprised, Ryan glanced around the lot, thinking.

"Sonya, how did you get this number?"

"Well, like you, we have sources." Sonya had a nice smile.

Ryan nodded, still considering the invitation.

"Seriously," she said. "One of our recent guests was Beatrice Clearfield with the *Finding Magda* group."

"Beatrice, yeah, I know her. Did she pass my number to you?"

"I can't confirm or deny, as people say." Sonya flashed that nice smile again. "Our episode with Beatrice was very well received. So, I continued researching Magda's case and you. The *Vanity Fair* piece you did a while back, about your search for Carrie, broke my heart. It was so well done, so moving."

"Thanks. I appreciate the invitation but, look, I like to keep a low profile. I don't like people knowing where I am or what I'm doing. Don't want to tip them off, you know?"

"I get that. Totally. We wouldn't reveal anything like that. We'd disguise you, your voice. It'll add to the intrigue."

"I don't know."

"Ryan our audience is in the millions. We'll promote the show and we'll offer a call-in segment. You never know, someone out there may know something. We're talking millions of people."

"Hmm."

"You just wear a Covid mask, dark glasses and a ball cap, we can alter your voice. We'll use your real name and you can tell your story, but nobody will know what you look or sound like. And we won't reveal anything about your location."

He stroked his chin.

"Ryan, Magda scammed the system. She beat the death penalty, broke her deal and is living free, while the families of the people whose lives she took—well, I don't have to tell you—"

"I'll do it."

51

"WHAT'S YOUR TAKE on Gilbert Croft?"

Benton, at the wheel, asked Pierce once they got onto the freeway back to Seattle.

"I don't know," she said, biting her bottom lip and consulting her notes. "He's seventy-nine, he seemed a little confused."

"And working in the garden, he could barely lift the brick, which would be about the same weight as the stones on the cliff."

"Yeah, but..."

"But what?"

"We're not done yet."

"Well, we're closer to nailing things down, like the prosecutor wants," Benton said. "You know, Heidi rarely loses cases because she makes investigators bust their humps to make sure everything is airtight."

"As it should be, Carl."

He nodded, changing lanes.

"So now we're heading to the Focus woman, Hamilton?"

"Marilyn Hamilton."

"And once we're done there," Benton said, "I bet you we'll go full circle back to Katie Harmon."

"Don't do that, Carl."

"Do what?" He checked his mirrors to pass slower traffic.

"Don't get tunnel vision."

Marilyn Hamilton lived at the Blue Rose Bay Apartments in Seattle.

When they arrived, Pierce and Benton went to the parking lot, found Hamilton's Ford Focus and confirmed the plate matched the one in the security footage. They entered the building's secure lobby, Hamilton buzzed them in and they took the elevator to the sixteenth floor.

When Marilyn Hamilton opened the door, she was wearing stylish glasses and little makeup.

"Come in," she said, taking them to the living room.

Pierce detected the aroma of freshly brewed coffee and a hint of lilac. The apartment was cozy, tastefully balanced with love seats and a small coffee table. Everything appeared perfectly placed with no clutter: a bookcase and framed photos, plants, a nook with a desk, a laptop, a wall map. Pierce noticed the words *Field Guide* on a book on the desk.

"I just made coffee. Would you like some?"

"Absolutely," Benton said. "Thank you."

Hamilton brought their coffee on a tray from the kitchen. They fixed their cups to their preference, then began the interview. As they had with Croft in Issaquah, the detectives related a summary of the case and explained this was a routine follow-up, since investigators didn't get Hamilton's statement at the outset.

This time, Pierce pulled Benton's tablet from her bag and gave it to him. He logged in and cued up the park's security camera video, set it to play, then handed his tablet to Hamilton, who held it while watching.

When it ended, Hamilton shook her head slowly.

"It's so sad," she said. "I followed it on the news. It breaks my heart to know I was there when it happened. Such a waste of a young life. How can I help?" Hamilton handed the tablet back to Benton.

"What time did you arrive at the park that day?" Pierce asked.

"Oh, let me think, it was early. Isn't the time marked on the video?"

"It shows when you left," Benton said. "Not when you arrived."

"Oh, I see, well, it was early when I left here. Maybe around six? It was an hour's drive, so I'm guessing I got there around seven a.m."

"Why go there so early?" Benton asked.

Hamilton nodded to the field guide on her desk.

"I'm a birdwatcher."

"You got up before six and drove out to Sparrow Song Park to watch birds?" Benton said.

"Yes, it's relaxing. I enjoy it. That day, I was looking for western meadowlarks and western bluebirds. They're so pretty. I'm not an expert, but it's been a hobby for years." She indicated the wall maps next to her desk. "Sometimes I go with nature groups."

"Are those bird maps?" Pierce asked.

"Yes, the birding groups know the best bird trails in the state."

"You were alone on that day, though?"

"Yes."

"What trail were you on?" Benton cued up a map of the park on his tablet and handed it back to Hamilton. "Tap your route."

"Mmm." Hamilton studied the map, then touched her finger to the screen. "Here, and went along here."

"Did you take binoculars?" Pierce asked.

"Oh, yes, tool of the trade."

"And you listen to the birdsong?"

"Yes, I have an app on my phone that can identify the bird according to its song."

"Did you see anyone else that day?"

"No, I was there fairly early because that's when the birds are most active. By late morning they settle down."

"Did you hear anything out of the ordinary?"

Hamilton shook her head, returning Benton's tablet.

"No. I'm sorry. I don't think I'm being very helpful."

"You're doing fine," Benton said.

"I was shattered when I learned about the girl's death on the news when I got home. When I realized I was there when it happened, it just broke my heart."

The detectives waited for her to collect herself.

Benton surveyed the framed family photos on the bookshelf: a little boy at an ice rink in hockey gear, a little girl on a pony, a little girl with an umbrella wearing a bright raincoat and splashing in puddles. A boy and a white-haired man fishing, several wedding and graduation photos.

Benton nodded to the array. "Your family, I take it?"

"Yes."

Glancing briefly at the pictures, Pierce said: "You have a nice family. Are you married?"

"Widowed. My husband, Frank, died about ten years ago. He was a mortgage broker. Had a heart attack at his desk."

"I'm sorry," Pierce said.

"Do you work outside the home?" Benton asked.

"I did. I was a legal transcriptionist, but I'm semi-retired. I do some contract work at home."

For the next several minutes, Pierce went over aspects of Hamilton's account of her time at the park. When they'd finished, Benton passed his tablet to Pierce, who slipped it into her bag. They thanked Hamilton and she walked them to her door.

"It's awful, just so sad," Hamilton said. "The news said she fell taking a selfie. Is that what happened?"

"We're still investigating," Benton said.

"What else could've happened? She didn't commit— I mean—what else?"

Pierce and Benton traded glances.

"We're still investigating," Pierce said.

52

Seattle, Washington

KATIE RAN HER thumb over the smooth neck of the hand-carved giraffe.

"Where in Africa did you get him?"

"Senegal," Dr. Mehta said. "That's a country in West Africa."

Sitting on the couch in Dr. Mehta's office, holding the carving, Katie traced her fingertips along its sides.

"Did you buy him at a store?"

"No, it was a market, a big, busy market."

"It's so pretty."

"Like your necklace."

Katie nodded. "I wear it everywhere, so I'll always remember her."

"I see that. Tell me, how are you sleeping these days?"

Keeping her eyes on the giraffe, Katie shrugged.

"Are you still having bad dreams?"

"Yes."

"Want to tell me about them?"

"Well, they're really weird," Katie said, her eyes on the giraffe.

"Go ahead."

"In one, Anna and I are in the park but it's me, I'm the one falling and I'm feeling what it's like to fall. I'm flying down to the ground and my body smashes on the rocks and there's blood everywhere. The river is all blood and I'm floating in it and I'm dead."

"Is that how it ends?"

"No, as I'm floating away Anna's looking down from the cliff and screaming at me, screaming *why, why, why?* Pretty weird, huh?"

"I think that's how the trauma, the shock of this, is still rippling through your mind."

Katie said nothing.

"You know your mom showed me the drawing you made? Are you okay to talk about it?"

Katie shrugged.

Dr. Mehta got her phone and brought up the drawing so she and Katie could see it together.

"What does this sketch mean to you?" Dr. Mehta asked.

Katie shrugged, her face registering unease.

"It's what happened on the cliff," Katie said.

"Why did you draw it?"

"I don't know. I just did."

"Why don't you tell me exactly what's happening in your picture."

"We're on the cliff and Anna goes to take her selfie. I tell her to be careful but she doesn't listen to me. She keeps backing up and I'm reaching out, like, to save her—but—"

Dr. Mehta waits for Katie to finish.

"But I have these good and bad thoughts." Katie stops, her face is blank.

"What are your thoughts?" Dr. Mehta asked. "What are your good and bad thoughts?"

"I want to help her, to save her. At the same time, I see her there, I— For like, a second, it's a lightning flash in my head and—" Katie freezes with her mouth open, staring at the sketch. "No, I can't even say what the bad thoughts are because then—then Anna's gone, she falls."

Katie blinks several times.

"And Anna's screaming for me to help, with screams I still hear, and I'm like why, why is this happening? Why didn't you listen to me? Why? Why was I thinking those thoughts— why, why, why?"

Dr. Mehta put her phone away and made a few quick notes.

"We've had a number of visits now, haven't we, Katie?"

Katie nodded.

"Do you feel comfortable talking with me like this in private?"

"Uh-huh, I like it."

"That's good because there are a couple of new things I'd like to talk about today. Would that be okay?"

"Yes."

"Katie, has anyone ever hurt you in any way that you haven't told anyone about?"

She lifted her head from the giraffe. "Like punch me or call me names and stuff?"

"Stuff like that. Or anything else, like touch you in a way that you felt was wrong. Or made you do something that made you feel awkward, or uncomfortable. Has anything like that ever happened to you, with grown-ups, or kids, with relatives, or friends, or strangers?"

Katie took a moment to comprehend what Dr. Mehta had asked her.

"Katie, even if someone told you to never tell anyone about it, or made you scared, it's okay to tell me here, in private. I'm here to listen and to help."

Katie thought for a long time.

"No, nobody's done anything like that to me, but once I—"

Katie's head snapped back to the giraffe in her lap.

"Sorry?" Dr. Mehta said. "You once what?"

Katie played with the giraffe.

"It's okay, Katie, finish what you were going to say."

"Once a boy said mean things to me. Then something happened that—"

Katie halted.

"Then what, Katie? Go ahead."

"No, I forgot, I'm not supposed to talk about it."

"It might help me to help you if—"

"No, I don't want to say any more today."

Dr. Mehta let Katie's answer stand for several seconds, deciding not to push the subject, while watching her closely.

"Okay, if you want to talk about any of this at any time, you know I'm here to listen and help you, okay?"

"Okay."

53

ON PHONES AND monitors across the US and around the world, the intro and montage for *Tell-Tale Hearts* fades to completion and the hosts appear.

"Hello and welcome." Sonya, in her red-framed glasses and headphones, waves from the studio table.

"I'm Sonya. This is my brother, Shane."

Beside her, Shane taps the brim of his New York Jets ball cap.

"Welcome to another episode of *Tell-Tale Hearts*," he says. "We're so pumped for this one because of our special guest. But first things first."

They give a rundown of the show's background, the advisory about disturbing content, then acknowledge their ever-growing audience.

"As you may recall," Shane says, "in a previous episode we looked at the case of Herman and Magda Vryker."

"They're the married couple who committed at least seven murders in 1994 and 1995 across Montana, Idaho and Washington," Sonya says.

"Your response was phenomenal," Shane says. "So, today we're going to revisit it from a different perspective."

"Whoa, bro, look at everyone joining us today already— it's awesome."

"Let's get to it," he says. "For new viewers and those who aren't familiar with the Vrykers, a little refresher."

For the next several minutes, Sonya recaps events as a slideshow of photos from the case appears on the screen, culminating with Herman and Magda's arrests, Magda glaring into the camera with icy intensity.

"It's one of the most horrendous stories we know, and it's far from over," Sonya says. "To take us deeper into it, we're honored to have Ryan Gardner as our guest. Ryan's sister, Carrie Gardner, and her friend Willow Walker were among the people murdered by the Vrykers."

"A show note," Shane says. "Ryan keeps a very low profile. We're protecting his identity by disguising his appearance, voice and location, for reasons that will become evident. And in addition to our live texts and posts, we'll have a call-in segment, for you to ask Ryan questions."

The screen splits and Ryan appears. He wears a long-sleeved, faded denim shirt, a Covid mask, dark glasses and a ball cap. His backdrop is a plain wall with no window or details.

"Welcome, Ryan," Sonya says.

"Thank you for inviting me." His voice sounds normal, but it's not his.

"We thank you," she says. "We know you don't usually do interviews, but you lived, and continue to live, with the pain of this case."

"Yes."

"Off the top, you believe Magda Vryker gamed the system?"

"I do."

"Do you believe that wherever she's living, she remains a danger to the public?"

"I do."

"And do you believe she knows where the bodies are located?"

"Yes."

"And your goal, your quest, really, is to find her, confront her and get her to reveal where your sister, Carrie, and all the others are located?"

"That's it."

"You've pretty much devoted your life to finding Carrie— appearing even more determined in the last seven years after Magda's release from prison and her vanishing into a new identity and new life."

"Yes."

"I have to say," Sonya says, "in doing my research, I was really impressed with how you presented everything in your in-depth piece for *Vanity Fair* several years ago. I urge everyone to read Ryan's article." A link pops up on the screen. "It's as much a mind-blowing piece of first-person journalism as it is a study in anguish and love. It's so good."

"Thank you." Ryan clears his throat.

"Take us through your family life and what it was like for you growing up with your big sister, Carrie. Help us get to know her."

"Well, Carrie was a lot of fun."

"You were kind enough to share some personal photos, which we'll put up now, and we've blurred anything recent that might identify you."

"Yeah, so Carrie was full of life, you know, she radiated with it."

As Ryan reminisces, photos of them laughing together in the photo booth at the Westfarms mall near Hartford, Connecticut, appear. As he continues, a montage of images plays of Carrie with him, their parents, during family events, outings, parties and milestones.

Then the photo his mother took at the Hartford airport, seeing Carrie off for her return to Arizona State University. Carrie is hugging Ryan.

"That's the last time we saw her," Ryan says.

While the photo remains up, Sonya continues.

"Ryan, do you recall what Carrie said to you that day? You don't have to say, I mean, if it's too personal."

"Yeah, it's okay." He clears his throat. "She said: 'Watch over Mom and Dad for me and be good. You're the best little brother in the world.'"

When the image changes to the split screen, Sonya brushes her eyes, then resumes.

"Can you take us through what happened next, the impact the case had on your family and how you came to pursue Magda?"

Ryan relates the horror of Carrie's disappearance and how things played out over the years for the families of other victims, his parents and for him. As he speaks, the screen displays photos of Carrie and Willow, with the van loaded with their belongings.

"They were so excited about driving to Alaska. My mom was worried, really worried. I think she had a bad feeling in her heart about it. Not long after they left Tempe, we stopped hearing from Carrie."

The screen shows photos of the Burger King in Idaho Falls,

EVERYTHING SHE FEARED   301

where Carrie and Willow were last seen. Then a photo with their faces on the FBI missing persons poster.

"And when the FBI told my parents Carrie was dead, it broke them. It was as if this claw had ripped a hole in our lives."

"I'm so sorry, Ryan," Sonya says.

Ryan continues on about how the case evolved, what he'd learned about the Vrykers: how Magda cheated the death penalty, worked her deal and beat the system. How, after becoming a reporter, Ryan had vowed to find Carrie's remains and bring her home.

"Magda refused to allow me to visit her in prison," he says. "She granted no interviews to any news outlet. She never answered my letters.

"As a reporter, in Hartford, then Chicago, I used every skill, every source, every resource and avenue I could to learn every detail of Magda and Herman's lives.

"I found out that Herman was in a doomsday cult, but followed conspiracy theories that were so strange they kicked him out. He was a prepper, a trucker who knew every back road in the region when he hooked up with Magda at the slaughterhouse. She thought he was her destiny."

More photos appear of Herman Vryker; in most of the images he has a full beard and his eyes are burning through the locks of his wild mountain-man hair.

"Magda was like something that fell from the sky. No one ever determined where she came from," Ryan says. "She had an extremely high IQ. She's suspected of killing a neighbor girl by luring her to her death in a well months after a dispute over a doll. They were both seven years old at the time and nothing could be proven. As she got older, Magda became fascinated with death, was obsessed with numbers, dates. She had a passion for numerology. Ultimately, she read her daughter Hayley's birthdate as a sign and used her to lure victims to their deaths. Hayley was a toddler at the time."

"Horrifying."

"When Magda's sentence ended, I was certain I was on top of things, that I was ready to confront her, and I went to the prison," he says. "But a few days before her release, she'd been secretly transferred to another facility and released quietly to avoid media attention. My complaints and demands for information were futile. She'd changed her name and vanished. The fact that while in prison she learned Spanish and French opened the possibility of her disappearing to any number of countries.

"I traveled across the country and around the world following leads, searching for Magda, always working alone. Sometimes the amateur sleuth groups would pass me tips, but I preferred to work alone.

"And despite all the records I have, and as much as I know about her, I don't have all the pieces," he says. "Many records are sealed."

"Thank you for that," Shane says. "We see messages are flooding in and the phone line is lit, so if you're ready, Ryan, we can go to them now."

"I'm ready."

"Okay, we ask for first name and location. On the phone we have?"

"Nick in Newark. Ryan, I just want to say what you're doing is noble, man, and Magda is a monster who should burn in hell."

"Thank you, Nick," Ryan says.

"Next caller," Shane says.

"Hi. Judith, Virgin Islands. We've got to let people rehabilitate. Magda served twenty years. It's been seven years since her release and she hasn't killed anyone since, has she?"

"Not that we know of," Ryan says.

"Let me ask you something, Judith," Shane says. "Would you be comfortable having Magda as your neighbor?"

"Well, I think, uhm, well…"

"You don't sound comfortable pondering it," Shane says. "Next caller?"

"Yeah, this is Sean in Boston. My family knew the Worrells, so I've been following this, too."

"Their case is believed to be the first," Ryan says.

"Yeah, Ryan, so are you also looking for Magda's daughter, Hayley? It might help you find Magda?"

"Yes, Sean," Ryan says. "I'm looking."

"Next caller," Shane says.

"This is Jesse, from Kingston, Canada. She served less than three years for each person she killed—that's a horrible injustice. I hope you find her, Ryan."

"Thanks."

"Next caller?"

"Nicole in Atlanta. Ryan, do you think you'll ever find Magda?"

"I do."

"And what will you do if she refuses to tell you what you need to know?"

"I'll cross that bridge, Nicole."

"We're getting texts, too. This message is from Lauren in Dallas. 'What's with your obsession, Ryan? What are you getting out of this? The woman served her time. Let her be.'"

"I respect your opinion, but I don't agree with it," Ryan says.

"Back to callers. Next," Shane says.

"Hi, I'm Darby from Melbourne, Australia. Magda will never be a proper member of society. I doubt her claim that she was a victim of her husband's abuse. I think she was the brains behind their killing rampage. The sickest aspect is how she used her child, her own baby. So evil. She should be locked up."

"I agree," Ryan says.

"Next caller," Shane says.

"Juanita, from Mexico City. I hope you find Magda and can bring your sister home, Ryan."

"Thank you, Juanita," Ryan says.

"Next caller," Shane says.

"I'm Lynn, calling from Chicago. Ryan, you can save yourself a lot of grief. You're wasting your time."

"Excuse me?"

"I have concrete information that Magda was using the name Sharon Ellen Vernay when she was killed five years ago in a car crash in Ontario, Canada."

A long silence follows before Ryan breaks it.

"You have this verified?"

"Yes."

"Lynn," Sonya says, "Ontario's a large province. Do you know where this crash happened?"

"In the northern part along the Trans-Canada Highway."

"That doesn't really narrow it down," Sonya says. "Are you sure about this?"

"Absolutely. Magda's dead."

"How did you come by this information, Lynn?" Ryan asks. "Is it documented?"

"I have relatives in law enforcement, with the Ontario Provincial Police."

"Would you be willing to help me verify this information?" Ryan asks.

"Just do a little digging. You're a skilled pro, you can confirm it yourself."

The call ends, punctuated with a moment of silence.

"What do you think, Ryan?" Shane asks.

"I don't know. I'll definitely look into it."

"Next caller," Shane said.

"Wendy in Salt Lake City. I think Magda has to go back to prison. We're not safe with her out there after the unspeakable crimes she's committed."

"Thanks, Wendy," Ryan says.

"We have an interesting text message from Michelle, in New York. She writes, 'Ryan, a relative of mine, who was knowledgeable about Montana Women's Prison, passed away a few years ago. Among their belongings I found some records related to Magda Vryker that were never made public that you may find helpful. How do I get in touch?'"

"Wow. Thanks, Michelle," Ryan says. "You can reach me through Sonya and Shane. I'd like to see those records, thank you."

"Very interesting," Sonya says. "We'll reach out to Michelle as well."

"Last caller before we wrap up," Shane says.

"Ian from Christchurch, New Zealand. God bless you, Ryan, we must never forget the victims."

"Thank you, Ian," Ryan says.

"Any parting words before we sign off, Ryan?" Sonya asks.

"Only to reiterate that I believe Magda knows where the bodies are. I think she'll reoffend because she feeds on the power. And to your audience, I say, she could be living next door to you, which is something to consider. And thank you for having me on, guys."

"A huge thanks to Ryan Gardner and to you, our audience," Shane says.

The show's opening music plays again against images of deserted gritty city streets at night before the screen fades to black.

54

Seattle, Washington

BEFORE RETURNING TO their office, Pierce and Benton stopped at forensics to see Kelly Jensen, a senior analyst.

Jensen looked at the laptop and tablet Pierce had set on her worktable beside her and said, "Just these two?"

"Yes," Pierce said. "We completed the request, and the chain forms."

"We wiped the surfaces clean before going out," Benton said. "And we tagged Pierce's laptop for Gilbert Croft and my tablet for Marilyn Hamilton. Anything you get beyond our prints for them would be helpful."

"I'll see what I can lift, but it's going to take time. We're preparing court cases, and we're short-staffed and backlogged."

"Isn't that always the way?" Benton said. "Any luck recovering prints from the rock?"

"That's going to take time, too. It's next to impossible to get prints from a stone," Jensen said. "But we're consulting with the FBI, police in Israel and a university in Scotland on new techniques. You never know."

"Thank you, Kelly," Pierce said. "Keep us posted."

"Wait," Jensen said. "Do you have everything you need from these devices? Because I may have to keep them for a bit."

"Everything's backed up on our desktops and phones," Pierce said.

Two hours later, Pierce and Benton were at the table in the conference room, ready for the next case-status meeting.

Acker, Grotowski and Tilden were there, too, studying their phones and checking notes in advance of others joining.

While waiting and reviewing her notes, Pierce thought back to what Gilbert Croft had said while they were looking at photos of his family—how teenage girls were *boy crazy*, could be rebellious, and a handful. You have to be stern with teens.

Anna Shaw was seventeen and had just broken up with her boyfriend. But Croft wouldn't have known that before the tragedy. His comment couldn't be related. Or could it?

Dismissing it, Pierce's thoughts shifted to Marilyn Hamilton. Something about her, and her apartment, niggled at Pierce.

Something felt off, but I can't put my finger on it.

Notifications chimed and Oscar Neale, a commander from the North Precinct, then Heidi Wong from the Prosecuting Attorney's Office, logged into the conference. Their faces appeared on the large screen at one end of the room.

"Sorry for the delay," Wong said.

"No problem," Acker said. "We're good to go. Kim, if you will?"

"Just a quick update," Pierce said. "We interviewed the two people recorded on the parking lot video, who were leaving the park at the time of Anna Shaw's death. Here's a refresher."

Pierce replayed the video, showing the man walking to his Camry.

"Gilbert Croft, seventy-nine, from Issaquah. Widowed, retired Boeing worker. He was at the park for a walk. Heard nothing, saw nothing. He seems weak, almost forgetful. We're looking to cross him off."

"We found no criminal history for him," Benton said.

The video then showed the woman walking to her Ford.

"Marilyn Hamilton, sixty, semi-retired transcriptionist who lives alone in town. Birdwatching is her hobby. She said she was at the park looking for meadowlarks and bluebirds. Heard nothing but birds. No criminal history. We're ready to cross her off, too."

"We're waiting on our forensic people who're endeavoring to get Hamilton's and Croft's prints and run them," Benton said.

"How did you obtain them?" Wong asked.

"Shared our laptop and tablet during the interviews," Benton said.

"Alright." Wong made a note. "So, it appears we're on the verge of eliminating Hamilton and Croft. We've eliminated John James Smith, and we have nothing beyond circumstance for a case against the boyfriend, Tanner Bishop. So, where are we elsewhere?"

"Larry, Lyle?" Acker said.

"Regrouped with the North Precinct with divers to search again for Shaw's phone," Tilden said. "We looked on the bank and in the water. Negative."

"It's possible an animal took it," said Oscar Neale, the commander from the North Precinct. "We'll go at it again, farther downriver."

"We ran Sara Harmon's background again through all the databases," Grotowski said. "Nothing. Also checked with SPD.

No complaint history on Harmon's house. To be thorough, we'll try some other avenues."

Grotowski paged through his notes. "And, we've gone back through all statements from the Sunny Days kids and the supervisors. We recanvassed and ran background on every person in the park when deputies first responded."

"And?" Wong asked.

"No change, nothing emerged," Grotowski said.

"And the time gap?" Wong asked.

"We checked it again," Grotowski said. "We still put it at approximately four to six or seven minutes."

"So, the only person we can put on the cliff with Anna Shaw is Katie Harmon," Wong said, then raised another aspect. "Where are we with getting prints from that rock with Shaw's blood and hair traces that the ME identified as a weapon?"

"Forensics says it's a long shot, but they're still working on it," Pierce said. "They're consulting with other agencies on new techniques."

Wong flipped through notes on her legal pad.

"And have we established that a nine-year-old girl, like Katie Harmon, can lift a six-pound rock, carry it about seven yards to the cliff, lift it up, then drop it like a weapon on Anna Shaw?"

"We're still working on that," Grotowski said.

"Anything else to update?" Wong asked.

"That's it for now," Pierce said.

Wong paged through her notes, tapping her pen on her pad.

"Heidi, it looks clear," Benton started, "that Katie Harmon was the only person with Anna Shaw when she fell. The rock is a weapon and Katie came out of it with Shaw's gold necklace."

"It *looks* that way, Carl," Wong said. "But I refuse to move on her until the case is solid. You guys are doing good work, diminishing doubt, making the case stronger little by little. But to charge a nine-year-old with murder is a complex matter. We're not there yet. We need to keep working."

55

DR. MEHTA SAW Sara waving to her in the bustling food court of Northgate Station, a mall in North Seattle.

It had been a couple of days since Dr. Mehta's last session with Katie, and, aside from a short conversation that day, she'd been unable to talk to Sara about it until now.

Dr. Mehta had been swamped with lectures and commitments. She preferred not to see patients outside of her office, but Sara wasn't her patient. In fact, it was Sara who'd requested they meet here because she was ending her shift at the diner and would be here.

Meeting at the mall wasn't ideal, but the time worked.

Moreover, after talking to Katie about the drawing, Dr. Mehta needed to convey her concerns about the other unresolved issues. She'd only touched the surface of Katie's deeper problems, especially with Sara raising the possibility of violence in her family's history.

Maneuvering through the hectic food court, Dr. Mehta arrived at Sara's table.

"Thanks for meeting me," Sara said. "I'm sorry to put you out."

"Not at all," Dr. Mehta said. "I was coming from a lecture and I have a meeting soon at the medical center nearby. My apologies, I've been busy."

Sara surveyed the tables around them, satisfied that the activity and din of the crowded food court would make it impossible for anyone to overhear them. Still she leaned toward Dr. Mehta.

"So, in our last chat in your office, right after you talked to Katie about her drawing, you said you had new concerns."

"Yes." Dr. Mehta withdrew her phone from her purse and began tapping. "I've made a few notes."

"What does the drawing mean?"

"According to Katie, it's a sketch of what happened. Anna was taking a selfie, backing closer to the cliff's edge, and Katie pleaded with her to stop before she fell."

"So, in her drawing, she's trying to save Anna?"

"Yes," Dr. Mehta said. "According to Katie."

"It's not an attempt at confessing to doing something wrong?"

"Well, no." Dr. Mehta looked at her notes.

Sara covered her mouth with her hands, blinking tears of relief.

"Sara, that's one level of interpretation of the drawing."

"One level?"

"I have to put this within the context of Katie's cryptic references to her *bad thoughts*, and to the boy, who you said died in her presence. I also have to weigh it with your raising the subject of inheriting violent traits from violent relatives, and violence in your family's history."

The relief left Sara's face.

"What're you saying?"

"The trauma of Anna Shaw's death may have triggered something about past actions, or abuse."

Sara shook her head.

"At the outset," Dr. Mehta said, "I attributed Katie's sense of guilt as a by-product of Anna's death. Fallout arising from the trauma of being with her when she died. But Katie's conflicting thoughts appear to be intensifying."

"What're you thinking?"

"I need more information."

"More information. What kind of information?"

"What happened with the boy that Katie keeps bringing up?"

"What do you mean?"

"I think there's something beneath the surface with the boy, or in another previous incident. Was Katie bullied? What exactly happened?"

"No, I don't want to—"

"I also need to know, for a clear understanding, about any violence in your family history, how, or what impact it's had, or *is having* on Katie—what all of this brings to bear on her."

Sara stared down at the table, shaking her head. "I'm not— I don't know." She bit her bottom lip.

"Sara, I need this information if I'm going to help."

Sara looked at Dr. Mehta. "You said you also have a duty to report any suspicions of abuse."

"Yes, but I'm here to help."

"I'm afraid, terrified actually, of you misconstruing or misinterpreting things and revealing them to other parties."

"Sara, I understand your hesitation," Dr. Mehta said. "But you must put Katie's safety above your fears. I'm asking you to trust my professional judgment."

"I don't know," Sara said. "It was a terrible thing. I just don't know."

Another long moment passed before Dr. Mehta broke it.

"Let me be as frank and honest as I can," she said. "You and Katie are grappling with significant inner turmoil over other issues I believe are related to, or have arisen from, Anna Shaw's death."

Sara looked at her.

"But you won't tell me, or help me understand, anything about them. And I can't help you if you won't help me with the information I need."

Sara said nothing.

An alarm bleated on Dr. Mehta's phone before she silenced it.

"I'm so sorry, I need to get going to the medical center," Dr. Mehta said. "Sara, think about what I said, and we can talk some more when you bring Katie to the next session."

Sara thanked Dr. Mehta and watched her disappear into the crowded food court. Then Sara sat alone for the longest time, her thoughts swirling, not aware that far across the noisy food court, one person had been watching.

56

IN THE TIME after he was on *Tell-Tale Hearts*, Ryan drove through the Seattle metro area, the miles rolling by as he sorted his thoughts.

The person on the show who'd promised him documents hadn't followed through. And the back of his mind still echoed with the claim from the caller insisting Magda was dead.

Maybe I am wasting my time?

It had always been a fear that he was chasing a ghost.

Will Seattle be another failure, like the other cities?

Stopped at a light, he glanced at his phone and Carrie's picture.

No, I'm not done here.

He couldn't rule out any of the women on his list yet. He was still waiting on his request for DNA analysis. It wasn't over in Seattle. Not yet. One thing he needed to do was deal with the claim that Magda had died in a car crash in Canada.

Ryan returned to his apartment to work on it. When he got to his desk, his phone rang. The ID displayed and he answered.

"Hi, Mom."

"Hi, Ryan, how are you?"

It'd been a long time since their last call.

"Hanging in there, and you?"

"Day by day, son. So, I see from the return address, you're in Seattle this time?"

"Yes."

"I saw the show with you in disguise, the *Tell-Tale Hearts* show."

"What did you think?"

A heavy silence passed between them.

"You know what I think, Ryan."

He didn't respond as the quiet between them grew taut.

"I am concerned," she said. "When will this end?"

"You know when."

"It's been years. You need to build your life. This can't be your life."

"Mom."

"I can't lose both of my children and my husband to that monster."

"Mom, please."

"Maybe you could get back with Olivia, you know, settle down and—"

"Mom, how's Dad?"

She said nothing, as if deciding whether or not to answer.

"He called me a week ago. It was three in the morning, he'd been drinking, and—" Her voice broke. "He said Carrie had come to him in a dream to say she was alive."

Ryan allowed her time to compose herself.

"I told him to go back to sleep," she said. "He has to accept that she's gone forever, we know that, and—and that monster—"

"Mom, this pain is why I can't stop, I'll never stop. And this time, part of me feels I'm close."

"Are you? Were you close in Brooklyn, were you close in Pittsburgh, or Minneapolis, or Dallas, or any of those other places?"

"Mom, please."

"Maybe the monster's finally dead, like that woman on the show said."

"We can't believe that. We can't let her keep Carrie and all the others. We can't let her win."

"Ryan, I'm so tired."

"Me, too. But we can't give up, alright?"

He glanced at his files stacked near him.

"Mom, you've had all the samples I sent you by courier for some time now. You're analyzing the DNA at your lab and sending it to Willow's dad, right? His police friends are still helping us? You're still helping me like you promised?"

"Just like every other time, but, Ryan, we don't know how much longer we can do this, how much longer I can get other people to help us."

"You know it's crucial, Mom. Magda's DNA is in the system. Our only hope of finding her is comparing the samples I send you to hers. It's the only way to confirm we've found her."

His mother said nothing.

"We're still a team, right, Mom?"

"Ryan, I'm tired. I don't know how much longer *I* can do this."

"Mom, we just have to keep doing this until we get a match."

"We can't go on like this forever."

"Mom, we're going to find her. We'll find Magda and we'll find Carrie and all the others. I swear."

57

Shoreline, Washington

"HOW ARE THINGS GOING?" Pierce asked her son as she drove.

"Alright, I guess."

She glanced at the gift-wrapped box on the console between them.

"It was nice of Amber to invite you to her birthday party."

"Yeah."

"I was surprised you said yes. I mean, you don't even know her. I'm proud of you, willing to meet new people and maybe make new friends."

Ethan shrugged.

"Your drum is coming along."

"Yeah, I like making it. When are we going to Arizona?"

"A month, or so, maybe. We'll see." Pierce knew Ethan had

something on his mind, something he'd been carrying for a while. "Anything you want to talk about?"

"Mom, did kids call you and Dad names when you were my age?"

And there it is, Pierce thought.

"Is someone calling you names?"

Ethan turned to his window.

"Just one kid at school."

"Who?"

"Arlee."

"What did Arlee call you?"

Ethan didn't respond.

"It's okay to tell me."

He dropped his voice. "Half-breed."

She tensed as a million hurts in her life knifed through her heart. Her first reaction was to go all momma grizzly on the situation, call Arlee's parents, call the school.

But it's not a perfect world. Besides, that wouldn't help Ethan.

She pushed all of it aside, glad that he'd found the courage to tell her.

"What did you do when he said that?" she asked.

"I just walked away."

"I don't know this Arlee—is he a friend?"

"Not really, he's just in my class."

"Did you tell the teacher?"

"No."

"Does he keep calling you that name?"

"Yeah, but he never used to."

"Really?"

"He started when I saw he got an F on a science test. No one else knew or saw, but I saw it, by accident, walking by his desk. He looked like he was all embarrassed and said, 'Mind your own eff-ing business, half-breed.'"

"I see," she said. "Well, maybe in that moment, he needed to feel he had the power over you to make you feel bad, too. And it sounds like he wants to keep it, you know? So don't give it to him."

Ethan considered that.

"What do you think you should do next time Arlee says it?"

"Just keep walking away, hang out with other kids."

"See how it goes."

"Okay, I'll try that."

"Is this why you decided to come to the party, to meet new kids? I mean, like I told you, I'm going to help because Amber's dad is my friend from work. And it's nice that she invited you, too. But you surprised me."

"You said there was going to be hot dogs, cake and ice cream."

"Ah," she said.

"How could I resist, Mom?"

They both laughed as Pierce continued driving to Shoreline, a few miles north of the city at the edge of King County.

Over a dozen girls and boys squealed and shouted, dodging and darting, playing tag in the big backyard of Lyle and Rita Tilden's bungalow.

Their daughter, Amber, was turning ten today.

"Thank you for coming to my party, Ethan."

Amber and her mother welcomed them. The yard and deck were festooned with ribbons, pinwheels and balloons. Thanking Ethan for his gift, Rita placed it with the others while Amber took him to the snack table for a drink and chips. Pierce found an empty lawn chair, and sat with Lyle Tilden, Art Acker and Larry Grotowski.

"Carl couldn't make it," Acker said.

Pierce nodded, knowing what none of the others knew.

Benton had taken his wife to the hospital for a new treatment. But she said nothing as the conversation fell to sports and then the case.

"We're going farther downstream searching the river tomorrow," Tilden said.

"Going to run background on Sara in Canada," Grotowski said.

"Sounds good," Acker said. "Let's see how we do."

The afternoon progressed with the kids sitting at picnic tables to eat hot dogs, pizza and nachos. Then came the cake. Everyone sang to Amber, who blew out the candles before her mother cut pieces, serving them up with ice cream. Then the celebration moved on to the opening of presents. Ethan's was a bracelet-making kit, which Amber loved.

Later, Lyle Tilden issued a sharp whistle.

"Kids, who wants to play a game where the winners get an extra goody bag?"

All the kids cheered to play.

Tilden glanced at Acker, Grotowski and Pierce.

"Okay, watch me, this is what you do."

In a corner of the yard, Tilden had placed six vinyl cement circular weights from his dumbbell set. Each one weighed 7.5 pounds.

"You pick up one of these, if you can. Carry it as fast as you can to this spot." Tilden had used ribbons to make a path about ten yards away. "Lift it up as high as you can and drop it. We're going to time you. Whoever's fastest, wins. Can you do that?"

The kids cheered.

"All girls aged nine, put up your hands. Okay, thanks. You go first, Marcie. Then Emily, Amy and Lorella, and anyone else. You can go, too, Amber."

The detectives got ready. Grotowski was the timer. Pierce prepared to record a video.

One by one each girl hefted the dumbbell and hurried the distance to the drop point. Grunting and straining, each girl hoisted the weight high—some got it over their heads—then thrust it to the ground.

"Okay, girls ten and older, Isabel, Miranda, Lucy."

Each girl completed the task before Tilden moved on to the boys, with Ethan taking a turn.

"What's the result, Judge Grotowski?" Tilden asked.

"I think it's too close to call. Everyone wins!"

The kids cheered, then moved on to play Pin the Tail on the Donkey, under Rita's supervision.

The detectives huddled in a corner of the yard to discuss their experiment. Acker stressed it was unscientific, unofficial and definitely not evidentiary.

"But it demonstrates that it's possible for a nine-year-old girl to lift the rock, quickly carry it several yards and drop it over the cliff," Grotowski said.

All the detectives nodded as Pierce replayed the video.

The strain in the girls' faces as they labored with the rock evoked other images in her mind. She thought about how in the *Lord of the Flies* a boulder was rolled onto Piggy, stirring the horror of children killing children.

And watching now, as girl after girl threw down the weight, Pierce thought of Katie Harmon thrusting a rock on Anna Shaw to end her life.

58

SARA CLEANED HER house with vigor in an effort to escape her torment.

There was no school today. Katie was out with Tamika and Adina while Sara was home alone, agonizing over everything.

She regretted having told Dr. Mehta about Katie's drawing, and asking her if violent behavior could be passed down.

The research shows it can happen.

But Dr. Mehta had misunderstood and taken the situation in another direction.

She wants to know more about everything—including the boy.

No, I can't tell her how Katie almost seemed content after what happened with the boy. How Katie had nightmares, then made a drawing. I burned it because I had to. I had to because she had nothing to do with what happened to the boy. I had to keep it secret then. I have to keep it secret now. It's the only way to stay safe— especially now. Dr. Mehta has made it clear she's obligated to report her suspicions of any harm or abuse. And now it seems like she intends to do it.

What have I done? And those detectives had their own suspicions about Katie. But ever since they came to talk to Katie, I haven't heard a word from them.

Why?

Sara's worries spun amid the loud cyclonic suction of her vacuum cleaner. She felt like she was losing control when her phone vibrated, pulling her out of it.

She checked the message.

It was an automated, timed reminder that she'd pledged to participate in the upcoming book sale for a North Seattle charity for literacy. There was a deadline for donations. She'd forgotten and needed to deliver a box of old books she had promised the group.

The box was upstairs.

In the attic.

She'd forgotten to bring it downstairs.

She was rooted where she stood.

Just go get it.

Steeling herself, Sara hurried upstairs, opening the door at the end of the hall. She switched on her phone's flashlight and climbed the creaking stairs.

She glanced at the cardboard box in the shadows near the wooden chest that held the old news stories about Magda and Herman Vryker. Those headlines were still buried deep, but she could feel them, almost hear them screaming at her, beckoning her to the undeniable truth of her life.

No, no. I am not like them. Katie is not like them.

But did Katie inherit their traits? Dr. Mehta said it was possible.

Sara thought of the sketch.

What did Katie do on the cliff?

Sara forced herself to turn from the wooden chest. She raked her light across the attic floor. Turning, she found the box of books. She picked it up and carried it carefully down the narrow staircase, kicking the door closed behind her.

Taking a breath, she placed the box of books on the kitchen table. She used a damp cloth to wipe them, one by one, smiling to herself at the titles. Most were her mom's and dad's hardcover editions, *The Great Gatsby*, *Oliver Twist*, *East of Eden*, *To Kill a Mockingbird* and some textbooks.

Remembering how her dad would use a ten-dollar bill, a lottery ticket, practically anything, for a bookmark, she flipped through pages, starting with a copy of *Moby Dick*. Sure enough, tucked inside was an envelope from Levi, Huttner and Sanchez, the firm that handled their property and estate matters. Inside was a letter about adjusting the will. Pretty dry, formal stuff, signed by their attorney, Constance Huttner.

Sara hesitated when she picked up a large book, a pictorial about holy sites in the Middle East. There was something peeking out between the pages.

She opened the book to find a business-sized manila envelope addressed to George and Marjorie Cole at this house.

The return address was the Montana Attorney General's Office in Helena.

What's this? I've never seen this. It's like it's been hidden.

The postmark showed 2015.

Inside, on letterhead for the Montana Attorney General's Office, was a covering letter.

Dear Mr. and Mrs. Cole:

The enclosed correspondence came to us by way of the law office of Katherine Marie Powell, attorney for Magdalena Kurtz, via the Montana Child and Family Services.

The correspondent is nearing the end of her sentence issued

*by the court and could make a case that any court-imposed re-
strictions will cease to apply. This could be contested, of course.
However, after considerable discussions with attorneys with Montana Child and Family Services, and the necessity to avoid the
risk of potential open court challenges by the creator of the correspondence, this office has determined that the enclosed material is rightfully yours and therefore is being forwarded to you.*

The correspondent will be informed of your receipt.

*We wish to emphasize that any decisions arising from it are
yours.*

*We also stress that your personal information remains confi-
dential and shielded. To ensure this is done, any further communication should be sent to my attention and would proceed
through official state channels in Montana.*

*Again, the decision on how to respond, if you respond, is
yours.*

*Respectfully,
Brett MacRitchie
Supervising Attorney
Child Protection Unit*

Inside were other envelopes, one from Montana's Child and
Family Services. Inside that, there was another envelope from
the law firm of Katherine Marie Powell in Billings, Montana.

The covering letter from Powell stated:

*On behalf of my client, Magdalena Kurtz, I have been in com-
munication with the Montana Attorney General's Office and
Montana's Child and Family Services.*

Permission has been secured to forward the enclosed, on be-

half of my client, and Women Healing in the Forgiving Light,
the group my client is working with.

Inside was the last envelope with the return address: Inmate
#3877465, Montana Women's Prison, Billings, MT
A note inside said:

To Whom It May Concern:

For several years, our support group, Women Healing in the For-
giving Light, has been working closely to help Magdalena Kurtz
prepare for her return to the community. The date for the end
of her sentence is six months away. She has made remarkable
progress and wanted our help in ensuring her letter reached you.
Our hope is that you will be merciful,

Thank you.

Sara's fingers shook as she looked for Magda's letter.
She found nothing.
I never knew Magda wrote to my parents—and she appears to
have dropped the Vryker name.
She looked again and again. The envelopes were empty.
She checked the pages of the books. Nothing. She returned
to the attic and scoured it for the letter.

59

Seattle, Washington

RYAN'S KEYBOARD AND mouse clicked.

He'd heard nothing more on the person from the show offering to provide him documents. He got back to checking the claim that Magda had been killed in a car crash in Canada five years ago.

If it's true, then that leaves only the daughter. She'd be my last hope to find Carrie. Would she even know where Carrie is? Could it really all fall apart? Have I been deluding myself with false hope all these years?

Glancing at Carrie's photo, he shoved the prospect of failure out of his head.

The caller, Lynn from Chicago, had been certain that Magda was using the name Sharon Ellen Vernay at the time of her death.

Ryan dove into news databases he subscribed to. Lynn had put the crash along the Trans-Canada Highway, in the northern part of the province of Ontario. Ryan opened a map on his screen showing Ontario. It was huge, larger than California and larger than Texas.

He submitted *Sharon Ellen Vernay* with the words *Ontario* and *crash* to databases for all Canadian news reports. He liked using one called *e-NewsHawkQuest*. It offered files from all major and regional news sources from 1980 to today.

Within seconds he had a story that was five years old, out of Kenora, Ontario. He consulted the map, following the highway northwest, locating Kenora not far from Manitoba. He went to the story.

KENORA, Ont.—Police have identified a Manitoba woman killed in a single-vehicle crash near Kenora, Ont., last week.

Sharon Ellen Vernay, 46, of Winnipeg, died at the scene, Ontario Provincial Police in Kenora said in a statement.

Vernay's minivan was traveling westbound when it left the road after it struck a deer near Sugar Bay Marina about 20 kilometers west of Kenora, on Highway 17, part of the Trans-Canada Highway.

Vernay's passenger, Brenda Nyakachuk, 49, of Winnipeg, was treated for non-life-threatening injuries.

The women were returning to Winnipeg after attending a country music festival near Kenora.

Ryan considered the story.

The date was correct for Magda's age. But he needed more details.

He went flat-out, checking obituaries online and in news databases for Winnipeg newspapers. He found the obit and began reading.

VERNAY, Sharon Ellen (née) Stornerk, passed away tragically in Ontario... Born in Brandon, Manitoba, in 1972.

Graduated from Colonial High School…married Leon Ford Vernay, her high school sweetheart in 1998…

Wait.

The dates didn't make sense. Sharon Vernay couldn't be Magda. In 1998, Magda was in prison in Montana. She couldn't have been out and free to live in Manitoba to get married. It didn't make sense.

Ryan continued searching social media sites, and soon came upon memorial postings on Instagram, Twitter and Facebook by Sharon Vernay's husband, her relatives and friends, marking what would have been her birthday.

Sharon Vernay's birthdate matched Magda's.

Ryan studied all the photos posted of Sharon Vernay's life, high school, wedding, with her children. Then he studied all the photos he had of Magda, and began shaking his head. *No way. Not even close.*

Why would Lynn from Chicago call in to *Tell-Tale Hearts* to make this bogus claim?

Ryan's first thoughts were to let it go, to move on with the relief that Magda wasn't dead. But he went back to his question: why call in to make a bogus claim—a *detailed* bogus claim?

Analyzing the call yielded a few theories. What if Lynn was only half right? What if Lynn had stumbled onto something? Magda had stolen Sharon Ellen Vernay's ID because her birthdate matched hers?

Ryan reached for his phone.

Finding the number for Sonya Rule at *Tell-Tale Hearts*, he called.

After three rings she answered.

"Hey, Sonya. Ryan Gardner."

"Hi, Ryan! I was going to contact you. The response to your episode was wild. We set a few records."

"That's great. The reason I'm calling is to ask your help reaching one of the callers."

"We'll help if we can."

"She's the one who claimed Magda was dead."

"Yeah, I remember that."

"Right, Lynn from Chicago—she called right after the woman from Mexico. I see you record episodes, but do you have caller ID, or some way for me to reach this Lynn? I'd like to talk to her."

"I'm not sure about all that. It's sort of technical. We know people use false names, or block their calls at their end. But Owen is our IT support expert for the show. Let me see if he can get a number or something for her. It shouldn't take long."

60

AT HER DESK in headquarters, Pierce smiled at Ethan on her phone as they talked over FaceTime.

"So how did things go with Arlee at school today?"

"He wasn't in class."

"Oh."

"Mom, I forgot. At Amber's party, I met this kid, Rayne, and he let me play with his Nintendo Switch. It's so cool. Can I get one?"

"We'll see. Can I say hi to Dad?"

"Okay." Ethan turned his phone to Webb at the wheel of his pickup. She heard Ethan whispering, "Tell her about Nintendo, Dad."

"Not now, buddy. Hey, hon," Webb said. "Going to make it home for supper?"

"Not sure. I'll let you know later."

"Alright, maybe pizza, maybe chili? We'll letcha go." Webb waved.

Ethan turned the phone back to himself.

"Think about Nintendo. Love you, Mom, bye."

"Love you guys."

Hanging up, she glanced at their photo in the new frame on her desk. The wisp of a thought about the birdwatcher lady stirred, but Pierce failed to grasp it, distracted by Benton's arrival. He had told Acker he had a dentist's appointment, but Pierce knew otherwise. He'd taken his wife to another specialist.

"How'd it go, Carl?"

"Still waiting on some results, but this new doctor's optimistic."

"Hey, that's something."

"What's up here? Did Lyle's experiment work?"

"Well, we—"

Acker appeared at their desk.

"Good timing, Carl. Okay, we're set, briefing in my office. Let's go."

Grotowski was out canvassing on another case and Tilden was working with the North Precinct. Benton shut the office door and sat next to Pierce. Acker pushed buttons on his phone, activating his speaker feature for a teleconference call with Heidi Wong at the Prosecuting Attorney's Office, Kelly Jensen in forensics and Oscar Neale in the North Precinct.

"Everyone's on the line," Acker said. "You all have our summary of the unofficial, unscientific aspect of the investigation, indicating that it is more than likely Katie Harmon, a nine-year-old girl, could lift the rock, carry it to the cliff's edge and drop it on Anna Shaw."

"You know, Art, none of this is admissible," Wong said.

"We know. But it helps us," he said. "And we've been

working on ruling out other options, removing or diminishing reasonable doubt."

"Yes, you've established that the girl could conceivably lift the rock and use it as a weapon," Wong said. "But what about the time gap and the two other possible suspects?"

"Yes," Acker said. "Marilyn Hamilton, and Gilbert Croft, who were in the park, on security camera footage."

"Hi, this is Jensen in forensics," she jumped in. "We got clear latent prints for Croft and ran them. Other than being fingerprinted for his job at Boeing, his don't come up anywhere."

"And Hamilton?"

Pierce felt another ripple of nagging vagueness about Hamilton that she couldn't pinpoint.

"In her case," Jensen said, "we're still working on lifting something usable. We have a lot of smudging and it's slowing things."

"Again, we believe we're likely going to rule out Croft and Hamilton," Acker said.

"One more development," Jensen said. "This just came to us from police in Israel. They've had success lifting prints from rocks and indicate that the new technology they're using, which they're willing to share with us, could help us get something from our murder weapon."

"Really?" Wong said. "Wow, okay."

"I think it's clear—everything takes us back to Katie Harmon," Acker said. "How do you want us to move on this, Heidi?"

"Give me a moment. I'm going to mute. Standby."

Nearly a minute passed before Heidi Wong came back on.

"As we know, the prints you obtained surreptitiously from Croft and Hamilton are inadmissible and used for information, or elimination, at this stage."

"Right," Acker said.

"Moving to build a case on the girl remains challenging," Wong said. "We still have no probable cause for arrest or charges at this point. We need to proceed carefully. We have a narrow window under the Fourth Amendment to collect her fingerprints as part of a criminal investigation, even if there is no probable cause for arrest. Let's say under the principle of elimination prints."

"So, our next step is to fingerprint Katie Harmon?" Pierce said.

"Yes. Formally. We do this by the book now, so it doesn't come back on us. At this stage we'll use Katie Harmon's prints as comparison with the evidence, should we obtain a print from the rock."

"Want us to question her again, go further?" Benton said.

"No, not at this stage," Wong said. "Mirandize her, obtain her prints, and we'll see where the science takes us."

"I'll get in touch with Sara Harmon and set it up," Pierce said.

61

Seattle, Washington

PERPLEXED AND NUMB, Sara stared at the envelopes on her kitchen table.

She hadn't known that Magda had written to her mom and dad six months before her release.

Since Magda was freed, she'd vanished into the world with a new identity, as if she never existed. *Except in my blood and my nightmares.* All her life Sara was told, and believed, that there had never been contact between her family and Magda.

Why didn't Mom and Dad tell me about this? What did Magda say in her letter? Where is it? I have a right to see it.

Sara was jolted when her phone rang, the screen showing a blocked number.

"Hello?"

"Sara?"

"Yes."

"Detective Kim Pierce."

Sara caught her breath. "Hi."

"We're almost finished our work and we'd like to set up a time to come to your house. We'd like to collect Katie's fingerprints."

Sara tensed.

"Her fingerprints?"

"Yes."

"But why her fingerprints?"

"This is pretty much a routine follow-up."

"I thought you were done with her?"

"We need to collect her prints so we can wrap things up. It won't take long. Would today be good?"

Sara's pulse raced; she tried to think of an excuse to buy some time.

"No, today's not good. Tomorrow would be better. Later in the afternoon, say four?"

"Alright, we'll see you and Katie tomorrow at four. Thank you, Sara."

She ended the call with her mind racing.

Fingerprints. The detectives wanted Katie's fingerprints.

Why? And why now? What do they know? Is this related to confiding my fears and showing Katie's drawing to Dr. Mehta?

Still gripping her phone, she examined her options while staring at the envelopes. She focused on the letter from Levi, Huttner and Sanchez.

She needed help.

She called the firm's number. While it rang, her worries whirled. She couldn't afford a lawyer for Katie.

But I can't afford not to get her one.

The receptionist answered.

"Could I speak with Constance Huttner, please?"

"I'm sorry, Ms. Huttner's no longer with the firm. She's retired. How may I direct your call?"

"I'd like to talk to a criminal defense attorney."

"Criminal, I see. But we don't— Hold, please."

Hold music played. A Beatles' ballad, "Yesterday." Then the receptionist came back.

"Sorry for the delay. I'm going to connect you."

The line clicked, then a man answered.

"Lincoln Berdell."

"Hello, Mr. Berdell. Are you an attorney?"

"I am."

"And this call is confidential?"

"Yes, go ahead and tell me about your situation. Let's start there."

Sara began by saying that years ago her parents had been clients of the firm for property and estate matters. Sara never mentioned Magda and she didn't think it likely Berdell would be aware of any connection. She began summarizing Katie's circumstances but didn't get far.

"Excuse me, Ms. Harmon," Berdell interrupted her. "I understand." She could hear his keyboard clicking. "We don't handle cases like this. You're going to want a juvenile criminal defense attorney."

"But I don't know any."

"I know a firm, and an attorney there, Rose Aranda. I'll get your information and have Rose reach out to you as soon as possible."

Unable to concentrate, Sara kept busy flipping the pages of books, preparing the box for donation while mentally contending with her confusion and dread. Time went by slowly until her phone rang with a call from Rose Aranda.

Sara outlined Katie's predicament to Aranda, reiterating the fact that she was with Anna Shaw when she fell.

"I recall the news reports," Aranda said. "If detectives are coming tomorrow at four, I'll be there at three to talk further with you and Katie. You did the right thing, Sara, by agreeing to cooperate and seeking legal help."

"Thank you, Rose. I have to ask, what's your fee?"

"It's normally three-fifty per hour. The first consultation is free, so I'll count tomorrow as a first consultation. We also do pro bono work. We'll work something out, Sara. Don't worry."

Adina and Tamika got Katie back home in time for supper.

Over homemade tacos Sara explained what would be taking place tomorrow with the detectives.

"Fingerprints?" Katie said. "Does that mean I'm getting arrested and going to jail?"

"No, sweetie, it's police stuff. We'll have a lawyer here helping us. You'll meet her tomorrow. Her name is Rose and she sounds nice."

Katie stared at her plate with a blank expression. Then Sara said: "What is it?"

"I didn't make Anna fall, Mom."

"Are you ready to tell me more about that day?"

Katie shook her head.

"No, because if I did, you would think I made Anna fall, but I didn't."

"Did you make Anna fall, Katie? Even by accident?"

Katie shook her head.

"Is that the truth?"

Katie nodded, then looked at the necklace Anna had given her. Sara let her be and cleared the table.

"What day do I see Dr. Mehta again, Mom?"

"I don't know," Sara said. "I don't think you need to see her anymore."

"But I like her office. I like watching her fish."

"We'll see."

Sara's sleep was troubled that night.

She got up around two thirty and went into Katie's room, finding her curled under her sheets. Watching her, Sara's stomach tremored.

Did you tell me everything, honey? Are you lying to me?

Why do the detectives want her fingerprints? What about Dr. Mehta? Was I wrong to confide in her? Sara flicked a glance to the ceiling, where everything about Magda had been locked away until now. Why hadn't her mom and dad told her that she'd written to them? What had Magda wanted?

What if they try to take Katie away from me?

Sara leaned down and softly kissed Katie's cheek.

I won't let that happen. We are not like them.

Sara returned to her bed.

As she slept, her own unspeakable memories crawled from the dark mists of her mind...*the screams...the thudding...the digging...*

The next day, Sara got off a little early from her shift at the diner to get Katie at school. For an appointment, she told Mel.

At three, the doorbell rang and Rose Aranda arrived. She was in her forties. She wore a blazer and pants, and carried a briefcase. Sara invited her inside to meet Katie and have a quick chat.

"I'd like to talk to your mom," Aranda said. "Then you and I can talk alone. If that's okay?"

"Sweetie, go up to your room and watch a movie, then I'll send Ms. Aranda—"

"Rose. Call me Rose."

"Then I'll send Rose up to see you."

Sara made tea and talked with Rose in the kitchen. Sara's voice quivered as she related Katie's case. It wasn't easy telling a stranger, even one who was going to help. Sara told Rose that Anna had been Katie's sitter, about the Sunny Days trip and how Anna fell taking a selfie. She touched on every key point, about the trauma, Dr. Mehta. She showed Rose Katie's sketch. But Sara withheld any mention of Magda or the little boy in Canada.

Rose asked questions and took notes.

"First," Rose started, "under state law, it's presumed that children under twelve years of age are incapable of committing a crime."

"But why are police coming to fingerprint Katie?"

"Well, it's possible that children aged eight to twelve can be prosecuted for murder if the prosecution can establish that the child fully knew the act was wrong. It's a difficult and complex burden to prove."

"Katie told them Anna fell. Why're they still investigating her?"

"Any number of reasons. They're not required to reveal to you details of their investigation. They could have a witness, or new evidence. They might be establishing *elimination prints*, meaning that they have something and want to rule Katie out. They can collect prints without a charge or arrest. The best thing is for you and Katie to cooperate with me present."

Rose then went upstairs and talked alone with Katie.

A few minutes after four the doorbell rang. Sara led Pierce and Benton to the kitchen table, where Katie joined them.

Rose Aranda introduced herself.

"I'll be sitting in on this."

Benton maintained a poker face. Pierce nodded and smiled.

Sara's heart flipped when the detectives advised Katie of her Miranda rights—"Just routine, by the book," Benton said— in the presence of her mother and attorney, and a form was signed by all the required parties. Then Pierce opened her bag to withdraw a portable fingerprint scanner, which resembled a smartphone.

"I need you to touch your fingers one at a time on the square here, Katie."

Sara's throat dried watching Katie touching the square. Her little fingers were shaking.

"Don't be nervous," Pierce said.

"I'm a little scared."

"Katie," Rose said. "Remember what we talked about."

Benton shot Aranda a glance and Pierce recorded finger after finger.

"Why are you scared, Katie?" Benton asked.

"You all think I made Anna fall," Katie said.

"Katie, you shouldn't say anything."

Benton shot a look to Aranda, to Sara, to Pierce, then Katie.

"Did you make her fall?" Benton asked.

Katie glanced at Rose, who was shaking her head.

Katie remained silent until the detectives left.

62

GROTOWSKI GOT BACK to an empty office.

Tilden was in Sparrow Song Park with the North Precinct people; Pierce and Benton were out collecting Katie Harmon's fingerprints.

With the investigation shifting back to the girl, Grotowski got to work double-checking background on Sara Harmon and Katie. He settled in at his computer and once again searched every local and state system for any reference to Sara or Katie. Beyond being charged or sought for anything criminal. He searched to see if they had filed a complaint, witnessed a crime or been questioned in another case. He checked other databases that were part of the ACCESS network.

Nothing surfaced.

Again, he went to NCIC, the national databank managed by the FBI. He also submitted queries to other national databases, like those holding no-fly lists or terror suspects. He checked others, like ViCAP, running through networks for unsolved homicides, parental abductions and missing persons.

Again, nothing.

Even though he submitted Sara's name, date of birth and social security number each time, he knew there were exceptions that would not confirm a hit. In rare cases people were protected if their information was sealed by the courts, say in spousal abuse cases, violent custody disputes, or if someone was in a state or national witness protection program.

He also made a call to Ottawa, Canada, where the Royal Canadian Mounted Police managed the Canadian Police Information Centre. Similar to NCIC, it was a database holding information on crimes and criminals. Grotowski was directed to Corporal Rachel Taylor and left her a voice mail.

Then, for good measure, he went to Interpol. He'd just finished requesting a search for any international warrants, wants or notices when Tilden entered the office, holding up a clear evidence bag.

"The divers found Anna Shaw's phone way downstream in the rocks."

Grotowski stood to take a closer look at the phone. It was rose gold, and the same color, brand and model as Shaw's parents had described. But the screen was shattered and the body of it cracked in several places so severely components were exposed.

"It's in rough shape, Lyle."

"Yeah, pretty banged up. And it's been in the water all this time," Tilden said. "I called the forensic IT guys. They weren't hopeful but they'll see what they can do. I'm going there after I show this to Art."

"Good work," Grotowski said before his phone rang.

Corporal Taylor with the RCMP in Ottawa had returned his call.

"Thanks for getting back to me," Grotowski said, then explained his request to run Sara and Katie Harmon's names and details in all databases in Canada.

63

DR. MEHTA LEFT the Rosling Center after a meeting with other professors and walked across the campus to her car.

Leaving departmental politics behind, she'd just begun thinking about her upcoming afternoon sessions with patients, starting with Katie Harmon, when her phone rang.

It was Nadia from her office.

"Hi, Sally. Calling to let you know we have a cancellation. So, you have some free time."

"Who canceled?" Dr. Mehta reached her Subaru and pressed her key fob. It chirped, unlocking the doors, and she got in.

"Katie Harmon. Sara called to cancel."

"Sara canceled? Did she reschedule Katie?"

"No. Actually, she said she thought Katie didn't need any more sessions."

"Really?" Dr. Mehta thought for a moment, then said: "Can

you send me Sara Harmon's contact information? I've got it on my laptop but it'd be faster if you sent it. Thanks, Nadia."

After hanging up, Dr. Mehta tapped her phone to her steering wheel, processing what had happened. The phone chimed with a notification from Nadia. Dr. Mehta then debated calling Sara.

No, I won't call her. Not just yet.

She drove off.

Halfway to her office, she stopped at a coffee shop. It wasn't busy. She found the aroma relaxing. She got a latte and a table in a quiet corner. Amid the subdued clatter and drone of the TV on the wall behind the counter, she put her laptop on the table.

Sara canceled and wants to end Katie's sessions.

Dr. Mehta went back over their meeting at the mall. Maybe she'd been too forthcoming and made Sara uncomfortable about her thoughts on Katie and the subject of abuse. Sara's decision to end Katie's therapy sessions was the wrong approach.

It concerned Dr. Mehta, deepening her dilemma.

She opened her laptop, logged in and examined Katie's case. She went through her notes, Katie's guilt, her nightmares, her anguish with conflicting "bad" thoughts that she'd either refused to articulate or was unable to bring forward. She looked at Katie's sketch of herself with Anna Shaw on the cliff.

Is it a depiction of what happened? Or could it be something else? Have I completely overlooked another aspect to this?

There was Katie's unwillingness, and Sara's refusal, to provide any details about a past traumatic incident concerning a boy who died in Katie's presence. Katie had been on the cusp of opening up a little. She'd said that a boy had said mean things to her in the past—but she wasn't supposed to talk about it. Was this the same boy? What happened?

Was the boy's case an accident? A violent death?

Most troubling of all were Sara's cryptic questions about a history of violence in her family, and whether violent traits could be inherited. It signaled so many concerns.

Had Katie been abused? Had Anna's death triggered a deeper traumatic psychological wound?

Still, none of this fit.

Dr. Mehta knew that all families had secrets and would do anything to keep them behind closed doors.

If she were correct about Katie Harmon being abused, then she had to get to the root of the abuse. Was it happening at home? With a relative? A friend? A stranger? Was it happening at school?

Or what if Katie's the abuser?

Dr. Mehta studied the sketch, looking at it in a whole new light.

Either way she had a duty to report what she knew, to advise social services, or even police.

What if I'm completely wrong?

But the risk of harm was so great it had to eclipse every other consideration.

I don't know what happened with the boy two years ago. And all I know about what happened on the cliff is what Katie and Sara told me.

Dr. Mehta studied the sketch again.

Adjusting her glasses, she began typing on her keyboard, digging up some of the early social media chatter about Anna's death. As a rule, she never gave any weight to these observations, which were fraught with offensive comments, fakery, cyberbullying and scams.

Nothing new had emerged about Anna Shaw.

Still, curious, Dr. Mehta went to the original, earliest news stories about Anna Shaw's death. She read through them and looked at the comments. Skipping over ridiculous theories, coming to one she remembered.

Maybe there's more to this story than we think? one person had posted.

"Turn that up."

Dr. Mehta looked from her work to the counter. A customer staring at the TV had made the request. A staff member, a young man with a ponytail, picked up the remote control.

A **BREAKING NEWS** graphic topped the screen as a news anchor said:

"...learned that the tragedy of Seattle teen Anna Shaw, who fell from a cliff in Sparrow Song Park southeast of the city, is now being investigated as a *suspicious death*, according to sources close to the investigation."

A quarter of the screen displayed a photo of Anna Shaw, smiling beautifully while file footage from the ground and air, taken the day of her death, showed police, emergency crews and grief-stricken children and families at the park.

"To recap, the case of the tragedy of Seattle teen Anna Shaw, who fell from a cliff in Sparrow Song Park..."

Dr. Mehta's jaw dropped slightly.

This changes everything.

64

BY THAT AFTERNOON the report on the investigation's status had moved like a tsunami, reaching some families at Rainier Pine Elementary just as they arrived to pick up their kids.

Amid the commotion of buses, cars, and running and shouting children, Katie Harmon stood in the pick-up zone. Spotting Val Rossi in the distance, Katie moved toward her. Val did the same, both unaware of the news and what was unfolding.

Among the dozens of people in the pick-up zone were parents who knew Anna Shaw's family, or were associated with the Sunny Days Youth Center. Gathered in clusters, they studied their phones, conversing. Mouths agape with shock, some shot glances at Katie.

Immediately picking up snippets of what the adults were saying on what was developing, Dylan Frick and his friends left their circle, overtook Katie and surrounded her before she got to Val.

"It's on the news." Dylan smirked. "You killed her."

Shaking her head, Katie tried to step back.

"My mom says your babysitter didn't fall by accident," Dylan said.

"That's not true," Katie said.

"Yes it is and you're a liar." Laughing, Dylan looked over his shoulder at parents staring at their phones. Some were headed toward the group of kids. "It's true." He grinned. "You pushed her. You're a murderer!"

"No!" Katie shrieked.

"Murderer!" one of the other boys chimed, chanting it over and over.

Katie pleaded for Dylan Frick to stop. She tried to escape but Dylan and his friends blocked her, taunting her.

"You leave this girl alone, young man!" A woman emerged, putting herself between Katie and her tormentors. "If you know what's good for you, you'll go home now! All of you leave her alone! Do you hear me?"

Sobbing hard, her teary vision blurred, Katie couldn't see her defender clearly. She didn't recognize her voice as the chastened boys returned to their families.

"You poor child." The woman put her arm around Katie, squeezed a gentle, protective hug. "Those boys have no idea."

Katie covered her face with her hands, struggling to stop crying.

"What happened?"

Rubbing her eyes, Katie now saw Val Rossi. She'd arrived breathless, fumbling for a tissue in her bag to brush at Katie's tears. Able to see better now, Katie glanced around. The woman who'd rescued her had disappeared into the chaos. Two staff members from the school made their way to them.

"Hi, Katie, Ms. Rossi," Alice Jenkins, a staff member often assigned to the pick-up and drop-offs, said. "Is everything okay?"

"I think some boys upset her." Val surveyed the crowd and hubbub. "One of the parents, I think, chased them off."

"Which boys?" Jenkins scanned the crowd. "Which parent chased them off? We can make a report."

"I don't see her," Val said. "Katie, do you know who?"

She buried her head into Val and shook it.

"I want to go home," Katie said. "Can we go?"

"You're sure you're okay?" Jenkins said.

Katie nodded.

"Alright. I think it's best if we leave," Val said to Jenkins while putting her arm around Katie's shoulder. "My car's this way."

As Jenkins watched them leave the zone, she was nudged by her partner, who was reading the breaking news story on her phone.

"Maybe it had something to do with this, Alice?" she said, turning her phone so Jenkins could see the screen. "Anna Shaw's death may not have been an accident."

65

SARA DROVE HER Trailblazer home from her shift at the Jet Town Diner, grappling with the upheaval in her life.

My nine-year-old daughter has been fingerprinted and read her rights by police!

She stopped at a red light and took a deep breath.

The detectives said it was routine. The lawyer said it doesn't mean they suspect Katie. But I don't believe it. I can't believe it. The police know something.

A horn sounded behind her. The light had changed.

As she drove, Sara's thoughts shifted to what she'd discovered in the attic. That Magda had written to her family.

I need to ask Mom what Magda wrote and if she answered, and why they never ever told me.

Nearing her neighborhood, Sara found a little relief knowing Val had picked up Katie from school today. It would give Sara time to decompress before she got Katie home.

Sara's phone rang. She recognized the number and used her hands-free voice-activated feature to answer.

"Hey, Val."

"Have you seen the news about Anna?"

"What news?"

"It's just coming out now about the investigation."

"Hold on. I'll pull over."

"I'll send you the link to the story. It's very short."

Wheeling over to the shoulder and stopping, Sara read the story that said the police now considered Anna Shaw's death suspicious—the words piercing her.

"Oh, my God!" Sara drove her fingers into her hair.

"It's just happening," Val said. "I think people, some from Sunny Days, were finding out at pick-up, and some boys at school upset Katie."

"Is she okay?"

"Yes, she's with me here," Val said.

"Can you put her on, Val?"

Sara heard muffled voices and Bingo's barking, then Katie said: "Hi, Mom."

"Oh, honey."

"Mom, is it true the police think I made Anna fall?"

"Oh, sweetie." Sara put her hand over her mouth, then pulled it away. "It's complicated, very complicated. I'm going to find out some more. You stay with Val and Bingo, and I'll get you as soon as I can."

"Love you, Mom."

"Love you, too."

Val came back on the line.

"Sara, I just saw a news truck go down your street. I think I should keep Katie here for a bit."

Sara's mind raced.

"Sara?"

"Yes, thank you. Yes, please keep her while I deal with this. Thank you, Val."

Gripping her phone, Sara took a breath, then called Rose Aranda's office. Her assistant answered.

"I'm sorry. Ms. Aranda is unavailable at the moment. May I take a message?"

"It's Sara Harmon. Please have her call me. It's urgent."

Hanging up, her fingers trembling, Sara sent Rose a text with a link to the news story and wrote: What do I do? We need help now!

She set her phone aside, took another breath, collected herself, then resumed driving home. She braced for whatever awaited her there. Minutes later she turned the corner for her street and saw them down the block. News trucks and camera crews on the sidewalk in front of her house.

Once again, Sara figured the media had gotten her address from the parents with Sunny Days; some had kids at Katie's school. People knew her connection to Anna's death.

The press may have my address but I thank God they don't know anything more about us. What if this makes them dig deeper? But they can't uncover our history. Everything's sealed, buried, names have been changed. But what if— No! All these years, no one has found us. No!

Fortunately the newspeople hadn't blocked her driveway. But they gathered around her Trailblazer the moment she parked. That's when her phone rang. Rose Aranda was calling. Sara ensured all the windows were up and all the doors were locked.

Camera lenses from either side and the front were aimed at her as she remained behind the wheel. She answered the call and spoke softly with her hand cupped over her mouth and phone.

"Sara. I got your message and read the story."

"What should I do, Rose? I've got reporters in my driveway and cameras pointed at me."

"Say nothing. Speak to no one. I'll get hold of King County and find out more."

"This is scary, Rose."

"I know. Hang in there. I'll call you right back."

Sara collected her phone, her bag and got her keys ready, steeling herself. She unlocked her car door. The moment she stepped from her SUV, the questions came.

A man thrust his microphone at her as she locked her car. "What is your reaction to police saying Anna Shaw's death is suspicious?"

Sara headed toward her house without speaking as camera operators jostled to get closer to her.

"Sara," a woman with a microphone said, "your daughter was the last person with Anna Shaw—do you have any comment?"

A man recording with his phone said: "Is it true Anna Shaw babysat your daughter? How did your daughter end up with Shaw's jewelry after her death?"

Sara made it to the house, fumbled to get her key in the lock, got inside, shut the door and locked it. She slammed her back to the wall, sliding to the floor, struggling not to sob.

She stayed that way until she recovered a degree of composure. Her phone rang and vibrated several times with calls from news outlets. She ignored them all while monitoring for Rose Aranda to get back to her. Sara went to her desk, logged on to her laptop and searched online for more information.

Told'ya. It's the girl pushed her, one person posted on a thread after linking the breaking news report of Anna's death being suspicious. A nine-year-old? Come on, another posted. Gotta be something else, said another poster. Sickened by the comments, Sara searched social media for more news reports and came to a clip of a Seattle TV news station at the house of Anna Shaw's parents.

"No," Lynora Shaw, Anna's mother, said at her door. "We haven't been told anything."

"But can you confirm that just before her death, Anna had a bad breakup with her boyfriend?"

Lynora Shaw's face was pained.

"I'm sorry, we have nothing more to say."

Sara's phone rang and vibrated. It was Rose.

"I reached Detective Sergeant Art Acker."

"What did he say?" Sara asked.

"It was a short conversation. All he would say is that the investigation is ongoing."

"What about it now being suspicious?"

"I pressed him on that. He wouldn't confirm or deny it, only that the investigation continues."

"What does that mean for Katie? What do police know? What are they doing? Why did they take her fingerprints?"

"Could be any number of reasons. I know this is a terrible time, but you're going to have to ride this out."

After the call, Sara sat alone while her phone vibrated with more media calls.

She held her head in her hands in a futile effort to stop the terrifying thoughts swirling in her mind.

66

ERIK FOY, A LATENT fingerprint specialist at the King County Sheriff's AFIS Section, went to his supervisor, Kelly Jensen, who was hunched over her worktable.

"What's up, Erik?"

"I think it's a no-go collecting anything from the detective's tablet."

"Carl Benton's tablet?" she said without looking up.

"Yeah—" Foy glanced at his notebook "—the one they tagged for Marilyn Hamilton. For what it's worth, I ran Hamilton's name through AFIS and nothing comes up for her."

"You said earlier that the latents were smudged?"

"Yeah, they're smeared, not enough information. I think her fingers were moving slightly when she touched the surface, distorting the ridge details."

"Try spots where there may be overlap. I know it's trickier. You can do it. You got usable stuff from Pierce's laptop."

"Alright, but we're so backlogged."

"Keep at it, Erik."

Jensen continued working on her aspect of the case: the rock considered to be the murder weapon in Anna Shaw's death.

Nearly seven inches in diameter, seventeen inches in circumference, it weighed six pounds. Earlier analysis found traces of hair and blood consistent with Anna Shaw's hair and blood.

Getting a fingerprint from the rock was critical.

Late yesterday a kit had arrived by courier from Israeli police, via the FBI, with resources that could help Jensen develop prints from the rock. Recovering prints from a rock's surface had always been considered next to impossible.

But recently forensic experts around the world had begun developing new techniques with positive results. At first they found that time was commonly crucial when examining rocks. The early breakthroughs allowed for collecting prints that were less than two or three days old at most. That was because as the fingerprints saturated the surface, it didn't take long for them to break apart. But recent advances in the new technology had pushed the time frame back to four or five weeks.

Still, that depended on the kind of rock in question and how porous it was. Different methods were applied to different rocks. This analysis, with so much at stake, was challenging.

Jensen could have sent the rock to the Washington State Crime Lab and let them analyze it. But she wanted to do this in-house. She wanted to learn this technique. She had worked late into the night and resumed early this morning.

The whole time she considered the kit's guidance for various methods.

Now, as her gloved hands worked meticulously on the rock that the medical examiner said had likely smashed into Anna Shaw's skull, Jensen caught her breath.

Something's taking shape here.
Hold up. No. False alarm.
Jensen looked at the rock.
Okay, no prints yet. Nothing to compare.
Jensen resumed studying the information kit.
This is going to take more time.

67

Seattle, Washington

ALL CONVERSATIONS STOPPED.

Detective Sergeant Art Acker's eyes went round to the faces of the people at the meeting room table, then to those standing against the walls.

"This will be quick," he said.

Everyone was there: Pierce, Benton, Grotowski, Tilden and several others under Acker's command. Soft coughs, pen-tapping and throat-clearing rippled as Acker's jaw tensed.

"By now, you all know what's happened on Shaw. The fallout from the leak to the press shot up the chain and they tore me a new one."

Acker placed his hands on his hips.

"We've taken calls from Katie Harmon's attorney, from Anna Shaw's parents, the prosecutor and the media," he said. "This does not help our investigation. We don't know who put it out there, could be anybody. But if we find out, there will be hell to pay. You got that?"

When Acker looked around at the group again, some people shifted in their chairs or where they stood.

"Nothing is a lock on this case," he said. "No matter what some may think, we're not done."

Acker let his message sink in.

"Alright, get back to work."

Pierce, Benton and the others returned to their desks.

"Why would someone leak?" Benton said.

"I don't know, Carl."

Pierce studied files on her computer while Benton threw his question to the other detectives who'd resumed working at their desks.

"Lyle? Larry? Any thoughts?"

Grotowski shook his head.

"No idea," Lyle said. "Could be anybody."

Benton leaned closer to Pierce and changed the subject.

"Kim, don't you think Katie was acting strange when we were getting her prints?"

"You mean, what she said?"

"Yeah, but more the way she said it—*you all think I made Anna fall.* And the way the lawyer had her clam up. It seemed odd."

"Maybe, Carl, but we have to follow the evidence."

Benton's phone rang and he answered it.

Pierce continued checking messages for anything from forensics on prints. Kelly Jensen had said she was determined to recover something from the rock. If that happened, and they could compare it to Katie Harmon, then that could nail it. *We've covered everything, haven't we? Unless we missed a key piece with the boyfriend, or Anna's phone, or an element unseen or not pursued.*

Jensen and her team had also indicated that they were not likely to get any usable latents for Marilyn Hamilton, the birdwatcher. Something about their visit to Hamilton's apartment still bothered Pierce, but she couldn't identify it.

She left that thought, then noticed a couple of forms she'd completed for HR and opened her drawer for her stapler. She spotted the paper stock photo from the picture frame she'd bought at Walmart. The one of the little girl with the bright umbrella and raincoat.

Why's that still there? I should put it in the recycling.

Before she moved it, Benton ended his call.

"Hey, Kim, Martin at the front desk says a psychologist is here to see us."

"That could mean so many things on so many levels, Carl."

"Seriously, she's here. She says she has information that may be pertinent to the Shaw case."

"No appointment, just walked in?"

"Martin says she seems legit but nervous. Couldn't hurt to talk to her."

"Alright."

Pierce closed her drawer and they left.

Passing by Grotowski's desk, they overheard his end of a phone conversation.

"What's up, my Mountie friend?... Really?... Something out of British Columbia?... Vancouver?... Could be. Hold up, I want to take some notes, and could you send me..."

68

Seattle, Washington

ONE CONSEQUENCE OF leaks to the press on active investigations was that it motivated people to come out of the woodwork.

You got all kinds: disturbed individuals who wanted to confess, those who claimed to have a tip and wanted a reward, even well-meaning people who just wanted to help. No matter what kind they were, they tied up investigators because each one had to be assessed.

But until your case was cleared, you had to keep an open mind and guard against tunnel vision, Pierce thought as they met Dr. Sally Mehta at the front desk.

After signing her in and issuing her a visitor's badge, they found a small empty office. They checked her driver's license and confirmed her license as a psychologist and her position at the University of Washington.

Mehta was poised and carried a professional air about her, Pierce thought.

"I'll record our conversation for my own notes," Pierce said.

"But this will remain confidential?"

"Of course."

Pierce adjusted her phone and set it on the table before Mehta.

"You have information pertinent to our investigation?" Pierce said.

"First, I need to stress that the fact I am here comes after an enormous amount of difficult thought. I could be taking a professional risk with my license, but I have a duty to report if I have reason to believe a patient has been harmed, or will harm others."

"We understand," Pierce said. "What is your relationship to the case?"

Dr. Mehta gathered her thoughts.

"I volunteer with a crisis counseling network. In the aftermath of Anna Shaw's death, we worked with the Sunny Days group to provide grief and trauma counseling to the children, families and staff who were touched by what happened."

Pierce nodded.

"Katie Harmon was among the first I saw. After that she became a patient, and I've had several sessions with her."

Dr. Mehta related Katie's case, her observations and growing concern. Katie's cryptic references to bad thoughts and guilt over Anna Shaw's death. How Sara had suggested her family had a violent history and was concerned if violent traits could be inherited. Sara had acknowledged Katie was present when another child, a boy, died years earlier.

"She was present at another death?" Benton said.

"Can you provide the name of the boy, and dates?" Pierce asked.

Dr. Mehta shook her head.

"I tried. But when I asked Sara for more information to help counsel Katie, she refused and ended Katie's sessions with me."

Dr. Mehta reached for her phone.

"And there's this."

She showed the detectives her photo of Katie's sketch.

Pierce and Benton studied it.

"At first, I interpreted it to represent just what Katie said it was, a depiction of Anna's fall with Katie trying to help."

"But now?" Pierce asked, her eyes on the sketch.

"Now I'm not sure. The bottom line here is I think Katie could have been abused, or she could be a violent abuser, or both. I'm just not sure. I only know that when taken together, there are sufficient factors for me to act on my professional duty to report this to you."

Pierce and Benton traded glances.

"Can you send us that picture of the sketch?" Pierce asked.

69

SCROLLING THROUGH SOCIAL MEDIA, Ryan read reports on how that wilderness death of the girl who fell taking a selfie was now considered a suspicious death.

Wow.

None of the coverage identified a suspect. There were few details, photos or names, likely because minors were involved. Yet the reports stirred Ryan's curiosity again about whether the case had any connection to one of his subjects, Sara Harmon, from the Jet Town Diner.

He went back, pulling up the first reports from when the incident happened in Sparrow Song Park. He reviewed the news photos taken at the time of emergency units, police and families in shock.

He concentrated on one news image that he'd been drawn to earlier. It was tightly framed and showed a woman, her arms wrapped around a girl, their faces covered by their hair and buried into each other. They were photographed between two parked SUVs. The caption above the photo said *Wilderness Tragedy*. The cutline below it said *An unidentified mother and daughter embrace after a teen was killed at Sparrow Song Park, southeast of Seattle*. Photo credit was given to Newswire Services.

From what Ryan could see, and he was in no way certain, but to him, the woman resembled Sara Harmon. That's what had caught his attention then, and it had him asking the question again now.

Is that Sara Harmon?

With the development on the tragedy, the possibility nagged at him. *What if it is?* The idea that Sara and her daughter were at the park when the teen died, and what that might imply, was hard to fathom. But the more he looked at the photo, the more he thought about it.

And after thinking about it—thinking how he was waiting to hear back on his DNA requests, and those he'd made to *Tell-Tale Hearts* on the bogus tip and the offer of documents— he decided to try something.

During his time as a reporter, when a vague aspect or inexact potential new thread of a story surfaced, he'd sometimes drive by the locations of the key players while thinking about it.

Because you never knew what could emerge.

And he had Sara Harmon's address from his investigative work. In fact, he'd driven to it since his arrival in Seattle.

Ryan got into his SUV.

He didn't know what to expect, or if driving by made sense, now that it was a day after the story had broken. He made good time getting to North Seattle. He turned onto Sara Harmon's quiet street. As he neared her house, he slowed down.

A news van was out front.

Something's up.

After parking a few doors away and across the street, Ryan got out and approached the SUV. Its station and logo on the doors in red, white and blue said *KT96-TV NEWS "WE'VE GOT SEATTLE'S STORY."*

A man in a ball cap, jeans and a flannel shirt was loading a tripod into the back. A woman wearing a jacket with the station crest stood on the sidewalk, ending a phone call.

"Hi," Ryan said. "Are you guys here for Sara Harmon?"

The TV people eyed him and nodded.

"Who are you?" the woman asked.

"Ryan Gardner. I'm a freelancer."

"For who?"

"Mostly magazines." He reached into his wallet for his old press ID. "Before that, I worked for the *Chicago Tribune*."

The woman studied Ryan's ID.

"Got a second?" he said. "I'm just trying to catch up on this story. Can you bring me up to speed?"

The man slammed the tailgate shut, then said: "We got about two minutes, Ash. Then we gotta get to Ballard."

"So, you know," the woman said, "that KIRO reported that the case of the girl who fell taking a selfie in Sparrow Song is now a suspicious death?"

"Right." That was about the extent of what Ryan knew. "And Sara Harmon's connected?"

"Kids were in the park on an outing organized by the Sunny Days community group. Anna Shaw, the teen who died, was there with Sara Harmon's nine-year-old daughter, Katie. Anna was Katie's babysitter."

Ryan nodded.

"Rumors and speculation are flying," the woman said, "that Katie pushed her babysitter to get her necklace, and police have questioned Katie."

"Really?"

EVERYTHING SHE FEARED   371

"Those are the rumors that most of the Sunny Days parents are floating. They're the ones who put us on to her home here."

"Ashley." The man was now behind the wheel and started the engine.

"Look, our organization's being careful. There's no evidence, no proof, no charges," the woman said. "And with our policy, we won't name or show the faces of Sara or Katie, because she's a minor. We'd blur them."

"Right, that's standard practice," Ryan said. "Did you get an interview?"

"Nope. She didn't talk to anyone yesterday and she's not talking to anyone today. Everyone's struck out and moving on to other stories." The woman got into the passenger seat, buckled up and lowered her window.

"Wait," Ryan said. "One last thing. What can you tell me about Sara Harmon's background?"

"Not much. We heard she's a single mom, works at a diner."

"What do you know about her family history?"

The woman shook her head.

"I think her mom is in a seniors' home."

"Which seniors' home?"

"Pal—" the man leaned toward Ryan "—she's told you enough. We gotta go."

"I don't know which home," the woman said, reaching into her pocket and giving Ryan her card before they drove off.

He turned to the house.

He stood there, rooted staring at the door, struggling to grasp that he was on the cusp of an entirely new dimension.

All these years he'd searched.

Are Magda's daughter and granddaughter on the other side of that door? Sara's mother is in a seniors' home—is it Magda? Is Katie a killer like her grandmother?

Ryan's breathing quickened as he struggled to decide on what he was going to do.

He had no proof of anything. He couldn't just ring the doorbell and ask Sara Harmon about her family and plead for her help, especially with all that was happening.

She would shut him down.

No, now was not the time.

His stomach tensed as he walked back to his SUV.

70

PEERING AT THE street through the crack in the curtains, Sara watched the KT96 news crew and a second reporter leave.

Grateful fewer media people had come to her door today than yesterday, Sara continued her call with Mel at the diner. He'd allowed her to take another day off.

"I get it," Mel said. "A couple reporters were poking around here looking for you."

"I'm so sorry about this, Mel."

"Well, we'll just have to figure it out. I'll juggle things with Polly and Beth and the others, see if we can keep covering for you."

"Thank you."

"Do what you need to do, Sara, for you and Katie." Mel softened his voice, grappling with his unease over the situation. "But if this gets to be too much, we'll have to talk."

"What does that mean?"

"I'll have to see how this plays out, look at the impact on the diner."

"What?"

"Just do what you need to do."

After all these years? I started there when I was a teen. I thought Mel considered us family. I guess that all goes out the window now.

Sara's stomach churned.

She couldn't lose her job.

Feeling as if the walls were closing in on her, Sara clenched her eyes shut for a moment, then shifted her concern back to Katie. She'd kept her home from school today. Val had offered to come over if Sara needed to go out. Katie was sitting at the kitchen table, flipping through a favorite book, *The Lorax* by Dr. Seuss.

Sara's thoughts went to the attic and the horrible truth about Magda. Her stomach roiled as she watched Katie gently turning the pages.

"At school Dylan Frick and his friends said I pushed Anna. They called me a murderer." Katie's tears fell on the pages as she stared blankly at them. "Why did he say that?"

"Sweetheart," Sara said.

"I told you what happened on the cliff. I told the police and I told Dr. Sally, too."

"I know, I know, but—"

"When will I see Dr. Sally again?"

"We're going to take a little break from Dr. Sally."

"But I like going to her office, to see the fish and the giraffe from Africa."

"Katie, listen, this is important." Sara struggled to keep from coming apart. "What happened, what really happened on the cliff?"

Katie took the heart of the necklace into her fingers and stroked it.

"Pullleeesee, Mom! I told you a million times!"

"Honey, you said you had bad thoughts, scary thoughts. You have to tell me what they are so I can help you, and so I—" Sara's voice grew tender. "So I can protect you."

"I didn't push Anna. She fell."

Katie sobbed, shaking her head, gasping.

"I'm not bad, Mom! I'm not bad!"

71

"WE GOT THIS from her psychologist, who was concerned enough to come forward," Pierce said.

Sitting at his desk, staring at his monitor, Art Acker glanced at Pierce.

"One little girl and two deaths, Art," Benton said.

"So she was present at another death." Acker scraped his hand over his face. "How did we miss this?" He glanced at Benton, then resumed studying his monitor. "How?"

The sketch was titled *The Park*.

"Art." Benton leaned forward as they all took in the two stick figures and the dialogue. "This is a damning admission or confession of a disturbed young mind."

"That's your read?" Acker said.

"Think about it. Anna goes over the cliff, and guess what? Katie's got her necklace. No witnesses. Perfect crime."

Acker continued studying Katie's drawing.

"Maybe not so smooth, though," Benton said. "Katie either hit her with the rock first, or Anna did fall to the branch and Katie used the rock to finish her off. Whichever, I think Katie's artwork here is damning."

"Could be she's trying to help her," Pierce said.

"Come on, Kim. She may have been involved in a previous death."

"Just keeping an open mind, looking at all possibilities," Pierce said. "What do you think, Art?"

Acker shook his head. "How the hell did we miss this?"

A soft knock on the doorframe and Grotowski stood there, holding his notebook.

"Come in, Larry," Acker said. "What is it?"

"This is big." Grotowski consulted his notebook. "So, from the get-go, I've been running background on Sara and Katie Harmon—our local and state databases, NCIC, the usual. We got nothing but the traffic violation, a speeding ticket years ago for Nathaniel Harmon, Sara's deceased husband, Katie's dad."

"Right. We know that," Pierce said.

"And I checked with the Canadians, got the RCMP to check on their national databases. And they got nothing."

"So?" Benton said.

"So, I just got off the phone with my contact at the RCMP in Ottawa. Corporal Taylor. Apparently, she went further. She checked with the territorial, provincial and larger municipal databases. She also put out a request for smaller ones to run a check for absolutely anything that came up. Didn't have to result in charges, could be a complaint, anything. The request took time."

"And?" Acker said.

"We got a hit with Sara and Katie."

"A beef in Canada?" Benton's eyes widened. "Maybe that's how we missed it, Art. Maybe this is the previous death?"

Grotowski nodded while consulting his notes.

"I just have a summary, no specifics. This is out of Delta, British Columbia, a suburb in Metro Vancouver. About two years back, Katie Harmon, who was seven at the time, was at a community swimming pool. She got into some kind of verbal exchange with a boy, who I think was eight. He bullied her and she may have threatened him."

"That's it?" Benton said.

"Not long after that, the boy was dead—he'd drowned at the bottom of the pool."

The detectives glanced at each other.

"Man, oh, man," Benton said.

"She was seven at the time?" Pierce said. "What were the circumstances, the result of the investigation? Were there even charges?"

"We don't know any more," Grotowski said. "I got a request in with Delta PD and they're going to hook me up with the lead investigator."

Benton whistled through his teeth. "This thing's breaking wide open," he said. "We gotta take all this to Heidi, Art, and move on Katie."

Digesting the revelation out of Canada, Acker studied the sketch and nodded slowly.

"Alright, let's go."

72

Seattle, Washington

RYAN'S HEART WAS still beating fast.

In the corner of his mind, his journalist's voice warned him to be cautious, to get the facts on Sara Harmon. Just because Sara and her daughter were caught up in the tragic death of Anna Shaw, it didn't make them descendants of Magda.

I have no concrete evidence.

Yet every instinct told him he was closer than ever to Magda. He needed to process it all. He needed to be 100 percent sure about Sara Harmon.

Then he needed a plan, he thought as he rolled his SUV into the car loading lot for the Bainbridge ferry. The trip across Puget Sound to Bainbridge Island and back would be calming and help him decide on what steps to take.

He boarded, secured his car, and got out and took in Seattle's skyline as the boat set sail.

They hadn't gone far when his phone vibrated with a message.

Hi Ryan: I'm Owen Sikes with *Tell-Tale Hearts*. Sonya Rule told me to get back to you re: your request concerning your episode and the woman who identified herself as Lynn calling from Chicago. Unfortunately, we don't have the ability to obtain detailed information on people who contact the show. However, I can confirm that her call did not come from Chicago. It came from Seattle. Wish I could be more helpful. Owen.

"Seattle?" Ryan said out loud to his phone.

That's strange. This "Lynn" gives me bogus information and she's calling from Seattle? Of all places. What's up with that? Could it mean I'm on the right track here in Seattle and this was an attempt to steer me away by getting me to believe that Magda's dead?

He sent Owen a thank-you message.

For the next several minutes he assessed the new information further.

Then he received a call.

"Hi, Ryan, it's Sonya Rule. Is this a good time to talk?"

"Sure, go ahead."

"Did you get Owen's message?"

"I did. Thank you."

"I have another update. The woman who said she has documents just got back to us and wants to talk to you. Do you want to talk to her?"

"Yes, give her my email."

A few seconds passed.

"Done," Sonya said. "I'll keep you posted in case I hear back. Good luck, Ryan."

"Thank you, Sonya."

As the ferry cut farther across the water, Ryan felt a renewed energy, that things seemed to be going in the right direction. He was reinforcing the need to take careful steps when his phone vibrated. A new email had arrived.

Hi Ryan: Your appearance on *Tell-Tale Hearts* broke my heart and I'm hoping I can help. My aunt passed away several years ago and I was going through her belongings with my sisters when we found some interesting things she'd kept. She'd had a troubled life, which led to her spending several years at Montana Women's Prison in Billings. As an inmate there, she got to know Magda and kept a journal. After discussing it with my sisters, we've decided that we'd like to give you a copy of her journal by courier. If you give me your address, we could get it to you as quickly as possible.

Michelle
Queens, NY

He stared at the message.

A journal about Magda?

This could be something. He'd never had access to records of this sort. A prison friend who kept a journal. Yes, he needed to see it. As soon as possible.

But he didn't want to reveal his Seattle address.

Just in case this is some sort of ploy or stunt. You never know.

Michelle had left her phone number with a 917 area code at the bottom of her message. He called. It rang four times before she answered.

"Hi, this is Ryan, is this Michelle?"

"Oh, yes, hi, Ryan."

"Thank you for your message about your aunt's journal."

"Do you think it might help you?"

"It might. I'd like to see it, but I was wondering. If the

journal's not too long, could you scan the pages about Magda and send them to my email in a compressed file? I think that might be the best way."

Michelle took a few seconds to answer.

"I'm not very good at stuff like that, technology. I'll get my nephew to help me with those pages, if that's okay?"

"Absolutely."

"It might take us a little while."

"I'll stand by. And, Michelle, thank you for this. Thank you."

After the call, he listened to the ferry chugging as it slowed for its arrival at the terminal. He got back to his SUV, intent on returning to Seattle.

73

Seattle, Washington

THAT EVENING SARA listened to the low rumble of running water as Katie prepared to take a bath.

While Katie was in the bathroom, Sara waited in Katie's room. Sitting on the bed, Sara touched her trembling hand to her temple, her mind swirling in the wake of the news media, the police investigation, her lawyer.

Just spoke with police and the prosecutor, Rose Aranda had texted her moments ago. No movement to take action. Stay strong.

Sara looked down at Katie's sketchbook.

It was on her lap, open to the drawing of Anna and Katie. Sara's heart broke again. She could not deny the truth about her biological mother and father: Magda and Herman. And the mystery of Magda's prison letter to her mom and dad continued to anguish her.

Why did Magda write to them? Why did Mom keep it secret? I have to know the truth.

Sara's world was spinning, spiraling with dread that something was coming.

"Done, Mom."

Sara looked up to Katie, freshly scrubbed, her teeth brushed, hair combed, fragrant with soap, shampoo—*and innocence.*

We're not like them. We can't be like them. She's just a child.

Sara's fingers shook ever so slightly as she caressed Katie's cheek, then moved so Katie could get into her bed.

"I think you should stay home from school tomorrow."

Hesitating at the tremor in Sara's voice, Katie nodded.

"I might go to work. Val will come over, or you can stay with her. I have to see Grandma later."

"Can I see Grandma, too?"

"I need to go by myself, to talk to her about important stuff."

Sara followed Katie's gaze to the sketchbook she held in her hand.

"Honey, I need to know what happened with Anna. It's more important than ever."

Katie stared at Sara.

"And—" Sara's voice cracked. "I love you and no matter what you tell me, I will protect you and never let anything happen to you. But I need to know what really happened, while we still have time."

Sara's hair slid, curtained over her face. Her fingers shook as she brushed at it. She saw Katie processing her devastation, as if it unnerved her, but Sara pressed on.

"Did Anna give you the necklace on the bus?"

Katie nodded.

"Did she fall taking a selfie?"

"Yes."

"But you said you had terrible thoughts, scary, bad thoughts?" Sara held up the closed sketchbook. "Horrible thoughts, like with the boy, but worse."

Katie's face went blank.

"Tell me what they are. I won't think you're a bad person. I will always love you, but you have to tell me now."

Katie shut her eyes while Sara waited.

"When Anna backed up to the edge, I told her to be careful. I did. But right then, just seeing her standing on the edge of the cliff, this thought jumped into my head. I don't know why or how. It came like an electric shock, or lightning flash, like a voice and…"

"What was it? What did it say, Katie?"

"It said—*what would it be like to push Anna over the edge and watch her fall?*"

74

THE NEXT MORNING Pierce joined Acker and the others for a crucial meeting with Heidi Wong to respond to developments in the investigation of Anna Shaw's death.

Wong's office was in the newish Judge Patricia H. Clark Children and Family Justice Center in First Hill, south of Seattle University. Wong, facing a heavy court load, had requested they meet there.

Pierce, Benton, Tilden and Grotowski gathered in the lobby with Acker. After clearing security they found Wong working on her laptop at the end of a table in the conference room she'd reserved for the meeting.

"Hey, guys," she said as they settled in.

Wong reached for her commuter cup next to her laptop, sipped some coffee, then set up the video call with two others from Juvenile Division downtown. The screen at the end of the room split, with Wong's colleague, deputy prosecutor

Edgar Leichter, and their boss, Victoria Mullen, who headed the division.

After the introductions, Mullen started.

"As Heidi has emphasized from the outset, charging a nine-year-old with murder is extremely rare and challenging," she said. "The law presumes that children under twelve are incapable of committing a crime, unless this presumption can be removed. The offence has to be the magnitude of a homicide, and you must prove the child committed the act and understood what they did was wrong. All to say, our job here is to remove the presumption. I've been briefed on the background. Art, your people can update us on what you think are the new deciding elements."

"Thanks, Victoria. I'm going to pass it to Kim Pierce, who's leading."

Pierce looked to her laptop and the notes she'd made last night working at home on the kitchen table.

"Katie Harmon's psychologist was concerned enough to come forward with a number of troubling concerns. The first being the sketch, which we've shared with you."

"You believe this could be considered an admission?" Mullen asked.

"Yes, taken with the other considerations, including Katie's mother raising questions that have us assuming a history of violence in Katie's family."

"And what do we know about that?"

"We've learned that Katie was present when a boy drowned in Canada two years ago after a verbal disagreement at a community pool. We're expecting more details from Canadian police."

"Alright," Mullen said. "Where are we on all the other aspects of the investigation?"

"You've read the ME's report?" Acker said.

"We have," Mullen said.

"We're confident we can recover prints from the rock to compare with Katie's," Pierce said.

"Have you proven that Katie can lift the rock that is considered to be the murder weapon?" Mullen asked.

"We're confident she had the strength to lift the rock," Acker said.

"Other suspects? And reasonable doubt?"

"We've canvassed and interviewed, and in every case possible, have run background and checked fingerprints. A few forensic aspects are being completed, but we've essentially ruled out all other possibilities," Acker said. "We've recovered Anna Shaw's phone, but it's too damaged to be of use."

Mullen glanced at her notes.

"You've presented a compelling case," she said. "Give me the bottom line here in plain language."

"Everything points to Katie Harmon killing Anna Shaw in a number of scenarios—striking her with the rock and pushing her off the cliff, or pushing her off the cliff and dropping the rock on her. Maybe for the necklace, maybe not. But everything points to Katie killing Anna Shaw and knowing it was wrong."

"Alright," Mullen said. "Can you give me a few minutes with my team?"

Pierce and the others left to get a coffee at the cafeteria.

By the time they'd returned, Mullen and the others were ready.

"We think we're as close as we're going to get," Mullen said. "While you tie up loose ends with forensics, we'll proceed preparing a charge of second-degree murder against Kaitlyn Jean Harmon."

75

DEVELOPING FINGERPRINTS FROM the rock used in Anna Shaw's death was more challenging than Kelly Jensen had expected.

At times the senior forensics analyst had to interrupt her effort for cases coming to trial. Still, she always returned to processing the rock. But even with the kit and guidance from the Israeli police on new techniques, every attempt seemed futile.

She wasn't giving up.

At her worktable she resumed studying the guide. Using cyanoacrylate and ninhydrin hadn't worked. For the past couple of hours, she'd tried the more advanced chemical and imaging methods set out in the guide.

Now she was completing her analysis of the latest results.

She looked at them. *What?* She looked again.

Jensen sat stock-still.

Something was emerging.

She waited.

It's for real. It's emerging. Oh, my God, it's really working. We're getting something!

She turned the rock to view different angles.

There and there.

Jensen captured images and soon filled one of her large monitors with fuzzy patterns. Tapping on her keyboard and using her mouse, she adjusted, enlarged and sharpened the focus to distinct groupings of loops, whorls and arches. They were good enough to run a comparison to a suspect.

Jensen shot a quick glance to one of her other computer monitors.

The one that displayed Katie Harmon's fingerprints.

76

THAT AFTERNOON, WHILE VAL ROSSI read *Crime and Punishment* on her tablet in the living room of the Harmons' home, Bingo left her side to trot up the stairs to Katie's bedroom.

Panting, tail wagging, the retriever put his head on Katie's lap and she rubbed her hand over his back.

She was at her desk, working carefully, drawing on a sheet of paper.

Mom had gone to Bothell to see Grandma. Katie wanted to go, too, but Mom said she needed to go alone.

It was serious. Everything was very serious now.

Katie angled her head to examine her drawing. It was stick-figure Anna standing on the edge of the cliff, taking her selfie. Pulling her head back to study it, Katie stroked the tiny heart on her necklace she was wearing.

I'm in more trouble now that I told Mom what my bad thoughts were. Mom pretended she wasn't upset. But what happened to Anna wasn't my fault and nobody will believe me. It was like a big war in my brain, a huge horrible war between good and bad.

Katie lowered her face next to Anna on the page.

It's a good thing I didn't tell Mom all of my bad thoughts.

77

Bothell, Washington

SARA FELT LIKE she was being kicked in the gut, again and again.

She'd gotten little sleep the previous night, tossing and turning until the hour before dawn. When she was at work, she'd kept customers waiting, then messed up several orders. She'd eaten nothing all day; she was in a fog.

Now, while she was driving to Bothell, her knuckles whitened on the wheel. She struggled to endure the agony of the maelstrom grinding around her as Katie's words thundered in her mind.

What would it be like to push Anna over the edge and watch her fall?

In the wake of Katie's revelation, Sara couldn't escape the dread that police, media—*the world*—were closing in on her with one question tearing her heart: *Did Katie kill Anna?*

Sara didn't know the answer, didn't know what police knew.

She was lost, helpless. She needed to talk to her mother. Only her mother knew the truth about Sara's life, her bloodline— about Magda's letter and what it meant.

If the horrors of my past have come to life in Katie…

Sara had been so consumed with worry she found herself in the Silverbrook Hills Senior Living Home parking lot without remembering much of the drive. She went to register at the desk, disappointed that Hetta Boden, the manager, was there.

"Hello, Sara." Boden's voice was calm, icy. "Kaitlyn isn't with you?"

"No," Sara said while signing in. *Does Hetta know?* she thought. Sara took quick stock of the lobby, where some of the residents were playing cards or reading. *Do they know? They can't know. Our names haven't been made public. No.* "No, Katie's with a friend. It's just me."

"And have you been receiving our notices of the adjustment? We need you to complete the financial form. It's due now."

"Yes." Sara pasted on a smile for Boden. "Thank you." She left, stepping into an open elevator, reaching for the button to close the doors.

"Hold it, please." Bella Spencer hurried to join her.

Sara held the doors for her, then pressed the button for the fourth floor.

"Thank you, Sara." Smiling, Bella caught her breath. "Oh, how nice to see you again. Where's that pretty daughter of yours?"

"She's home." Sara looked up at the display, her chin crumpling.

Bella noticed.

"Is everything alright?"

Taking a breath, Sara managed to say: "Thanks. I'm fine." The car droned, then the bell chimed. The doors opened for the fourth floor and Sara went down the hall, turning a corner to Suite 404 with the large-lettered sign Mrs. Marjorie Cole. The door to her mother's room was open. She was watching *Wheel of Fortune.*

"Sweetheart," Marjorie said and switched off the set.

Sara closed the door and embraced her, holding her for a long time. She sat on the bed next to her mother.

"You know everything that's going on, Mom?"

"From what you've told me and what I've seen on the news."

"It's horrible." Sara squeezed the tissue in her fist. "I'm so scared."

Marjorie rubbed Sara's shoulder.

"They didn't show you, or Katie, on the news. Or say your names," Marjorie said. "I don't believe for a second the things being said. This could be a big awful mistake."

Sara shook her head.

"Mom, we both know what's really happening."

"Do we really know everything?"

Sara recounted everything to her mother about Anna Shaw's death, about Katie, the necklace, Katie's bad thoughts, Dr. Mehta, the police, getting a lawyer, every detail, every fear. She held nothing back. She reached into her bag for Katie's notebook and flipped to the sketch of Katie and Anna on the cliff. Looking at it, pain and love filled Marjorie's face.

Then from her bag, Sara pulled the old envelopes related to Magda's letter to her parents.

"I found these hidden in the attic."

Marjorie looked at them in Sara's hand.

"You never told me that she contacted you from prison," Sara said. "You never told me what she wanted. Why?"

Staring at them, Marjorie released a soft groan, then said: "I wanted to protect you."

"What did she want?"

Marjorie looked off to her calendar on the wall at today's date, which she'd marked with a tiny heart.

"You know, it's funny," Marjorie said. "Today's the day you officially and legally became our daughter."

"Yes, Mom. But tell me, I have a right to know. What did Magda want?"

"She wanted to see you when she got out of prison. She wanted to know if she had grandchildren. She wanted to be part of your life."

"Part of my life?" Sara was stunned. "Where's her letter?"

"I burned it. Dad and I decided no good would come from sharing that with you. So, I told Magda no."

"You wrote back to her?"

"Yes."

"But what if she got your address and came to our house?"

"I was careful to go through the Montana Attorney General, to protect us. Magda didn't even know our names."

Sara stared at the envelopes.

"Maybe I was wrong," Marjorie said, "to deprive you of the decision to see her. I only wanted to protect you."

"What did you tell her?"

"I told her in no uncertain terms that she could never be part of your life and to never try contacting you again."

"What did she say? Did she write back?"

"No. We never heard from her again. Even after she got out of prison and disappeared. It's been more than seven years now. That was the end of it. I'm sorry I never told you. I wanted to keep it buried in the past. I would do anything to protect you from her. Maybe I was wrong to bring you up with so many secrets, seeing what it's done to our family now. I am so, so sorry." Marjorie searched her eyes. "Did you ever wish to see her?"

"Never." Sara looked at Katie's sketch. "But we know the truth, Mom. It's not the end of it. Look at what's happened."

"Sara, no. I don't believe it."

"Believe it, Mom. Not a day goes by that I don't think about who I am and what they did. And how no one will ever forget. I will always feel the pain and shame. I can't help bearing some of the responsibility for their acts.

"That's why, like you and Dad, I always guarded against being found out and persecuted for being the child of monsters. That's why—" Sara held up her wrist "—as soon as I was old enough, and you said you understood, I got this tattoo to hide the mark that ties me to them. I can't change who my biological parents are any more than I can wash away the awful shame."

"No, no, Sara. You and Katie are innocents. What they did has nothing to do with who you are. You have a right to live free of their crimes."

"Do we? My God, look at Katie, Mom. *There is an evil in us!*"

"No, Sara, don't say that."

"It's why I never wanted to have children. I never wanted to pass on their vile bloodline. Then I met Nathaniel and he had such a good heart. He filled me with hope."

"Nathaniel was so good."

"But after that first time I looked at the news photos of their victims—I don't know how old I was then—but I imagined myself being one of them, feeling their terror, their pain. It haunts me because…"

Sara caught her breath.

"Because they brought me with them. I was there. They used me to lure those poor innocent people." Again, Sara looked at the tattoo covering her scar. "They cry out to me in my dreams. I can still feel the woman clawing, gouging into my arm—I can hear her screams."

"Sara," Marjorie said. "You must listen to me. There is a line between good and evil and you never have crossed it, and you never will because we raised you right. You might have your thoughts, but I know you have a moral spine that will not bend to evil. Nathaniel had a good heart, and Katie has his goodness and your goodness in her. She may be struggling, but she's not evil. You have to believe that."

"But what if some kind of strong force in her blood has pushed Katie across that line?"

They both shot a look to the door and a noise that sounded just outside. Sara opened the door, glancing both ways down the empty hall.

Nothing.

She'd just returned to her mother's side when her phone vibrated with a text from Rose Aranda.

A friend in the prosecuting attorney's office tells me they are poised to charge Katie. We need to prepare.

Sara covered her mouth with her hand.

"What is it?" Marjorie asked.

"Police are getting ready to charge Katie. I have to go."

78

A SOFT CHEER floated across the forensic section to where Erik Foy was working, drawing him to the analysts gathered at his supervisor's worktable.

Kelly Jensen had succeeded in recovering fingerprints from the rock used in Anna Shaw's death. Developing prints from a stone was no small feat, Foy thought. This was significant on several levels.

"Thank you. Alright." Jensen smiled a little, keeping her eyes on her monitor, the screen spilt, displaying large clear images of fingerprints from the rock on one side and Katie Harmon's prints on the other. "I still have comparison to do. So, everybody back to work. Erik, we really need you to finish on Carl Benton's tablet, so we can wrap up this case."

"I'm on it."

Encouraged by Jensen's achievement, Foy returned to his effort to get a single clear usable fingerprint from Benton's tablet.

It wasn't easy but he eventually recovered something from the area where fingerprints had overlapped. He enlarged the image on his monitor. Now his challenge was to separate the entangled impression into two distinct prints and compare them.

Foy had to locate the endpoints and real-branch points of the overlapped image. Enhancing it would involve several steps, including image binarization, ridge thinning and minutiae extraction. He was making progress, but it was meticulous work.

He'd lost track of time when he saw Jensen stop working on comparing the prints she'd recovered. She left her worktable and hurried out of the section with a grave expression.

Something's up, Foy thought.

Meanwhile he'd succeeded in recovering two prints for comparison.

The first was easy; it was Benton's.

The second print belonged to the woman who was in the park, Marilyn Hamilton. Foy was pleased because it was a detailed image, good enough to run through the Automated Fingerprint Identification System.

After several commands and adjustments, Foy submitted Hamilton's print to AFIS.

Pressing the last key, he said: "And away we go."

79

Seattle, Washington

THE HANDWRITING WAS NEAT, legible on the lined pages of the journal belonging to Tracy Linda Loman, from when she was an inmate at Montana Women's Prison in Billings.

The attachments had come through from Loman's niece Michelle.

Ryan had checked them for viruses. Then he called the Montana Department of Corrections and an official there confirmed that Tracy Linda Loman, Inmate #3875647, had served time there.

Ryan began reading immediately, Loman's observations taking him deeper into the darkness that had consumed Carrie.

He came to the first reference to Magda.

So as fate would have it, not long after my arrival, I've become friends with the infamous Magdalena Vryker, or

Magdalena Kurtz, as she prefers after hubby Herman hung himself. She's now got just 5 years to go and seems chatty.

He continued to other passages, reading carefully.

She tells me she's learned Spanish, French, studied theatrical makeup so she can make herself look completely different (we have a very good library) and is working on a new life plan for when she rejoins the world.

Ryan slowed to reread the passage, then continued.

One day she tells me about her devotion and belief in the power of numbers, how the numbers told her of some great meaning, a sign, that her daughter was born on the date she was. How it was all woven into her destiny, or some cosmic thing. Then she said the date she met Herman Vryker, and what it meant, something about being selected to do great things. She'd go on about why things happened, what the numbers mean. She has this fanatical weird obsession with numbers.

So she's fixated on numbers.

One time after lunch Magda tells me about all the psych sessions, tests and counseling she's had. How she told every psychiatrist who assessed her what they needed to hear so it would help her. She told them that Herman abused her and made her go along with his sick fantasies. How she had to do it or he would've killed her and their daughter, Hayley, which was pretty much all lies.

A liar, no surprise there.

We were out in the yard, walking alone along the fence, when Magda stops and says: "The truth is I loved hunting and luring them. I loved the power of the kill. It was our destiny. It was written in the stars and the numbers for us. If it was in the numbers and the stars, I would do it again. I would have to."

What the——? Ryan took a moment, then continued reading.

I asked her if she actually knew where the bodies of her victims were. She gave me a smile that turned my blood to ice. Oh, this woman is a piece of work. Very intelligent, manipulative and very dangerous. Very dangerous.

She knows where they are. She damn well knows where Carrie is. Ryan slammed his fist on his desk, then continued, coming close to Magda's release and the final passages in Loman's journal.

Magda's time inside is short now, and she tells me about wanting to find her daughter, Hayley, who was taken from her and adopted by another family. Magda says she has no idea who the family is, where they live, their names, nothing. But she vows to find them. Magda says that with her sentence ending, she's working with Women Healing in the Forgiving Light and her lawyer to find a way to find them. She wanted to find them so she could make a plea for reunification with her daughter, Hayley. How Hayley would be a grown woman now and Magda may have grandchildren.

Ryan couldn't believe what he was reading.

Magda tells me that she finally was able to get a letter out to Hayley's family through the group and her lawyer and she's filled with hope.

Ryan skimmed ahead, past a few mundane passages.

Magda got a letter today. The family's response. It has left her seething. At times when she tells me, her entire body shakes. "They stole my baby from me and this is what they say." Magda showed me what they said: You are not her mother. She never wants to see you. Stay away. As far as we're concerned, you have no role in our lives. You mean nothing to her. You do not exist. I looked at Magda and it was as if a switch had been thrown, something behind her eyes was burning.

That was the last passage.

Ryan took a moment and a breath to digest it all.

Then again and again he read it over, looking for any missed reference Magda may have made in reaching out for her daughter. For any reference to the people he had pursued in the past and was pursuing now.

He found none, of course.

He was steepling his fingers and touching them to his lips when his phone rang. It was his mother.

He answered.

"Ryan, oh, Ryan."

Surprised by the excited nervousness in her voice, he feared bad news—maybe something had happened to his father.

"What is it, Mom?"

"We got the DNA results back. You found her!"

80

Seattle, Washington

IT WAS EARLY evening when Sara got home.

Bingo was first to greet her, nuzzling her leg as she went to the kitchen where Val and Katie were finishing cleaning up, drying dishes.

"Hi, Mom," Katie said.

"Hi, Sara," Val said. She put the dish towel away. "We just had chicken sandwiches for supper. Would you like me to fix one for you?"

"No, thank you, Val. Katie, you go upstairs and I'll be up."

"Okay. Come on, Bingo."

After Katie and the dog left, Sara sat at the table.

Reading the fear in her face, Val went to her.

"It's all wrong," Val said. "What they said on the news, at the school—I refuse to believe it for a second, you know that."

Sara nodded weakly.

"Tell me what I can do to help," Val said.

Swallowing her pain, Sara shook her head.

"You've already helped us so much."

"Want me to keep Katie with me for the night?"

Sara shook her head.

"You know you're like family to me. I'll do anything to help you."

"I know that, Val. Thank you."

"Want me to stay a little longer?"

"No, thank you. You've done so much for us and it means the world to me, but I've got some things to do."

Val smiled at Sara.

"I'll get Bingo and give you guys some space." Val hugged Sara. "If there's anything, anything at all, just call me."

Moments later, after Val and Bingo departed, Sara called Rose Aranda.

"What more do you know?"

"From what I gather, they're working into the evening."

"Oh, my God, are they coming to arrest her tonight?"

"Not likely. They don't have the formal charge ready yet."

Sara released a creaking sob, as if she were breaking.

"They're going to charge my nine-year-old daughter with murder! I can't lose her!"

"Sara, hang on."

"What if we left, right now? We have friends in Canada. Or we could go to Mexico?"

"Sara. You've got to hang on. First, we've got to see what they're going to do, okay? I'll be over first thing in the morning. We can fight this."

Sara collapsed into a chair at the table.

Was it Dr. Mehta? Did she go to police? What does it matter now? This is the hardest thing. Is God taking Katie from me? Just like Nathaniel. Just like Dad. God is punishing me for who I am, for being part of what they did to all those people.

She looked at the tattoo that covered her scar.

Because I was there.

The stairs squeaked.

Katie appeared at the bottom of the stairs, startling Sara. "I'm in big serious trouble, aren't I, Mom?"

Sara swallowed and went to her, every nerve ending tingling.

"Yes."

81

ELBOW ON HIS DESK, phone pressed to his ear, Detective Larry Grotowski took notes and glanced at the time.

Still early evening.

He had an apple in his desk to snack on before he got something more substantial later. This was going to be a long night. He was on the line with the lead investigator from Delta, British Columbia, who was detailing the case of the boy who died when Katie Harmon was present two years earlier.

"It happened at the Elmside Heights Community Pool." Detective Dennis Sandler read from Delta's case file. "The boy's name was Myles Henry Zuter. Age seven. I'll give you his DOB."

Zuter and his family were from Switzerland. They were visiting family in Delta when they went to the pool. The boy was big for his age and was known to have teased, some said "bullied," other children, Sandler said.

Katie Harmon, aged seven, was with her mother. They were from Seattle and were visiting friends in Delta.

"At poolside Myles was snapping his towel at some girls and calling them names, according to witnesses. Then he pulled Katie's hair. She told him to stop. Amused, he pulled her hair again, only harder," Sandler said.

"This time she told him that if he didn't stop, something, and I'm quoting, 'something very, very bad would happen to him.' Myles laughed at her and left."

Sandler said that the pool was near capacity. The lifeguards were busy breaking up horseplay of older teens. It was estimated that fifteen to twenty minutes after his exchange with Katie, Myles Zuter was found at the bottom of the pool. Adults jumped in to rescue him. Efforts to resuscitate him failed.

"Some witnesses noted Zuter's exchange with Katie Harmon and rumors circulated that she caused his death," Sandler said.

The investigation and statements from adults who dove into the water to rescue Zuter showed that he'd been trapped under the water. The drawstring of his swim shorts got tangled in the filtration mechanism and tightened around him. He couldn't remove them to free himself. Katie Harmon had never ventured to that area of the pool.

His death was an accidental drowning.

"Katie Harmon was distraught, traumatized because of what she'd said to Zuter in the moments before his death. I imagine she'll carry the guilt of this with her all her life," Sandler said.

"But she had nothing to do with the boy's death?" Grotowski said.

"Absolutely nothing. Witnesses said she was at the opposite side of the pool at the time. It was a tragic accident," Sandler said. "I understand she may be connected to a recent death your way?"

"That's what we're investigating," Grotowski said. "Thank you for this, Dennis."

"Sure, you bet."

Grotowski sat back in his chair, then swiveled to tell Tilden and the others. But he was the only one there. While on the phone he'd missed the activity. Everyone was in Acker's office, including Kelly Jensen from forensics. Grabbing his notebook, Grotowski joined them.

"You're certain, Kelly?" Acker said.

"Yes. We definitely got prints from the rock. I compared them with Katie Harmon's and we have zero points of similarity, nothing with minutiae, pores and ridges. The prints on the rock are not Katie's. But I haven't run the new prints through the databases yet, or compared them with the others we collected for the case. I wanted to tell you guys right away that those aren't Katie Harmon's prints on the rock."

Benton cursed under his breath.

"Where does that leave us?" Tilden said, turning to acknowledge Grotowski.

Acker interrupted his concentration to read Grotowski's concern.

"You got something, Larry?"

"Actually, I do." He glanced at his notes. "Just spoke with the primary investigator on that case in Canada. Turns out Katie Harmon was present when the boy drowned, had words with him, but had nothing to do with his death."

"What?" Benton said.

"Yup. It was an accidental drowning. She just happened to be there."

Acker folded his arms, his face creased in thought as he rocked.

"I'll have to get the prosecuting attorney's office to stop everything," Acker said.

"Wait." Pierce turned to Jensen. "We still need to run the prints from—"

Jensen's phone rang.

"It's Erik. One sec." Jensen held her palm to Pierce and took the call.

"Kelly, I got a hit from AFIS after running the tablet print on Marilyn Hamilton, and boy, did we get something!"

"Go ahead."

Foy began telling her, and Jensen's eyebrows lifted in disbelief as she turned to the others who were waiting. She held up a finger.

"Erik, Erik," Jensen said. "We need to compare your print from the tablet with the one from the rock. I'll be right there!"

82

Seattle, Washington

THIS TIME RYAN'S sources had been right.

Sara Dawn Harmon was Hayley Vryker, the daughter of Magda and Herman Vryker.

The Vrykers' DNA was in the national database of convicted criminals. The samples Ryan had provided were tested against the Vrykers' DNA and resulted in establishing a "familial DNA" connection with Sara's, which Ryan had gotten from a discarded toothbrush he'd found the night he rummaged through Sara's trash.

After Ryan's mother alerted him to the successful DNA results, he drove to the Jet Town Diner, even though it was evening. He was aware from his research and surveillance of his Seattle subjects that Sara tended to work earlier shifts. But he was hopeful he might see her here.

Sitting alone in a booth, he ordered a coffee.

It wasn't busy.

But it took everything he had to remain still and think.

All these years he'd been searching for a way to find Carrie. Despite every close call, every miss, every false hope and every failure, he kept going. He'd never given up and now, now he had done it. He'd found the connection, the irrefutable path to Magda.

Years ago, DNA collected from the crimes, and later from Magda and Herman, had eventually been submitted to the Combined DNA Index System, CODIS, the national DNA database. Through his mom and police friends Ryan was able to have the cast-off DNA he'd collected from every major subject in his research compared with Magda's and Herman's DNA through familial DNA searching.

Time and time again they consistently found that nothing matched.

It was looking futile.

Ryan's mom had wanted him to abandon his search for Carrie.

But this time, they got a hit. This time the DNA he'd collected from Sara Harmon showed she was a biological relative of Magda and Herman Vryker.

For nearly thirty minutes Ryan studied the tranquil diner. Sara wasn't here.

He reached into his thoughts. For years he'd planned and rehearsed this moment in his mind, as to the best way to approach Magda's daughter if, and when, he found her. Now that he'd found her, he weighed his options and the dark deeper concern that Sara and her daughter had played a part in the tragic death of her daughter's babysitter.

Is there no end to the wickedness that runs in Magda's bloodline?

Ryan shut his eyes for a moment.

He'd held off on approaching Sara. But that was before he had confirmation of who she was.

He could call Sara or send her a message, requesting to talk. But she could ignore him. He could also show up at her house. No doubt it would upset her, even scare her. But, if he had that one moment to tell Sara that their lives were connected, that he needed her help, it might work.

This could be my only chance. I can't let it slip away.

He placed several dollar bills on the table. He was light in the chest, his entire insides vibrating when he left the diner for his car.

It had started to rain.

83

NIGHT HAD FALLEN.

Pierce and Benton were wearing body armor, sitting in their unmarked Ford Explorer half a block from the Blue Rose Bay Apartments.

As they waited for the all clear from the arrest team, Benton worked over the stick of Juicy Fruit in his mouth.

Events had unfolded with lightning speed once the forensic analysts had matched Marilyn Hamilton's prints from Benton's tablet with the prints on the rock used to kill Anna Shaw.

Again, they'd submitted Hamilton's name, date of birth and social security number to NCIC, the national crime database. Hamilton had no criminal record. But after submitting Hamilton's prints to AFIS, they found they matched the prints of convicted serial killer Magdalena Ursula Kurtz, also known as Magdalena Ursula Vryker.

Magdalena had been released seven years earlier, without

conditions, as part of a plea deal, after serving twenty years in Montana Women's Prison for a series of murders in 1994 and 1995 across Montana, Idaho and Washington.

Magdalena was living a quiet life under the alias Marilyn Hamilton.

Acker alerted the prosecuting attorney's office. A judge moved fast to provide an arrest warrant for murder that was emailed to Pierce and Benton.

"The way this all came down." Benton shook his head as he chewed. "We got this by the skin of our teeth."

"That we got that snippet of video from the parking lot of the park, that we got her prints and that Jensen and her team did what they did—yeah, it's a stunner."

"Birdwatcher." Benton eyed the apartment complex. "Serial killer."

"When we sat in her apartment," Pierce said, "I got a bad vibe about her but I couldn't put my finger on it."

Pierce and Benton were vaguely familiar with Kurtz/Vryker's crimes in a case that was largely prosecuted in Montana decades ago. The murders Magdalena and her husband committed reached back nearly thirty years. There were occasional TV crime shows, social media chatter, but for Pierce and Benton, the case had no relation to Seattle or King County.

Until now.

And now it deepened the mystery about Magdalena's role in Anna Shaw's death.

"Why was Magdalena in the park when the Sunny Days group was there?" Benton asked while watching the apartment.

"There was only a gap of a few minutes when Katie ran for help, so she had to be watching."

"So why was she there?" Benton asked.

"Maybe a connection to Katie?" Pierce said. "Remember,

Dr. Mehta said Sara Harmon raised concerns about her family's history of violence."

Benton's walkie-talkie crackled with a dispatch from the arrest team.

It was time to move.

King County and Seattle police had stopped traffic along the street. They blocked the exits and entrances to the building's parking lot. They quietly evacuated residents from all units near Hamilton's, then shut off the elevators and put officers in all the stairwells. The building superintendent helped with a key for Hamilton's unit, if needed.

It was.

The heavily armed arrest unit got no response when they banged on the door.

They entered the apartment, guns drawn, and searched it room by room.

Hamilton wasn't there.

Pierce and Benton arrived to check it before crime scene people seized her laptop and other items. As the detectives walked through the apartment, Pierce went to the bookshelf in the living room. Taking a moment, she surveyed the framed family photos, the girl on the pony, the boy at the hockey rink and others.

She froze.

The photo of a little girl in a bright yellow raincoat holding a rainbow-colored umbrella, splashing in puddles with her bright blue rubber boots.

It was identical to the paper stock photo in the frame she'd bought.

That's it. That's what was familiar.

Pierce then studied the other photos more closely: the wedding and graduation photos, the white-haired man fishing with a boy.

Like the little girl, they all looked like models, stock photos.

They're not her real family. Who keeps photos of a fake family? Someone with no family?

"Look at this, Kim."

Benton was staring at a wall calendar in the kitchen, dotted with handwritten notations on different days.

"What is it?"

"Look what she wrote on the last one, today's date."

Pierce read the tiny neat script in blue ink: *Today's the day!*

She exchanged a glance with Benton.

Neither one of them knew the significance of the date.

Pierce swallowed hard, because whatever it was, she sensed that they were too late.

84

Bothell, Washington

AT THE SILVERBROOK Hills Senior Living Home, a soft knock sounded at Marjorie Cole's door.

She'd been sitting up in her bed watching the rain web down her window and turned to see Bella Spencer at the entrance to her room.

"Your door was still open. I'm sorry, did I disturb you?"

"No."

"Would you like some company?"

"Okay." Marjorie's weak smile couldn't mask her torment. Bella sat in the chair next to her bed.

"I saw Sara on the elevator a little earlier, and my, she looked upset."

Marjorie's chin quivered but she was silent.

"And now you look upset. Forgive me, I don't mean to pry, but is something wrong?"

Blinking at her tears, Marjorie turned back to her window. "That's quite a storm we've got out there," she said.

"Goodness, I am prying. I'm sorry."

"No, no, don't apologize." Marjorie looked down to study the crumpled tissue in her hands. "It's just family matters, you know?"

A moment followed with only the sound of the rain on the window.

"Family matters," Bella repeated. "We know all about that, don't we?"

Marjorie nodded.

"In fact—" Bella stood and closed the door, then locked it "—I wrote to you about a family matter."

Marjorie was puzzled.

"And you wrote back to me," Bella said.

A new wave of concern rolled across Marjorie.

"Do you remember what I said?" Bella stood at the foot of the bed. "I told you my dream of starting over with my daughter. I told you that after twenty years I was a changed person. I sought forgiveness. I begged you for mercy. I begged you to let me see Hayley."

Marjorie's face whitened.

"Ahh, it's all coming back to you now," Bella said. "Then you'll remember what you wrote to me. You showed me no mercy, no forgiveness. And you present yourself as a good person, always helping others, holier than thou. You took Hayley from me! You turned her against me! You said I didn't exist! Well, I do exist!"

Marjorie reached for her button to alert the staff for help.

Bella slapped her hand away.

"It took me a long time to find you. But, when you use a lawyer and go through the state and county bureaucracy, flooding them with every sort of written request, well, things like names and addresses slip through the cracks. And I crawled through one of them. Here I am."

"Please leave."

"You may have turned Hayley against me. But when I learned about Katie, my beautiful granddaughter, my heart soared."

"Please. Just leave."

"You look uncomfortable. Let me take care of that for you."

Bella looked at the large pillow next to the bed. She picked it up with both hands.

"How I've waited for this day. You know today's date and what it means?" Bella slowly raised the pillow. "The numbers and the date align. Today's the day you took everything from me." She stepped closer to Marjorie. "And today, I'll take everything from you."

85

HETTA BODEN PRIDED herself in keeping all her client files up to date and orderly.

In every case the notices of the fee increase at the Silverbrook Hills Senior Living Home had been addressed by the families or estates.

All but one.

The case of Marjorie Cole.

This annoyed Boden because the deadline was looming and it was as if Cole's daughter, Sara Harmon, didn't care. Didn't Sara realize that the home may be forced to deliver her mother to her doorstep?

Working into the evening in her office, Boden bit her bottom lip.

Then she snatched the keys for Suite 404. Perhaps if she stressed the situation directly to Marjorie, she could convey it to Sara.

Boden took the elevator to the fourth floor and stepped into the hall. She turned the corner and stopped at 404.

She knocked on the doorframe.

"It's Hetta Boden, Mrs. Cole," she said to the closed door. "I need to speak to you."

Boden waited in the silence then knocked again.

"Are you in need of help? I'm coming in, Mrs. Cole."

Her keys jingled. She unlocked the door and swung it open.

"Mrs. Cole?" Boden stepped inside to a still room.

Her bathroom door was open, the light off. The TV was off. Boden stepped toward the bed and froze.

"Oh, my God!"

86

"WHAT'S WRONG WITH ME, MOM?"

Sara was now with Katie in the kitchen and took deep breaths, struggling to keep up the facade of being in control.

"Honey…" Sara searched for words. "Anna's death was traumatic, like getting a wound in your heart and your mind, you know?"

"Everybody says that I killed her and that police are going to get me because I'm this terrible killer."

"Honey—"

"And you got a lawyer person—I don't understand. I'm so scared."

"Hold on, let's get you back upstairs to your room."

Sitting on the bed, Sara took hold of Katie's shoulders gently and, with all the love and resolve she could summon, stared into her eyes.

"Yes, it's scary, because it's complicated. That's why we have

Rose to help us. She'll be here in the morning, so listen to me. No matter what police say or do, nothing bad will happen. We will protect you, but, and this is so important, you can't keep any secrets about what truly happened on the cliff. Do you understand, Katie?"

She nodded.

"Now, you said that when Anna was taking her selfie, a bad thought came into your head like lightning, asking what it would be like to push her over the edge. Is that true?"

Katie lowered her head.

"Is that true, Katie?"

"Yes."

"Is that all?"

Katie was silent.

"Is that all, Katie? I swear to God, you have to tell me because police will be here tomorrow. So, is that all?"

Katie shook her head.

"What else?"

Katie, her voice barely above a whisper, said: "The thought that jumped into my head also said—" Katie stopped.

"What, honey? It also said what?"

Big tears rolled down Katie's face.

"It also said do it! Push her!"

Sara recoiled, mentally absorbing what Katie had revealed.

"Did you do it?"

"No!" Katie shook her head. "It was like this big war in my brain! A huge horrible war between good and bad. Seeing her standing so close to the edge and the voice telling me to push her."

Sara blinked, absorbing the revelation.

"But another thought, like a voice, said no, don't do it. I knew, Mom, it would be wrong. So I didn't do it. I just kept telling Anna to stop backing up. But she didn't listen and she fell. Then everything happened so fast, like an awful, awful dream! I thought, she fell because of me, because I was thinking about it. What is wrong with me? I was so scared. Why did I have those thoughts? Why didn't she listen to me and not go so close to the edge? I saw her hanging on to the branch. She was looking up at me, crying for help, then I ran and ran!"

Katie sobbed.

Sara put her arms around her.

"Okay, it's okay. Honey, bad thoughts are bad thoughts. Everybody has them at some point. I've had some but it doesn't mean I want to hurt people. Oh, sweetie, I know you feel it's wrong to have them but you must never do what they say— and you didn't. You didn't because you're not a bad person. I'm so happy that you told me."

Sara's phone rang. But she'd left it downstairs.

Thinking it could be her mom, or Rose Aranda, she pulled away from Katie.

"That could be important. Stay here, I'll get my phone."

Sara hurried down the stairs with a measure of hope rising in her heart. Grabbing her phone from the kitchen table, she was drawn to the window by the headlights of a car stopping in front of her house. Without looking at the caller's number, she answered.

"Sara Harmon?"

"Yes."

"This is Hetta Boden at Silverbrook Hills."

Hetta Boden. Sara winced. If that woman was calling about payments—but her tone was different; it sounded frayed, urgent, and there was background noise.

"Yes."

"Ms. Harmon, Sara." Boden sounded uncharacteristically human. "Sara, I'm so, so very sorry to have to inform you that your mother has passed away."

Sara's knees buckled.

Her mother's face, voice, her fragrance, her touch blazed through her. Steadying herself on the counter, a bile-soaked cry erupted from her gut, shooting up the back of her throat.

"Oh, God."

"I'm so sorry, Sara."

"I'll be right there."

"The paramedics took her. I think they were still attempting to revive her all the way to the hospital."

"What hospital?"

"Sunline—"

The doorbell rang along with insistent knocking, distracting Sara.

"Hold on, Hetta, please, I need to—please hold on—oh, God!"

Still gripping her phone, her mind reeling, Sara, fearing it could be related to her mother's death, went to her door and opened it.

At first, she saw a stranger standing alone before her, a woman in her fifties in a rain-slicked raincoat and hat. Through her shock and grief, Sara recognized her from Silverbrook Hills.

"Bella?"

Bella Spencer saw Sara's anguish, and the phone in her hand. "I can see you must know about your mother already. I'm so sorry, Sara. Silverbrook sent me to help."

"What happened? My God, I was just with her!"

"Her heart, maybe. I'm so sorry. They sent me to come here as fast as I could, to watch Katie for you."

"Watch Katie? Why?"

"They need you at the hospital now, to tend to things."

"I just don't know, I just—" Sara's fingers clawed at her hair.

"It's a horrible time," Bella said. "Let me help."

"Mom?"

They both looked up at Katie standing at the top of the stairs.

"Did something happen to Grandma?"

"Oh, Katie," Sara said. "We're not sure. Please go back to your room."

"Hi, sweetheart." Bella smiled up at her.

Katie remained at the top of the stairs, staring at them, looking at Bella, assessing her while the tiny distant voice of Hetta Boden chirped from Sara's phone. In a moment of clarity, Sara became aware of her phone and the rush of wind-driven rain at the open door.

"Come in, Bella, I've got to find out—" she said, turning partway and raising her phone. "Are you still there, Hetta?... What hospital?... Bella Spencer is here..."

Bella stepped inside, pushed the door closed, removed her rain hat and smiled up at Katie.

"You get prettier every time I see you," Bella said.

For her part, Katie knew Bella from visiting Grandma at the seniors' home. But staring at her now, Katie discerned that she'd seen and heard Bella someplace else, too.

"You were at my school," Katie said, "when Dylan and his friends called me names."

"I was watching over you," Bella said. "I've been watching over you for a long time, like a guardian angel. I was at Sparrow Song Park on the same day you were there."

"I didn't see you."

"I was there."

Sara lowered her phone and turned to Bella.

"Hetta Boden at Silverbrook says she didn't send you." Sara's face tensed. "Why're you here?"

Bella looked at Sara, satisfaction, then triumph emerging on her face.

"Don't you know who I am, *Hayley?*"

Sara stared hard at Bella, and in that moment her heart dropped from her body, for she saw the answer, saw the truth raging behind Bella's eyes—*Magda stood before her.*

Icy fear wriggled up Sara's back like a spider.

"You know what today is," Magda asked, "and why I'm here?"

Sara stood rooted in shock, squeezing her phone, her thumb accidentally ending her call with Hetta as Magda stepped toward her.

"You and that woman who stole you from me said I don't exist! Me! Your true mother, your rightful mother! You never once reached out for me! You have my blood! I gave you life!"

Shaking her head, Sara stepped back, her mind racing.

"No!" Sara said. "No! You gave me pain!"

"I'm here to take what belongs to me!"

"Get out! We're not like you!"

"Katie is! She's exactly like me."

"Get out! You're a monster! Get out!"

"YOU'RE THE MONSTER, HAYLEY! AND TODAY'S THE DAY FOR DESTROYING MONSTERS!"

Still gripping her phone, Sara illuminated the screen to call 911.

Magda's hand shot in and out of her pocket. A steel blade flashed, and Magda struck Sara with several rapid thrusts until she collapsed on the floor.

Katie's screams vibrated off the ceiling, walls and windows.

Magda looked up at her. "Shh, sweetheart. It's going to be alright. I'm your true grandmother. And today's the day I've come to take you with me."

Horrified, Katie cried out, "Mom! Mom, get up! Why did you hurt my mom?"

"She was a terrible mother. She lied to you all these years."

Paralyzed with fear, Katie's eyes widened as Magda moved toward the staircase, still holding the knife dripping with Sara's blood.

"I watched over you in the park that day," Magda said, taking the first steps up. "I wanted to get you alone and talk to you. I followed a little behind you and that girl on the trail, keeping out of sight. I didn't see, but I heard a scream. Then, from the forest, I saw you looking down over the cliff. That's when I knew—you pushed her."

"No! No! I never pushed Anna!"

Magda took another step.

"How did it feel to have that power over life?"

"I didn't push her!"

Another step.

"I know you did it because we're the same. Your blood is mine."

"No."

"And after you ran, I looked down at her. She was hanging on to that tree root. I knew if they saved her, she would tell them what you did—"

"But I didn't!" Katie shook her head. "I didn't!"

Another step.

"If she survived, she would tell, so I got a rock and did what needed to be done, for you. For us."

"No!" Katie sobbed.

"You have to accept it. You have my blood. We belong together. I've been dreaming and waiting for this special day. We are destined to do glorious things. Together."

Magda neared the top of the stairs and Katie screamed.

"MOM! PLEASE GET UP!"

On the floor below, Sara's eyelids fluttered open.

Her body numb, her vision blurred, she heard Katie's cries.

Grunting, she pulled herself to her knees in time to see Katie run from Magda, fly into her room and slam the door.

Sara crawled to the stairs and began climbing them on her hands and knees.

Upstairs, before Katie could lock her bedroom door, Magda forced it open. Katie disappeared under her bed, watching for Magda, seeing her shoes, then a diffusion of light, creaking floorboards.

Magda's face appeared as she looked directly at Katie under the bed.

"Sweetheart." Magda extended her hand. "Come out of there and give me a hug. I've waited so, so long."

Shrieking, Katie kicked at Magda, whose face dissolved into anger. With the speed of a cobra, Magda seized Katie's ankle and dragged her out from under the bed. With talon-like fingers, Magda clutched Katie's arm. She yelped with pain when Magda yanked her to her feet.

When Magda turned to leave with Katie, Sara smashed a lamp into Magda's face, then with an explosion of adrenaline she wrapped the cord around Magda's neck, growling as she tightened it.

"Run, Katie!"

But the two women blocked her bedroom doorway.

Magda fought Sara, flailing and thrashing with the knife, some strikes landing on Sara's shoulders and arms. Their struggle continued to the top of the stairs, where Magda, her face a mask of hair and blood, had nearly removed the cord. Magda raised her hand with the knife high to plunge it into Sara.

Sara's blood-slicked fingers clawed at Magda's as they battled for the knife, losing their balance in the struggle. Both fell down the stairs, entangled, crashing and tumbling to the bottom.

Neither moved, their bodies crumpled and twisted.

In the stillness, Katie crept down.

Hysterical and quaking with convulsing sobs, she rushed to Sara and fell to her knees, cradling her mom's head in her lap.

"Wake up, Mom! Please wake up!"

Katie held her mother's bloodied hand, felt her mother squeeze hers.

Sara was alive.

That's when Katie felt Magda's unflinching glare.

She was on her stomach, lying on the floor a few feet away.

Meeting Magda's open eyes boring into hers, Katie was hit with one thought: *the knife!* She cast around. *Where's the knife?*

Alarm hammering in her ears, Katie never heard the doorbell, or the voice at the front door after it opened.

"I'm sorry but I heard screams— Is everything—?"

Ryan Gardner stepped inside.

The air froze in a surreal, timeless moment that took his breath away and he was staggered by the heart-stopping scene.

Two women were on the floor, bloodied and broken in the aftermath of an epic struggle. A child held the hand of one woman, tenderly cradling her head in her lap, gently rocking and whispering.

"Wake up, Mom, please wake up."

Then the woman's grip slackened, her hand fell and the child's screams merged with the wail of approaching sirens.

87

IN THE BACK of a yelping ambulance, a paramedic worked nonstop to revive Marjorie Cole.

She had no vital signs. An oxygen mask had been applied, a high concentration of oxygen was administered and he initiated CPR.

After a few minutes, he reassessed her.

Still nothing.

He resumed work but without results.

He readied the equipment and initiated defibrillation, then rapidly reassessed her.

He got a pulse.

Yes.

The paramedic alerted the hospital in Bothell.

Miles away, in North Seattle, events unfolded in the wake of the attack at Sara Harmon's home.

Sirens echoed in the quiet streets of her neighborhood.

Hearing help coming, Ryan stayed with Katie. She'd refused

to leave Sara's side while she and another woman lay unconscious. Ryan didn't know what had happened. After spotting
the knife, he kicked it away. Then, between his efforts to use
dish towels to stem their bleeding, he strained to understand
the words Katie was uttering.

Several minutes later, police swept into the house with
guns drawn.

Ryan complied, showing his hands, then lying flat, he attempted to relate what he thought had happened from what
Katie had managed to convey to him. Things moved fast in a
mix of order and confusion. Ryan, whose clothes were blood-
stained, was handcuffed and put in the back of a marked car.
Police secured the house and removed the knife, treating it as
evidence. Paramedics transferred Sara and the other woman
into separate ambulances. An officer rode with each patient
to take a potential dying declaration.

Out front, yellow crime scene tape cordoned off Sara's front
yard.

Neighbors watched from the sidewalk. Val Rossi was among
the first to arrive in time to see paramedics from a third ambulance treat Katie before taking her to the same hospital as
the others. A female officer went with Katie. Val rushed home
for her car and drove to the hospital to help.

At the scene, a uniformed Seattle officer questioned Ryan
in the police car, taking his initial statement as word of the
tragedy moved at viral speed. Bystanders posted texts, pictures and video clips on social media. The news drew more of
Sara's friends to the house, among them Adina Nichol; Polly
and Mel from the diner; people from the Sunny Days group;
and Dr. Sally Mehta. As they became aware, some went to the
hospital where Sara and Katie had been taken. Others went
to Bothell to be with Sara's mom.

Advised by Seattle PD, Pierce and Benton arrived.

They were further updated.

And as more details became known, Ryan's handcuffs were removed. Pierce and Benton were speaking with him when a Seattle detective informed them that one of the two adult women transported from the Harmon residence had died of her injuries.

The dead woman was initially identified as Bella Spencer, also known as Marilyn Hamilton. But in fact, she was Magdalena Vryker, also known as Magdalena Kurtz.

EPILOGUE

When the story broke, it made national headlines for days.

In Seattle it was major news for more than a week.

People were gripped by the horror that Magda had surfaced and murdered the teenage babysitter of her biological grand-daughter, then attacked her daughter and her daughter's adoptive mother in a bid to abduct her grandchild.

Early reports said that Marjorie Cole had survived Magda's attempt to suffocate her. And Sara, having lost a dangerous amount of blood, underwent surgery and survived.

Interest in the tragedy prompted intense chatter by the social media group *The Hunters—Finding Magda*. And *Tell-Tale Hearts* devoted episodes to the case, revealing their connection to it.

As questions about Magda swirled, Pierce, Benton and other investigators put the pieces together. Scrutinizing Magda's apartment, they discovered other maps of Montana, Idaho and Washington under her bird maps. The hidden maps pin-pointed the locations of where the victims had been buried.

After exhuming remains, examination by coroners and

medical examiners in Montana, Idaho and Washington determined that the victims had been strangled or stabbed within
a short time of their disappearance.

In processing Magda's computer, they unearthed her new
plans. After learning where Marjorie, Sara and Katie lived,
Magda took her time patiently stalking them, volunteering
at the seniors' home as Bella Spencer. Adhering to her path-
ological obsession with dates and numbers, Magda set out
on the anniversary of the date she'd lost her daughter to kill
Marjorie and Sara.

"It was vengeance for her perceived betrayal," Art Acker
told a reporter from the *New York Times*.

Acker said Magda planned to abduct Katie, her granddaughter, and win her over. Then Magda intended to approach the
families of her victims without ever revealing her true identity. She would tell them Katie had a deadly illness requir-
ing expensive treatment, in order to generate sympathy and
financial support. At the same time, Magda would present a
purported personal item of a victim, then claim she had information on the locations of their remains that she would
exchange for money "to help her granddaughter."

"She would use a child again—that was her vile, twisted
fantasy. We doubt the scheme would've worked. Families
would have notified police," Art Acker told the *New York
Times*.

Not long after clearing the case, Pierce and Benton reflected on it.

"It never went smoothly," Pierce said.

"We were one step away from her, but reality is more
complicated than the movies," Benton said. "What're your
thoughts on your first homicide?"

"You learn. About investigations. About people," Pierce
said. "How is Elizabeth doing, Carl?"

He smiled. "She's just started therapy with a new drug that has a seventy percent survival rate. We have hope," he said. "And you? You've got plans."

"We're going to Arizona next month to see family, join in some celebrations and ceremonies. Give my son a chance to show off his new drum."

Pierce showed Benton a picture of Ethan with his drum.

"Very nice," Benton said. "Very cool."

One afternoon, in the months that followed, Ryan Gardner drove his mom and dad into the countryside at the edge of Hartford, Connecticut.

They stopped at a small cemetery in a well-kept churchyard, shaded with stands of red maple and black birch trees.

They walked along the soft grass to a new stone that was inscribed:

Carrie Arleen Gardner
Feb. 21, 1973–1995
Eternally loved daughter and sister

Ryan's mom lowered herself and lovingly brushed dried leaves from the base. They stood there listening to the birdsong as butterflies flitted among the bluebells and wild geraniums that bordered the grounds. A long silence passed until Ryan's mother broke it.

"She would've had her own family and a wonderful life. But we finally have her home with us."

Ryan put an arm around his mother.

She'd never been the same after losing Carrie, but today he saw a small light flicker in her, soothing an unending aching.

His father looked like a man who had been repeatedly broken and reassembled. But he was going faithfully to AA and

Mom had invited him to move back home. Standing at Carrie's grave, Ryan's dad took his mom's hand, and it warmed him.

Ryan shut his eyes and he was with Carrie inside the photo booth at the Westfarms mall as she hugged him and they laughed so hard.

We're all together again. We're going to make it.

Across the country, there were similar moments at cemeteries in Boston, Baltimore, Denver and beyond to Manchester in the United Kingdom. In each case, after the recovered remains of Frank and Lydia Worrell, Willow Eve Walker, Brent Porter, and Sharon Lance and Jeremy Dunster had been returned, their respective families and friends had gathered to remember them.

With the case drawing attention, the family and friends of Anna Shaw also held a candlelight memorial service to honor her memory.

But in a remote corner of Montana, one death went unmourned.

By arrangement through King County, Magda's remains were returned to officials in Big Sweet Water for internment. Herman Vryker's remains had been returned to his family in Idaho after his suicide years ago. But his uncle refused Magda's remains for burial next to Herman in Hayden Lake. As a result, authorities in Montana thought it best if Magda were buried alongside her adoptive parents, Nelson and Scarlett Kurtz, in Big Sweet Water's cemetery.

But the plan outraged locals, who didn't want the reviled Magda resting near their loved ones, nor the notoriety that would surely accompany it.

Magda's remains were incinerated; no stone or marker was erected.

She'd left this world the way she'd come into it, with no one knowing who she truly was.

★ ★ ★

Now that Ryan had found Carrie, now that he'd tracked down Magda, he had the ending he'd sought for so many years.

He returned to Seattle, where he set out to write the book encompassing the horror, the anguish, the memories, hope and love that he, and the others, lived with every day.

Central to the story were Sara, Katie and Marjorie. Like him, they were victims, too.

More important, they were survivors.

Katie's fingers traced the smooth surface of the hand-carved giraffe in Dr. Mehta's office.

Holding it gave her comfort.

In the time after the attack, it was Katie who had insisted on resuming her visits with Dr. Mehta. During their sessions, Dr. Mehta worked on treating the psychological injuries Katie bore from Magda's rampage. And unlike their previous visits, Katie opened up this time.

"So, apart from the tragic night, are you still having bad thoughts like you had with Anna?"

"No, they're gone."

"Tell me how you know they're gone?"

"It's kinda hard to explain, but I think now I know that my mom and I are good people and if even a tiny bad thought comes into my brain, I'll fight it and kick it away."

Dr. Mehta saw this as Katie establishing a protective coping mechanism, reinforcing that the moral compass Katie had inherited from her mother eclipsed any of her grandmother's violent traits. The tragedy had strengthened it, and Katie's recognition of it was a positive step.

"That's good, Katie."

"Mom said that Bella was like a long-lost relative or some-

EVERYTHING SHE FEARED   441

thing, and people were saying things about us, but she's going to tell me more."

"That's true. I talked to her, too, and she will tell you more very soon."

Katie nodded, stroking the giraffe. "I like this giraffe so much."

"You know," Dr. Mehta said, "giraffes represent many things to many people."

"Like what?"

"Grace, beauty, and being able to rise above all trouble and see hope in the distance."

Upon her release from the hospital, Sara began seeing Dr. Oleva Krensic, a psychiatrist who treated her for her mental and emotional trauma.

Sara was still sore from her physical wounds, but she was slowly recovering on all fronts.

Dr. Krensic helped Sara understand how her heroic action not only saved Katie but reinforced Katie's own sense of morality by protecting her from the threat of evil in every sense of the word.

Still, it was difficult for Sara to grasp that she had been forced into a death battle with Magda, her biological mother. Sara continued to carry shame and guilt for the possibility of passing on Magda's genes to Katie, and agonized over having to tell Katie about her family's dark history.

"This is a natural feeling," Krensic said. "But it's unwarranted. You bear no responsibility for Magda. The guilt you feel is the pain of having a human heart," Krensic said.

"These feelings are inevitable. It may help you to frame it this way—you helped Katie break away from any biological hold or control from Magda. Magda's death is your victory over evil, a cleansing, a purging, a chance for you, Katie and your mother to start anew."

And so much had happened after the attack.

Marjorie faced a range of physical and psychological issues on her long road to recovery. But it helped that she was able to move back into her North Seattle home with Sara and Katie.

A lawsuit against the Silverbrook Hills Senior Living Home, for its failure to check Bella Spencer's background, and lax security, was settled out of court with a large payment. It enabled Marjorie to employ all the professional care she required at home, and provided for renovations to accommodate her needs.

In the early days Mel and everyone at the diner raised donations for Sara's family through crowdfunding efforts. But Sara quickly arranged to distribute nearly all of the money to the families of Magda's victims, including Anna Shaw's family.

Sara and Katie visited Lynora and Chuck Shaw to personally tell them of the funding they'd receive.

The Shaws used the funding to establish a memorial scholarship in Anna's name.

In the days after the attack, while Sara recovered in the hospital, Ryan Gardner got word to her. After learning who he was, and the role he played that night comforting Katie until help arrived, Sara allowed him to visit, and he told her his story.

When Ryan finished, he said: "So, we're connected to all of this, Sara."

"We are," she said. "And I'm so sorry."

"You don't need to be sorry for any of this."

They continued visiting, becoming friends.

Weeks after returning home, and after considering Ryan's

request for several days, Sara agreed, and convinced her mother as well, to cooperate fully with him for his book.

"This is how all of us can ensure the truth is finally told," Sara said.

Sara returned to working part-time at the Jet Town Diner and undertook courses to get her real estate license.

One sunny afternoon she and Katie went to Kerry Park.

"It's time to start telling you the truth about our family's history," Sara said as they took in the view of downtown Seattle. "You remember I told you how I'm adopted?"

Katie nodded.

"Well, there's more. You see, a long time ago, the people who had me, not Grandma Marjorie or Grandpa George, but the people in Montana who had me when I was a baby, they had problems," Sara said. "Big, grown-up problems that were so serious they couldn't look after me anymore…"

As Sara continued, Katie rubbed her thumb along the smooth neck of the hand-carved giraffe Dr. Mehta had given her. As she listened, Katie knew that no matter what, she and her mom could rise above any trouble. Together, they could defeat anything bad that came along.

Katie knew this because, as she watched the ferries crossing Elliott Bay, she looked beyond to the horizon where there was always hope.

★ ★ ★ ★ ★

ACKNOWLEDGMENTS & A PERSONAL NOTE

In writing *Everything She Feared*, I drew upon real cases of people responsible for unforgivable acts throughout history. My aim was to consider their children, then to make my imagined story as true to life as possible.

As a former journalist, I've had sources who'd supplied me with secret documents, or suggested where to look for them, when I was pursuing a lead. I have used legislation in several countries to gain access to government records on all levels. While most were protected, sealed or redacted, I learned that if you look hard enough, you'll unearth pieces of compelling stories.

My thanks to Tim Meyer, Captain/Media Relations Officer, King County Sheriff's Office, for his help on the basics. For law enforcement aspects in the story that ring true as they pertain to King County, Washington, thanks go to Tim for his generosity and patience. For any errors, blame me for taking creative liberties with police procedure, jurisdiction, the law and technology.

I have visited Seattle. I have traveled across Montana, Idaho and Washington. They are beautiful places. For those who know them better than I, my apologies for taking license with geography. For example, Sparrow Song Park does not exist. While the novel stretches reality, I did my best to keep it real.

In bringing this story to you, I also benefitted from the hard work and support of a lot of other people.

My thanks to my wife, Barbara, and to Wendy Dudley for their invaluable help improving the tale.

Thanks to Laura and Michael.

My thanks to the super-brilliant Amy Moore-Benson and the team at Meridian Artists; to the outstanding Lorella Belli, at LBLA in London; to the talented Leah Mol and the wonderful Emily Ohanjanians; and to the incredible editorial, marketing, sales and PR teams at Harlequin, MIRA Books and HarperCollins.

This brings me to what I believe is the most critical part of the entire enterprise: you, the reader. This aspect has become something of a credo for me, one that bears repeating with each book.

Thank you for your time, for without you, the story never comes to life and remains an untold tale. Thank you for setting your life on pause and taking the journey. I deeply appreciate my audience around the world and those who've been with me since the beginning who keep in touch. Thank you all for your kind words. I hope you enjoyed the ride and will check out my earlier books while watching for new ones.

Feel free to send me a note. I enjoy hearing from you. I

have been known to participate in book club discussions of my books via Zoom. While it may take some time, I try to respond to all messages.

Rick Mofina

www.rickmofina.com
www.instagram.com/rickmofina/
twitter.com/#!/RickMofina
www.facebook.com/rickmofina